EST. 1920

QUAERINT QUAE
METUANT

HERE LIVES
A CORPSE

HERE LIVES A CORPSE

EST 1920

ODERINT DUM
METUANT

TO REREAD SQUAD AND MY BETAS.
Y'ALL TOLD ME NOT TO GIVE UP.
TO PUBLISH THIS BOOK.
BECAUSE OF YOU, I DID.

EST 1920

ODERINT DUM
METUANT

SPECIAL APPRECIATION TO NICKI AND CASS.
I LOVE YOU BOTH DEARLY.

EST 1920

ODERINT DUM
METUANT

JUDGE IF YOU WANT, WE ARE ALL GOING TO DIE.
I INTEND TO DESERVE IT.

ANONYMOUS

EST 1920

ODERINT DUM
METUANT

PLAYLIST

BLOOD // WATER - GRANDSON

SARCASM - GET STARTED

BE KIND - HALSEY

MY IMMORTAL - EVANESCENCE

I'M NOT A VAMPIRE - FALLING IN REVERSE

BLACK SPIDERMAN BY LOGIC

MIDDLE FINGER BY BOHNES

OHIO IS FOR LOVERS BY HAWTHORNE HEIGHTS

IHATEIT - UNDEROATH

COUNT IT UP - FAME ON FIRE

SUCH A WHORE (BADDEST REMIX) - JVLA

REINVENTING YOUR EXIT - UNDEROATH

COMING BACK DOWN - HOLLYWOOD UNDEAD

BLACK SWAN - BTS

LITTLE POOR ME - LAYTO

THE MYSTIC - ADAM JENSEN

ALONE - I PREVAIL

MY HEART I SURRENDER - I PREVAIL

TRUE FRIENDS - BRING ME THE HORIZON

PROLOGUE

Death has a stench.

It's stagnant and stale but still pervades each hollow moment. Sticking to everything it brushes, death and its clinging nature surround the world.

But at this moment, it's enveloping me.

Is this the end? My… *end*.

Woods encircle me, trees tall and voracious in structure imbuing the forest around Arcadia. My feet hit the fallen branches, cloying the universe with the sounds of my retreating form.

Please, spare me.

I'm sorry!

My heart pounds, a rapt noise hitting my bones, instilling more fear than the footfalls I know are behind me.

Snap, snap, snap. Their feet bite at the twigs, crunching with every movement. How close are they? Are they friend or foe?

But my gut knows. It feels the danger and promise They're here to kill me.

My life isn't meant to be over. I'm still a teenager. haven't yet begun to live.

When you're forced into a family-based society saturated in blood money, murderers, and secrets that ensure danger a every move, this moment in my life isn't that foretelling, is it

It's too dark.

The lake is nearby, the boulder, too. If only the trees wer enough coverage from the brightness that seems to reflec down on me like a spotlight. But no, the moon hangs high shining, showing my retreating form.

Even the birds have taken a silence, almost predicting a end cut far too soon.

Everything that'll save the young ones, the informatio needed to save us all, is within the files.

They've only got to find them.

I'm impacted from behind, my body falling to the ground The thief of my breath tackles me, my air no longer inside me. Frantic, I brush off the figure and bolt in the opposit direction.

They'll save me.

They can help.

My chest heaves with adrenaline and the instinct to stay alive. I scream, begging for help, needing someone to know just one person.

"Please! Help me!" I screech, knowing my voice will travel carry across the trees, maybe to the ears of nearby students.

I need more time.

"Help!" My voice echoes, my throat growing drier from running and breathing too fast.

Fear is my only savior.

"Please—" I begin again before I'm once again taken down. This time, though, my ankle twists to the point of pain, and my scream is cut off short by a hand on my mouth.

Whimpering, I silently beg for my life.

I'm just a kid, my eyes say.

I haven't lived yet, my chest rises.

This isn't how my story is supposed to end, my tears offer.

The white light of the moon crests down upon me and the face of my murderer, and I gasp in recognition. He only moves his hand for a wink, a tiny moment lapsed in the blink of time, right before the knife he wields pierces through me. But that's not enough, is it?

The knife comes down.

Again.

And again.

And again.

CHAPTER ONE

Silence drags along my skin like my favorite blades. It'
voiceless, careless, staunching me with desperation to b
seen. My scars are ugly, big, and scraggly, too. They beg fo
attention, as a motherless child lost in the woods would.

Can you hear me now?

Can I die yet?

Most people wake up with the thought in mind t
conquer the day, but me? I pray that my lover, death, keep
me snuggled a bit longer.

Did you know the theory that sleep is your affai
with death? You're halfway there. You must keep your eye
closed longer.

This past summer, I begged my parents not to make m
go back to Arcadia Crest. It's not the same without Cassidy
It's not even remotely bearable with him gone, but thei

indulgence for my needs left the building when he did.

Nothing seems to be tolerable anymore. Even breathing is a chore.

Like the dicks my parents have always been about their *image*, they told me I'm going. They've invested too much into the school to allow me to transfer to Cello Academy for girls, but I couldn't help but try.

Arcadia Crest Academy—a huge preppy dick school in the middle of the mountains—is a wasteland for people like me.

Escaping Arcadia for good was the energy pushing me through the remainder of my sophomore year and the following summer. It kept me looking forward and not behind.

In the end, that final gavel—telling me that it wouldn't happen—ruined all hope for peace.

When founder blood runs through you, you're expected to bend for societal norms and to do what they expect and desire, a puppet of their own making. Being there sucks the soul straight from my body, plastering it over the halls for every elite douchebag to watch and smear.

It's one of those schools that promises everything and, in turn, takes and takes until there's less than nothing left of you. No one notices until it's too late. That's what it did to Cass. To me. To everyone who didn't luck out. Even when their souls aren't stolen, did they really come out triumphant? Or did they lose it all in another form?

Today, I'm supposed to move back to campus in a new tower. Crystal Tower, the one I was in before, only houses Student Gov. Since I'm no longer involved, I'm forced to relocate. We have live-in dorms at the school.

My mind falls to my brother while being reminded of th tower we shared. *Cassidy Amos Hudson.* Thinking of his nearl translucent silvery hair that used to match mine makes m sick. Not with nostalgia, no, with the memory of it coate thick with blood, tainting the ethereal appearance of it.

He's gone.

I shake my head at the memories of him. It's the only wa to survive, the only way I won't break down. Mom doesn' like a hysterical daughter. It's a stain on her perfect image She doesn't understand. If she did, she'd have allowed me t transfer to Cello.

Where *they* aren't.

Does she want me to live in a constant hell? In a schoo full of fakes, bullies, and trauma? There's no longer a choice– if there ever was.

I'm heading back to Arcadia, whether I want to or not It's in a remote area in the Fraiser Mountains, away from politics, publicity, and normal people. To be the opposite of a social pariah while being one… *interesting tactic.*

After dressing in my normal not-Arcadia-approve clothes, I head to my vanity to put on my face. Immediately, startle when connecting with my reflection. The once silvery hair is now a toxic green, matching the virulent lifelessnes seeping through me.

A virus, just like my existence.

It reflects the death of a girl, bringing forth a despaire zombie filled to the brim with hatred for herself, the world and every asshole whoever did her harm.

My silvery pale blue eyes, twins to my brother's, no longer stare back at me. I don't allow myself to look at them anymore. Every day since spring break last semester, I cover them with bright pink contact lenses. They don't even look fake. If you never met me, you'd believe it's the natural color of my eyes, and it's why I'm constantly wearing them.

I'm not him. He's not me. We look nothing alike anymore.

My parents appreciate my need to stop mirroring my brother. That's why they can still look at me. It's why they haven't entirely shut me out.

Changing my entire appearance saved them from the pain of seeing the near doppelgänger of the child they lost.

"Colton!" my mother yells from somewhere downstairs, her voice careless and almost empty, just like every conversation we share.

I ignore her like usual, take out my liquid liner, and mask my face as I've done for the past one hundred and thirty-seven days without *him.*

My heart squeezes in my chest as the image of my brother's lifeless body filters through the barricade in my mind, tumbling it down once more before I erect a new one in its place, this time stronger, less caring, more dangerous.

"Stop ignoring me!" she hisses, making me roll my eyes. When she pretends to care, it's almost funny. Mom hates being put aside as she's done to me most of my life. Tough shit. *Drink your own medicine, Mother.*

I hurry and put some mascara on and stare at the emo

7

punk staring back at me. A long distant memory of the girl I once was, that's for sure. *That girl was weak.* I'll never be weak again.

After grabbing my Poké Ball backpack, I dredge down the carousel of stairs to the foyer. Mom waits with her arms crossed. Her blonde hair—not as light as mine or Cassidy's—is perfectly styled, slick straight. Like a model about to command attention as she struts the runway, she stares at me without compassion.

Did she die too? Is there a person left behind the shell she hides in? Was there ever?

She's in her black pinstripe pants suit, tucked satin blouse, and Louboutins. You see, Mom is one of the strongest women in the Diamond industry. Shocker, right? She could've stayed a model, probably would have made her more caring. Or maybe I'm reaching. It's debatable.

"Where's Moms?" I ask, wondering where my other mom is.

Yeah, I have two. Destiny and Tasha Hudson. They're inseparable. Two peas in a goddamn pod. Moms—*Destiny*—doesn't know how to say no to me, so she always has Mom—*Tasha*—deal with me when it's anything of importance. Luckily for them both, I'm not bartering today. I'm just going to suck it up until I graduate next year.

"She had to be at Locust early today," Mom answers, avoiding my gaze.

Moms works from home most of the time, so saying she had to be at the winery at six in the morning on a Wednesday

8

is far from the truth. She hasn't had to be readily available at the winery for years, anything to excuse her inability to stand up for herself.

"Cool. Guess I'll drive myself then..." I muse, pausing because it's against the rules to have a car at Arcadia. We're literally like Hunger Games tributes out there, stranded, forced to fend for ourselves in the woods while getting an *elite* education. *Puh-lease.* It's a bunch of bullshit, but I digress.

"Absolutely not."

I stare at her and recall how she can only look at me since I hide any trace of my brother.

When he first died, she *wouldn't* look at me. Cass and I were Irish twins. Born eleven months apart and practically identical in appearances. We had the same lips, nose, eyes, and even the little dimple on our right cheeks. We never talked about how we were conceived. It's a *taboo* subject, and it's definitely not something our parents ever willingly discussed.

Rolling my eyes at the way she searches my face for recognition, I wait for her compromise. There's always a compromise.

"I can—"

"God, no," I interrupt. "Don't need everyone gawking at me for having the richest woman in Arcadia bringing me to school. At least Moms is discrete. We both know you're far from it."

She closes her eyes as if I'm the biggest pain in her life. She's not wrong. Cass is no longer here to be the bad one. While he partied and stayed out all hours, I didn't. He got

9

the better grades between us, but his desire to rebel made me seem like the golden child. Doesn't make me hate her less for forcing me to live at the cesspool most students willingly call home. Does her image really overrule my comfort?

Yes. Yes, it does.

"This can't be all you're taking?" She balks at my backpack that barely holds any books.

Her ignoring my comment makes me want to lash out and force her to care. Mom has been the least caring of my two parents. She always pushes me away, and I miss when she would get mad at my rampant hissy fits. I miss her wanting to teach me, wanting… *me.*

"Yang has all my stuff in her dorm as they relocate me," I lie easily.

Yang graduated last year. Not that Mom would ever pay attention. Yang was my best and only friend after Cass was gone. Without her, I'll no doubt be struggling.

To be honest, I have nothing and no one. After getting kicked out of Crystal, the third tower—the one that houses Student Government—my stuff disappeared. All the clothing, memories, everything that had traces of Cass… it's gone. To make things even worse, I'm a social pariah, and no one talks to me.

They kicked me out after Cassidy's funeral. Not just out of the tower, but out of Student Gov, too. When no one showed up as Cass was buried, it stole all my hope and made me realize they would never protect me as they promised.

Not that I care, anyway. I'm not the same girl from last year.

I'm reborn or, rather, re-deathed. Killed again, born again, whatever you want to label it.

"Oh, perfect. I'll get Sheldon to pick you up since you can't stand me on campus."

"Mom—" I start, not wanting her to think I don't want her around. I do, just not like this. She's the biggest donor at my school, a celebrity in the town, and a fucking spotlight of privilege. It's debilitating, to say the least.

"I'll see you fall break. Bye, sweetie."

She doesn't even kiss me or hug me anymore. Our relationship severed when Cassidy's lifeline did.

Sheldon drives me to campus. She doesn't bother me the entire way. One thing I love about my parents' best friend is that she doesn't prod.

I plug in my wireless earbuds and listen to *My Immortal* by Evanescence on repeat until we arrive. She taps my shoulder, forcing me to remove my headphones.

"Just want you to know I miss him, too."

I hiccough, choking on a sob lodged in my throat. Shelly's azure eyes stare at me with emotions that refuse to rise in me.

"Thank you, Shelly. Needed the reminder he existed," I whisper. My brother, my best friend, and the biggest pain in my ass, he's gone. Truly, utterly, *dead*.

"They haven't forgotten him, Colt. The pain his memory brings is just too fresh," she explains, but it doesn't help. It only makes the temperament rise, bringing resentment along with i

"His pictures are gone, Shelly! *Gone.* He's been erased lik
another shoddy diamond exchange."

She shakes her head at me, disappointment licking he
features as the anger only continues to rise in me. There's n
changing my mind.

I open my door and escape the car. Hiking my backpac
over my shoulders, I practically rush to the doors of Ivor
the second tower, where the plebeians exist. *That's who I a
now. A pleb.*

We're all rich here. That's a non-issue, but you're eithe
an elite or a pleb.

At Arcadia, there are three towers. Opal, Ivory, an
Crystal. Opal is the dorms for staff.

Ivory is for the normies, like me now. Crystal is fc
Student Government, which I no longer am a part of. Nc
after then. Not after spring break. Not after... Cass.

Ivory Tower isn't welcoming, not because it's any les
opulent, but because once you're kicked from Governmen
you're like a disease. No one wants you near them. All th
popularity you once had dissolves into dust, forcing you to tr
and fit in any way you can.

Making my way through the main floor to find th
assistant's desk, I'm stared at by every student I've ever me
and ones I've never seen before.

Yeah, it's a change for me, too, losers. Stop gawking.

"Freak," some freshman whispers under his breath.

His friends chortle along with him until I flip them th

bird. Their gazes narrow, and I hunt for the main desk that's basically the student center to get my new key and room assignment. Emo isn't an emotion. It's a lifestyle. It's not a common one at Arcadia, though.

Life without Yang this year will be miserable. She was the one person who got me through everything and was my protector from asswipes. Not that anyone messed with me. Student Government gives you a pass from scrutiny. It's almost a shield for the battlefield of bottom-feeders.

"Name?" the chick at the desk asks, her tone bored.

It annoys me that she hasn't looked up at me. Why can't people make basic eye contact while talking? This generation will be the death of human connection.

"Colton Hudson," I vexingly respond.

As soon as her eyes land on mine, recognition blossoms, but there's also confusion. It's probably the change. It's not like I'm Colton from last year. No, I'm a new brand of dead. Black and green. Beetlejuice's long-lost cousin.

"I-I'm sorry about your brother," she mumbles.

Don't react. Don't react. Don't react.

Yeah, most people apologize whenever they realize my brother died. They send condolences, and they act as if a simple word changes the fact that he stopped aging and breathing and existing. Well, fuck you all. It changes nothing, and it just pisses me off. No one was there to save him, so their words are useless annotations soothing no one's dead heart.

"Thanks," I mutter, not wanting to act out toward a girl with probably honest intentions. I'm not in this school year to make enemies. Only survival.

"You're in room six-twenty-two," she says while handing me a badge and key card.

My eyes water. Cassidy's birthday was the twenty second of October. Eleven months apart from mine.

"T-Thank you."

She gives me an almost knowing look, like she knew Cas or the number's significance. Wouldn't be a shock. He was one of Arcadia's rugby stars. Everyone was devastated, even if their only connection to him was his success on the field.

I try to smile, but it comes off as more of a grimace. Shuffling off, I head for the stairs. Elevators freak me out. Even though each tower has one for its ten floors, I'll never use them.

My heart hammers as I pass by it, feeling sweat slick against my forehead with the knowledge that tens, if not hundreds, of kids use it daily. My palms clam up as I make my way up to the sixth floor.

Gripping the straps of my backpack, I use it as a tether, hoping my anxiety settles. It's not like I'm riding the elevator. I don't even have to really see it. It's just the thoughts and overwhelming realization that people get trapped in those boxes all the time. *Like coffins. A forever home.*

Small spaces never used to bother me. Not until I watched my lifeless brother be buried in one. His everlasting home. An eight by two box, covered in dirt, malnourished by death, deprived of oxygen.

As my body shudders from the imagery, I make it to the

sixth floor. Stopping at the last stair, feeling dizzy, I take in a huge breath, praying for a swift and easy year. *Needing it.*

Not paying attention, I turn the corner, running into a big bulky form. We collide and tumble to the ground, a gruff *fuck* along with other expletives leaves the stranger's mouth.

His hands are on my sides, his fingers digging a little too harshly for a safety hold. I'm practically laying on him and start to apologize profusely, hating that I'm such a mess already. My words lodge themselves in my throat when my gaze connects with Bridger Clemonte's. His inky sable eyes stare at me with annoyance, the pitter-patter in my chest becomes a gallop from his expression. Underlying his distaste is an emotion neither of us will recognize for what it is. *Loneliness.*

That's who we are now. Nothing. All alone.

"Can you get off me?" he hisses.

His pouty lips curl into a sneer, nearly making me jump out of my skin. His voice never went this low or full of hatred. Not *before* anyway.

Once upon a time, his face alone would bring snakes of thrill slithering inside my body, pebbling my nipples with expectation and promise. Now, it only reminds me of what I hate most in life. Student Government.

I rise off of him, my heart pounding along with my head. We must've smacked into one another. He's emotionless like sand, a dry breeze of nothingness to pass in the wind. Even before, his emotions were held close to the vest. You would never know what he was thinking, feeling, experiencing. He hid that well.

15

Bridger, or Ridge, as his friends call him, is your run-of-the-mill charming dillweed. He's got rich brown hair that looks darker indoors than in the light. Catastrophic to the heart and damning to the soul, his eyes dissect everyone in his presence. An attacker of opportunity, he strikes when you trust him most.

Bridger's jaw could cut diamonds, and his body could give Stephen Amell a run for his money, but attraction aside, he's ugly everywhere it counts. When I was a different person, I crushed hard on him. If he even gave me five seconds of his time, a secret touch, anything, I melted like chocolate left in the sun.

But I'm no one's fool now.

"Sorry," I mutter, not willing to give more than that. He's not deserving of more than proper hostility.

He straightens his uniform as if I'm a leech that ruined it. Before he harshly brushes past me, he stares at my outfit up and down, reminding me how emo I appear to others. Baring his teeth like an animal, he makes sure his distaste is known. *"Freak."*

The word should upset me more, but it makes me smile, knowing he cares enough to want to be a dick to me. He's in for a hard lesson if he thinks I care that he doesn't like me anymore.

This isn't the first time the student body has witnessed me in all my goth glory, but it definitely still shocks the fuck out of everyone when they pay enough attention.

CHAPTER TWO

Being without clothes bites. Not realizing that tidbit until I got to school, I went to my favorite *Dark Princess* website and bought every black dress and skirt they had in an extra small. Then, knowing my moms wouldn't approve, I went online to *My Shirt is Better than Yours* and got every shirt, crop top, and lace coverall they had in black.

As my Onyx Visa card screamed for me to chill, I took it a step further and bought from Penn & Co., my secret thrill store. They sold the most expensive clothing in the elite world from five-hundred-dollar bras to thongs that cost just as much, all the way to clothing that could put a down payment on a car. I added some of their signature perfumes and hope it would get here quickly.

Tons of deliveries were made the next day, and it got me more looks than I cared to have. Since then, I've ordered

new things from new shops across the globe. My moms won
be happy about the twenty-thousand-dollar charge on thei
card, but I don't care.

They didn't bother to take me shopping before school, s
it's their own fault.

I've avoided students by going to the mess hall late ever
meal, sneaking in when everyone has left or before anyon
arrives. It's not easy being the only bright green-haired girl i
this school, but I want everything to skate by. Why not avoi
confrontation where I'll be most vulnerable?

Practically running down there now, I'm excited to se
the halls filling with people and not a single one notices me
It's nice, to have outlandish outfits—*their* words, not *mine*–
and not be looked at twice. It's not a phase. It's not a mood
It's a lifestyle.

After avoiding crashing into the row of rugby players i
the center of the hallway, I finally round the corner that lead
where I want to go. Upon entering, I see someone I wish I hadn'

Tennison Dellamore.

"You're beautiful, Col. Goddamn beautiful."

I shiver at the memory, feeling my skin prickle witl
awareness and distaste.

He's leaning against one of the classroom doors, talkin
to a pretty blonde. I've seen her before. She's on the dri
team, always smiling, but where she gets those smiles is th
only issue I have with her. She's not nice. Not to me. Not t
anyone who's *un*popular. She's only kind to Student Gov, anc
by Student Gov, I mean, *the boys.*

Last year, she didn't spare Yang or me a second glance.

Shaking my head, I look back over at Ten. My heart nearly catapults at the sight. He's as close to goth as any guy in this shithole. This year, he went more sporadic. Long, messy, inky locks on top hanging over his forehead in a heap and a bright red undercut that makes him look edgier than usual. His arms are crossed across his chest. They're thick and covered in tattoos beneath his charcoal gray sweater. He's sporting his signature black skinny jeans that show every toned muscle in his thick thighs, and I hate that my breath catches at the sight.

When his eyes drift to me, I swear my heart halts. Though he's too far away for me to see them now, I know what those silver eyes look like really close, like melted soldered metal pools. His sharp jaw looks like it would cut me if I touched it, angular and angelic in an ethereal way. His pierced lip has me near combustion, and when he excuses Blondie like she's a waste of air, I bolt.

"Don't run away, princess. I'll always catch you."

Another shiver racks my frame at his words. It's a promise, unless it comes to caring about me after Cass died.

Before he can get to me, I'm through the doors and running to the salad bar. It's an easy and safe meal. Until I'm used to buying and choosing my own food again, I'll have to avoid overindulging. That and the pills I'm forced to take.

"What can I get you, sweetie pie?" an older woman asks me, standing behind the bar.

I grab a biodegradable takeout tray and point to the spinach.

"Greens for the green girl?" she wits.

I laugh at the way she seems surprised. I'm not like othe people. I don't eat greens as a way to stay skinny. Usually, m form is a lot more filled out than it is right now. I eat the because when Cass died, I went catatonic to a point where didn't eat, went into a coma, and had to be tube-fed. It wasn purposeful. I'm not anorexic or hating myself. I just couldn fathom eating when my brother no longer could.

He doesn't get to enjoy food, so why should I?

I'm a pizza fiend. Wings, soda, Monsters, cand anything that's unhealthy, those are my favorites. Until m body can handle any of it, though, I'll be avoiding everythin in the league of grease, which breaks my fat-covered heart.

"Yes, ma'am," I finally respond with a fake joyous tone.

When she smiles, it makes me feel less bad about it. Sh must believe my front. After pointing to the cucumbers, beet carrots, eggs, cheese, and all the other toppings I want to us to make the salad edible, she leads me to the register.

The person she gives my tray to smiles meekly at me. He a student. I think I recognize him from somewhere. It's just no hitting me where. While I'm blatantly dissecting him with m eyes, he's trying to bring my attention anywhere but at him.

"Miss Hudson," Ike Rimbaur muses, gripping the base of m skull gruffly. "You should get on the table and dance for us."

My body felt light. High. Floating above the kids who abandone me when my brother was buried.

He assists me, helping me onto the table, handing me anothe drink. I've lost track of how many I've had, but I'm still somewha able to think.

"That's right, Hudson. Shake that ass," he presses, and I do. Attention isn't pretty when you're below your lowest low.

My mind fogs at the memory. This fuck. He's *that* dick.

"Fourteen ninety-two," he mutters, his face reddening. Why is he flushed? It wouldn't surprise me if he somehow got sent back to the time where he took advantage of my drunken state.

I peer down wondering if I have something on my shirt since that's where his eyes are directed, but soon realize, he's looking at the scar right above my cleavage, the one I've yet to hide with ink. It's not every day people try ripping out their own hearts, guess it's pretty gnarly to see.

Over the summer, I tried covering every scar with tattoos. It isn't easy. Finding tattoo artists who are willing to work on a teenager, let alone one who has tons of scar tissue from her own doing. They like using excuses. And while I've inked both my arms and thighs, my chest is clear as day.

I almost wish it wasn't. I've done a lot of body modifications. Piercings everywhere, even places a teen shouldn't put it, but that's a story for another time.

After I hand him my Onyx Visa, he stops ogling the tarnished skin and scans it. I'm surprised to see him working. His mom is the dean at this school. She's a no-bullshit kind of woman. It's something I admire about her. Some people have a shitty work ethic when it comes to teens, but she treats us all the same, expecting greatness. Ms. Rimbaur is as straight as it gets.

He hands me the card and receipt, and right before turn away, I make sure to look into his eyes.

"If you want to see my tits, all you had to do is ask. Haven you heard? I'm the school whore." His face flushes once more reminding me of how confident he once was, using me to tak pictures and upload them onto the school's forum board.

He's lucky I was out of my mind with loss because would have strung him up by his balls for his actions. It wa inexcusable, and now I'm labeled the Arcadia Whore.

Just another thing I've learned about myself.

Instead of giving him the chance to say anything I turn and walk off, taking my lame salad with me. Nex week, I'll make sure to add some carbs to my stomach. It' flatter than shit, and I'm sick of not absorbing my hatre in cheese and meats.

After lunch is over, I'm heading to History. It's one o my favorite subjects. I'm lucky to have been assigned Richter He's my favorite teacher. Hell, he's half the school's favorite Not only does he make learning fun, but it's also fruitful. W learn and absorb instead of reading a textbook and hoping to get somewhere.

Walking into the classroom, my pursuit is halted by th face I see.

Well, hello, fuckface.

My eyes connect with the one that quite possibly hurt me the most by saying the least. *Bridger.* When we collided i the hall on orientation day, so many emotions rushed throug me, and I didn't even get a proper look at my sociopath. He' empty yet full of *something* he only used to offer me. If I had to compare him to anything, it would be like never having ice cream in your life, seeing the creamy substance from afar and knowing it could possibly hurt you, and then one day, tasting it for the first time... just a little drop, though, something to satiate the curiosity, to delve into the depravity and then having it disappear once more. That's Bridger Clemonte.

Like every year since we met, his rich brown hair is messy and short on the sides. He's the definition of a jock from his white shirt that spans across his wide chest, hugging every inch of his strong body, all the way to his skater shoes. He's perfect in his sweet boy look, but behind the black eyes he sports is a demon that wrestles to be free daily.

Once upon a time, I let that monster free on me.

It changed everything.

"I like the way you look at me," I mention, peering up into his colorless eyes.

A smirky twitch to his lips is the only indication that he appreciates my comment.

"Why's that, Starless?"

I inwardly squeal at the nickname he gave me. Like his eyes, lack of light, the darkness within... it's our truth.

"Like you're trying to pick me apart, understand me..." I trail off, seeing the way his eyes slightly warm around the edges.

"Usually girls wouldn't enjoy that," he murmurs, thumbing his lip. It's one of his tells, something he does when he's trying to make me pay attention to anywhere but his expression. But right now, his face explains a lot.

23

He's fascinated with me.

"I'm not other girls, Bridger."

Why is it that I'm seeing him right after Ten? I close m eyes tightly, needing the memories to fade.

Bridger hasn't turned to see me yet, so he's unseeing an untroubled. At least, to the world that doesn't know him lik I do. He holds the windowsill like it's the map to hope, willin to take him wherever he needs to find peace. His fingers ta along the glass to a tune only he hears, but I know it's calmin him. He's the silent type, the kind that always says everythin without saying anything. I'm one of the only ones who know his language.

I move to a seat toward the back of class. I'm usually on to sit up front and be involved, but with Richter, there's not part of this room he doesn't animatedly speak to.

After I sit, students start pouring in. One by one, the seat themselves, talking absentmindedly while waiting fo class to start.

My gaze returns to Bridger, wondering what silence him, and then I chastise myself for caring.

He didn't care about me, so why should I still care abou him?

When most of the seats are full, our teacher strolls in with shades over his eyes, a coffee cup in hand, and a smile large than life. I can already feel myself returning the joy, sensing the energy coming off him in waves. It's addicting seeing person so passionate about something they speak about in manner that absorbs into the other person's mind.

"Class!" he booms, cheerful as ever.

When he removes his shades, a black eye is the first thing I see. *Whoa.* Wonder whose cereal he pissed in to get a shiner like that. He doesn't seem like the drunkard and douchey type. Maybe I've overestimated his personality.

Some people start whispering around me. Instead of listening to them, I lean back, uncap my pen, and wait for him to start. He smiles at me as if knowing I'm not going to ask questions. It's not my business, and it takes away from my learning schedule, so it's of no importance to me. Sending me an appreciative wink, he starts at the whiteboard.

"For those who don't know me. I'm Richter. *Rick-ter,*" he enunciates, marking the board with his name. "For those of you who have taken a class of mine before, welcome back. Hope you're not tired of overexuberance because it's not going anywhere anytime soon."

A brunette up front raises her hand.

"Yes?" He doesn't even attempt to ask her name. Smart man.

"Why do you have a black eye?"

He lets out a sardonic laugh that sounds more like a cough. "Well, sometimes… adults are stupid. Me, being that adult, I got what was coming to me. But enough about that. Let's get started on Stalin."

As he enthusiastically gets into the groove of history, my paper becomes black with all the ink I've spilled, recording every important detail. It doesn't even occur to me when the bell rings because my cap is still in my mouth and my pen is still moving.

"Colton?" Richter sounds out, breaking my reverie.

"What's up?" I ask, not peering up. I'm still writing dow
the last section of information he gave.

"You're always writing more than anyone else."

"That's because I'm not too busy ogling your ass," I bit
out.

It's true. Richter is hot. He's the youngest staff membe
at Arcadia Crest. Late twenties, nice athletic body, he eve
has kind eyes and a bad boy vibe when he smirks.

When he doesn't respond, I finally glance up at hir
looming over me. His face is red, and he looks uncomfortabl

"Sorry. Hate stupid questions." I add that for his benefi
since he appears two seconds away from running away.

"I understand," he responds, his mouth in a tight lin
"It's not news that the females at this school spread rumors."

"Not rumors, bro," I try jesting, but then realize I soun
illiterate and not funny. "You're attractive, and chicks can
keep that kind of thing to themselves. Either way... thanks fo
always bringing your A-game to the lessons. It really helps m
push forward."

He smiles.

I close my notebook, rising from the seat. "Keep it up."

CHAPTER THREE

I'm not surprised PE is added to my long list of *hated classes*.

The first day, we didn't have to do anything big. We weighed ourselves, got told our BMI, where we should be, and goals for the semester. Unlike in a normal high school, we're forced to be healthy in fitness. It's a drag.

I've always loved my food, but along with my food comes the requirement to exercise. The problem that's blatantly obvious is that I can't work out yet. Telling Coach Carter that I'm on restricted training made her roll her eyes. Not because she believed me, but because she didn't. It wasn't until she looked at my file, and her annoyance turned to pity. It made me realize how much I hate this class.

Fuck her.

Fuck this school.

Fuck them all.

They offer condolences for a kid they didn't save. He's dead because they didn't do their job. My brother is gone because of their lack of compassion, but still, they offer apologies like they give a single shit.

Truth is, they don't.

Mom's paycheck to their annual fund means being nice to the freak who hasn't coped with her brother's loss is necessary. So fucking nice.

As I enter the gym two days later, she's already gathering students. Class doesn't start for another five minutes, though.

If my parents weren't called with every single class missed, I'd definitely avoid this one and get high. That's one less burden for me. Too bad I can't. Luckily, I live in my dorm alone and can light up every time I damn well please.

Being a founder's kid has its perks, like having an entire dorm to myself. It also has its faults, like being forced to be involved, make good grades, and not be overly emotional. The perks don't outweigh the faults.

When I finally reach her and the surrounding circle, I notice the one thing I wish I could avoid or, rather, the one person. *Lennox DeLeon.* Student Government President.

Of course.

Of fucking course.

He's towering over Coach with his arm around her shoulder like they're best fucking friends. Maybe they are. Doesn't make him any less than the bane of my existence. Regardless of what his appearance says, he's not a good guy.

As much as Ten and Bridger have hurt me, Lennox is on

a level of his own with assholery.

Always dressed to the nines in his school uniform, tie, blazer, and all, he's the worst human. He doesn't see me as I watch him eagerly talk to the class. His words don't connect with me, but the way his pillow lips move does. Someone this rude shouldn't be this hot. It's unnatural and unfair in every way.

His hair is longer. It's dirty blond and messy but only when he's not in the halls. Usually, he's all done up—brushed slick hair and fashionable, like a Ken doll that will fuck you but tell everyone he's waiting for marriage. He's a bad boy in a good boy suit dawning this nice persona to get into every Arcadia girl's skirt.

And he wins every fucking time.

"Lennox is going to be my student aide," Coach announces.

I'm practically asking God to strike me down and end it all here. *Smite me, I beg of you.* How can there be Student Gov members in every class I have? Why do they have to infiltrate my life?

They couldn't just let me be alone in the divorce.

I try not to let loose the unladylike groan that wants to escape, but I don't have to. Lennox—*Lux*, as his friends call him—looks directly at me. A smirk tilts at his face. Cocksure and snarky. Good to know nothing has changed.

"Lennox will be assigning lockers to the boys while I do the same for the girls."

He mouths something at me, but I ignore him, giving my attention to Coach. She explains the mandatory uniform dress code, and by no means would the females be allowed t dress otherwise. The guys are lucky. Their uniforms are lon black basketball shorts and a heather gray shirt. The female had black tennis skirts—*gag me*—and heather gray fitted tee the school's emblem on both.

Luckily for me, I don't care about regulations given b the school. I'm not even dressed in the daily uniform. Mos Arcadia kids follow the rules, especially if they're Lux an have a reputation to uphold. My rep ended up fucked whei I got so tanked I made out with half the party-goers and tha loser recorded me.

People like me who have zero morals don't have reputation to sully. We don't care. Plus, when your parent are alumni with big wallets, paying out of their ass for specia treatment, that's exactly what you get. *Special treatment.*

We're separated, and as the boys leave, the girls are led to the locker rooms. These aren't communal like the school showers They're assigned each year. We're required to keep a locker an bring our own locks. They don't have the built-in kind. It's to giv us more privacy. Same drill, different school year.

Coach leaves us to change. I wait until the girls are gon to get into my own clothing. Once they've all left, I sneak into a stall and switch my clothes. Picking up my black sports br from my bag, I switch it for the lacy one. Slipping into m joggers, not wanting to show my tattooed upper thighs tha are painted with scars, my skin feels covered enough. Ever the ink can't hide all the damage inflicted to myself. No one gets to see those. My final touch is a long-sleeved crop top

30

that covers my scars there too. A mask within a mask.

After finishing, I put my hair in a ponytail, and with a quick snap of the door, all my shit is locked up. We don't get to have phones during classes. It's literally a rule, but they never said we couldn't have our iPods. I stuff mine in my bra and put my wireless AirPods in, leaving the room as soon as I'm ready.

"We're doing the timed mile," Coach explains when everyone's back in the gym.

Girls groan, and guys whoop. I stare at the field, feeling anything but happy. My moms won't let me work out, but you'll be damned to see me listen.

She sets us up with partners, and I'm surprised to see I'm alone.

"Miss Hudson," she calls while everyone is already dispersing to the track, "since you're not allowed to exert yourself, you'll be partnered with my assistant, Lennox."

Lennox. Lennox. Lennox. Please no.

Anything but that.

I'll sprint the entire mile. Take track. Donate blood. An organ. I'll go on the black market and sell my soul.

Anything but putting me with the biggest asshole in this school.

"Coach—"

"Uh, uh, uh. I've spoken to your mother. Until your body is well and ready to go any faster than a brisk walk, Lennox will be your partner and assistant."

"I don't think—"

She waves a hand, stopping my argument. "Lennox!"

she yells.

Mr. President himself dotes on her with a big grin. Behind that big grin, I know what resonates, and it's anything but pleasant. He's not what he shows the world. Everyone sees him as this innocent honor roll student. He's honor roll, all right. Just not innocent. He's cruel and callous, and his tastes are fucking with and torturing me.

His gait is confident as he makes his way to us. After he hands Coach the clipboard, she fills in me and Lux as partners. This is so fucked. He's going to terrorize me until I die, and even then, he'll make sure to stab my corpse a few hundred times for good measure.

I'm so fucked.

"Miss Hudson is to be monitored. She's not allowed to overdo it."

He raises a tentative eyebrow, giving away the fact that he didn't know something he wasn't meant to be privy to.

"You will time her, and when she's better, you'll do a solo run with her and time her again to show progress when she's been approved for normal activity." She flips the pages on her clipboard and nods silently while Lux's gaze digs into the side of my skull. I don't waver. He can stare all he wants. In no way does that make me responsible to give him any recourse.

"She's healthy with a four percent BMI. A little low for her age. Must be the—"

"Coach, that's none of his business. If you want to hear from my lawyers, I'll be sure to pass this little tidbit along," I bark.

He isn't allowed to know that much. Not that I had

ketoacidosis, that I can't eat forcefully, and that I'm below my normal weight because of it.

"You're right," she grouses and flattens her lips. She almost divulged information that's illegal to just toss out there.

Lux's stare feels more intense on me. My face is hot and sweaty, and I no longer believe he won't bother me. This will be an astronomical error, and with my luck, I'll have to beg for a class transfer.

"Off you go," she barks at us, not looking up from the chart.

Her whistle rings in my ear, making me cringe.

Heading toward the bigger group of students, she yells loudly, "Start your timers and go!" Everyone rushes off, besides me and Lux. We walk to the starting point. My stomach feels empty, and it's not from the lack of food. It's empty because he decided to march into this class and squeeze it to death with his hazel eyes.

"What was that whole lawyer bit about, Corpse?"

Corpse.

How Tim Burton of you.

"Put a can in it, dick."

He throws his hands up, and it's the first time he hasn't shoved himself into something that didn't pertain to him. Lux always pushes his agenda, always gets his way, and certainly puts himself into everyone's business.

But not this time.

What's your angle, Lux?

He pulls out a stopwatch, not looking at me more than a

specimen to study. For some reason, that's worse than whe
he pays too much attention to me.

"Go," he commands numbly.

Then I'm jogging.

"No jogging!" he reprimands from the side of me. "Yo
may not believe this, but I take classes seriously, so you'll liste
or I'll fucking make you listen."

My eyes meet his and see the warning written in hi
expression. He's not joking, which only makes me want to laugh

I pull to a soft stroll and roll my eyes at him.

It takes fourteen minutes for me to walk the mile. Th
entire time, Lux doesn't say a single word. This is how i
should be.

When we're finally done, my body aches, and I hate th
fact that I feel as exhausted as I do. My body will take time t
adapt, but it would be nice if it figured out its shit.

CHAPTER FOUR

The first week goes by without anything more than school and homework. Classes are boring, the regular stuff that drones on and on. It's nearly peaceful, quiet, almost too calm. I'm not even stressing about the ease of this year. It's going to be cake, and I'll be the glutton on its offerings.

PE, Math, English, and Science are my least favorite, while History and Psych are definitely my top two. The rest are inconsequential.

No matter how hard I try to avoid the guys of Student Gov, they seem to be in all my classes. They don't pay a lot of attention to me, which is fine by me.

It's different this year. Yang and I were the only females involved last year, but with her gone and me quitting, it's all guys. Lux, the president. Bridger, the vice president. Ten, the secretary. Ross, the enforcer. There's no longer a historian or treasurer. No one knows why we weren't replaced, but it stands as is. If they're waiting for me to come back or beg me to come back, they're going to be waiting a long time.

These guys are the same ones who ruined my life, but wait. My gaze lands on a paper pinned to the wall. The Arcadia Emblem is at the top, stamped like a brand of royalty. Looks like there's a new addition according to the wall announcements.

Welcome Jordan Winthrop, your newest enforcer.

Not sure who he is, but he sounds like a tool.

Maybe I'm being biased, but he's probably like the rest of them—dickish, self-serving heartbreakers.

My next class should be one of my favorites, knowing the teachings, but it will probably be as bad as gym.

Ten minutes later, I'm sitting in Psych, waiting for class to start when several girls huddle in the middle of the room, chatting conspiratorially. It's nothing unusual. We're in high school, after all, but I pay little attention to what goes on around me. It's less stress and drama for my mental health.

"I heard she kills animals in her spare time," a chick don't know whispers, catching my ear.

It's obvious *who* they're discussing.

"Maybe that's why she's in this class. Learning how to hide her psychopathic tendencies," another joins in.

"Getting away with murder would definitely be on my list of things to learn," I deadpan, barging in on their conversation, watching them jolt back as if I'm going to hurt them.

I would never touch a fucking animal. These cretins love their rumors. It's disgusting how much time and hatred people put in for five seconds of fame. I'd say fifteen minutes, but we all know a teen's attention span ends as soon as it begins.

"Nah, ladies. Miss Hudson only likes drinking the blood of men. Fresh from the tap. You know, since she's a bloodsucking vampire." *He* taps his throat methodically, receiving giggles from the stupid chicks who have nothing better to do than talk shit.

I don't know when he walked in or how I missed it. He was probably acting as a god, heaven-sent and otherworldly. *News flash,* that's inaccurate.

I would know his voice anywhere. If he stood in a lineup, no imagery necessary, his voice would be refined like aged whiskey. It's too unique, smoky, and promises havoc to everyone around him.

My head tells me not to react, but my heart tells me to make him eat it alive. That's what my heart wanted all last year, wasn't it? *Him.* His stupid blond hair that made my insides tingle and his piercing hazel eyes that couldn't decide which shade they wanted to be. It's the way he's arrogant as hell but doesn't cower or apologize for it. He's unapologetically himself; a cruel, rich, and unattainable asshole.

He hasn't said a single thing since he forced me to walk the mile. Assistant Lux isn't anything like Lennox DeLeon, President of the dickbags. *Shocker.*

They may physically be the same person, but Lux is who I know. Lennox is who scares me.

"Don't act like you didn't like it last time, Lux. We both know my mouth is your favorite," I taunt a little too late but still knowing where to push.

Whether he'll admit it or not, he *had* feelings for me. So much so that he begged me to pick him. Now, with my eye staring right at him, I feel power ooze from my pores, and it only increases as his jaw tics. It's not news that Lennox is the richest kid, besides me, and the most charming guy in school—unless he's dealing with me. He's constantly fawned over and eats it up, gorging on the attention like a leech. But shit, he's a gorgeous leech.

"I'd never let a vampire with pale as fuck skin touch me. Get some sunlight, Bloodsucker. You're starting to show your corpse."

"Fuck off, Lux." It comes off too heated, showing my cards when he shouldn't have control over the deck at all.

A smirk tilts at his lips like he knows he's won something, but he'll never win. Not again.

"It's Lennox to you." He sits back in his chair, crossing his arms like he's macho. It's a front for a boy with daddy issues, even if he'll never admit it.

"Okay, *Lux*. I'll take note."

He grunts before going back to his work.

Mr. Bautista announces our new assignment, telling us to pick a serial killer. He explains the requirements—that we're to research them and write a five-page theory on why they did what they did and whether or not they're a psychopath or a sociopath. *Or both.*

As he excuses us to start, Lux's hand raises, but when the teacher doesn't notice, he whistles.

"Yes, Mr. DeLeon?"

I don't turn to look at him, even if he's only a chair behind me. He's not worth the wasted energy.

"Can we pick *any* serial killer?"

"Is that not what I just explained?" Our teacher drones.

"So, I can write a piece on Vampire over here?" he asks, ignoring the fact that the teacher is giving him a death glare.

"Mr. DeLeon, don't waste my time on—"

"We all know she killed her brother and probably every animal in the forest. Might as well just prove it now."

I fist my palms so tightly that my gel nails break skin. That doesn't stop me from digging more and more as my skin prickles with embarrassment.

"Mr. DeLeon!" Bautista yells, his face reddening, the vein on his forehead making an appearance as well.

"I'm just saying—as someone who has seen what she can do, I think she'd be a great case study." His voice is one of consideration.

The fact that he brought up my brother so callously has me wanting to prove a theory. I'll be a murderer if that's what he wants. Bringing up Cass when we both know he was involved in the cover-up makes me sick.

Instead of sticking around to let him beat on me more, I raise from my desk, collect my shit, and race out of there.

Mr. Bautista calls after me, but I don't stop, not even after I leave the room.

39

Lennox can bully me all he wants, but he better learn to leave Cass out of it. I told myself I would keep my distance and I even left Government to avoid them all. Even if leaving Ten practically sawed out my organs, it had to be done. The refused to admit their involvement, and I'm not playing their little game anymore.

"Colt!"

I don't stop or turn to see who it is. The stranger's voice whoever it is, sends a familiar thrill through me. There aren't many guys who do that. Actually, I can count on one hand how many have the capability, but whoever this is, he isn't one of them.

"Please stop running!" The voice is insistent, almost desperate in a way.

"Not running. Just not stopping," I grunt in reply, trying to not be rude as I make my way out of the school and toward Ivory Tower.

A hand clamps onto my shoulder, making me squeak. turn toward him, ready to berate him, but my heart pounds as my gaze connects with the bluest eyes I've ever had the pleasure of seeing. They're so dark, almost black, but as the light shines on them, I can see they're a deep navy. My mouth hangs open as I try to form words. I'm not one for geeking out on a guy. I've made that mistake before, but this guy... his eyes... *omigod.*

His hand touches my chin poignantly, forcing it closed. "Like what you see?" he teases, his eyes hone in on my lips and I subconsciously lick them.

He's so damn handsome. His hair, like his eyes, is dark, but the lights overhead show the reddish-brown tones. He's sporting the regular uniform without the blazer. The arms are cuffed at the elbow, and his tattoos shock me.

He has to be a student. He appears young. Like me, his arms are swathed in detailed black ink. It's intense, like his penetrating gaze.

"H-How do you know my name?" I ask, hating that a bad feeling bubbles in my stomach. Not snakes, no. Spiders. Venomous, disgusting, and squirmy in the worst way. I've never seen this kid before, and yet he already knows me?

Red flag, Colt. Red fucking flag.

"I-I..." he stumbles. I'm not sure if it's because he's a terrible liar being caught, or such a good actor that he's able to seem stuttery. "We have three classes together. I've watched you."

That's not creepy, admitting to watching someone.
Joe Goldberg, is that you?

He runs a hand through that dark hair of his, making me lose focus once more. Before Cass died, I was one-thousand percent boy crazy. It's what got me into trouble last year with not one but *four* guys.

"Oh, well. Hi," I respond lamely. I'm not about to jump this dude's bones over him noticing me. It's hard not to notice me. I have toxic sludge green hair and black raccoon eyes.

"I'm Jordan Winthrop, but everyone calls me Walker."

"I'm—"

"I know," he interrupts with a boyish smile, revealing a

41

dimple. "I just wanted to see if you were okay. Lux isn't exactl nice."

That icky feeling comes back at Lux's name.

"How do you know?" The question comes out withou pause. I don't trust anyone, least of all someone who know Lux.

"I'm the new enforcer for Student Govern—"

"I've gotta go," I rasp.

He was listed on the bulletin board earlier today. Now have a face to connect with the name I know to avoid. *Good.* will not get involved with them. Never again.

He licks his bottom lip, revealing a tongue piercing tha has a shiver running through me.

Hurrying, I turn away and head for my room.

When I finally get there, I notice a note on my boarc All doors have one. It's for messages, notes, or even number from losers who want in your pants. My eyes connect witl several words that have my blood running cold.

Go home. No need to lose the last Hudson child.

Who wrote it?

Why did they?

Bet it was one of those assholes in Student Government

The words stare back at me as I gnaw on my li relentlessly. Instead of erasing it, I take a picture with my ce and go inside my dorm.

How the hell did I think this year would be easy?

CHAPTER FIVE

As soon as I enter my room, I notice him immediately.

It's been four months since I truly spoke to him last. He took something from me, something I can never get back. Not that I would want it back anyway. When he didn't show up to Cassidy's funeral, it solidified our separation, making it permanent.

"Ten," I whisper, unable to believe my eyes. *How did he get in here?*

His metal eyes pierce me like the silver they reflect. His facial expression isn't readable. It's almost… nothing. Not here nor there. It just is.

"Kid," he responds, his gravelly voice hitting me where it hurts most, between the ribs, a little to the left, right where it beats hardest.

To many, I'm just Cassidy's kid sister, even with less

than a year separating our age. *Kid.* That's what he calls me even when we grew up together. It's not blasé either. It's how I know he still cares. But I don't want him to *care.* I want him to hate me as I've forced myself to hate him. He was there that night. With them. *He's one of them.*

"This is Tennison," Cassidy explains.

This boy he's showing me lives nearby. I've seen them play a lot but I'm not allowed to hang out with them. His friend Tennison's hair is a brown color, like wet dirt, muddy and dark, but it's longer, and messy, like boys always are.

"I'm Colton." *I offer my hand. Since I turned ten, I've been sneaking around more, playing football with boys.*

Tennison stares at me, his shiny eyes meeting mine. They're so pretty, like the spoons Moms has just cleaned or even the shiny earrings she wears when they go to fancy dinners. They're pretty, and I can't stop staring.

"Nice to meet you, Kid."

"I'm not a kid," *I argue, pouting.*

He smiles boyishly, his mouth curving upward. "You look like a kid to me."

I shake myself of the memory, glancing at the boy who stole a vital part of me. He's such a sight right now. His appearance is dark and enticing and all him. It's a replication of his soul. Moody. Disturbed. Pained.

My heart hammers at how much he still affects me. He has a new piercing on his eyebrow, one I didn't notice in the mess hall. It's a little bar, and the inane desire inside me to lick it zings at my taste buds. To flick my tongue and taste the bitterness of the metal would be unnerving in the best way, just like when I used to with his spider bite piercings.

"Stop looking at me like you want to fuck, Greenie. We both know there's not much to stop me," he nearly growls as I lick my own piercings. Metal, the friend I never knew I needed. A distraction in my time of need.

My mind travels to what he just called me. "Greenie? What am I, a leprechaun?"

"Your hair is green. Seemed fitting. Plus, you're short. Leprechaun isn't far off," he replies with a shrug, sounding bored.

I hate that about him. There's never anything important enough—sans sticking his dick into chicks—to bring him to life anymore.

And he did that, dipped his stick into chicks. It's one thing I could never pretend to not be jealous about. Not even now, thinking of how many broads he probably bagged this summer. We were never exclusive, just two people who liked finding pleasure in each other, even if all I wanted and tried for was *more*. It didn't help that there were three others vying for my attention, and I was sharing it with them, too.

"Why are you here, Ten?" I hate how my voice lowers, sounding small and insecure. *I* left him. *I* walked away. Why does it feel like he's the one who left me? They all abandoned ship, but it was me who made the choice to cut all ties.

He steps closer to me. I shut the door, trying to back away from his close proximity, but his fingers pinch the green locks of my hair. He caresses the strands almost reverently, like he's shocked that I'm no longer blonde.

"I miss you," he drawls, making heat pool in my stomach. Whether his words are in reference to my hair or my body, his voice simmers in me regardless of the source.

"Don't," I whimper, feeling my confidence to stay away caving.

"Don't what?" he rumbles, reaching for the back of my neck, pulling me to his lips. "This?"

His lips connect with mine as the word leaves his mouth. His tongue seeks entrance, tracing the metal of my piercing. A moan escapes my lips and I open up for him. He takes advantage, swiping his tongue against my teeth. I bite his lip, dragging my teeth against the softest flesh.

He holds my throat, demanding my every noise, warranting each one, too. His jeans are tented with his very large appendage, one I've fucked, touched, and tasted once upon a time. We were always tumultuous. Every single time we burned bright, hot and heavy.

My brother's bloodied body flashes in my mind, reminding me why I hate Ten and why I left. Pain belies every inch of me as my hand connects with his chest and pushes him back. Tears well, and I would do anything to choke back the emotion. He can't win.

"Leave." It's barely a muster.

"Don't do this, Kid. You push everyone away."

It's a valid argument, but it's worthless to me nonetheless.

Bracing myself, I make sure my mind is as solidified as my body.

"I won't stop, Ten. Not until I'm far the fuck away from here and all of you," I hiss out harshly.

Sadness pools out of my eyes. I'll really look like a trash panda soon, a wet one from the sewer, black and white, messy from helplessness.

Ten needs to leave, and I need to be stronger in the future. This can't be a repeat situation with us.

"Just remember you chose this," he bites back, sidestepping me to leave.

The anger on his face as he walks out my door forces me to my knees all while sobs rack my frame. He's not wrong, but I can't just forgive them for lying and covering up Cassidy's *accident*. They can say all they want that he fell off the cabin and hit his head on a boulder, but I know it's not true.

I don't know why they lied.

Why I didn't call them out on it.

How they didn't come to his funeral.

Cass wasn't drunk at the party. He was my designated watcher, the person to make sure nothing happened to me while under the influence. My being too tanked caused them to blame me for imagining things, but I saw Cass. His body had been beaten to shit. Drunk or not, I know what I saw.

I don't stop sobbing until I pass out, and Cass lying dead on the grass invades my every dream.

I skip classes the next two days, needing to decompress

47

and sob it all out.

Abandoning Ten hadn't been easy on me last year. He didn't fight for me anyway and made me feel crazy for believing Cass had been murdered.

My darkness seems to be creeping up with each hour that passes. Doesn't help that Moms calls every few hours. The texts are nonstop, too. She's asking why I'm missing class, if I'm okay, and finally, she says she'll call the cops if I don't respond. Knowing her, she's not lying.

After I dial her up, my fingers itch to click End before it patches through.

"Cariña," her soft Colombian accent sounds out on the other end. It's full of worry and care, thick with emotion and trembling a little. I hate it. She can't be like this face-to-face, but as soon as I'm one hundred miles away, she's cool. "Talk to me."

"Pass," I bite out, barely able to contain my resentment.

It hadn't always been like this. Moms and me, we were always close until Cass died. She pushed me away. Can't blame her. We not only looked identical. We were always similar in every way—our hobbies, tastes in food, and even the way we dressed.

"Please, Colton. *Te extraño.*" *I miss you.*

"You could have driven me here, but you bailed."

"Don't berate me, baby girl. It's hard for me. You know this," she pleads, her voice thick and choked up.

Why do I hurt her back? Why can't I be a normal child and accept how much she hurts me? Why can't she be like normal moms and think about me first?

"That's a cop-out because you do whatever Mom wants." The words leave me, and I hate each one. She's trying, and I'm fucking it up.

But she only tries when I call her out.

"*Eso no es justo,*" she says, her voice small. *That's not fair.*

It's not her fault that she loves Mom as much as she loves me. She can't choose, but the decision is made for her every day, and she doesn't fight.

"She's stubborn," she continues. "You only have two years left. Why would you want to start over?"

"Because he's gone!" I screech, the anger and bitterness climbs up my throat. "I can't breathe here, Moms! He's in every hall and every fucking kid's expressions. I don't want their pity. I want my brother back."

She doesn't scold me for swearing like she normally does. Hell, both of my parents don't do much *raising their voices* anymore. They've let me flip my life upside down with whatever the hell I want since we lost Cass. Not sure what that says about them, but I'm done caring.

"How about I pick you up for fall break?" she offers, but I'm already done with this conversation.

"Sure thing, Moms. Gotta go."

"Don't forget that I love you past the stars."

"To the Milky Way," I respond like always before hanging up. It's our goodbye, but it no longer rings true to me. Moms isn't biologically my mom, not by blood, but that doesn't change the fact that she is in fact my mom. She raised me and Cass. We're hers, through and through.

Talking to Moms doesn't seem to help as much as it once did. Doesn't help that we're all a mess and can't seem to function as a family without Cass.

We're fucking hopeless, and I'm done trying.

CHAPTER SIX

Jordan and the rest of Student Gov seem to gravitate toward me. They're everywhere, and it's driving me nuts. At first, it was easy to ignore them. Avoiding eye contact, making comments, or even thinking about them seemed to work, but as school progresses, that's not the case.

I can't even skip class to smoke a bowl because they somehow always seem to show up when least expected.

Today, though, getting high is my only goal. It's not a little urge. I'm at the point of desperation. Alcohol used to be my go-to before Cassidy died. Sixteen, an alcoholic, living off the praise of seventeen-year-old boys and all the popular kids. What a fucking joke. Parties were constant occurrences at Crystal Tower. It's like they invented them.

But this year, it's different. Weed calms me but doesn't leave my mind foggy. That's what I need to get through this year.

Pulling out the little baggy I scored from Tanner in th
city before coming here, I escape to the woods near the schoo
After the debacle with Ten, there's nothing I want more tha
to hide. Student Gov is a bunch of annoying dicks who nee
to fuck right off.

The twigs and earth crunch beneath my boots, eac
step loud while class stays in session. The clouds, murky ar
gray as usual this time of year, clings to the sky, envelopir
the light in a cape of shadows. The chill isn't to my bones y
It's still a good time to sit near the little lake in the center
this godforsaken forest. *Technically,* we're not allowed to cor
here, but that doesn't stop any of us. We do what we wa
when we want. Regardless of how much I spit on the othe
with my distasteful words, I'm as entitled as the rest.

Near the lake, there sits a rock. Cass would take
there, and when he wasn't here, it became my escape, o
where I would draw and write, pretty much do anything to
away from Cass when he became overbearing. It's insane h
life changes and the only thing truly desired is my brother.
trade anything, even my soul, if that would give me anot
moment with him.

Just one.

A few words.

Goodbye, maybe.

Anything to feel this gaping hole mend a little.

The trees surrounding me are big and green, almos
moody as me. If you stuck a depressed filter on this landsca
that's what expresses itself now. I almost hate it, the

that it's so dank and dark, but that doesn't stop my pursuit. Depressing as it is, it's more soothing than sunshine with fake smiles and morbid fallacies shown to others.

My favorite stop comes up ahead as I drag my feet. Around some redwoods and pine is my rock and several others. They've always intrigued me. As if they fell from the sky in a heap, they're separated from the rest of the mountainous area around. There's no other way to explain the phenomena. Not a single boulder nearby could have created such massive rocks randomly.

Right as I'm rounding around the tree, a lone figure sits in the distance, and I catch my breath. From the twenty-foot distance, there's no telling who it is. All I know is that they're wearing the school's uniform and are broad-shouldered, big, wide like a brute.

Nestling behind the tree, I stay back. The desire to sneak over overwhelms me, begging me to see what the stranger is doing. He stands, pacing back and forth. *Is he arguing with himself?* His arms move vigorously, going up and down as if he's pissed. Well, this is awkward. Why am I watching him? Is this the equivalent to a train crash?

Deciding to move closer because I'm a masochist, I try not to crunch everything in my path. It's hard when you're wearing four-inch platform boots in a fucking forest, but attempting it is my only choice. The scent of tobacco permeates the air. Sniffing as little as possible causes me to scrunch my nose in displeasure. Yeah, smoking a joint or ten a week is my thing, but cigarettes are gross. *Hypocrite*, probably.

Regardless, cigarettes are gross.

My feet aren't light as I'm progressing toward the guy. He's still yelling, and as I get closer, I can hear some words.

"This is such bullshit, and you know it! I owe you fucker nothing. Absolutely nothing."

The voice is a bit muffled by the sounds of birds and wind rustling through the redwoods, but it sounds familiar.

"Well, fuck you guys and your dad!" a familiar voice hollers loudly.

When I'm a few yards away, a branch snaps beneath my foot, and I'm halting. Almost as if the birds, wind, and nature decided fending for myself was the result of stupidity, everything silences.

Adrenaline rushes through me, I attempt to slow my breathing, not wanting to be caught. He can't see me. I'm behind foliage and trees, but my hair is bright fucking green. With my luck, it'll give me away.

"Did you hear that?" a voice, deeper than the first, questions.

My heart hammers, and my palms suddenly feel clammy. There's no harm in spying, right? These are probably a bunch of teenagers pissed at their parents for something... right? They wouldn't hurt a Hudson. They wouldn't.

For the first time since Cassidy's death, I'm panicking. Fear slices through my veins like my razor always does when my mood drowns.

I back up a step when I see them shuffling. They're worried. Which means, one, they're doing something illegal, two, they're ditching class like me, or three, all the above and worse.

"Who's out there?" a third voice, deeper and angrier than the first two, barks, making my skin slick with sweat.

Shit. Shit. Shit. I just wanted to smoke a joint, not cause trouble. This year is supposed to fly by.

When the three figures are more visible, my body trembles from head to toe, and even though it's cold, I'm sure that the temperature has nothing to do with the sudden chill in the air.

"Let's split up." The words escape one of the three, promising danger with each syllable.

I rush away from the trees, no longer trying to be quiet, running for my life.

Is this how Cass felt?

Am I going to die, too?

"Come back here!" one of them shouts as I near my hiding spot, a cave Cass and I found my freshman year. He used it for whatever he wanted, and I used it to make out with Ten. We called it our bunker. Cass eventually made it a fully functioning place of escapism. It's furnished inside, and there's even a door. After escaping inside its small entrance, I hear feet running across the stick-laden ground, the sound of the wind whooshing, and the grunts as they pass by without seeing me.

Minutes go by. My heart still runs rampant in my chest. So much for taking it easy.

After I'm positive they're gone, I exit the cavern. Looking

back to where we came from, my body shivers. As I turn, I ru
into a solid chest.

"What are you doing out here, Colton?" Bridger asl
coldly, his voice scarily deep.

That's when it hits me. He's the first voice I heard.

My eyes meet his starless skies, burning, melting, an
dissolving into a puddle of death.

"I was simply trying to smoke a joint," I whisper, wishin
my words didn't sound ragged and my chest didn't heave wit
every syllable. It makes me look guilty—*I am*—but he doesn
need to know that.

"Eavesdropping, perhaps?"

Right now, in the middle of the trees, where life doesn
truly exist, fear is the only answer. He scares me. Not befor
that night, no, but now, surrounded by a gray sky and bein
dissected by eyes that are bottomless, fear is my only trait.

"N-No," I mutter. Damn, stumbling over my words mak
me feel and appear weak.

He doesn't care. He only wants to know what I know
It's apparent on his face as he eyes me, squinting ever s
slightly. He's nearly expressionless, yet it's like he's diggin
through my brain, tugging on every inch, making sure no vit
information resides there.

"*Weed*. That's why I'm here." It sounds less frantic an
smoother. Reaching into my pocket, I pull out the bag. "See?

He doesn't look, though. His eyes penetrate me, sti
dissecting me as if I'm a lab rat, waiting for results he ma
never see before an untimely death. Since he won't d

anything, I pull out my Zippo and the joint I've got pre-rolled. He doesn't hesitate, watching me like a freak, making my skin crawl and fill with dread.

Only he can do that—rip me apart with his blackness and tape me together with past lustful gazes that remind me we're all simply human. Maybe not, though. Maybe Bridger has crossed that path, becoming more creature than mortal. He's darker than black and scarier than elevators. He's the shadows on the walls at night, the promises of death, the warning of hell.

I bring a shaky hand to my lips, barely holding onto the joint. Instead of saying anything, he takes the metal from my fingers, flicks the roller, and lights the weed. The fire is a mirror of salvation in his eyes. If I burn, will he carry me away to my forever imprisonment? I was never meant to live, anyway.

While sucking in a long pull, our gazes collide, and I can't seem to escape his. He's so off-putting in his silence. It's always his aura. I blow out the smoke, feeling my body visibly relax. If a mountain's rock never moved or weathered, it would be a good comparison to Bridger at this moment. His eyes haven't left mine, yet his quietness perturbs me. How does it not bother him to be this closed off?

"Want some?" I offer.

He doesn't smile, flinch, or even relax, but he takes my hand holding the blunt, bringing it to his lips to inhale. It's single-handedly the hottest and most unnerving thing to witness. He hollows his cheeks around the tiny stick, all while gripping my wrist as if it anchors him here. When he lets out the puff, his hand doesn't drop mine.

"You should be careful in the dark, Colton. Monster don't mind kidnapping little things to use over and over again."

My chest tightens, making my heart pause along with it

"What do you mean?" I ask, feeling stupid for showing my fear and cards.

"Means that in the shadows are where monsters like my kind lurk. Next time you come out here with your short-ass skirt, tall fucking boots, and a halter top that leaves barely anything to the imagination, you might be dragged to the dark side where there's no escaping."

My breathing catches, my mouth falling open at the response. Cool wind whips at me as he moves closer, making our chests practically bump. Slowly, like a promise, his finger touches a stray neon lock, tucking it behind my ear, then somehow finds its way to my hand. Doing what he did before, bringing the joint from my hand to his mouth, he takes a long drag. Puffs of smoke dance in the air, its own ritual before dispersing into the sky forever.

Releasing his hold, he leans in, leaving me no room to breathe, and blows every ounce of toxic vapor into my mouth making sure our lips don't touch.

"Stay out of the woods, Colton."

Coldness is all that greets me when he leaves me here heading in the direction I ran from. It only takes me ten seconds to realize how unsafe it is at this school. My brother was killed less than five months ago. It's not old news. Being reckless isn't in the cards, and as that realization dawns on me, I run back to my dorm, locking it tight.

CHAPTER SEVEN

The next day, I head to the shared bathroom down the hall, m[y] caddy in hand, my mind in a negative space.

We have communal showers. It's kind of despairing whe[n] you think too hard, but they're trying to be less regressive[.] There are five showers on each side with curtains and hanger[s] outside for towels and laundry bags. The center has two lon[g] benches, and toward the south side, there are changing area[s.] Since we share with both guys and girls, it's helpful to hav[e] some sense of privacy.

Pushing open the door, I'm welcomed with noiselessness[.] Serene. It's never packed while classes are in session. Lucky me[.]

I hang my towel and undress. It should be noted tha[t] though this is a communal shower, it's implicitly meant fo[r] girls. It's the least frequented one in the tower since girls wer[e] only allowed at this school in the last decade. Guys generall[y] stay toward the east part of the tower, the chicks on the west. It should bug the staff, but they don't stop anything. It's like we're expected to be adults, do everything on our own, and pretend we have our shit together.

Plot twist. We don't.

As I turn the knob almost all the way to the left, the water runs. The heat of the shower invades the empty stall, scalding my skin, but it's a welcome ache. Experiencing pain and pleasure and everything in between instead of the mind-numbing void Cassidy's death brings me is freeing. When you live through someone's death, one so close to your heart, it ruins that soft part of you, the tangible one who empathizes with others, offering kindness and emotions. It steals every hope and dream too, promising only ruin and a never-ending ache on the soul.

That's what it did to me, took the naïve girl and forced her to become dead in a living world. They aren't wrong when they call me a vampire. I let life suck me dry and, in turn, suck the happiness from everyone closest to me. The way I dress doesn't help, but I'm not changing for a single soul.

Steam rises as my body absorbs each moment with the heat showering my skin. The kiss and pinpricks that lick each crevasse as I breathe in have me feeling removed from the world for once, allowing me an escape from my own damaging thoughts. I'm not supposed to use hot water on my hair since it makes the colors bleed out faster, but who cares? Certainly not me. I have to get my hair done every three weeks. It's almost time to get it touched up anyway.

61

Hopefully, Scotty, my hairstylist, will drive out here to do it. Paying to go to town for it sucks, and sneaking out of this campus isn't the easiest feat. Unless she absolutely refuses to venture here, then it'll be a must. She's not exactly a fan of this place. *Can anyone blame her?*

After my skin feels numb to everything with red and blotchy spots, I turn off the water, hating the chill that settles as soon as the steam escapes. Reaching for the towel hanging outside, my hand collides with cold unbothered tile. I pat my palm around, wondering if it's more one way than the other. Flat porcelain and the metal kiss of the towel rack are all that greets me. *What the fuck?* The shower curtain, currently the only thing hiding me, is my saving grace. As I peek around it in search of my stuff, my heart deflates. It's gone. Everything. My clothes, my towel, and my cell.

"You've got to be fucking kidding me!" I hiss loudly, hearing the words echo like a bad joke. This better not be a prissy bitch's doing, or I swear to God...

"No joke, Vampire. Seems you're without clothing," *his* voice sing-songs.

My blood runs cold, mirroring the tile my hands just touched, sending a newfound chill over my body. *Nonononono.* It can't be. No. Please, no. But I know it. The memories gnaw at my bones, sharp reminders that this boy has engraved himself onto each one permanently.

When death meets her maker, does she kiss him hello, or does she kick and scream the entire time he drags her away?

"Ross?" I question the hidden person, already knowing

62

the answer. *Ross McAllister.* Along with Lennox, he's the only true dick in my life, and we're not talking about the pleasurable kind. "Where the fuck is my stuff?"

"What? No, how was your summer, or, I'm sorry I bailed on you in Student Gov? What about I miss you, Rossy? You're my *favorite*."

"My shit. Where is it?" I growl, evading his questions. Deep down, he does want the answers. He may act with nonchalance, but inside that body is a guy who wants love and has more abandonment issues than a lost puppy.

My fingers tighten around the curtains, hoping he doesn't come closer. It's been months since I've seen him. Didn't expect to pass by him often. We don't exactly run in the same circles, other than the obvious one with his friends who like torturing me. *Student Gov.*

"Colty, Colty, Colty," he taunts, making me shiver more. Even when Ross and I didn't fight, we were never friends. Not really. He and Cass were the closest aside from Ten. He always thought of me as Cassidy's bratty little sister.

Some friend he was.

"Did you miss me?" His voice drips with both syrup and venom, the combination as sweet as it is damning.

"No," I whisper, clutching the curtain across my chest.

He finally comes into view, and my mouth dries up. In the last six months, he's gotten bulkier. Ross was never slim, but he didn't pack this much muscle before. He's not sporting his uniform, no. He's wearing only gray sweatpants that sit *very* low on his hips, leaving nothing to the imagination. Shirtless and charming as fucking night, he quirks a brow. His nipple are pierced and staring right at me, and his abs... *Jesus*. He' grown. I stare at his muscular arms and tattoos I didn't know he had. He's a sight, and I hate him for it. His hair, unlike las year, is gray and buzzed short. Really short. His eyes, green and mossy as ever, taunt me. An upside-down cross blesse his temple near his left eye, and it's got me gobsmacked. Tha goddamn mole that resides on the left corner of his lip taunt me as much as his words. Ross is a demon in and out of th uniform he rarely wears. His demerits are always stacked, bu mostly based upon his non-approved attire.

Another change in him is his dimples. *They're pierced.* My eyes are stuck on that tidbit. What I'd do to bite them. I lic my lips subconsciously thinking of it.

"I think you're lying." He smirks, making his piercing indent in such a churlish way. He seems mischievous ever while being a dick. His body is merely two feet away now The glint in his bright green irises has me pausing and tensing with expectation. Not the pleasant kind either. "I think you miss having me around to flirt with you as you blush sever shades of crimson."

"You're wrong," I squeak.

He closes the distance. "Too bad about your clothes princess. Quite liked the lacy thong." He closes the distance between us and thumbs my chin ardently, touching me like I'm his to touch. *I'm not.* He flames my skin as he smiles. "Much more tempting without makeup." He swipes my wet bottom lip, spreading the beads of water across.

With that last act of assholery, he walks away, leaving me naked and shivering in the bathroom.

Fuck him. Goddammit.

It takes me several minutes to get the shower curtain off the bar above me. It wasn't pretty and hopefully, no one hid and recorded that show.

I literally waddle all the way back to my room, praying he will give my phone back at the very least. Both my moms will kill me if not. It's only two weeks in. Being down a phone this early on will lead them to be less lenient with me.

The door to my dorm is somehow slightly ajar, saving me a trip for a new badge. In my haste, my body collides into someone.

"Fuck!" I shout, dropping the shower curtain.

My mouth falls open in an attempt to say something and cover myself up, but at this point, it's too late.

Ten stands there with a smirk hotter than a stove coil as I squirm under its weight. His eyes rake my frame appreciatively. "You've definitely grown up, Greenie."

It's been two weeks, and I've had encounters with every fucked-up Student Gov member, and the whiplash of salty and sweet thrown my way is just too much.

"Can you turn around?" I request meekly. He may have seen it all before, but it doesn't help that it's been a long time, and my body has changed a lot since. And the piercings. Shit. The piercings.

"Can't. Struck stupid." He hums his approval.

Finally, I bend down, and my fingers fumble a bit before

they grip the shower curtain, and I cower behind it once agai

"When did you get those?"

I open my mouth then close it. It happens a couple mo
times before he laughs.

"I remember everything about you, Kid. Those a
definitely new." He emphasizes by pinching his nipples.

I groan, my face feeling hot. "Why are you here, Ten?"

"After the other day... I needed to apologize," he answe

The honesty on his face has me caving in. He's a chink
my armor. Probably always will be.

"I can't force my friendship on you, but I miss yo
Colton, so fucking much."

He abandoned you, my mind parries.

I stare at him longingly, unable to escape how he affe
me. My heart not wanting to see what's right in front of n
He must see my yearning because he steps closer, holdi
my jaw. Tenderness meets me, so warm and welcomir
Human touch, you never realize how much it matters ur
it's happening after a long fast without it.

He abandoned Cass, my mind reminds. Making me diz
but too distracted by his silver eyes.

"I like the piercings," he adds, "especially the hip ones.

"Oh, the hip ones? Couldn't tell you noticed with h
you ogled my tits," I grumble, ignoring everything insi
yelling at me to walk away.

He chuckles, kissing my nose.

What are you doing?

The nagging voice in the back of my head telling me

left me alone, didn't come to Cassidy's funeral, and isn't here with good intentions is ever-present.

"Sorry, babe. Those are fucking hot."

Babe. He *can't* call me that.

"Ten—"

"Shh."

He silences me with a kiss. Our mouths meld, and the curtain barely held up of anger and resentment bows out with how he takes control of our mouths' movements. He grips my hip with one hand, his thumb tracing the barbell there while his other holds my throat. I like it there, his hand. It's where it belongs.

He pulls away, placing his forehead against mine, ragged breaths the only sounds leaving us both. This tension we've always carted is going to get me in trouble. I can't trust him. I won't. He's no longer the person I allowed to take my virginity last year. He's not the same sweet guy who brought me calla lilies when my period struck. He's definitely not the guy who stood up for me when Lennox belittled me. He's a new breed of asshole, and probably only pretending to care about me for whatever game Student Gov has planned. When it mattered most, he chose them. When Cass was buried, none of them showed up. When my life felt hopeless, shredding the last bits of humanity spared by my beating heart, he didn't say a word. He's something else now, and that realization is scarier than the fact that I've allowed him to touch and kiss me twice within days. The more power given up, the more I lose myself and the less Cass is honored.

"You should go," I suggest, pulling away, allowing th
tiny morsel of pride to stab through me. "This can't happer
Ten, no matter how good it feels."

"So, you admit. You still feel it, too."

"How many chicks did you fuck this summer?" I chang
the subject.

His face falls, and right there is where his truths ar
visible. There have been several others. The jealousy gnawin
my insides makes zero sense. He owes me nothing. He's nc
mine. Never was.

"Colt—"

"Please. If you actually care as much as you pretend, jus
go. I bet there are tons of chicks who'll beg to take my place,
I mutter, the bitterness seeping from each word.

"I don't want anyone else."

It's too late, though. I've already gone to my dresser an
thrown on some panties and a shirt and am moving hin
toward the door.

"It can't be me, Ten. There's too much history. I'm no
even part of Student Gov. Technically, we can't even date."

Not that the guys ever tried to get rid of the rules afte
Yang and I came on board. They wanted every reason to hi
it and quit it. There are rules at Arcadia Crest. Weird fuckin
barbaric ones, but rules nonetheless.

He nods with understanding and anger. No fight. Neve
any fight. "Can we at least try to be friends? Like before? Cas
would—"

"Out." My single word brooks no argument, and h

realizes his mistake immediately.

"My number is still the same, Colton. Try." He heads out after giving me another once-over.

I sit on my bed long after he has left, wondering why and how he could be involved with what happened to Cass. It's not like he could harm a fly. His heart, though not reflective of his dark outer appearance, is gold. Or it was.

He's changed.

They all have.

When I've finally calmed down, several knocks sound at my door. Turning toward it, I groan, wishing we had peepholes. Hopefully, no freshman decides the egging contest is great for the outcast. Opening the door, I see my phone sitting on the ground. Hoping Ross didn't get into it somehow, I search it for clues. Nothing.

What are you playing at, Dare?

CHAPTER EIGHT

"You are Colton Hudson?" a new student asks as I'm headir to Psych. She has bright eyes because she hasn't experience the toxicity of this place yet.

A few days later, I'd finally sucked it up and went back t classes. After the scolding from Moms, the visit from Ten, an the realization that the world doesn't stop turning becaus I'm miserable, I ended up back on track.

The girl waits for my response. She's being nice, and it different. She's the first person who hasn't called me a freak.

We couldn't be more different. She has natural strawberr blonde hair and freckles smattered across her nose and hig cheekbones while I'm dark and gory on my nice days. She charming in that small-town-debutante kinda-way.

"The very one, and you?" I'm nothing if not polite. It ingrained in me. Even when I hung out with the boys c government, I didn't treat anyone less than me. Why would I? There was never a rivalry for me with girls. While they may have had issues with me for being *popular,* I didn't have the same qualms. Plus, this new girl seems sweet and with good intentions.

She smiles kindly at me, the distinct niceness of her personality floating over me. Unlike half of the student body, she doesn't give me the *I hate your guts* vibes for being different. It's a pleasant change.

"Melissa Tompkins," she replies. Her voice has a little lilt to it. She's not from the Valley, where most Arcadia kids are. You're either part of the Valley—the rich and famous—or you came from other similar places around the world. She almost has a southern drawl. Maybe she's from the south or far east?

"I'm not—"

"Oh, my bad! My father is Roderick Krane," she interrupts as if it explains everything.

The name lights a switch, but I'm not sure why. I give her a pensive stare, not wanting to be rude, but unsure where this conversation is leading.

"I'm not sure who that is. I'm so sorry! I kind of live under a rock." Shielding my face from the first moment of actual embarrassment I've had, a self-deprecating laugh leaves me. It's a half-truth. It's not in me to care about status and all the other bullshit they drill into our heads. They want us to know our place on the scale, as if it makes us worthy or not.

She giggles. "It's okay. He owns half of Tennessee. He's old money. But out here, the west coast, I can completely understand why you wouldn't know. It's kind of refreshing, she says on a sigh. "Usually, people are terrified of me because of him."

The name repeats itself in my mind over and over, and finally, it clicks. "Is your father that Movie Mogul? The one with Irish ties?" *The mobster.* It's coming to me, the scandals court cases, lies upon lies, and the family dragged apart by them.

"That's the one," she whispers. "It's why I don't go by Krane. Don't need to start here on a bad note. Being the new girl is hard enough without that name tying me down."

I smile at her, offering her my hand. "Nice to meet you, Melissa. Welcome to hell. Hope you like it warm," I tease. I'm not even slightly lying now.

She stares at me, almost as if she's trying to dissect my brain. Good luck, girl. Not even sure I could do it myself.

"You're not going to prod?" She bites her lip, her face one of confusion.

"Not my place. Why ruin a new friendship by diving deep?"

Almost deciding something in her mind, she nods. "I'm not sure where I'm headed." She hands me her schedule. "Please, if you don't mind."

This is the strangest yet most pleasant conversation I've had this year. It's insane that a new girl is kinder to me than anyone I've known my entire life. It's sad, really.

Perusing her schedule, I notice she's headed the same place as me. "Oh, you have Psych like me. Not many new kids do. They generally don't take this class."

"Oh, psychology fascinates me," she drawls, her voice taking on a passionate tone. "Knowing how the brain of a killer's works and people with mental health issues intrigues me to no end."

The enthusiasm in her tone reminds me of the me from before, with Art, back when my life wasn't a living hell without my favorite person to experience it with me.

"Me too. Not sure what that says about me."

"Maybe you're a knowledge fiend like me?"

"Not really. My grades are decent but nothing to write home about. If not for my parents, I'd never get into Providence Hall."

"That's a nearly impossible school to get into," she muses thoughtfully.

She's not wrong. Providence Hall is an Ivy League University far outside Arcadia. It's where both my moms went. The difference between them and me, they're actually eclectic, wanting to be the best of the best. I just want to survive high school.

"It's not as if your parents own half the country," I say.

"Your mom is Tasha Hudson, the Multi-Billionaire Diamond Trader?"

"Unfortunately," I deadpan.

She's not just a Diamond Trader. She's *the* Diamond Trader.

The warning alarm for class rings out, cutting our conversation short. She follows me as I rush to Mr. Bautista.

He'll lock us out if we're late. By the time I'm rushing inside the room, there are only two seats available, both next to Lux and the new guy, Jordan. Though Jordan was kind, he's also in Student Gov, which means he's practically an asshole without the confirmation. Instead of forcing myself to suffer at the hands of Lux, I take the seat in front of Jordan and immediately regret my decision.

"So, you're back to class. Does this mean we get to be friends?" Jordan's voice sounds out from near my ear. He had to be leaning in really close for me to hear him so profoundly.

My response sticks to my tongue and absolutely obliterates itself when Lux jests nearby.

"You should keep your distance, Walker. Might catch an STD."

"Are you fucking joking?" I hiss, turning toward him. "Get bent, Lux."

"Are you offering, Vampire? Not sure if I'm into blood play and sacrifices."

It's a lie. We both know he's down for blood play.

"Fuck off." It comes off as a grumble, not a full attack.

My eyes catch onto the new girl while she studies the situation. She literally analyzes it with that big brain of hers. Her wheels turn as she absorbs the information and comes up with whatever conclusion she sees fitting. It's present in her eyes.

"Class. Today's the day!" Mr. Bautista announces like we're at some goddamn award show. He's excited for the subject, I'm sure. Any psyche is. It's like a thing.

"Boring," Lux complains.

Our teacher turns to him with a conspiratorial grin. "Sounds like Mr. DeLeon volunteers."

"Shit."

"Shit is right," Melissa comments, barely stifling a giggle.

That little comment has me liking her even more.

Lux practically drags his feet to the front of the room. It's surprising, just for the simple fact that his loafers cost more than my entire outfit. He's not one to scuff his precious *things.* Once upon a time, he made it a point to claim me as one of those things. How times change. Unlike me, Lennox isn't scared to spend every penny his father offers, while I shop at Dark Princess as if it's the best I can afford. It's not. It's just my preferred attire nowadays.

In his hand is a notebook, and the wicked gleam in his expression scares me. It's one I know too well. A promise really, of destruction, pain, and callousness.

"I decided to do my paper on a serial killer who hasn't been caught."

Bautista nods, acting like he doesn't know where this is going, but I do. From the way his eyes seek mine out and connect, it's clear. He's going to hurt me. Nerves claw their way to the surface, begging me to leave before this gets worse. Before he embarrasses me. Before he ruins what's left of my sanity.

"In Arcadia Crest, no less," he starts, waiting for the collective gasp.

Bautista doesn't seem to know what to make of this, but he can't know of every serial killer in this rural town. Not when he's an outsider. But I do. There's two. Since this tin town was founded, there's only been two.

"A person in this town pushed a young boy, an Arcadi Crest student. The fall ended his life as he bled out from hi skull in messy heaps. There was so much blood that when th crime scene photos leaked, no one could erase the horror."

"Is he talking about Cassidy?" a grade eleven bo whispers loudly.

"Didn't he fall off a building?" one mutters.

"Yeah, that's the freak show's brother," another adds.

"Some say the killer will strike again, and at homecoming no less," Lux explains solemnly like he's telling a sad stor instead of a true one. "Some say the killer is a teenage frea with green garbage hair."

A whimper escapes my lips before I can swallow it down A chorus of laughter mixed with hushed whispers sprea throughout the room.

Bautista realizes where this is going a little too late "Class, settle. Settle down!" His voice carries across the room brooking no argument.

Lux's eyes haven't left mine, and the triumph there ha me barely holding in tears. He accused me once again o killing my brother. What about Lux? He's the one who ha been there, not me. I'd been losing my virginity to Ten ir Crystal while he and his fuckboys disappeared on us, doin, whatever it was they were doing.

What do they know?

The class doesn't stop their incessant whispers, but

can't move or look at any of them. I'm stuck in the disgusting hazel thrall of Lux DeLeon, the worst kind of monster. He smirks evilly at me. It stays on me as he sees himself out. No matter how long he's gone and the next students talk about their chosen serial killer, there are still whispers of me and my poor brother. They don't know us. They don't know our story. They don't know how much pain comes with even the mere mention of him. He's gone, and he's never coming back, and the asshole elitist snobs at this school know what happened.

"Miss Hudson, you're up," my teacher announces as my body numbs to everything around me.

"She did it. She's only in this class as a cover," a grade eleven snubs at me.

"Her brother was such a good kid. This godless whore took him away," another bites.

Tears sting my eyes. The emptiness in my steps as I make my way to the podium only increases the dread. It's all I know. When things start to look up, everything crashes down. It's how this school works.

My hands grip my paper tightly, so much so that it's crumpled around the edges from the force. When I make it to the podium, everyone's whispering under their breaths and pointing at me. Everyone but Melissa and Jordan. Using them as anchors, whether they know it or not, I stare at them as I deliver my research on Pedro Rodrigues Filho, a Brazilian man who killed over one hundred people. One of which was his own father. It's said he ate a piece of his father's heart to prove a point, which to me makes me feel like he was hurt and needed something to prove that his father wasn't heartless. By the time I'm finished explaining tyranny and Pedro's knack for killing bullies and murderers alike, people are staring at me as if I'm Pedro, and I'll kill anyone who speaks ill of me.

My assignment goes from something that harbors passion to something despicable and fearful. It feels as if my body closes in on itself at the whispers going around. It shouldn't bother me, but it does. Classmates stare at me in horror and fear. It's something I'm used to. This time, though, after Lux has ruined my whole reputation, it somehow seems worse.

"Thank you, Colton. You can have a seat," Bautista announces.

Even in his eyes, there's doubt, an inkling of sorts, or maybe I'm reading into things. Either way, my stomach eats itself as the wait for class to be over seems to go on like a snail in a race.

When predicting this year would be easy, I never accounted for others openly working against me every step of the way. Lux will be an issue. Not that he'd been anything less than a prick since we met, but now his charming and addictive charisma only sets itself to turn the entire school against me.

Colt + Lux = screwed.

CHAPTER
NINE

"I didn't mean to come off so strongly."

"You're fine. I'm not a people person anyway," I mutter, walking toward my next class.

After saying the words, I realize how inaccurate that used to be. Last year, when my brother and Yang were my best friends, life was good. Popularity, fame, you name it, I had it. It was fake, of course, but it was mine for the taking. Then Cass died. Then they all abandoned ship.

My only stresses surrounded four guys who make my life hell but also made my life something more. They weren't afraid to reveal how much they liked me.

Ten was always first, pushing for us to mess around, but I didn't want only him. Call it greed or the need to be single so when I went to college, boys wouldn't break my heart or academic goals. Either way, our relationship was everything but the title.

Then, there was the rest. They were mine without eve saying it.

It was obvious in the way they kissed me, held me, alway kept me close. We were a group of people who just loved bein around each other.

Yang didn't approve.

At first, I thought jealousy drove her, since I had th school's four hottest guys for myself. After everythin happened, I realize it was because she recognized thei darkness.

"Hey," Mel mentions, stopping my pursuit to the gyn "I'm sorry I didn't say anything more to Lennox in class."

That's what she meant.

I raise an eyebrow. It's not her job to protect me Especially not to the likes of those guys. If anything, sh should stay far away from me and them. Collateral damag is a real problem.

"Don't apologize. He's a dick. He always will be." Th nonchalance in my voice isn't to be avoided.

"What's the story there?" she asks animatedly, grippin her books to her chest. Is she asking because she wants dirt, o is she asking because she actually gives a shit?

"A long story that doesn't deserve repeating," I let out.

She bites her lip like she wants to say more, but sh doesn't.

I appreciate that. Holding my bag strap tighter wonderment fills me. Not many people can hold back thei nosiness. It's a curse. We, too, have to deal with the bullshit that spills from their lips, all from their lack of restraint.

"That's fair," she muses. "What's your next class?"

I grimace, thinking of PE and how I'll be seeing Lennox again. It's not going to be pretty. Whenever we're put into the same classes, something goes wrong, especially this one when he's my babysitter. My doctor called and let me know I could start eating regular food. She specified it to be small amounts so that I could monitor changes. My pill dosage is being lessened every day as well.

Tonight, I'm eating a goddamn pizza.

"Fitness," I groan. "With Coach Carter."

She laughs, literally tips her head back and laughs, her books bouncing with each jolt. "I like you, Colton. You're definitely not normal."

"Thanks?" I mutter, not knowing how to react, but I'm glad she's honest. We need more people in the world who don't hold anything back. Continuing my pursuit for greasy happiness, she follows.

"It's a compliment. Being normal is overrated. I have to go to Lit, but I'll definitely catch up with you later if you have second lunch?"

Stopping my escape, I turn toward her, but she's several feet away by now. "I do!" I yell after her. "Have second lunch!"

"I'll find you!" she hollers back while retreating down the hall.

Her heels tap in the other direction while my boots sound like loud reverberating stomps. It's in no means intentional.

I would never do it on purpose. The last thing I want is t
garner attention from this cistern.

After arriving to the changing rooms, it's apparen
everyone is already outside, making me late. Shit. No one'
here, which means Coach will start without me, and Lu
will—

"You're late, Corpse."

—be a bigger dick than usual.

"Why are you in the girl's locker room?" I gripe, fastenin
my fingers around my bag's straps as if they'll protect me fron
him.

What is it with these guys thinking they can invade m
space? First Ross, and now Lux. When will they let the past die

When you do.

It's never going to end because my brother is gone, an
there's no stopping me from getting answers.

"Why are you still wearing your gothic ensemble tha
makes Bellatrix Lestrange seem like a Muggle?"

"The fact that you know what a Muggle is and wh
Bellatrix is makes me believe you're a lot nerdier than you'v
let on."

"Are you going to get dressed, or are you going to mak
us both look bad?" he deflects.

Mentally, I save this information for later. Who knows
Maybe he's a true Potterhead, and I can use that to m
advantage. My mind immediately travels to Slytherin jokes an
how Ross would appreciate them. *Fuck. Stop thinking about them*

Lux stares at me. If he thinks I'm undressing in front o

him, he's got another knee-to-the-balls coming.

"Well, if you're going to be standing here, we'll be waiting all day." Heat spreads through me as I pull off my backpack and use it as a shield against my chest.

"When did you become self-conscious?"

His curiosity grates on me. He's acting as if the last five months didn't pass without a word from him or the others.

"When did you become a dick?"

He scoffs. "Do you always answer a question with a question?"

I give him the *really* look. "Why do you act like this, Lux? It's not like you know me."

He sidles closer to me, forcing me to take several steps back, my bag landing between us at my feet. This sociopath side of his, the one that terrorizes me, it's one I'll never get used to. He's always been terrifying, but at least before, I'd been aware of what he'd be giving in the deal. Now, he's an entirely different creature, and that's a scary realization.

"I know you, Corpse." He slides the bag away with his foot, trying to erase the gap between us. "Sometimes more than you know yourself," he finishes.

His hazel eyes, the green more prominent than the brown today, throw me off. He hasn't been this close in a long time. There are mere inches between us. It would take him leaning in to eat the last few breaths. He would, especially if it would unsettle me further.

Lennox DeLeon has a reputation from dismantling groups, terrorizing them to concede, and rising from their ashes after he's destroyed everything they hold dear.

"You don't know me," I mutter, not wanting to push int him and force him back. With my condition and his brut strength, it wouldn't be a battle, and losing isn't an option.

"I do," he mocks, gripping a bright green strand of m hair, tugging it enough to make me yelp. "I know you so muc that even though you just made a noise of discomfort, you pussy is hot and wet for me." Lux bridges the gap so that hi lips aren't even centimeters away. They're practically touchin mine. "If I pull up that black little number and touch you, wi you already be a mess between these thighs?"

A gasp absconds from my lips, expelling itself like wanton wish as his other hand grips my hip right where m piercing is. It's such a sensitive spot, and I hate how mucl his words illicit warmth to spread through me. He's right too knowing my body loves pain with its pleasure. They worl side by side, driving me both crazy with need and hatred. lover's quarrel where there's no winner, only loss and despaii Someone as monstrous as Lennox shouldn't make me so ben up inside. He shouldn't have a single effect on me.

But he does.

The silent ones always do. They bring out the baser sid of me, the side needing to be handled and fucked until carin is the last emotion riding me.

"We're going to be late," I try, shrinking back as much a the metal grate behind me allows.

His arms and hands box me in as he places one on eithei side of my head. Licking his bottom lip, he breathes agains my throat. Its slow, heady, murmuring promises he'll never follow through with.

"We're already late. You have two minutes to change. After that, all bets are off."

His unnerving last words makes my body tremble from head to toe. Opening my locker, I shove my stuff and grab my change of clothes, taking it to the stall and undressing faster than I ever have. Lux may be menacing, but unlike normal teens, he's not an idle threat. He's deliberate with his words, his threats. As much as fighting him sounds good, this isn't a battle worth losing.

As soon as I'm out of the stall, he's there, waiting. Two minutes, my ass. He probably barely wasted a second to pop in here. A smirk tilts on his face, letting me know he's aware of where my mind just went.

Fuck off.

I throw my stuff in my locker and follow him out. This is going to be the worst class since the first day, or maybe tormenting me is his favorite past time. No matter what, I lose.

The class wasn't too bad. We worked out in the fitness portion of the gym—weight lifting, treadmills, and bikes. Since I'm on regulated duty, I could only do the bike, which, by the way, isn't as easy as people make it out to be. After doing intervals for thirty minutes, my thighs feel like Jell-O, but at least, they feel *something*. The weakness they've had isn't appealing in the least.

Since being sick, I've felt frail, which is not me. I used t
dance and do drills and workout as if it was my religion.

After class ends, we change. Most girls won't showe
because they're nervous. Me? I have zero qualms for that shi
even after Ross barged in. I refuse to feel sweaty for the las
two hours of school.

Hurrying into the shower, I make quick with removin
my makeup and washing my body. No one sees me withou
makeup. Not during the past year, at least. Even then,
didn't leave my dorm without a full face. It mattered. Muc
differently than now, but it still mattered.

As soon as I've finished, it's a race to get dressed. N
one's in here. They're probably all at the end of roll call. I'r
okay with that. There's no reason for me to come back.

It takes about ten minutes to get my full face back t
where I like it.

Adding a gloss layer on my lips instead of my norma
black, I head out right as the bell rings. Well, would you loo.
at that? Lunch time.

Instead of checking back in with Coach, I make my wa
to the cafeteria. Not rushing to hide. It's something I haven'
done since the start of school. Luckily for me, I've got a nev
whatever-she-is, Mel. She's not quite a friend, but she'
definitely not a foe. It's a happy medium of existing in hel
alongside one another. A camaraderie of sorts.

As I scan the room filled to the brim with students, i
takes a moment before seeing a familiar face. How does ever
single Student Gov kid have the same lunch as me every day

Can't they have the opposite of mine and not make me want to die more than I already do?

The five of them are huddled at a table, along with three of the drill team girls and several people I don't recognize. One girl sits in Ten's lap. Another is draped over Lux, and I'm internally vomiting.

Mel, where are you? My eyes are practically racing to find her. The anxiety of being surround by this many people is as claustrophobic as the elevator. It's daunting in the worst way.

My stomach begs me to fill it with carbs. I'm about to turn and leave when her voice stops me. "Colton!"

Did she have to say it so loudly? People's heads, along with five guys' from Student Gov, all turn my way. It's like silence has been masked upon the entire room while she makes her way to me.

"Great. Just want I wanted."

"What was that?" Mel asks, coming right beside me.

I gape at her, not knowing what to do with my life. Students staring at me is somewhat normal, but stopping all conversation just to watch how this plays out? That's new.

"Pizza. Need pizza."

She smiles. It goes across her entire face, making her eyes crinkle with the motion. "I honestly thought you'd be a salad girl," she murmurs.

I would laugh if it wasn't true. Instead, I scrunch my face in displeasure.

"I'm sorry. I didn't mean to offend. You're just so nimble."

I want to reassure her and tell her it's fine, but my body

being so small makes me uncomfortable. I've been a curvie side of skinny for a long time, so being on the bony side isn't appealing. Wanting to offer her a little reassurance, I offer a grin. "Greasy food is my favorite," I say. "If I could live off carbs, I would."

"With a body like yours? Why not?" She says it like she has to care about her own figure, but she's gorgeous in every way. People would be stupid not to notice.

"Oh, shut up," I mock. "If I had an ass like yours, I'd be flaunting it."

With that, it's almost like our kinship is growing. We're breaking barriers, and lord knows I need any push I can get. We both get pizza after finding a table away from everyone. Arcadia, being one of those hoity-toity schools of course had full barstool type seats. It's convenient when you want to leave easily, but crappy when you bend too far one way.

Chatting, I notice Mel can tell I'm deflecting questions, but she always backs off without crossing into the annoying zone of getting to know someone. I'm starting to understand why people keep friends around. They're pertinent to existing in high school. Without Yang here this year, drowning was the norm. Having Mel might just save me.

CHAPTER TEN

"Look at what we got here," Ross muses from nearby, reminding me how much I hate knowing all of their voices like the back of my hand.

He sidles up to me as I'm about to take a huge bite of pepperoni. His hands come down on my shoulders. Nervousness sizzles inside me as my spine stiffens, feeling like he hit me with a hot poker. Skin contact shouldn't feel like a brand, a marking of ownership, or a fucking kindling stoking my fire.

It should be unwelcome, unpleasant. At the very least, it should feel unwanted.

But like a year ago, I'm a marionette, and these fuckers are my masters.

His fingers bend into me, squeezing none too lightly. It's not enough to bruise a normal person, but it's definitely enough to discolor my anemic state.

Mel searches my eyes for a guide, as if I'm accustomed t this and what to do.

Newsflash, southern comfort, I'm not.

"Aids, tell me it's aids," I ask in a faux girlie tone, like I'm a mad groupie and he's offering me his body at my disposal.

His hands lift off me, and he's turning me around. Thos eyes of his, the greenest ones that give my hair a run for it money, narrow at me. He's gauging my reactions, like a vipe ready to strike, waiting to know and understand its prey from the inside out first.

"Ah, Tim Burton special, wouldn't that be grand? Tellin the entire cafeteria how you—"

I push into him, smacking a palm over his too-evasiv mouth. He bites the skin and then licks it right after, makin me shiver and cringe all at once.

I hate him.

I hate them.

I hate life.

After dropping my hand, I wipe it on my skirt.

Ross seems amused at the movement, like he got th reaction he wanted out of me. I'm not sure when the other made their way over, but now, next to him, they're al surrounding the table behind us. Lux sits, staring at me witl eyes that portray how hungry he is for me. Fuck, the way he' spread wide, his elbows resting on his thighs, it does something to my insides. Beside him, avoiding me, is a grimacing Ten. H refuses to glance this way—not a surprise. On the other sid of him stands Bridger. His blank stare gives me no reprieve, and did I really expect it to? Out of all these guys, he's the only sociopath who openly admits it when asked. He doesn't care that people know, but he would care if they knew he wasn't born one and it was a learned trait. I know he has daddy issues. Hell, all these boys do. But if you asked, he would fuck you up and then pretend it never happened.

I think of all the times he's made me a frazzled mess, and I cringe. Why is he so perfect in an ungodly way? If he was carved from stone, it wouldn't be a surprise. It must go deeper than that. Maybe his parents sacrificed souls to create such a haunting child. He's too perfect and too inhuman. Unnatural.

It takes me far too long to respond that Ross taps my nose to get my attention. It's too late, I'm entranced by a numb boy who doesn't know how to feel.

Maybe he secretly does. Who knows?

"What?" I snap.

"I was asking why you're sitting in the mess hall. It's not your style."

Anger ignites in me as my eyes roll in response. Didn't know eating food was a fashion statement.

"Good thing no one asked you for your opinion, Dare."

He swallows slowly, his Adam's apple bobbing slowly, surely, like he's unsure how to respond. Bet no one knows why he's called Dare, and they probably won't. It's a secret we're told to take to the grave.

Too bad I'm already dead.

"One of these days, I'm going to mess up that pretty little

mouth of yours, Colty."

I smirk back at him, loving the edge he just gave me. He doesn't realize kind words are an opening for cruel ones.

"Never said you could handle me sucking cock, Dare. Guess you've just realized it, too."

He flinches, and the rest of the guys, except Lux, seem flummoxed, but Lux—*the fucker*—he grabs his groin and winks at me. What that means, I'm not sure, but that doesn't stop me from feeling knocked down a peg or five. Fuck. He's too hot for his own good, and I'm too weak for mine.

And stupid. There's a whole lot of stupid flooding my mind.

"What the fuck was that?" Mel whispers after the guys fuck off.

I stare at her, not knowing how to explain it.

"I feel like I just witnessed a dick measuring contest, and you definitely won."

At that, I'm chuckling. She isn't wrong. I would beat them in that contest any day. I've got nothing left to lose.

"But seriously, what is going on with you and that Dare guy?"

"If I knew, I couldn't tell you. They're Satanists."

Her eyes widen.

"They'd have no qualms in sacrificing my soul for their own twisted games."

Of that, I'm absolutely certain.

As soon as my teeth dive into the greasy masterpiece between my fingers, I gag. It's an uncontrollable reaction to something I've tried to overcome in the last two months. The slice drizzles that perfect oiliness that I love, but seeing it now, smelling the cheese and pep as it touches my tongue, I can't control the repulsion.

"Are you okay?" Melissa asks, her face full of worry.

She's staring at me as if I'm dying. Maybe I am. This must be what absolute torture feels like, sitting in front of the thing you love most, wanting to eat it, and then it telling you *nice fucking try.*

"Yeah, yeah," I mutter, trying not to let the overwhelming sadness be present in my eyes. It's hard being a foodie without the ability to eat. It's unfair. I put a napkin to my mouth and spit out the cringy bite, barely holding back the heaving.

"Are you sure? You look paler than normal."

"Thanks, Dr. Phil. Want to add therapist to your resumé?" I bark, hating the acrid tone coming from me. She doesn't deserve my malice any more than the pizza. "Shit. I'm sorry," I apologize.

She stares at me with an open mouth, grabs for her bottle of Snapple, and drinks a hefty gulp. After, she nods her head as if deciding something in her head.

I'm sitting here, waiting for her to blow a gasket, telling me how big of a cunt I'm being.

"I can see there's something here you're touchy about, Colt," she murmurs and looks directly into my pink eyes. "I can even understand your displeasure and know a little thing or two about eating disorders, so I won't fight with you over your asshole remark."

I can't even smile at her words because I feel like a total

shit, and she's seemingly angry—rightfully so—but doesn't retaliate like most teens.

She lets out a long breath and gives me a small grin of reassurance. "When you're ready, you can tell me all about what you're going through, and then I'll share my story."

Nodding with pure gratefulness, I feel the nervous swelling of my body deflate like a balloon. She's seriously the chillest girl I've met in a long time.

"I'm sorry," I offer. "It's just hard not being able to enjoy life's simple pleasures."

She nods in return. "I get it. Just remember, I'm not your enemy."

Wanting to hug her—which is weird for me—I offer her a reassuring smile. "You're right. I'll try not to forget that."

Because let's be honest. I'm a hormonal teenage girl. Making promises to not overreact isn't in the books.

After grabbing my Poké ball backpack, I pick up a granola bar. It's bland without even chocolate, but it'll give me enough energy for later. It seems salad, greens, and those god-awful protein shakes are the only meals I'll be having for the time being.

As we both eat in mere silence, Mel's eyes keep wandering over to the table seating my five terrors. *Jordan isn't a terror.* My mind and heart battle with that. Even my gut has an argument with that sentiment. He may not be *like* them, but he's one of them, which means, he's an enemy. And I'm fucked.

As I try to see who she's looking at, Bridger's eyes flit to mine. It's not usual for him to give me attention, or anyone for that matter. He's not exactly one for words or more than gestures, but he eviscerates my body with his dead gaze. Maybe it's just because he scares me, or there's something hidden in those black eyes. Either way, I'm trembling from how he doesn't blink or look away from me, and also shivering from the way I know he can practically shed my clothes from that look alone.

Why do my tormentors have this kind of power over me?

"Hey," a male voice sounds out from behind me. "This seat taken?"

It's only when Bridger's eyes narrow to near slits that I realize the guy is talking to me. What throws me most off balance is the fact that my sociopath doesn't seem to appreciate it very much.

Which, in turn, only makes me want to defy him.

Turning to the guy next to me, I offer a big grin, probably seemingly like the happiest emo girl in the entire universe. He's tall—really freaking tall—his hair is curly and messy, boyish and charming. I don't recognize him, but smile anyway. "Hiya," I respond. "It's *not—*"

"It's taken," Ten barks, making me wince.

The poor dude stares at me as if he can convince me to say something.

"No, it's really not," I hiss at Ten, wondering when he came back, hating the smirks he gives me as if he's been waiting for this very moment. Ignoring the massive asshole next to me, I give every ounce of my attention to the new dude. "What's your name?"

"Terrance," he offers a hand.

Ten smacks it away in an instant.

"I'm Colt." I once again avoid the big body taking th seat next to me. "Sorry about this caveman. He has small dic energy, if you know what I mean."

Placing quotations over the small dick part is a nic touch. A grin resurfaces, and my lack of appetite is all bu forgotten when my arms are snatched and my body is lifte by Lux himself.

"Fuck off, DeLeon!"

But he carts me over his shoulder, smacking my ass i front of half of the school. I squeal when he does it again.

I hate him.

He starts walking out of the mess hall, and panic sets ir I'm yelling and pounding on his back. My skirt isn't exactl long, and I'm sure people are spotting both my scars and m tattoos on the back of my thighs.

"Let me down!" I hiss.

A resounding slap sounds out as his palm connects witl my flesh again.

"Who knew a corpse could get pink skin?" he muses.

When I flatten, no longer an ounce of fight in me, h puts me down. We're outside the cafeteria and in the hallwa nearest the drama club. Great. These classes only run in th mornings. Which means—

"No one is allowed to sit with you," Lux grouches, hi face contorted with annoyance.

—they aren't giving me a choice but be cornered.

His arms are crossed, as if that gesture will keep hin

from touching me. With each breath that hisses from his chest, my body heaves in return, wanting him to attack and wanting to hit him in return.

"Fuck right off. You won't control who I hang out with."

A chuckle escapes him, and he throws his head back, exposing that thick throat that I'd love to taste again.

What the hell? Stop.

My inner ramblings are starting to make me uneasy as hell.

Lux pushes into my chest, and with the heat of my sore ass and the close proximity of this guy, I'm flushed and hot. Where's my buffer? Where's Mel? Ten didn't follow us. He must be keeping her back. Dicks.

When my back hits the brick wall, Lux boxes me in. He loves to do this, doesn't he?

"You will not sit with Terrance Reid. You got me, Corpse?"

It takes everything in me not to laugh in his face. He thinks he can demand a single thing from me? No. That's not how this works.

"Fuck. Off." The steely edge to my tone shows he's pissing me off. Fuck. He knows he's getting to me. That simply won't do.

He grabs a toxic lock of my hair, and I'm thrown back in the past when he grabbed silvery blonde strands before taking my breath away.

I shake in an attempt to thwart him, but he only pushes in closer.

"Seems like you need a lesson in who has the powe Corpse." His words are as harsh as they are confident.

But there's nothing he could do to me that'll hurt me. M brother is dead. My grades are suffering, and school is a lie.

Not like any of us need it. We can pay any university fe a roster spot. It's as simple as that.

"You seem to need some guidance in the fucks I dor give because I'm running short on explanations, Lennox."

"Ah, but it's so fun to watch that mouth move, especial as it's wrapped around my cock."

His words are venomous, but that doesn't stop my bo from reacting. My piercings always keep my nipples hard, b they suddenly feel like the metal inside them only tells he much he's affecting me.

"Lux," I whisper, not wanting him in my space anymo

His eyes cast down to look into mine, devouring, monstrosity, waiting for its next meal. For a fleeting mome he's softened, and that's exactly what I need. When he lea closer, I lift my knee and connect with his balls. As he cring and bends over, gripping his jewels, I make my escape for Not even caring that my bag is still in the lunchroom and tl I didn't get to eat my granola bar, I allow my feet to carry to my dorm, all while praying Lux doesn't catch up with m

CHAPTER ELEVEN

I hide out for the next few hours like I'm being hunted. If they wanted, they could easily get to me. That's the thing about Student Gov. They have all the power. Hell, they even have a master key to every room that's not in the Opal Tower.

Basically, if they decide I'm too much trouble, my life is fucked.

It's only been a couple weeks into the school year, and I've already embarrassed Ten, kneed Lux, and found Bridger doing some suspect as fuck things in the woods. It's not looking good. Yes, I want to find out what happened to Cass. Yes, I want to hurt the guys like they hurt me. But most of all, I'm fighting against all of them. They're bound to destroy me.

After grabbing my stash, I roll a joint and head to my balcony, hoping no one is outside to see me ditching class. There's something so freeing about being where I'm not supposed to be while everyone else follows the rules.

Cass always used to call me out on it.

"You can't keep missing classes, Col. What are you going to d
when it's time to graduate and you don't have enough credits to wal
with the class?"

"Convince Mom to pay them off," I mope, hating how right h
is. School and I have never gotten along. It's always a constant battl
one where we're wielding pool noodles, neither able to truly win.

"No, you're going to get your shit together and kick ass." Hi
arms drape over my shoulders as he pulls me into his embrace. "You'r
going to make me proud and show the world that you're a badass."

My throat tightens with emotion. While he's a boy and a dic
most days, my brother has never ceased to protect me, love me, o
push me to be my best.

"I love you, Cass."

"I love you too, Col."

Tears prick my eyes as the memory shakes my mind an
heart in equal succession. If he wasn't gone, he would give m
shit for skipping. Just like he used to when skipping with th
guys. *Those were the days.* When they didn't want to hurt m
unless I begged them.

Now, hurting me is their only agenda. I'm only waitin
for the other shoe to drop.

They're being too nice. Other than the cafeteria, they'v
been too quiet. Laying too low.

Something is bound to happen.

Lighting up, I pinch my joint between my thumb an
forefinger. It's burning to a pretty ember, and my body feel

relaxed. Maybe it's not about the weed. Maybe it's the action itself that brings the contented sigh of relief.

Inhaling a big drag, I let the smoke stay. My body visibly relaxes. With one hand, my palm flattens on the rail, and my other holds the bud. It has this calming effect on me that's missed. Being at ease comes few and far too little these days. But this? Me and my light on the back canopy, staring at the green mountains, is exactly the kind of release I need.

Actually, an orgasm would be nice too, but asking one of the fuckers who are tormenting me to give me one would be a stretch.

I sit in the little lawn chair I stole from Scotty, and smoke until my lungs feel exhausted.

No one comes for me, and my body finally feels at ease. Maybe it was a reach, thinking they would—

The sound of my door's lock being undone has me jolting up from the chair, dropping the stub left of my smoke.

—come for me.

"Colty," Ross sounds out, making my body shiver.

Since that day in the communal showers, I've been on edge. He's seen me entirely naked, well, as much as the curtain revealed. He could know about my scars and tattoos, witnessing my body jewelry and the secrets my clothing hides. While I never show my arms, right now and in the shower, they aren't covered.

His eyes land on the ink that resides over the marred flesh, hiding my pain, keeping it like a dirty secret while it watches over me.

"What are you doing here?" I complain, wanting nothing more than to smack him and then fuck him for good measure. My body tingles. The weed must've wired my mind wrong again. He can be a hot fuck, but he won't ever be mine.

"Came to see if Lux visited yet."

Closing my eyes tightly, I feel my body warm and freeze at the same time. Shivers and chills break out over my skin. Not just his name brings these reactions, but the knowledge that he plans on coming after me for my little stunt does too.

"Kinda wanted to see you before he wrecked your pretty—"

"Don't finish that sentence. I'm not fucking him *or* you."

A wide churlish smile breaks free, his dimple poking through to make me even more prone to bending for him. He's the worst of them. With his charming smiles, devilish looks, and the goddamn tattoos, he's weakness conjured into human form.

He's my sad boy.

Not yours, Colton.

That's what I've always called him. Whether or not he intentionally permeates the air with his melancholy, he does. Maybe it's only me who notices and that's why I've always been drawn to him, but he does.

His sadness seeps into me as I walk closer. There's no way I'm going to say a single thing to him. I just want to see what I missed.

"You seem to think you can avoid it, Vampire."

"If you think that's going to get me to suck you off, you're sorely mistaken."

He chuckles. It's warm, less sad, something strong and potent, like a cup of coffee before your eyes fully register anything, a hot bath when your body feels deteriorated beyond comprehension, or even a smile for the first time after months of absence, filling a void that always felt barren.

"That's not why I said it, but since you brought the idea up…" he trails off, sauntering toward me, closing the gap.

I stay rooted now, not wanting to show him how unnerved he makes me.

If it's possible, his grin widens. Like Jared Leto's Joker, his grin is unnaturally wide, devilish, ready to cause mayhem wherever it reaches.

Heat wraps itself around me as his hand comes to my jaw. It's covered in ink like mine. While mine is pure black with no intricacies, his are roses and thorns, as if he wanted to depict the pain that comes with love all while showing the beauty in it too.

"I like it when you shiver, Colty. Drives me mad."

My breath catches at how wicked his green eyes look this close with his admission. As I stare at him with every emotion, he practically groans. Unlike most women who think giving a guy emotion means you're weak, I feel it has the opposite effect. If you give them love, lust, and hatred, if you offer a morsel of your humanity, it taunts theirs, begs theirs to come out and play. And when you're finally wrapping your barbed wire dripped with malice thorns around their hearts, they kneel for you, nearly begging for more.

When I'm like this, he's mine.

So, no, I don't have to hide behind numbness. My hea does all the work for me.

If only I could tell my heart not to reciprocate.

Ross seems enamored. It's daunting. Enticing. It's wha we always do whenever we're alone. That's the problem wit these guys. Alone with me, like *truly alone*, they're themselve Almost like they shuck their armors and come in here naked Their souls bleed. They just don't intend it to.

"I like when you make me come, yet here we are," whisper, feeling every ounce of my weed infiltrating th intelligent part of me.

He groans at my response and has his other han gripping my naked hip. After coming back here, I spare myself the discomfort and traded my goth garb for som night shorts and a crop top that says *Fuck your opinion*. It's on of my favorites.

Ross continues trailing up my thin waist, then over m bony ribs, and it takes everything in me to hamper down th sadness that overwhelms me when he notices.

"You are thin, Colt."

Gone is the sensual mood and bubble I felt myself sinkin in. Now is a troubled boy who doesn't have making me orgasn on his mind. *Great.* His fingers trail over each rib, even if hal are covered. His eyes are full of concern, and I hate it.

Pushing him back, I point a finger in his direction. "Sto looking at me like that," I hiss.

It hurts, seeing the care in his expression. He's no

heartless, no, far from it, but seeing how he's trying to recognize something that he won't find makes me uncomfortable. With me standing there, being scanned like a patient in a hospital, I no longer feel safe and calm. My heart starts beating irregularly.

"You're *incredibly* thin," he practically repeats his first sentiment.

"Glad to know your eyes work, Dare."

His eyes collide with mine. Who would've thought that using someone's nickname would set them off so much? Ross hates being called Dare by me. It could be the reason behind it, but I think he likes how intimate it feels hearing me say his name.

"What happened?"

I scowl, feeling my blood boil and my body tense. "Hmm," I mock, disdain dripping from my voice. "First, four guys… fucked me over. Then, my brother fucking dies. Sounds pretty obvious to me."

I almost let it slip that four guys made me fall in love with them. That can never leave my mind or lips. Though emotions hold power for my benefit, that admission would do them more good than it'd do me.

"Colt," he starts.

I rub my forehead, forgoing the need to let him comfort me. Ross is great at cuddling and bringing warmth back in my body. He's like a big cuddly tattooed bear that knows exactly what is needed when it's needed it. He and Ten are the same in that sense. The difference is, I would trust Ross with my heart before I would ever let Ten touch it again.

"Please, don't." It comes out as a plea.

Tears prick my eyes. Not only does emotion clog my heart and soul, but a little too much green compromises me. That's the kicker, isn't it? What these guys do to me isn't welcome, but it happens anyway. They make me forget how they were somehow involved with covering up what happened with my brother. That's not okay.

"Talk to me. Are you eating? Starving yourself? My sister—"

A derisive laugh escapes me. "Do not compare me to Olivia," I bark.

Once upon a time, that girl was as close to me as Yang was. Her addiction to diet pills came before my health. She fucked me over. Guess it's a family dynamic.

"She had issues—"

"She thought she was fat!" I yell, feeling my heart ache at the comparison. Olivia was thin by *choice*.

Or maybe it was conditioned into her, and I'm being too harsh. The real difference between us is that I'm forced into a starvation because I forgot to sustain my body by not mourning my dead brother. She loved her bones poking through her skin. Always telling me I needed to stop eating what made me happy. She was toxicity personified.

"That's not what's wrong here." The words escape me more a sentiment and not anger. I could eat all the food, chug all the booze and soda, but my body wouldn't tolerate it. It's not used to fats, carbs, or much of anything that will keep me alive.

It's broken.

Like me.

My heart and what's left of my hope.

Big fat tears roll down my cheeks, making my face feel hot and uncomfortable. Crying should be labeled a disease for how it wreaks havoc on the body and mind. It's such a burden to be capable of such an ugly act.

"Colty," Ross soothes, his voice softer.

He comes up to me, holding onto my arms, bringing me in for a hug. My body melts like butter sitting out in the sun, becoming less and less of the hardened material it once was. An ache in my heart reaches for connection, anything to offer it hope, peace, a viable thing to live for because my life sure as hell isn't enough to live for. Before everything happened, four guys made me feel alive, giving my heart a reason to beat, offering everything. Now, loneliness is all that meets me. I'm suffering, at the cusp of a mental breakdown, all while trying not to think about the brother who was stolen from me.

"I didn't mean you're sick in that sense," he offers.

His voice is so serene, like when I tried meditating for a week and listened to the soft teachings of people who made me sleep. But it's not tiredness enveloping me. He's making me come to life in his arms, healing me in a way that shouldn't happen. He's worming his way inside, burrowing deep, and I hate it.

"I'm not broken."

It comes out a broken sob, but we both know that's not true.

He holds on tighter, bringing one palm to cradle my hea
When he pulls back, it's only to look into my eyes. Sweetnes
fills the air as if my nose catches his scent for the first time–
sugar and honey, two things Ross offers in lungfuls.

Emotions sift across his eyes like glitter floating in
snow globe. He's so sincere when he wants to be, but it's neve
when it matters. Ross has all the control in the world, and th
ability to absolutely destroy me. When he's not tormentin
me, he's giving so much more. It confuses me more than
comforts.

"You're not. You're right, Colton. You're a survivor. M
strong girl."

Tinges of yearning flood my veins, pushing me into hin
taking his mouth with mine in the next breath. He's thrown of
for only a second, a little hiss his only sound as he cups my face
devouring my lips like they're his last sustenance on this earth
It's consuming and breathless, but neither of us pull back.

Backing us up a few feet, he only stops to lift me. I moan
softly when his hands cup my ass. They're so warm and strong
He starts to carry me to my room, but my body screams to
take off his clothes now, to not hold back, and I listen and
reach for the hem of his shirt. He presses me against the hal
wall and uses his thigh to hold me up as I help him take of
his shirt. Underneath his clothes, he's breathtakingly hot. Th
new tattoos he's inked since this summer and the piercings..
I'm practically melting.

Ross palms my ass, lifting me again, taking my mouth
with a fierce desperation that mirrors mine. When he pull

back a second time, it's with an awe-filled expression. He licks both of my piercings through my bottom lip, and as if only noticing my double tongue ring, he licks those, too.

"Fuck, you're killing me." His words are filled with grit, heavy with unresolved emotions he's probably tucked away in his faux joker attitude.

I can't help but smirk, though. If he knew the power he had over my body, he'd be jumping with cocky indifference, or at least, if the guys were here, he would. He puts up a front with the outside world, but with me, he's Ross. Not Dare, the asshole who doesn't give a fuck.

"These," he almost grumbles, flicking his tongue over the black metal of my venom piercings again. "They're giving me ideas."

"Like?" I ask, batting my eyelashes.

"Thinking of how they'd feel against my cock as I throat-fuck you."

That has me squeezing his hips. He finally takes me to the room and tosses me on my bed. It hugs me as he takes residence of the space above me. Not touching, only hovering above like a king waiting for his subject to please him in every way.

It takes no time for him to lower down my body with his confident lip bite just to kiss my bare stomach. His tongue swirls over every inked inch, and he only stops to look me in the eyes.

"I'm going to taste every inch of you, Colt. I'm going to lick and fuck every hole of yours, and then when I'm done, I'm going to repeat it until my cock no longer works," he rasps.

He lifts my crop top, baring my breasts to him. He takes one look at the newest jewelry slicing through my skin and growls. It settles deep in my body, vibrating as chills kiss my skin in response.

"Fuck."

I feel his hiss between my legs.

As I grind into him, he doesn't stop looking at my black dangling bat barbells. "What else do you have pierced?" he asks.

A coy grin crosses my lips. I forget the fact the boys haven't touched me since *I've* changed. The only thing they got was my belly button ring.

"You'll just have to see," I taunt.

This has him practically jumping to remove all my clothing. He spares no time to remove the rest of my top, and then he's sliding my shorts down.

"No panties?" he hisses, his face dark and desperate.

I shake my head. "Didn't see the need."

He's leaning down, and his nose is running up my slit slowly. "Fuck, Colt. Fuck."

He inhales my pussy as if it's the best aroma he's ever smelled, and I squirm. It's so depraved and primal. I can't tell if I'm disturbed or turned on.

He uses both hands to spreads me. Another groan rips from him in reaction. I'm starting to learn that sound as my favorite noise from Ross.

"Fuck. Fuck. Fuck."

I can't help the giggle that escapes. He's so entranced by the piercing on the hood of my clit, and I love the way he's amazed.

Without another word, he leans forward and bites it. I let out a mewl, and he pulls on it, making me sweat profusely. When I think he's going to torture me further, he opens my folds as wide as they'll go, and he dives in, licking long and slow strokes. After I'm canting off the bed, he's faster, more aggressive, grunting as he eats me out. I'm a mess of moans and cries as he teases my clit and hole with his tongue.

"Ross," I moan loudly.

"That's right, princess. Come for me. Let me hear you say my name."

I cry out his name, my legs shaking, all while his mouth continues to torture me.

When he's finally done, he leans back and smiles. His chin is wet; his eyes are wild. Using my finger to call him over, he travels across my body and takes my mouth. The taste of me mixed with the flavor of Red Bull and Twizzlers has me groaning. He's always been a foodie like me. It helps that we both smoke a lot and have similar tastes. We kiss and kiss until I'm rutting against him for more.

"What are you waiting for?" I question, breaking our make-out session.

He grips his shaft through his jeans, rubbing slowly over it. The need in his eyes can't be avoided.

"Trying to be a gentleman."

"If you cared about being a gentleman, you'd have fucked

me without asking."

"Oh, princess," he coos harshly, bringing me down th
bed more. "I wasn't asking."

He undoes his belt and pants, and then he's moving ove
me. "Now spread those thighs wide for me, Colt. My cock i
fucking famished."

That's all the warning I get before he's thrusting in me
My back arches at the instant pleasure. Ross has always been
hung, but I almost forgot how wide and long he is. My bod
barely adjusts before he's slamming into me mercilessly. He'
a few pumps in before he flips me over, making me ride him
I start bouncing on his dick, making us both growl and hiss
He holds my hips, his thumbs digging into my piercings as m
body comes up and down over his.

When he's getting close, he grips me even harder an
fucks into me from the bottom. Not being able to keep u
with his pace, I just let him control every thrust, and screan
when he hits that spot inside me.

"Fuck, Colt. You're so tight."

That's the last thing he says before he's slowing dow
and grunting his release. My body relaxes on top of his. Ou
sweat mixes together. Knowing we fucked so hard our bodie
are overheating makes my body shake with pleasure.

He helps me off him, and my body wobbles from exertion
After I fall over, he pulls me into him, tucking me under hi
arm, and I can't imagine a better place to be.

His left arm wraps around me, and it's beautiful seeing
our ink blend together. In his arms, I shouldn't feel this saf

and secure, but I do, and while I'll regret this tomorrow, it's exactly what I needed to stop me from breaking apart.

CHAPTER TWELVE

At some point, we must've passed out, or at least, I did. When wake up the next day, there's no Ross and no note left behind Why didn't Lux come after me? What is he planning?

Staring at the empty bed, I try not to be upset at th fact that I'm alone, but I can't seem to shake the feeling tha he's either regretting our time together, or he's not too fon of cuddling now. He used to be a snuggle whore, I'd alway teased him for it.

It's not my fault he pulled me into his side and snuggle me, but if he's pissed about that, he needs a reality check.

This changes nothing, I'm sure, but hope blossoms in m chest anyway.

As I'm drying off after a quick shower, I notice the mark across my skin. Shit. I didn't realize how frantic we were Hickeys litter my throat, breasts, and hips. With my pale skir they won't be easy to cover up. Finding a foundation as pale as I am is hard.

The first time I bought the lightest foundation offered at Penn & Co., I found out really soon that 'fair skin' is *not* pale enough for me. Yang and Cass made fun of me all day for that mishap, and it took me ages to try makeup again.

Orange against pasty whiteness doesn't add up, believe me.

As my eyes catch all the places he left his own personal brand, a smile creeps forward. Liking this shouldn't bother me, but it does. Wanting him to mark me as his makes me feel desired, but it's a lie. He doesn't want more than my body.

I hurry to my closet and grab another long sleeve crop top and a skirt that's a tad longer than the one I wore yesterday. The skirt is pleated with tulle underneath. If goth chic was a thing, my outfit would be definition of it.

After putting on my face, I make sure to cover all the love bites and head out soon after. It's Saturday, I'm smuggling myself into town to get my hair done. Scotty—my hair stylist for the last five years—doesn't travel, and since my blonde roots are coming through, I need a touch-up.

Lacing up my boots and grabbing my wallet, feeling lucky it wasn't in my bag yesterday, I leave. Texting an Uber to pick me up at a location near campus, I sneak away.

My feet are sore for some reason, and as I walk, my thighs and calves start to ache too. Shit. Shit. Shit. As I'm mentally cataloging my need for magnesium and potassium vitamins tonight, my body starts to ache, reminding me

I've once again mistreated it.

Glancing at the clock, it dawns on me that I haven't eaten in twenty-four hours. Not only did I miss my meds yesterday, but eating never happened either. Food and consistency is important when trying to refuel my body and retrain it to consume regular foods.

Soon, I make it to the meetup point I'd pinpointed for the driver, and I only have to wait ten minutes before my Uber shows up.

Upon opening the door and sitting down, my heart nearly stops. The pitter-patter of my chest becomes a slow exploding cacophony, whether it is lack of sugar, the face staring back at me, or not breathing correctly, I'm not sure. My ears ring with the power of my heartbeat.

"You know it's against the rules to leave school property when you're not a senior or part of Student Gov, right Corpse?"

His words swirl in my mind, but my attention sticks to the smirk making his face too snarky for his own good. My eyes linger on Lux's lips a moment too long before I cross my arms over my chest.

"So?" I grumble.

He caught me, and he's not against writing me up for it either. Lux is all about being a prick for prick's sake.

"Where are you headed, Dracula?"

Nowhere that includes you.

"Town," I mutter. "Need tampons."

It's a lie, but he doesn't need to know that.

"School shop has plenty. Now, where are you really headed? Running away? Couldn't handle fucking Ross and need to go pout about it?"

My eyes widen at his words. It's only been a day. How could Ross already spill his guts? He's worse than Charlotte Ohara, the biggest school gossip who doesn't know how to keep a secret to save her life.

"How—"

"You think Ross didn't make sure to record that little tryst?" he taunts. "Your moans made me come twice, sweetheart."

I growl and cringe in the same go, hating Lux even more. Ross usually isn't that much of a tool.

You don't know him anymore.

"Jealous much?" I poke, knowing that's not why he's bringing it up. He's doing it for power. That's what this entire thing is to him—a power play, a way to win and beat me and make me weak. He wants to win, but fuck, what are we even fighting for?

"Yes, maybe I am," he muses, touching his chin. "The fact that Dare got to dirty up the Corpse Bride in less than a month of school is quite demeaning. Didn't know you'd slip onto a cock so easily."

"Fuck you," I hiss.

He pushes between the divider of the backseat and grips my jaw. "If you want me to fuck you, Corpse, you're going to have to beg. My cock is needy, but it's not desperate enough for you."

Instead of giving him more ammunition, I shake from his grasp and leave the car. That's when I notice my driver standing in wait five feet away.

Rushing over to him, I bark out Scotty's salon's address. Yes, he already has it from the app, but this way he can't fuck it up and give Lux another reason to be a dick.

Lux doesn't follow us, and I finally breathe easily. We make it to town in an hour, and my chest aches at the heady breaths I've taken. Not eating is making me feel weightless, and regardless of what others believe, feeling this way isn't nice. Yeah, being small is great and all, but not being able to stomach food and be able to work out like a normal person is maddening. I hate feeling weak and small, and that's all this disease does.

My depression ruined me

Cass' death destroyed me.

My parents' lack of love killed me.

If it wasn't for those things, Lux calling me a corpse wouldn't bother me, but it does because I *am* dead.

He's winning by calling me that name, and I let him by allowing it to hurt. Either way, I'm losing this battle.

The car ride is swift, luckily. A little awkward too, especially since I yelled at him when getting in the car. We arrive at Scotty's shop, *Colormore*. It still brandishes its uniqueness in Arcadia Township. It's quirky and black. The only shop appearing gothic in any sense, it stands out against the rest. I'm happy to see her chatting it up with a local. As soon as she sees me, she lets the person go and screams running toward me. "Colton!"

It's such a high pitch shriek that I'm smiling nonstop.

"My goth princess returns! Touch-up? New do?"

"This is a lifestyle, Scotty, not a phase." I laugh when she gives me that iconic *okay, honey* face. She thinks that once I get over my heartbreak—that's what she thinks is wrong—then I'll go back to normal.

Joke's on her. This is my new normal.

"I need a touch-up and wanted to maybe go black underneath?" I question myself and tap my chin. It would give me a little more umph.

She nods. "I like that, maybe even give you a little trim." When I shake my head, she laughs.

"Not a cut, just chop some of these dead ends. Let's get started!"

Her fingers trail through my hair. Usually people touching me would make me wince, but right now, it's like being around Cass or the guys before they fucked up. It's comfortable.

She skips, and I follow her to the back where her station is. Her shop was recently remodeled and is now fancy. It's the only place updated in Arcadia Township. She sits me down and wraps the black tarp around me, humming some melodic tune that makes zero sense.

"Any new cute guys in your life?"

Her eyebrows raise at her question, like the motion would allow me to feel cornered enough to answer. It doesn't. There are no new guys, only the same ones who make my life hell.

Heat flames my cheeks anyway, and I shake my head, hoping to deny it. "Not in this lifetime. They're all losers."

"The sound of a jaded woman," she tsks. "Just imagine when you find an Antonio. Then, you'll never doubt love again." She grips her chest with happiness.

Antonio is her French lover. He came over for a modelling gig, and Scotty did his hair at one of his shoots. They literally banged on set while she was supposed to get him ready, and they fell madly in love.

Scotty is gorgeous. She's Asian, her skin fairer than mine, her hair never the same shade twice, but what always captures my attention is her tattoos. Unlike mine, hers are woven across her, peonies and pythons, a mixture of dark and intriguing.

Right now, her hair is bubble gum pink with coon tail underneath. The name comes from the tail of a raccoon, stripes dyed another color to give it the same appearance. She's slender and bright, always smiling and joking.

"You're right, but not all of us can find a French lover on the set of a Penn & Co. runway show," I muse, pursing my lips.

"Yeah, but your guy will come. He'll sweep you off your feet and fuck you like there's no tomorrow."

My mind flashes to Ross. Yesterday, he did exactly that. What if I'm not meant to have one love but four? *No.* There's no way. I bite my lip as she talks about how she and Antonio are travelling across Europe for an entire month this summer. I'm excited for her. Scotty deserves a break.

She parts my hair and divides the top half into three

sections. We meet a silence where I'm stuck in the thoughts that plague me and she's trying to decide which part of my crown would layer best. After she splits it from top to bottom, she starts by dyeing the bottom first.

"So, why the change?" she asks.

"First, you want me to change it. Now you're wondering why?" I mock, incredulously. I'm not mad, more curious why she cares. She didn't question me when I'd gone goth, but now, she's intrigued for some reason.

"Honestly, when you came to me wanting to go green, I thought a guy tore you up inside. Whenever teens get a drastic change, whether it be clothes, hair, makeup, or entire appearances, it's usually heartbreak, but it wasn't just the hair with you, it was everything, including all these piercings and tattoos. What happened?"

"My brother died," I mutter.

It's not an easy admission. This town covered it up. It's almost like Cass never existed past the huge vaulted walls of our mansion.

Scotty looks at me with sadness. "That makes sense. I'm so sorry, Colt."

I shrug, hating how it makes me feel to talk about Cass in the past tense. In my mind, he's happy and travelling the world. In reality, I can't bear thinking of him in the casket I was forced to watch lower into the mud.

After that, we don't talk. She doesn't bother me, and I'm too stuck in my head to be bothered with mundane questions.

Maybe one day, my mind won't torture me with

memories, but right now, the only thing I see is my brother'
coffin being buried and not a single one of the guys bein
there to comfort me.

CHAPTER THIRTEEN

PAST
CASSIDY'S FUNERAL

Pain.

You're taught it's something natural, that everyone will experience it from time to time. Common practices while enduring it usually tend to be crying, flinching, and discomfort.

But they never explained how loss hits the pain scale beyond measurement.

Once the moment occurs, the sadness of *never again* is not easily dealt with, it burdens the soul, tarnishing the light inside you. How do you cope with the unavoidable?

He's dead.

Cassidy's gone. Those two words don't depict what the aftermath promised—the emptiness, the tears that won't stop coming, the absolute endless detrimental heartbreak.

You can be taught about suffering, but no matter how

much you're told loss is part of that equation, the impact isn
felt until you're forced to endure it.

The dull throb in my head doesn't compare to th
resounding beat inside my chest. My knocks on the door
to the chapel are louder than the soft and melancholic ra
against my ribcage.

I'm no longer me somehow.

My feet move, but my mind stays. I'm walking toward th
gravesite, the family mausoleum. The grass squeaks beneat
my Mary Janes. The blades are wet and damp like my eye:
the constant moisture unable to ebb and flow naturally.

Squishing is my only tether as I'm led to the final restin
place of the boy who singlehandedly taught me everything.

He showed me love when my parents didn't.

He gave me strength when my body felt desolate.

He comforted me when no one else cared.

He told me stories when I couldn't sleep.

He was my entire livelihood in the form of a brother. H
was my protector, keeper of the keys to the dungeon of m
soul. He reminded me to live, and without him, I'm not sur
how I'm supposed to continue to do so.

Someone's hand wraps around my arm, but the numbnes
has already settled in. The care to see who it is no longer exists
but they seem to be guiding me outside the chapel to wher
Cassidy will be at rest.

With the sky dark above, cloudy and ill-tempered, I wai
for the rain. We get it often this time of year.

Spring.

Flowers are bursting through the ground around me, but they're alive, and Cass isn't. It's unfair. The flowers will be rebirthed in the future, but my brother will forever stay in a box beneath the muddy scant earth.

Dead.

Without me to be there for him like he's always been here for me.

The tightening on my arm begins to tug, a pulling that should bring me away from the detached world I've latched onto, but it fails.

My eyes aren't even truly taking in my surroundings, the misty air, the tomb marked with Cassidy's name.

Cassidy Amos Hudson.

I get caught on the middle name I only used when angry or when he rebelled my belief of a perfect brother.

But that's not true, is it? He's always been a good brother, a guide through the horrible world I've been begotten upon, someone I could depend on, love, and know above all else. He would always be there for me.

Staring at the tombstone, I know that isn't the case any longer. He won't be here any longer.

It's my fault for drinking and partying while I could have been watching him. He didn't kill himself. The more I think of him, his life, his goals, I know that's not his story.

"Colton," Mom tugs, forcing me to reattach to the world around me.

I turn to her, only peering away from the grave to brace for impact.

125

She narrows her eyes. It's like she remembers Cass and shared the same hair, eyes, and most facial features.

We mirrored each other, yet he was the successful one.

Life gave him intelligence, athleticism, and hope.

It decided to steal all those attributes from me.

"Fix your face. The sermon hasn't even begun." Her voice is void of emotion, not struggling with pain or anything other than her annoyance with me.

With her words, the part of me which carted hope of a relationship with my parents after Cassidy's death dies along with him.

A preacher comes. He speaks of the accomplishments my brother succeeded with, his dreams cut short, the way life should have been, and the future he'll never know.

My sobs, barely abated, crawl up my throat, choking me while random strangers stand around us. A man I don't recognize seems to be almost ghostly as he stares at me while I break apart.

When Mom nudges me, I'm forced to look away. After I've placed my single rose on his closed casket, he lowers, and I break.

He's gone.

Cassidy's really gone.

Peering at the crowd once more, the man who stared at me is gone, and the boys I'd dumbly thought loved me never showed up.

I can understand Lux and Bridger not coming. They only would've come to support me.

But Ross and Ten? They were Cassidy's friends for years. They betrayed me.

Left me alone.

And now he's gone, buried deep, and I feel like I can't breathe.

Can I die too?

CHAPTER FOURTEEN
PRESENT

"Homecoming is in three weeks. Got a hot date?" Melissa asks me as she sits on my desk chair. I invited her over after the whole mess in Psych two weeks ago, praying to keep at least one friend in this school.

Lux's actions disgusted her, and she decided right then and there that she would pick me. It's refreshing, not fighting with girls.

It's something I've always dreaded about social ladders in this school. We're literally put against one another to get the title of *best* and *richest*. It's belittling and gross.

Her question has my mind shifting to Jordan, the new guy. Would he want to go to some lame dance with me? He seemed just as upset with Lux as Melissa, but he hasn't tried being cute with me since. He's kept his distance, and I can say I blame him much.

"Ha!" I mock. "Me, the green-haired emo freak… *Yeahhh*." I can't stop the self-deprecating laugh that escapes my lips.

It's true. No one gives me a second glance nowadays. It makes me question last year when they actually paid me attention. Every guy at Arcadia seemed interested.

"What are you talking about? You're so hot. Like, if I rolled that way, you'd be at the top of my bang list."

"You're insane."

"You're beautiful. Your green hair with those fake pink eyes, gothic changes to the uniform, and that ass… You're like an anime wet dream, Colt." She shakes her head as if not understanding my obliviousness. "Seriously, if I could have your curves, tiny waist, and tits, I would."

"Staahhpp," I complain, hating that she's complimenting me. "You're gorgeous!"

"See? Now I know you're a big phony."

I side-eye her, hating that she's unable to see her own charm. We don't even know each other, and I've already grown to like her. Ever since we met, she's constantly around. I like it. Too much. It's like with Yang but more freeing. Melissa doesn't want to constantly hang out with guys and go to parties. She seems to be interested in just hanging out with me.

"What about you, Miss Georgia Peach?" I poke, knowing she's quite the catch. I've seen Salvatore Stevenson eyeing her and a few others from the Rugby team. They're intense and scary, but only because I know nothing about them.

"Well, there's this guy…" she starts, her eyes nearly glow with affection.

I miss that, the feeling of desire, the craving to know more, have more, be *more*. Ten used to make me feel that way. Hell, Lux, Ross, and Bridger, too. They lit a fire in me I couldn't explain, but in the end, I had to choose, and apparently, I chose wrong.

"Tell me more," I urge, pretending to grab popcorn.

Her gaze sparkles with fondness. She sits on it a moment longer before releasing out a huge breath of air. "His name is Ridge Clemonte," she swoons.

Right there, in this room, my heart explodes with displeasure. *Ridge.* My good boy who's really a bad boy, the one who teased and taunted me for his own amusement. He never harassed me like Lux, but he's not exactly nice either.

"I-I know him," I mutter softly.

Her mood immediately changes on me. "Oh, no. What's that expression for? Is he bad?"

I cringe slightly, not wanting to ruin it for her but also secretly wishing this wasn't happening. Bridger and I shared something special. It wasn't something the others could touch or really compare. It was different, but somehow, it was ours. The pain of knowing he could be with Melissa makes me upset for reasons I can't pinpoint. He's not mine.

"He's just… someone I used to know, but if you guys like each other, go for it." I try giving false bravado.

Inside, my heart deflates. My palms sweat as the visual of him kissing her, dancing with her, and fucking her fly across my mind. This can't be happening. He's no one to me. Just a cute boy who made my chest flutter before stabbing it repeatedly in hopes he would see what color it would bleed.

"He's so hot," she continues, missing the obvious discomfort in my gaze. "Whenever he smirks, my entire body warms."

She chats about him and his perfectly sculpted body as my mind wanders to the first time we had a moment.

"Col!" Bridger yells after me as I leave Study Hall. My all-around GPA isn't doing that great, and with Cassidy being best in the class, our moms are grilling me to up my game. It's not easy. It's like the information won't absorb. Don't even get me started on reading material. Reading is gross.

"Hey, Ridge," I say simply, my face feeling warm as his depthless gaze roams me greedily. Something about how his eyes show no emotion while being endless has me putty in his presence. He has this smirk that just burns through me, making me hot all over. It's been this way since last summer.

"I noticed you're taking Sociology this semester."

I stare at him and his blanket statement, wondering what that has to do with anything. "Yeah?" I ask in confusion.

"It was my best grade. Studying people amuses me."

What he's hinting at, I'm not sure.

He places a palm on my shoulder, pushing me into the locker. His face hovers inches away from mine, and he smirks with that panty-melting expression. I'm sure he could get anyone to do anything he wanted. Anything.

"Cass may have mentioned you're struggling."

This little tidbit has me wanting to strangle my brother. He means well, but doesn't understand that stupidity isn't attractive. I'm just not intelligent like others. It's hard to focus and give my work the attention necessary to excel.

"He did, huh?" It comes out angry, and he can tell because his face softens.

"He cares about you. Honestly, it just gives me a reason to offer you my undivided attention."

My heart rate picks up, and my belly warms with desire. The way his eyes hone in on my lips has me wanting to lean forward and make a move, but what if he's just being nice?

"Is that so, Ridge?"

"Yes," he hums and leans closer. "Would you like that, Col? Me, you, uninterrupted."

"Yes," I breathe out pathetically.

"Then make sure you call me Bridger when I'm around."

He nips my nose and leaves me to wonder what the hell just happened. Bridger isn't one for many words, but if he has his sights on me, who am I to deny him?

"What do you think?" Melissa asks.

My mind tries to wrap around our conversation, but nothing comes to mind.

"Huh?" I say pathetically.

"Haven't you been listening? Bridger texted me and wants to know if I want to go to something called Crystallites on the Friday before Homecoming. What's that, and should I go?"

Dread fills me. There's only two reasons Ridge wants to invite her to this party, and both are horrible.

"You just met him. Is that really something you want to go to?"

She raises an eyebrow at me, her face unreadable. "I'm not even sure what it is."

It's an unspoken rule. You don't speak about what happens at exclusive parties. If you do, bad things tend to happen.

They're get-togethers with the elitists, or whoever they want to ruin or invite to the club. It's where orgies tend to happen, bets that end in bloodshed, and pranks up the fucking wazoo. It's like a secret society, one I'm not super privy to out of choice.

Ten took me once. That's the night I lost my v-card. And my brother. Cass told me not to go, but my stupid star-struck heart didn't fucking listen, and look at me now.

"Can you bring someone?" I ask instead of answering. I'm not sure on that part of the rules because Ten brought me, and even being the Historian in Gov, I'd never been invited before.

"I don't see why not." She shrugs noncommittally. "Want to come?"

"Not sure if they'll allow a freak in, but I'm in."

"You've got to stop calling yourself that," she complains, shaking her head. "You will come and assist me since you seem to know more about them. I'll just tell Ridge I'll meet him there."

Does he want her to call him Ridge?
Does he want her?

133

Does he think of me anymore?

"This may end badly. Not for you, of course. For me. I anything happens, call the cops."

She looks taken aback, her shoulders stiff and postur even straighter. "You're scaring me."

"Mel, you should be scared. Terrified, even. These partie aren't for the likes of you. You're too sweet and kind an innocent..." I let out a ragged breath. "The last exclusive went to was the day my brother died."

"So, what they said in class... is that true?"

I balk at her absurd question. "I didn't kill my brother," hiss, feeling attacked and on edge.

"No, Colton, the murder. Was he... murdered?"

I nod, unable to get his vacant look out of my mind. "Yes and this entire school and town covered it up."

She exhales noisily, her eyes wide with shock and sadnes: "Tell me what I need to do."

"Why are you doing this? It's practically social suicide, I begin, seeing understanding lick her features. "You don' even know me. What if I'm a psychopath leading you to you death?"

She full body laughs at that, and I narrow my eyes. "You couldn't hurt a fly, darlin'. I can tell," she drawls, her accen thick.

I'm not sure who Mel is for the long run, but she doesn' seem so bad.

CHAPTER FIFTEEN

Homecoming. It's meant to be this big deal, and hey, last year, it was. I made a huge day of it, had four people vying for that spot even. Now? I'm not too sure. I'm not all into huge frilly dresses anymore. This year might have a different theme.

Either way, I'm wearing black.

I'm so excited for the dance tomorrow! Mel's text comes through. Then another. *It almost makes me miss my dad and brothers.*

I stare at it, wondering about that tidbit. She never mentioned brothers.

You have brothers?

The feeling of absolute desolation hits me square in the chest. If I could trade my soul for my brother's, I would. He would at least do something with his life. He had dreams, hopes, a future. I'm wasting my life and can't give a single fuck as to why that should matter.

Two. They're twins. They're my older brothers.

My heart beats in this erratic rhythm that makes me sadder than I've been since summer. School has helped me be distracted, so I don't think about my brother constantly, not until one of the dickbags bother me.

What are their names? I ask, hoping it doesn't sound weird. Maybe being close to her brothers will ease some of my struggle. Probably not, but it's worth trying.

Justice and Prudence. They like Just and Pru, since they're rebels. Very uptight parents, right?

I laugh, loving that their names aren't normal.

Could be worse. I'm Colton, after all.

But that's charming. Their name makes us sound like hillbillies that wanted to run for the presidency at some point.

I'm full body giggling at her response. No one burns their family like Mel does hers.

I'd love to meet them.

Was that too forward? What's wrong with me?

Hard to do when they're still in Tennessee, but if you come with me for fall break, I'm sure we can make it happen.

My stomach clenches uncomfortably at that. Fall break Cass and I always went home and spent the week hanging out with our moms, but what do I do now? Especially since they're basically zombies...

Let's make it happen. I always wanted to see the southern states

First of all, no one but west coasters say that weird stuff. And two, really? I'd love for you to come. It'd make it easier to not dea with my father alone. He insists I come back even though we're not on speaking terms and he's trying to avoid being in prison. Her text saddens me. Much like my relationship with my parents, hers seems to be suffering too.

Isn't prison for rich people nearly staying at home with an ankle cuff? I joke.

Practically. He's laying low, only leaving to attend his court appearances.

That's sad and must be hard.

We should just have sleepovers at this rate. We're still teens after all. It's true.

We're teens who never truly act like teens. Maybe it's being wealthy or forced to live alone once we turn fifteen. Either way, we should be allowed to act our age.

You're welcome here whenever, Mel.

Be there in ten then.

I just chuckle.

No more than fifteen minutes later, she's dragging in a duffel full of chips, drinks, and snacks. I'm staring at her disbelievingly. She has come prepared. I would have never had that much stuff on hand.

"How did you get all of this?" I ask in wonder. These snacks make my mouth water—jelly beans, jujubes, taffy, and everything in between. I've been slowly implementing foods. I'll have to keep my consumption low, but I'm enjoying getting back to feeling human again.

Last week, the school-appointed concierge doctor checked me over while on a voice call with my primary

physician. They agreed to take me off of my pills as long as
kept track of my lethargy and continued taking my vitamins

"Remember those twin brothers? Well, they keep m
stacked high. I'm not sure how they get them to me, but there'
always a package from administration stuffed full of treats."

I smile at that, knowing my brother would do the sam
if he wasn't stuck on campus.

Or dead.

"Well, we should thank them."

She looks at me with an *as if* expression and shakes he
head. "You're either into trying out twins, or there's somethin
more and I'm not privy to it."

I practically choke. While I haven't been with twins,
know what it's like to want to be with several guys, and that'
not in the realm of what I'm thinking.

Letting out a self-deprecating titter, I smack her arm
lightly. "I just miss my brother," I mention, trying not to cr
over it.

Understanding dawns on her features. "I'd be los
without mine. They may be total jackasses who love ruinin
my high school experience, but they're—"

"Worth every ounce of trouble they cause," I finish fo
her, knowing exactly how she feels.

"Yes, that. They're my pain in the asses, but I wouldn'
trade them."

New sadness festers inside me, and I bring her in for ;
hug. I'm not a hugger. Hell, I'm not too into being touched b
people, but I think we both needed it. Case in point, she take

a second to realize we're hugging before she squeezes the life out of me.

"He'd be proud of you for pushing forward," she comments.

She doesn't realize how untrue her statement is. I didn't push forward. I'm stuck. The only difference between then and now is my parents forced me to come back here. More like, they're unable to work around the fact that I practically starved myself nearly to death. They didn't want to look at me and take care of me. My being gone was their easiest solution.

"Yeah," I mutter, not meaning the word. "So, homecoming. Are you excited?"

She passes me a bag of chips, then flops a pillow on the floor, sitting cross-legged on top of it. After grabbing some tootsie rolls—the flavored kind that aren't waxy chocolate—I start untwisting a blue one. Imagine my surprise as a kid when I realized the blue one wasn't blue raspberry. It was the first ounce of betrayal in my life.

"We had these huge dances back where I lived. They're obscene with their monstrosity." Her face takes on an annoyed gleam. "You had to do some outrageous asking skit, making sure you weren't boring and simple. It was like a requirement." She rolls her eyes, pops in another candy, and chews. "Then, we had to wear these big pins—*mums*, I think—that were more ostentatious than the frilly dresses they forced us to wear."

I start to say something.

She begins again. "Not like your elegant dresses either. Think pilgrims went Hollywood. It was *not* pretty."

I'm laughing at the distaste all over her face. If it wasn
for the hilarity of this entire situation, I would think she at
a nasty candy.

I eat my chips as she goes on about how they made suc
a big deal about the events that she never went to a dance.

"Never?"

"Nope, not ever. Plus, my brothers would've scared th
poor lad away."

"That's kind of my first experience."

"Oh, tell me more." She readjusts and grabs a coupl
tootsie rolls, leaning forward like we're at a summer cam
about to tell ghost stories.

"Last year, I was in Student Gov."

She nods, then makes a face like this is gossip. Maybe i
a way, it is.

"Four guys wanted to take me to the dance."

She stops mid-chew and stares at me as if I'm some kin
of hussie, but she digs it at the same time.

"I didn't look like this," I add, gesturing to my entire body

"You're hot. That isn't a question. I'm just trying to thinl
of a day you actually liked humans, and I'm coming up blank.

I throw a chip at her, hitting her on the forehead. Th
orange dust leaves a mark. We're both a fit of giggles as sh
realizes it.

"Well, Cassidy—my brother—wasn't too fond of any o
them, especially since they were known as players."

She's nodding and watching me intently. Like any gir
who lives for snooping, she's waiting on each bated breath fo

my next words.

"All of them asked me, not in some crazy way, but with a kiss," I say conspiratorially.

Yes, they all kissed me when they asked, wanting to know if that would help me make the decision. The problem? It didn't change the fact that I wanted them all and couldn't just show them off as my boyfriends. Even as a group of people open about the idea, we never labeled it.

"All of them?" she whispers, as if that's the only part that matters.

Maybe in the gist of it, that *is* all that matters. Four guys. All vastly different than the other, but all a part of me the same.

"Yup, they all wanted to date me, but I liked them all." The words come out, and I'm so embarrassed. My face feels hot, and the way she opens her mouth makes me feel even more self-conscious.

"Four. Guys. Omigod," she squeals. "Did they know you wanted them all?"

This is where it gets tricky. I don't want to spread rumors. While they all liked me and knew I liked them and were okay with me being only theirs, they never admitted to being mine. People never witnessed me with anyone but Ten. He was the only one who didn't care about my reputation and his crossing paths. Even still, I wasn't *his*.

"I'm not sure," I lie. Keeping them protected is still at the forefront of my mind, even if they are all psychopaths who brutalized my heart whenever they deem fit. "But I didn't ever pick just one." *Another lie.* "Kept it platonic." *Liar, liar, pants on fire.*

Imagine if our pants really caught fire if we lied. There would be a lot of scarred people. Lying is a trait carried through people, a natural one you don't learn but is something ingrained before birth.

We come out lying, not screaming. They just don't understand our language.

"Tell me what happened?" she pokes after I've gone silent.

"Come to homecoming with me, Colty. I'll make it worth your while," Ross muses, winking at me.

His eyes are full with promise, and I know it's definitely auspicious. His tongue is wicked and not just with words. He grabs the back of my neck, bringing our lips together. With one swipe of his tongue, I'm a mess. As I give him access, he groans into me. When we part, his eyes are wild.

It's not news I'm a virgin. All the guys know it. But the way he's looking at me right now is anything but innocent.

"Don't decide now," he says, seeing the gears in my head moving at his question. "Tell me later. All the guys want you over. Movie night."

With one last chaste kiss and a wink, he's heading off to class and I'm stuck in the campus courtyard, wondering how I got myself entwined with four other lives.

"Princess!" Lux calls out.

I gaze at the clouds. They're puffy today, like marshmallow cream but less melted.

It takes Lux grabbing my chin for me to pay attention. Sometimes, my mind wanders, leaving me to wonder how it can fog so easily.

His hazel eyes meet mine. They're so light and boyish today. No moodiness or brute arrogance. Soft. Serene. Mine.

He grabs a strand of my silvery blonde hair, staring at it as if it guided him across the universe to find me in this exact spot.

"Homecoming... got a date?"

It's such a casual asking, nothing like the strong exterior of the boy I'm starting to care for. Out of everyone, he's who I imagined to make a huge deal of it. He's always stressing about perfection and making everything right.

"I—" I start to say.

But he's using the grip on my chin to bring his lips to mine. Unlike Ross, he doesn't use his tongue. He holds me there, memorizing, breathing me in, holding me in this moment. When he lets off, his eyes darken. He's just like Ross in that sense. He wants more. They all do.

"Tonight maybe? Movie night?"

Do they not all talk? Is this what they all decide? Come to me and repeat? I raise an eyebrow at him and cross my arms over my chest, more than likely pushing my breasts forward.

Finally, I nod, and he turns, running toward class. That should be me, but I don't want to go to Frasier's class. It's literally the first few weeks of school, and he's already talking about how textbook this entire course will be. He's my least favorite History teacher. He doesn't love the craft, the knowledge, or teaching it as such. He makes us read a chapter and tests us on that chapter. Nearly word for word, too.

As the warning bell rings and I'm still in the same spot, I decide to ditch today. Why not? What's the risk?

Heading back to my dorm room at Crystal Tower, I smile at the sight of Tennison standing, waiting, leaning against my door all chill-like. In his hand is a single kaleidoscope rose. It's rainbow and bright. My favorite.

"Wait, wait, wait. You like roses, and bright ones at that?"

I roll my eyes at Mel and give her the finger. "I did. Now it's black on black on black."

"Wow. I'm just shocked. Next, you're going to tell me you're an *it* girl."

Heat flames my skin, and I hurry to continue my story.

His eyes meet mine, pewter and shiny, metallic and bright. They're my favorite part of my moody boy, and yes, that's what he is, the soft and moody one. He smiles at me, not a full one, just a small grin that tilts a little. It's boyish and charming, just like the suitor.

Ten has always been my favorite. They tell you not to pick favorites, but we are always on the same wavelength, especially when it came to how I felt.

"Had a feeling I'd see you here, pretty girl."

A blush warms my neck, and I'm sure it rises to my cheeks. Unlocking my door, I open it and wave him in.

"Didn't feel like being bored to death, Ten. Nothing dramatic."

"Or maybe it's because you needed a little TLC from your moody boy."

"You did not just call yourself my moody boy."

"I did, and if you pretend you haven't said it out loud—which is exactly how I heard it—I may scream."

"You, scream? Now who's dramatic?"

He grabs his chest, a low chuckle leaving him, and it's only another reason why he's my favorite. He just gets me.

"I'm sure every guy has asked you by now, but I think we both know who would make you have the funnest time," he teases, twisting the rose in his hand.

Watching his strong fingers grip the stem, his rings shining against the light, makes my heart beat faster.

Moms always called me boy crazy. She's not wrong. They make my belly flutter and my body ache. They're the bane of most people's existence, but they make me thrive.

"While I know you'll bring the most to the dance floor, I'm not sure who I'm picking."

He pouts, but it doesn't reach his eyes. There, I see the cockiness I admire, the sureness that he'll win, and the moodiness that says he's not giving up. He stands from the office chair he took upon himself to sit on and makes his way to me. Smiling because that's what he does to me, he taps my nose in response.

"Let me show you a good time, pretty girl. You deserve to have more fun than any of those losers can offer."

Unable to help the eye roll, I try covering it with a giggle. "You guys are relentless. What if I wanted to go with someone else? Someone that isn't you four?"

Ten growls, his face darkening. It's like I've stolen his toy and ran off with it. He grips my hips, bringing them flush with his, and trails his palm up to my jaw. He cups both sides, his hardened palms rough and inviting against my softness.

"There is no one else," he barks before kissing me, taking every

145

argument away.

He doesn't stop there. He slides his tongue between my lips, making my body shake with awareness. Then, he's lifting me, my legs are wrapping around his, and we're taking it to the bed. Our mouths don't break, he teases me with his fingers and mouth until I'm moaning his name and promising him it's only them four and no one else.

CHAPTER SIXTEEN

"Wait." Mel throws her hands up in exasperation. "What about this forth guy?"

I stare at her, not realizing Bridger wasn't mentioned.

For some reason, him asking me seems too personal. The way it happened still throws me. It's probably what tipped me over the edge to go stag. Not that I didn't get wined and dined by each of them. I just refused to be shackled to one. It would set a bad precedent to choose only one.

Why would I ever choose?

How would they feel if I did?

"Oh, him. Well, he… It wasn't worth remembering." My face flushes, thinking of how big of a liar I've become in the last year because it was definitely worth remembering. It was something I used my BOB for. Often.

At some point, Ten and I passed out and slept through half the day in each other's arms. It was perfect. Waking up to a scowling Cass was not. You see, he and I share a key to my dorm. When I miss class, he tends to become a father figure and yell at me.

Right now, it's worse. Ten and him are having a stare off, and I'm too grumpy to care. I haven't had a lick of caffeine today, and that sets for a bad and grumpy Colt.

"The fuck is this loser doing here?"

I scrunch my face at that. My brother doesn't swear in front of me unless he's mad mad. It's his way of showing he's not respecting me. I don't care if he curses, the moms do, though. They're all about leading by example.

"We fell asleep," I grump, rubbing my eyes.

Ten doesn't move, but his stance is not any less frigid and protective. He stands over me, almost like he'll punch my brother if he so much as says the wrong thing.

"I'm sorry I missed class, Cassidy. It won't happen again. I'm just a little exhausted after last weekend."

He looks at me with understanding. Moms confronted Mom about cheating. And it didn't bode well. We were stuck in the middle, as usual, fighting our sadness with every minute that passed.

"Don't bring him here. You know the tower rules. No boys in the girls' dorms."

I nod numbly, hating how much of an enforcer he is. They picked the right guy for the job. My brother never bats an eye to writing students up for mistakes.

"Can you go away?" I ask. "Tonight is movie night."

He groans and walks away. My brother doesn't know I'm practically dating four guys, but he definitely hates every single one of them and our Friday night movie hangs. We watch a random movie and end up fooling around a bit. Then, I either fall asleep in someone's arms, or they convince me to stay the night with them. Our movie nights are at the cabin in the woods, a place no one quite wants their kids going to hang out. It's a Student Gov and Emerald building meant for get-togethers, not the fuck pad most of them use it as.

Ten gives me time to shower after he leaves, and I know I'll be trying to look my best. When I say we fool around, it's usually all four of them bringing me orgasms that make my toes curl and them working out their frustration through their fists.

I've wanted more. So many times, I've wanted to have them all inside me, sharing me while they share each other too. I'm a freak, and I'm sure it has everything to do with the books I read. It's not helping that I'm obsessed with reverse harem high school books where a chick has five plus guys to her disposal.

I'm addicted.

A-dick-ted.

I smirk at my inner ramblings and towel off. In ten minutes, I'm fresh-faced, dressed, and headed out the door to meet my guys.

It doesn't take long for me to go to the cabin. As soon as I'm at the door, Bridger is opening it. I haven't seen him in days, so seeing his warm brown hair that's messy and boyish in the best way makes me smile. He doesn't return it, but that's Bridger for you. He's not one to fake anything, let alone give away what he's feeling. It used to polarize me when he would practically ignore my questions, but he isn't for small talk, and I've grown to admire it.

"I've missed you," I mutter.

Unlike the others, Bridger keeps his distance. Not just his heart,

but his body. We don't kiss. Not since initiation and even then,
almost feels like something I've made up. I often think of his lip
and how they're most often in a straight thin line, and I wish I coul
soften them up with my own as he moans my name.

He stares at me, and those eyes of his gleam. It's so subtle, but
know he's happy I've missed him.

"Where are the others?" I question.

"Giving us a few minutes."

His low voice sends chills across my skin. He has that effect o
me. I'm not sure if it's because he's not touchy, and I can't tell wh
he feels without him giving me that skin-to-skin contact, or if it
because he secretly scares me a bit.

"What for?" I ask before turning right into his chest.

I start to tumble, and he grabs my shoulders, making emotion
and feelings sizzle up and down my spine. My body shivers, lovin
how aggressive his touch is and how silent he is when he thinks peopl
don't notice.

I do. I notice.

He releases me, only to stare into my eyes as if he needs me t
feel what he feels without the words.

"Homecoming?" I offer.

A smirk tries breaking free before he stops it. "Yes."

"Are you asking me, Bridger? Or are you wanting me to?"

I place a hand on his face and watch as he trembles a little. Whe
I swipe those flattened lips, he drags his teeth over it and bites down.
moan without meaning to, and his eyes flash with lust. It's so sexy to b
on the receiving side of those eyes. I'm stunned. His body warms min
with every inhale and exhale. It's beautiful. We're beautiful.

"Come with me, Col."

Only my brother and Bridger called me Col. Not Colton or Colt. Col.

"But I-I," I stutter, wanting to say yes. He makes me want to say yes. I imagine it's where our bodies would rub against one another and his hands wouldn't leave mine. It's all I can think about, and it has me melting against him.

"If you keep making those little sighs, I'm going to have to do something about it," he grumbles, his voice deeper than before.

It's thrilling, knowing I can make him react even when he refuses to bend for anyone. It's sexy. Power. Having control over a situation all while giving it to him.

"Then do something about it," I whisper.

That's all it takes. He hauls me over his shoulder, smacking my ass roughly. I squeal at him, loving every second of his hand on me. As we pass four rooms that I've never been in, we finally make it to the media room. The screen isn't lit, but the dim lighting is. He sets me down on a recliner, and within seconds, he's shucking his shirt.

I can count on one hand how many times I've seen him shirtless. That's three. Three times. He's not a swimmer like Ross, or into rugby like Lux and Ten. I can't watch him shirtless whenever I want. He crouches down, putting us at eye level, and I'm practically melting at his stare.

When he leans forward, I make it my mission not to go the rest of the way for his mouth. This moment, when he's finally letting me taste him again, I want him to offer that to me. He moves slowly, finally relaxing those stiff lips, and I'm a goner. His mouth, without the constant contempt or grimace, is haunting. His bottom lip is a

little larger than the top, but they're both soft-looking, and I want *to*
taste them.

He growls, as if knowing my intentions. Leaning even farther
he closes the gap and bites my bottom lip. I bow upward, pushing into
him, needing more, so much more. A moan escapes me when he licks
the bite as if to say I'm sorry, *and then he's kissing me.*

Bridger. Is. Kissing. Me.

I melt into him as he brings me to his chest, holding my hips as
if I'll disappear. It's rapturous and sensual. It has me hot and needy,
and when a whistle sounds out around us, it isn't me breaking us
apart. It's him.

"Getting started without us, dick?" Lux taunts from the door.

Bridger's lips are red and puffy, but as soon as he peers back at
Lux, they flatten, and he scowls like it's his job, and the heat is gone.

It was such a special moment for us, and as soon as it
came, it left.

"I'm sorry it wasn't anything special," Mel says,
interrupting my long daydream.

I nod nonchalantly, using my inner Bridger to seem
uncaring, but in reality, that moment meant everything. It
changed the game. Too bad the game ended up changing us all.

"Let's watch some Golden Girls. You can pretend you're
not Gigi, and I'll laugh and nod like I believe it."

We both chuckle, and we open up Netflix and dive in.
She's definitely going to change the game even more, even if
I've told myself I'm quitting.

Secrets have a way of getting out.

They never stay hidden for long.

I'm just scared to unfold the biggest one.

The one where the person who murdered my brother went free.

CHAPTER SEVENTEEN

"Colton!" Jordan's voice rang out somewhere behind me.

Once again, I'm rushing away. I'm not a fan of anyon who's a part of Student Gov.

His feet smack the linoleum obnoxiously, reverberatin in my ears and turning heads of everyone passing by. It's ba enough I stand out, between my hair and my past with th boys, but now, he's being a freaking elephant galloping dow the halls.

"Go away, Jordan," I hiss, not quite under my breath bu not quite yelling either.

"Why do you put off the vibe that you hate everyone? He ignores my comment entirely and stops me with his arms

This dude likes touching. I'm about to knee him and te him where to shove it.

"That's because I hate everyone. It's a fact."

His mouth tilts at the edges as my eyes roll. We're stopped in front of Barker's class. Barker's my old English teacher, and one of the hottest topics at Arcadia. Apparently, there are rumors he fools around with students. I'd say scandalous, but it wouldn't be the first time.

"A girl as pretty as you shouldn't have so much hatred," he muses.

The scoff escapes me before I realize it. "Does that work on every girl you flirt with, or is the Grinch's heart supposed to grow two times larger?"

"Are you calling yourself the Grinch?" He chuckles, shaking his head.

I point to my green hair as if it isn't an obvious reference. "My heart won't grow, dude. It's a dead horse. Stop beating it."

"You're something else, Colton. Not sure what that is, but you're it."

Now, it's my turn to laugh. "Yeah, okay. What do you need? Lunch is only thirty-five minutes away, and there's a slice of cheese pizza begging for my mouth."

As soon as I say the last part, my face heats. Shit. He probably thinks I was flirting. His smile confirms it.

"Before you go to Perv Town, remember, I've got four-inch platforms on that I'm not afraid to use." The threat is in my voice, but he's not taking me seriously.

"Believe me—" He winks. "—I'm very aware of your boots. They make your legs look longer. And that ass..." he trails off as I smack his shoulder. "What?" He blushes a little

155

while chuckling at my discomfort. "It hasn't flown past me that you don't wear the regulated uniform. You're like Goth Barbie with a nice ass. I dig it."

I'm sure my face is redder than wine with my pale complexion. The amusement in his expression makes me want to run. It's been a long time since anyone has flirted with me.

"I'm going to—" I try.

He puts a finger to my lips. "Go with me to the lame Crystallites party tonight," he finishes for me.

Except that wasn't what I was going to say, even if that's what I'm doing tonight. With Mel.

"I-I, um. I'm not invited," I stall, hoping he doesn't see anything but uncertainty in my eyes and not the truth of the fact that I'll be crashing one way or another.

"You are now. They say you can bring a date. That's you. My date."

Sweat lines my head at the implication. He wants me to go... with him. Why? What angle is he playing?

"They'll shun you for bringing me," I try, hoping he drops it but secretly wishing he doesn't.

"Who cares? I want you there. If they can't suck it up, it's not worth my time." He twirls a lock of my hair, staring at my mouth intently. "You'd make it fun anyway."

He leans in, and I can smell the pine-mint scent of him. I'm trying not to be affected.

He's so close.

So close.

His lips hover mine, brushing against my lip rings. "Com

with me."

His words literally touch my lips, and they feel good. Too good. He needs to step back and give me my brain back. It's all mush right now with him so close.

"Walker!" Dare yells from somewhere behind us. His voice dances across my skin devilishly. It always slices into me like a switchblade. Fuck.

Jordan doesn't turn to him. He waits for my words, my answer, my funeral in waiting.

"Okay," I get out as his smile brushes my mouth boyishly.

"Give me your number," he demands gently.

I shake my head, knowing if I give my number out, it'll cause hell. What if he's one of them? He could fuck me over with just my cell number.

"Fine." He grabs his backpack, rifling through it. He pulls out a Sharpie and drops down, uncapping it.

"What are you doing?" I whisper, unable to look away.

The marker touches my midriff before he starts writing. Shit. Shit. Shit.

"Stop!" I swat him away, only successfully leaving a big stripe on my hip.

"Just writing my number, twitchy. Calm down."

"What the fuck is this?" Dare barks, coming toward us. His face reddens the more I breathe, and his eyes narrow the closer he gets. A smile breaks free from me. Something about him sets my soul on fire while bleeding me dry in the same succession.

"Bro, lay off."

"Don't *bro* me, Walker. The meeting started ten minute ago, and you're here with the Corpse Bride."

The amusement doesn't leave my face. It really shoul since he's degrading me, but it's just too bittersweet. He hate me for an unknown reason, and the more I think of it, the mor it makes me wonder if it's because I picked Ten and not hin He acts like the other day didn't happen and he didn't fuck me

If whiplash was a style, Ross would outwear it.

"Jealous, Rossy?" I provoke, crossing my arms unintentionally making my boobs more prominent. They'r not small by any means, but any chick who does this offers little more show.

His eyes drop almost immediately. I watch as he lick his lips with his nose scrunched, almost like he's in pain an pleasure simultaneously.

The way his face looks, the pierced dimples an downcast expression, it's driving me mad. Attraction is bitter bitch, coming when you want it least and hiding whei you want it most.

"Why are you with her?" he growls at Jordan, ignorin me completely.

My gaze follows his anger and sticks to his metal. Fuck He has a lot of it too. His nipples might be my favorite, though My mind travels to the other day and his shirtless body. It' insane how much is beneath his uniform.

It's unfair how ugly dickholes can be the hottest guys o the outside while ruining me with their words and actions.

"Colton? Why, do you have a problem with hot chicks?

Jordan challenges, and I blush.

Ross turns to me, his eyes greener than ever. They're inhuman. I'm calling it now.

He leans in, his nose brushing mine. "No problem at all, Walker. This one is off-limits, though." A derisive noise escapes me, making my nose brush his again.

"What? It's a new rule this year. Colton Hudson, Vampire, Corpse Bride, Greenie, or—as I like to call her—*mine*, is off-limits," he enunciates slowly, making sure Jordan catches his message. But I'm not his. Not even close.

Ross reaches behind him, smacking Jordan, and then he's standing against me, Sharpie in hand.

"Ross, please," I nearly beg. "Don't."

An evil smirk lilts at his lips. Then, he's leaning toward my ear.

"Stay still. Don't want to fuck something up."

The way his words seep through me should be criminal in itself. They're like ink, the ink he's about to imprint my skin with. I'm not sure why I don't push against him or knee him. Maybe it's fear. Could even be stupidity.

"Going to pretend nothing happened?" I ask.

Ignoring me, he bends down where Jordan just was, and I feel his breath on my stomach near my belly button ring. It's hot, too hot. It takes everything in me not the squirm, but he said to keep still.

He's one to attack. All of the counsel is. The marker touches my skin, and a little noise escapes my mouth, making both pairs of eyes look directly at me. I close my mouth harshly, forcing it completely closed.

Ross hums a little as he continues whatever the fuck he's doing to my skin. Luckily, Sharpie is removable with some acetone. If it, for some reason, doesn't go away, I can wear an actual regulated uniform. Either way, I'm fine.

He stops, reaches back, and gives Jordan the marker back, and I close my eyes to my reality. It's like I'm a glutton or something. These guys aren't nice, though Jordan seems to be kind, and I'm letting them touch me.

Ross towers over me once again, leaning close. "Don't ever let anyone touch you, Vamp. We don't need another mishap, do we?" His voice is so calm and eerie. It almost doesn't feel like a real threat.

He kisses the side of my throat before backing away. He grabs Jordan by the back of his neck and leads him away, and I stand here like a fucking broken doll.

He just kissed my throat.

In front of someone else.

All while pretending he didn't fuck me only days ago.

I run toward Ivory Tower, praying whatever he drew on me isn't a dick.

It takes me no time to get to my dorm, and with only a few stolen glances, I'm sure I've passed under the radar of prying eyes. I'm throwing my backpack in the foyer as soon as I enter, running to the mirror. As soon as my eyes catch what's on my hip, my hand goes to my mouth. The gasp that leaves me isn't quiet.

Property of Student Gov.

Who the fuck does he think he is? On the left side of my hip there's six digits of a number, and a long line that hits my hip piercing. Hopefully, Jordan can find me tonight. I'll be there. I'll be wearing something that'll make them all shit bricks.

They want to fuck with me, so be it. I'll fuck with them right back.

CHAPTER EIGHTEEN

The mirror stares back at me, or rather, the girl in the mirror
It's me, yet it's not. The person reflected oozes confidence
security, and no-fucks-given. The person inside my bod
screams fear, disappointment, and cares-far-too-much.

My hair, like normal, is acid-green. The black underneat
that I got touched up by Scotty gives it a new darker edge
Before I looked punk. Now, I look goth goddess. Corps
Bride, just like Ross says.

My chest aches with the blue hues of a melted iceberg
staring back at me. It's the first time since he's been gone tha
I've really seen my eyes. I'm not sure what came over me afte
my shower, why I didn't immediately stick my contacts back
in, but as the Icelandic eyes stare back at me in shame, I know
it's a necessary evil.

"Why do our eyes match?"

Cassidy stares at me, his face almost comical at my question. "We're siblings, Col. Why wouldn't they match?"

We've always been close. There's a connection between us two. Time with him is laid-back. It helps that we have the same hobbies, but we also love doing extreme sports. Whether that's biking or skateboarding—which I suck at, by the way—we always find things to do together.

"But we don't have Mom's eyes," I think aloud.

Mom's hair isn't the same, and her eyes aren't either. When Moms told me and Cassidy she wasn't biologically our mother, we knew, but we always wondered who our dad is. Being young was the only reason we didn't understand.

We'd only ever known two moms, we didn't know you had to have a dude to make a baby.

Being a thirteen-year-old struggling with identity issues isn't easy. Cass is better at disguising his wants to learn more about our dad, but curiosity gnaws at me constantly.

Did he not love us?

Are we not good enough?

Were he and Mom in love?

What is their story?

I shake the memory as I think of my brother's eyes, his boyish charm, and the moments we shared before he was stolen from me. It takes all my will not to sob. Not tonight. It'll be different at this party. I know what to expect, what not to drink, and the right questions to ask.

Trading my silver lip rings for black ones give me an edge. Winging my eyeliner, I make it less dramatic than usual.

Topping it with gray eyeshadow makes me appear fierce, when I'm anything but. What truly makes my outfit, though, is the transparent top and huge X's over my nipples. When I went to Spencer's after Scotty did my hair, I found tape in their adult section. It's definitely not for this, but who's to argue?

The single tattoo on my ribcage, a raven, one I got to signify the loss of Cassidy while also proving my intent of ill will on the boys if they ever came for me, shows through the black mesh of my top. My belly ring that I changed for my bat dangle shows too. My skirt is beyond short. It's tulle underneath leather pleats and blacker than activated charcoal.

My entire outfit is black. The only thing of color is my hair.

Death should be depicted this way—savage, feral, untamed.

It's exactly how I feel in my outfit. Ready to avenge and take no prisoners.

I miss you, Cass.

Instead of putting my contacts in, I leave without them. It feels right. Might not be, but my brother feels present somehow, almost as if he wants me to do this, to see what the students are all hiding. Let's hope I don't get quieted like him.

What were you into, Cassidy?

Why didn't you come to me?

I'm not even done shutting my door before my phone goes off. Staring at the caller ID, I notice my best friend's name. A tiny sigh of relief escapes as I answer.

"I miss you." Usually, that wouldn't be my first response, but our conversations have been limited to texts and quick phone calls when we're both free.

It's been hell without her.

"If I liked pussy, I'd marry you," Yang jokes.

We're both laughing. It feels good to genuinely enjoy living for a moment.

"I miss you too, Colty."

"How's Duponte?" I ask.

It's been a few months since we've seen each other and caught up. She's busy settling into college. It's not exactly easy when you're as energetic as Yang Park. She's so spacey, I'm surprised her grades were ever better than mine. We were inseparable the last two years. Then, she had to graduate, leaving me in this hell alone.

"Pretty sure coming here's the biggest mistake I've ever made," she says, her voice both sarcastic yet somehow serious. "The guys here are bangable, though."

My face breaks into another big smile. She's the only living person who gets me, who truly gets me.

"But enough about me. We both know you're hiding around my life to avoid talking about yours."

"Hmm. Not sure what you're referring to."

"Bullshit."

"Let's not. When're you coming to visit?"

"At that soul-sucking hellhole? Never would be too soon."

It's not a joke, but we both let out forced laughter.

"I'm serious," I mutter.

"So am I."

Yeah, I get it. I do.

"I'll come for Christmas. I'm sure you're avoiding both moms, no?"

"God. I almost hate how much you know me," I groan. pass by the elevator, and my heart crumbles into a bazillion ashy speckles. I need to be off the phone when they finally notice me. "I've gotta go, babe. Text me." I hang up before she can argue.

If only there was another way down. My eyes catch the metal box, and sweat lines my forehead. By the only staircase sans the emergency exit that's always locked and armed with an alarm, stands the boys. Standing is a loose term, especially since two aren't.

Ross leans against a wall, one foot up against it as he stares at his phone. He's dressed in skinny jeans, a fitted but long tee, sporting his expensive watch, the only thing that shows how rich he truly is.

Lux stands opposite him in a fucking suit. It's blood red and so fitting it shows his bulky figure. He's the only one out of the four who has zero piercings and tattoos. Lennox DeLeon has always looked like a goddamn politician's son. Guess it's fitting that he is.

Bridger, the coiffed pretty boy with eyes darker than ash and a soul to match, is crouched down, nearly touching the floor as he talks to Tennison. They're gazes are locked, and whatever conversation they're having must be a deep one since Ten looks seconds away from punching Bridger in the face.

Ten rocks board shorts, high tops, and a Coheed and Cambria tee.

He's the only guy who reminds me of me. Tennison, my Ten. He's still in conversation with Bridger, whose expression is relaxed, the mood shifting from when I first glanced at them. I know their conversation is more cohesive than it ever is with me. Those two could discuss the world and never run out of a single thing to converse about.

Bridger's attire is more basic—fitted black jeans, a button-up with the sleeves rolled to his elbows, and loafers of some kind.

Of course, it's Lux who notices me first. His eyes connect with mine on a level that scares me. With a single stare, he dissects me. He always has. It's like he takes the bare bones from me, analyzes each of them, and then spits them out with distaste because I'll never be enough for him, even if he won't admit it's because of how broken he is and not the other way around.

"Bloodsucker," he taunts, biting the inside of his lip like he knows a secret I don't. I'm sure he does. They all do.

It's on me to find out what that secret is.

"Fuckface," I respond coolly, wondering where Jordan is. He's supposed to pick me up.

Three other sets of eyes connect with my body. I would say my eyes, but we all know they're looking anywhere but.

It's Bridger who gets to me this time. His eyes are so dark, even more endless than usual. You could see the entire world reflect in them normally. Now, it seems like nothing can be visualized but black and more black. His jaw ticks as

167

he devours me from head to toe. It's unnerving, having a guy
stare at you as if you're beneath him while also memorizing
every inch.

These boys are hot and cold, and I'm not interested in
either.

Right?

Sometimes, we lie to ourselves because the truth is both
damning and terrifying.

"Why are you here?" The question slips out, and I'm not
sure which guy to stare at in hopes of a response. They're
staring at me like I'm a meal, and if they think that's going to
happen again, they're fucking mad. It never truly happened.
just almost.

"A little birdy admitted he invited you to a Crystallite
get-together."

I bite my lip ring, hating that said little bird is Jordan
Was this all a ploy? They wanted to get me alone to corner me

"Is that so?" I ask.

"Yes," Ross responds, pushing from the wall and coming
straight for me.

My body wants to retreat, but my mind says to stay and
not show any type of anxiety. They'll eat it up.

"But like that little message on your hip, he's
overstepping." He's in front of me now, lifting my top, seeing
how hard I scrubbed until it was gone. "Looks like you're in
agreement."

I swat his hand away. "Why are you here?" I repeat, my
voice faltering a little.

He touches my chin the way he always seems to, all the guys behind him watching. "Because you're mine."

It's such a simple response, like there shouldn't be an argument.

I glare at him. "No, I'm really not."

My skin prickles as he pinches my flesh with intent. "You've been mine since you kissed me, ragdoll."

Ragdoll. That's a new one. I roll my eyes as I notice Lux approaching. Dammit.

He pushes Ross away, taking his place in my personal space. "He's wrong, you know. Technically, you're ours. Student Gov's."

Their cocky standoffish attitudes make me want to stab a knife in their hearts, to make them feel what it's like to live without the one person who loved you unconditionally.

"Good," I provoke. "That means Jordan can have me."

Immediately, four sets of eyes glare at me.

"What? He's a part of your bullshit posse. That means he gets a piece of the pie."

It's really just me trying to push them back, but it seems to have the opposite effect on these guys.

"Oh, Greenie. We were hoping you'd see it that way," Ten muses with a smile.

He's faking it. All the niceties, fucking me at that party, and playing good cop since school started… They're all up to something, and fuck if I won't find out what.

"You can come out now, Walker. Seems she's ready for this show to go on," Lux drones out, but unlike his bored voice,

169

his eyes are molten with promise. Whatever that promise i
I'm scared.

"Fuck, Colton. You clean up good." Jordan whistle
coming from behind Bridger. His voice is hardened and low
not soft, not boyish, not at all like he pretended to be sinc
that day in the hall.

How I missed him, I don't know, but the nice new bo
from the start of school is nowhere to be seen in the navy blu
of his eyes.

"Glad you finally took off those contacts," he continue
coming face-to-face with me. "They ruined the whole package
deal."

"Get bent," I nearly spit, not understanding what I'v
gotten myself into.

"You guys weren't lying," he comments, looking at eac
member. "Cassidy's little sister is one helluva spitfire. Hot a
fuck, too."

The way he says my brother's name with suc
familiarity has me finally backing up. My gut warned m
something was off with Jordan the first moment he walke
up to me. They say the gut is an early warning system t
danger. Why didn't I listen? Why am I always betraying m
body's knowledge for dicks?

"Don't scamper off now," Lux drawls, following m
retreat. "We've got a lot planned tonight."

"I'm not playing your games. None of yours." It's directe
at each of them, but comes out fragile like my heart an
confidence.

Bridger stays near the stairs as I continue retreating. Warm hands clasp my shoulders from behind, and I'm screaming. One hand clamps over my mouth to stifle the noise. Right as I'm biting into it, Ross is hushing me.

"Shh, Colty." Ross removes his hand as I stare back at him.

"Don't be scared," Jordan adds.

"It'll be a perfect night," Lux promises.

Too bad his promises are always dark and never enjoyable.

Instead of regarding them, I watch Bridger and how he seems disinterested like normal. He's the hardest to read, and it's why my gut reactions never work with him. Or any of them. My hormones got me in trouble when we met. Seems like they continue to fuck me without protection.

"It's time," Bridger finally speaks, tapping his watch before trailing down the stairs.

"Hope you're not this scared when you finally figure out what tonight's about," Lux mocks. "You're going to wish your parents moved you to Cello, Bloodsucker. We weren't lying when we told you to go home. You don't belong here anymore."

What is he talking about?

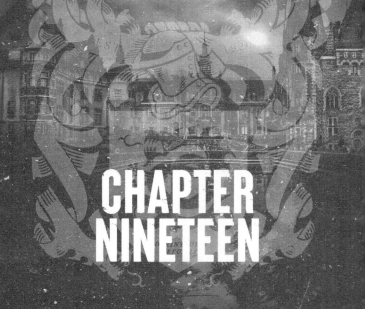

CHAPTER NINETEEN

"So, it was all pretend?" I question Jordan, hating how broke
my voice sounds. If I were half as strong as I pretended to be
I'd be able to cover up how upset his lies truly made me.

He eyes me as if it's simple and I'm over-thinking it. Hel
maybe I am.

"The nice-guy bullshit? Yeah." He nods. "The thinkin
you're fucking hot? Absolutely not." Jordan winks as if tha
makes this all better.

"Why lie?" The guys all escort me toward Crystal Towe
as my body shakes with anticipation. It's not excitement, eithe

"Needed to see if you'd give in. Can honestly say, I'r
surprised you held out so long. Chicks tend to fall at thei
feet for me."

"Do you not hear how fucking ridiculous that sounds?"
grit, hating all these guys even more.

"It'll all make sense one day."

"Cryptic bullshit, how nice," I mutter, ignoring him and running to catch up with Bridger. While he's never been super emotive, he doesn't tend to lie to me. "Why do you do it?"

He stops for a second before he continues walking. "You think you know me. You don't," he bites out.

"I could argue that."

"Then you're fooling yourself," he answers, frowning. "You should've stayed away. Made life easier on us all."

"Why? So you guys can get away with murder?"

He fully stops then, glaring at me. "You don't know a goddamn thing, Freak. Don't push for information. Stop chasing. Forget Student Gov. Us. Fuck, forget Cass, too. Let it go."

He rushes past me, and I don't have the heart to chase him. What does it all mean? They talk in circles with their stupid secrets and lame excuses. It's getting to me, though. All of it.

My phone beeps several times again and again.

Where are you?

We were supposed to meet.

Colttttttt. Don't ignore me.

Mel's messages keep coming before I text her. *Totally forgot. Meet me there. I'm here.*

Really?! You went without me? What about our plan?

"What plan?" Ten asks from behind me, making me jump.

I lock my phone and shove it in my bra. "Nothing."

"You're a horrible liar, babe."

"You've really got to stop calling me that, Ten. It's not… *fair.*" That's the only word I could settle on.

173

And it's not fair. He and the rest of these menaces fucke
me over. Even as I play nice, I'm going to keep digging whil
playing dumb. If they would have left me alone, this would b
over. But unlike their lies, they keep pushing *me*. I'm not th
one prodding them.

"Can't change facts. You've never stopped being mine."

"Yes, I did. I stopped being yours the night my brothe
was taken from me as you fucked my innocence away."

He stops me, holding my shoulders. "If I recall, you wer
there, your legs spread wide, your moans against my lip
and your orgasms at my fingertips. Doesn't sound innocer
to me, Colton."

Colton. Not babe, Greenie, or Vamp. He's mad. Te
is the softest of all of them. There's a side he gave me h
probably shouldn't have. It showed me the truth beneat
his mask, how broken he is. They all are, cracked puppets c
their parents' making.

Isn't that us all?

"Fine, but it was all fake."

He pushes against me, his pelvis hitting mine, the har
ridge of him rubbing against the softness of me. "Does it fee
fake? Do you really think I can pretend that well?"

A tear trails my face, surely making the black of m
makeup run with it. Even with setting spray, tears are th
blood of the makeup industry. You can't hide or waterproo
the saltiness of emotion.

"You guys done being emotional?" Lux sneers at us.

What broke that guy's heart? He's seriously soulless.

174

"Done being a dick?" I counter.

He laughs derisively.

"Guess that's a no for us both," I insult, hoping he'll someday break the hard shell protecting his heart like Alcatraz. Such a lonely life he must live.

We make it to the tower, and nausea overrides all thoughts for me. Though this isn't the last place I saw my brother, it's where the entire night began.

PAST

"I need you to stay at the dorm tonight, Col."

My eyes connect with my brother's, and I notice the bags underneath, how his cheekbones seem gaunt, and his lack of color.

"Why?" Ten wants me to go, practically begged me. I can barely say no to the guy.

"It's not a place for you, sis. Believe me. You're meant to be happy and alive and not at a Crystallites shindig."

What he's saying doesn't make sense. Alive? What does that even mean?

Why is he going if he's unwilling to let me go? Sounds pretty ass-backward to me. Cass isn't secretive, at least not until I started Arcadia. He's in the grade above me, but it never broke our bond being separated.

"Just tell me why, Cass. Why can't you just tell me?"

He closes his eyes, and it's then I realize how much weight he lost and how stressed he's had to have been to appear this frail.

My brother has always been way bigger than me. While I'm curvy, I'm shorter and smaller. He's built and strong. Right now or maybe it's been for a while, he's slimmer. He's almost too thin. I've been so preoccupied with Ten, Bridger, Ross, and Lux to notice but Cass hasn't been around. He's never in the classes we share, and he's never at our shared dorm. Come to think of it, he's always busy. Away. Nowhere to be found.

"What's going on?" I ask.

He still hasn't opened his eyes. They remain closed as his face shows pain. Is he hurting? Is someone the cause? What is going on? My mind rushes over every worst-case scenario and still, he doesn't say anything.

"Please, Cass. How can I help you if I don't know what's wrong."

"Don't need your help, baby sis. Need you to stay home tonight." His voice cracks, only slightly, but it's enough to have me nodding.

"Okay, I'll stay."

Too bad neither of us listen to each other.

Not even two hours later, Cass is at Crystal Tower, and I'm trying to hide the fact that I came here, too, with four guys.

It started by drinking too much with Ten at his dorm, which led to dancing with Bridger and making eyes at Ross and Lux. It's dangerous dance the four of us do, one that won't end well when I've finally got to make a choice. A girl can't possibly have them all. They know it. I know it. The world knows it.

It's not natural.

Not normal.

Not acceptable.

"Come with me?" Ross whispers in my ear, coming from behind me as Bridger holds my waist fervently. They glance at each other, a silent conversation flowing between them.

I nod at them both. As Ross leads me away, Bridger follows. Maybe they all do. I'm too entranced in the heat radiating from Ross' hand to be certain.

We make it to a room. There's a huge bed in the center. A California King, I'm sure. It's too big to be anything smaller. Plush, fluffy, and wide as fuck, offering me a pillowed comfort for what's about to happen. He directs me there, backward, and my heart rate picks up. My legs connect with the bed and bend naturally. His fingers find my silver hair, the strands almost like silk in his hold. His hands, calloused and warm, cup my cheeks. Our lips connect soon after, and it's like melting in the sun on the hottest day in July. A little moan escapes me, and a growl is the only response.

Bridger comes toward us. His hands brush my shoulders reverently, gently, with purpose, but as Ten stalks in, they both back away, as if they had a silent conversation that makes no sense.

I see Ten's eyes, and they say so much. He and I are the closest. We're passionate. He knows how to tease my body until it blushes everywhere. He understands the way I need to be touched to get a release. As the recognition in his eyes flicker at me, the other two back away and watch as Ten kisses me with every emotion he carries.

He grunts when my hand brushes his hardened flesh. The two watch, and I wish they'd all touch me, take turns, all at once, anything as long as they're all here. My heart misses Lux. Why didn't he follow? Does he not want me anymore? Is it because I'm too close to Ten?

When Ten's fingers slip past my panties, under my dress, I

forget about anyone else. As he flicks my bundle of nerves gently, knowing where, when, and how much pressure to add, I'm falling apart and Ten's the only one I see and feel.

"Do you trust me?" he whispers after I've come down from my release.

I nod, my heart still pounding, but almost in a gentler beat instead of frantic. Ten kisses me harshly, making my lips feel swollen and then, he's pulling out a condom.

"Do you want me to stop, beautiful? I'll stop if that's what you want."

My heart shatters into a million butterflies, fluttering above me, soaring in happiness. In that moment, I fall for Tennison Dellamore.

I nod again, and he enters me in one swift thrust.

They always say it hurts the first time, but it doesn't. All I feel is good. All I experience is pleasure. All I taste is Ten and our bodies colliding sweetly. He grips me, thrusts harder, and we both cry out in ecstasy.

We're barely escaping our high when a high-pitched scream pierces my ears. It's blood-curdling, the kind you hear in movies and on the news. It's deadly, like all the terror in the world is encompassed in that single sound. I'm shoving my dress down and racing outside toward the sound. I can't find the origination, but it doesn't stop me from searching.

Ten doesn't follow. That's weird.

As my hazy state clouds me a bit, I recall how I've had a little too much to drink. Maybe I'm dreaming? But then I hear the screech again, and sobs, loud and heartbreaking ones. Is this girl hurt? Did someone rape her? Is she okay?

I chase the cries and stumble upon something I never thought I would see.

My brother.

Unmoving.

Bloodied.

Lifeless.

A girl, Dolly Maez, if I remember correctly, leans over his form distraught.

I rush to him. My heart stops beating, and I think I stop breathing. It's a dream, a really fucking bad one. Shock overwhelms me. I pinch myself and realize it's not fake. It's real. He's dead.

A scream, loud and piercing, escapes my throat. It hurts my ears, shakes my entire body, and physically pains me to let it out. The screams don't stop there. They continue as my hands touch his face, his silver hair now garnet with blood. I cry, and cry, and cry. The screams don't stop, not even when the cops show up or when they try taking his body. They don't stop when both moms show up or when they take him in a body bag.

They just never stop.

Not for days.

Weeks.

Months.

Until one day, I feel nothing.

They claimed he jumped off the cabin.

They said he hit a boulder.

They swore he was drunk.

That he was suicidal.

That he wanted to end it all for quite some time.

They all fucking lied.

CHAPTER TWENTY

"What's with that blasé message?" Mel asks ten minutes late

We're on the tenth floor where it all happens. Mo
times, it ends at the cabin, the one at Moonstone Lake. It
a fifteen-minute hike. If they go there, I'm not sure if I ca
follow. There are too many memories surrounding that plac
ones not worth reliving.

"What message?" Lux pipes in, putting an ownership
type palm on my shoulder.

"None of your business, DeLeon," Mel snaps, giving hi
a death glare.

Lennox raises an eyebrow, confusion and contemplatio
barer than his ass in the shower.

"Can we talk in private?" she whispers, but I'm sure Lu
heard. He's like a goddamn bat.

"Sure," I mutter, not even positive the guys will allow i
They're bossy and think they rule the entire world. It's n

entirely false. They rule Arcadia. And me.

We walk over to a nondescript sitting area. It's not away from everyone, but definitely away from the boys. Not sure if I'm more scared of the secrets or the boys. Either way, it's not safe here.

"First," Mel says, grabbing my arm gently, "you look like a goddamn snack."

I laugh at that compliment. It's one you can't resist to giggle over.

"Second." She rubs up and down my arms like she knows this isn't easy for me. "Why are you with them? *All* of them. Even Ridge?"

The accusation is light, but I get it. We had a plan to come here and snoop and hopefully not die, and she's crushing on the dude. My showing up with five guys who are far from kind isn't exactly smart.

"I was right," I whisper conspiratorially. "Jordan is one of them. He was pretending to be nice to me the entire time."

Her eyes widen as she mulls this over. "How do you know?"

I lean into her. "He came to my floor with the guys and admitted he only pretended to be nice to get me close to him."

She pulls away abruptly, and we look around to see if anyone's listening. Not even ten feet away, Ross stands watching us. His face isn't too readable. He's like a fucking vault with his emotions right now, and it's the most annoying part of the male species.

"What do we do now?" she asks.

"We can't snoop. They're here with me for a reaso
Maybe go cozy up to Ridge. He seems to like you."

She blushes a bit and then fixes her face. "You sure?"

It's like she needs my permission to go after one of n
guys. A pinch of annoyance which is more than likely jealous
tries leaking from me, but it's not fair. He's not mine. None o
them ever were.

"Go," I urge. I'll try sneaking around. It'll probably ge
me hurt, but I'm not willing to stop.

She sees that, my trepidation. Leaning in, she kisses m
cheek just to whisper in my ear, "I'll try keeping them busy
Act like we're flirting. Lux is right behind you."

I giggle and bring her lips to mine. We brush gently, he
face warm in my palms as I use her for clout and distraction
She only hesitates for a breath before she's into it with m
Girls have never interested me, but her lips are soft and swee
It's not gross at all. It warms me up as if a guy did it.

"That's enough," Bridger hisses, pulling us apart.

She winks at me as I stare at the guy who's the leas
unkind to me. His eyes burn with something. Rage? Envy
Hatred? He's Pandora's box, and opening him isn't in th
cards for me.

I make the phone gesture with my hand. "Call me," I flir

She smiles so fucking huge and allows Bridger to tak
her away. They aren't even five feet away when arms are o
my shoulders. I feel his breath on the shell of my ear befor
his voice comes.

"I'll admit that was hot, Corpse, but no one, *no one* touche what's mine," Lux hisses.

"Ours," Ten corrects with a grunt.

This could work to my advantage. In so many ways, this could benefit me. Just imagine if the most popular, rich, and powerful kids in school were on my side? Could I find out what happened to Cass? Would it be them?

My heart pumps. Its beat echoes in my ear as if I'm underwater. With the music blaring in the background, I'm nearly overwhelmed with senses. One of the two boys licks my ear lobe then nips it shortly after. There isn't a feel of metal, which means it has to be Lux.

"It's time for the big surprise," Lux coaxes, but in reality, the soft yet gravelly sound of his voice has me hot and nervous. Two very opposite reactions for the scariest kid in school. How fitting.

They practically drag me toward the elevator.

My chest constricts. "No, absolutely not!" My words come out frantic and pitchy.

They stare at me with confusion. Either they're purposefully fucking with me, or they don't realize how absolutely terrified I am of that stupid silver death trap.

"Really? Come on. Stop fucking around," Lux complains.

Ten watches me curiosity.

Stop being curious, fuckface, and stop this, I want to scream.

"Stop, Lux," Ross says, coming from wherever the hell he just was. It's the first time I've seen him care in any sense since we fucked. He's not one to really show his emotions to anyone. He hides it, keeps it tucked away like a secret. He may

be nice to everyone, overly joyous to hide his sad boy interio
but he never shows when he cares for someone. That's whe
he feels weakest.

Tears prick the corners of my eyes as I silently thank hin
It warms me in a way it shouldn't, kisses the most sensitiv
parts of my flesh like a wish.

"Why?" Lennox barks, his eyes narrowing on Ross. "Ar
we going to have a problem, Dare?"

Ross rolls his eyes at that. "She's fucking terrified. Don
force her to go on the elevator. Stop being a lazy fuck, an
walk the stairs."

Lennox immediately swivels his gaze to mine, analyzin;
almost debating whether or not he's going to force it. My che
heaves with terror, hoping for once in his horrible existenc
he doesn't make the worst choice of all and break me.

Bringing his mouth to my throat, he whispers, "Only
get to scare you, Corpse. Let's go."

It's the only reprieve I get before he's shuffling down th
stairs and pulling me with him. At least going down stairs
easier than up. These guys aren't slow by any means. Gues
sports will do that for you. Not football or any sport lik
that, the other unconventional ones—motocross, skatin;
BMX, baha'ing through the dunes. They're extremists, both i
life and extracurriculars. Lennox and Bridger are definitel
gym hounds, though. Once upon a time, they made a jok
that I was a goddamn gym bunny. Only for them, though
Only ever for these assholes.

"Remember this place?" Lux prods, forcing us toward th

spider tree near the lake.

Something inside me breaks as each step brings me closer to Cassidy's last living moment.

Don't cry, Colt. You're strong enough.

But I'm not. I'm only seventeen. I'm not strong enough for what's in store for me. I'm not ready.

"Yes," I grit out, seeing the tree come into view, lit by the moon, stars, and the reflection from the water.

Moonstone Lake got its moniker from the full moon. Whenever it's at its crest—like now—it illuminates the entire lake and the single tree and rocks nearby. The spider tree, the only tree near the foot of the lake, has been uprooted. A storm tore it from the earth, and the winds and constant change in climate made it a skeleton of the tree it once was. Still, it prospers. It grows leaves every spring and loses them every fall.

"Remember our first kiss, Corpse?"

I cringe. I've never told anyone about it. Not the guys, my brother, or even Mel. When I peer at the other three, they don't seem bothered, like it's not new information for them.

"How could I forget?" I whisper, reaching up to touch my lips as if it was recent and not a year ago, before that party, before Ten and I spent stolen moments under the stars, before Bridger in the halls and that one time with Ross in the janitor's closet... They're all moments I remember. Forgetting them would be useless.

"I think the guys need a demonstration. Show them how a real man kisses."

The jab in his words has me wondering which guy makes

him feel threatened. I'm not any of theirs, and they're far from mine. If they were, they wouldn't hurt me. If I were theirs, they wouldn't need other women.

It would be me.

I would be enough.

"If she needs a demonstration, it should be me," Ross snarks, pushing past Ten and Jordan. His eyes are trailing my form. They're hungry, wanton, *angry*. He's always angry.

My angry yet very sad boy.

Some things don't change.

Lennox smirks at us both then pulls me to him. His height is astounding compared to me. He's a tower—no, skyscraper—and I'm a measly half stack of pancakes. His dark scent wafts through my nose, burning me straight between my thighs. I squeeze them, unable to resist the affect he's always carted over me.

"Tell me, how does a vampire kiss?" he insults with a curl of his lip.

"With teeth," I respond and bite his thick bottom lip, waiting until blood prickles.

He doesn't yell or reprimand, no, because the secret about kissing Lennox DeLeon is that he likes swapping blood over spit. He loves the pain, to punish, to attack and hold no regard to feelings. His calloused hands, big and too strong, grip my throat, as he walks us backward toward the tree, just like the first time. His hard erection grinds into my scantily clad body. Heat zips up and down my spine as he owns the kiss.

As he owns *me*.

He grunts when I nip him again, and I enjoy the feel of his barely abated dick through his slacks. Lennox isn't one to lose control. It's how he became president, how he rules the Gov, and how he takes every step possible to win every duel.

Not this time, not as he loses with me. His tongue lashes mine, a whipping. Hatred seeps through my taste buds. It fills me to the brim, and when he's rolling his hips into me, I learn Lux isn't as unmovable as he pretends. No, he's malleable, bendy, and mine to test.

I thrust back, and he hisses.

"Fuck," Ross mutters underneath his breath somewhere by us.

"Porn has nothing on this," Jordan muses.

"Okay, guys. Jesus," Ten chastises, his displeasure only making me push into Lux more.

Ten deserves pain.

They all do.

They warrant ruin.

Lux pulls back, dragging his teeth over my mouth and lip rings. His eyes swim with feelings.

Yes, feelings. Lennox DeLeon can pretend until he's black and blue, but when his lips touch mine, it's me who's in control. He licks where I split his lip, and his smirk and darkened flickers of lust have me wet.

Fuck. I can hold my own or make them weak, but they do the same for me. They make me lose control, and my body enjoys them even if my heart isn't so easily fooled.

"Not bad for a bloodsucker," I tease, feeling the savageness

of our make-out session. Even my piercings are a little sor
He's all about being rough, and you would think with ho
sweet Ten gets, I would be opposed to it, but sometimes, a gi
craves unbidden lust.

"Not bad at all," he musters angrily.

Wonder if he felt himself coming undone like I did.

"Stop making fucking eyes and let's go," Ten barks.

When I turn to him, all that's there is green, bright an
toxic like my hair. His aura is full of greed and envy, an
something about that makes me insanely happy.

"Where to, boys?"

While I sound excited, I'm anything but. A storm rage
inside me, one with mixed emotions and rain clouds promisin
to sink me if I'm not careful.

The thing about losing your reason to live? You becom
reckless. It's been half a year of nothingness. Starting a ric
seems right up my alley.

CHAPTER TWENTY-ONE

"What the fuck was that?" Ten growls quietly at Lux.

We're headed to the cabin, and I'm sweating bullets. This place brings horrors to fruition. It drags me back to the night I witnessed my first dead body.

"This isn't the plan."

"Fuck the plan, Dellamore. You're just pissed because you're fucking bent over this girl." Lennox and Ten argue at the lead of the group while I trail several paces behind with Jordan and Ross nearby.

"Me? What about you? Tongue-fucking her and nearly coming in your pants. Who's the real bent one, Lux?" Ten's voice carries.

It takes everything in me to pretend I'm not listening and enjoying their little one-on-one.

"I think it was hot," Jordan comments, making me swivel

my head to him. He's not looking at me, but his stance relaxed.

"Of course, you do. You've always liked watching. Whethe dick or pussy, you're always fucking gawking," Ten scolds.

How do they know him? Where did he come from? Wh is he here and with them?

"Don't know why you're bitching, Ten. We all know yo got to fuck her last year and that you've broken several rule since school started," Ross interrupts to jab at Ten.

My ears prick at the mention of rules. What rules?

"You're one to talk. We know you fucked her the othe day, Dare."

Ross visibly swallows.

Silence encompasses the crisp, empty air, but not for lon;

"Bet he was a two-pump chump," Jordan tosses in.

It takes every ounce of control not to bark out a laugl They're fucking ridiculous with their petty jealousies. Do the share all this information? Who bags Colt? Who kisses Colt Who one-ups the other? They're worse than chicks.

"Shut the fuck up, all of you," Lux demands, turnin his head toward me. "Have you ever met the Emeral Vestige, Colty?"

I cringe at the shiver that racks my frame. The Emeralds A memory smacks me in the face.

"I don't like scary stories."

With my words, Cass smiles. He's become a bit of a jerk sin starting at Arcadia Junior. It's like he's becoming someone els Different. Popular. Not my best friend.

"Too bad. Gramps told me about this story of these elitists who owned the town."

The mention of the town interests me. I've always heard ghost stories about this place. We're told to behave, that our actions are the basis of the town's reputation and that we're not allowed to tarnish what has been built over generations and traditions I'm not even aware of.

"What's that?" I ask.

"They're called Emeralds, apparently. He used to say they had so much power they could destroy any person."

I shiver, staring at my brother as he animatedly speaks of this group.

"I'm sure it's not true, but wouldn't it be insane to be raised in a town that has a secret society?"

Shaking my head, I deny that. "No. Imagine being raised in a town where it's ran by someone you can't even see."

With that conversation in mind, chills break across my skin. Whether these douchebags are discussing that or not, I shouldn't be here, but it makes sense. A secret society who destroys those around them...

My mind travels to the last few weeks with my brother. The secrets. Weight loss. Sleepless nights. All those times Cass came home covered in bruises, hanging out with new people... It only makes sense if the Emeralds had a hand in it.

"No. Meeting the Emerald Vestige is not on my to-do list," I grit out, my fists tightening with each step toward the cabin. "They're just a scary story told to Arcadians to keep them from doing stupid shit."

191

At least, that's how it's been told. Was Cass somehow alluding to this all along?

"Wrong." Lux's face morphs into disappointment.

"They're definitely real and quite the fun crowd," Jordan explains, only confusing me further.

They're real?

"Why are you here?" I deflect, finally getting the nerve to not be scared into silence. I direct my question at Jordan, who smirks, amusement present. "I understand the guys. They all want to fuck me or fuck with me, but you make zero sense. You came from nowhere and saddled up to me. What gives?"

Ross chuckles. Ten scowls. Lux smirks.

Jordan narrows his eyes, glaring at me in a haphazard way. "Why, Colton Hudson. You must not remember me." A sardonic laugh escapes his sharp lips, his tongue piercing glints in the moonlight as he licks his lips.

"Am I supposed to?"

Lux full belly laughs as Jordan gives him a glower that would make a normal person think twice.

"Think back. Really fucking hard, Vamp. Back to a day when you came to this cabin for the first time."

My mind travels over the first trip here, to what led me here the first time. Though that night was my first invite to a Crystallites party, it wasn't my first trip down to Moonstone Lake.

If memory serves, Jordan is the kid in green. My body and face heats as awareness kicks in.

"Ah, there it is. You remember," he says gleefully.

My mind drifts to that night.

"Do you think we'll get caught?" I ask Yang, wondering if she's as scared as me. She's older, more mature, and generally fearless with everything.

She gets this devious glint in her eyes. "What's the fun if there isn't a chance?"

She grabs my arm and leads me to the cabin. There's a curfew during the week at Arcadia, and we're out past the ten o'clock rule. If we go back, we'll have to convince one of the boys to let us in. Luckily, my brother is one of them.

We sneak around the cabin, and nearby, I hear something loud fall.

Yang eyes me, and then she puts a finger to her mouth. "I'm going to go this way. Stay right here, Colt. Don't move." It comes out as a shaky whisper. For the first time in our friendship, she actually seems scared. Not sure why it makes goosebumps climb up my skin, but it does. She leaves me here, shaken and afraid.

Another loud bang sounds out, seemingly closer to me. Instincts take over as I rush around the way Yang went. It isn't until a little light catches my eye that I realize I'm near a bottom floor window. As the sounds get louder, I open the window. Why isn't this locked? People are crazy. Wanting to hide from the noise, knowing Yang went in the opposite direction from the new noise, I shimmy into the small space, and my back scrapes on the metal awning of the window. I wince.

Shit.

Shit.

Shit.

It's nearly dark. The light illuminating the room casts more shadows than it reveals dark. I'm tiptoeing, hoping not to get caught up in anything on the ground and praying no one decides to axe murder me. It's practically soundless in this place, which is creepier than you would think.

My foot stubs into a beam of some sort, and a string of curses come out under my breath. Bending at the hip, I rub my boot covered foot as best as I can before making it to some stairs. My heart hammers uncontrollably as I trail my gaze upward. My only hope is that if there is a killer, they won't hear my excessive panting.

Low noises tickle my ears, and I go toward the sound. Seems stupid, but maybe there's someone in here who can protect me.

The sounds get louder, and I realize it's groaning. My body warms up on its own accord. Fuck. Someone's having sex. I've watched enough porn to recognize pleasure. A male's low growl makes my chest furl with lust.

I think back to some of my favorite topics—men with men, dominance, breath play, knife play... I prefer the amateur clips the most. It's more personable.

Smacking fills my ears. Deep breathing and gravelly grunts make my core clench. I've never had sex, and every orgasm I've had has been with my own hand.

When I make it around a corner in the hallway, light escapes a room. How did I miss the only lit room? It's not bright, more like candlelight than anything lamp-like.

In the middle of an old clandestine carpet is four guys. Two are watching from the side as the other two are fucking. The two fucking are seniors, Robert and Flint. I've seen them around Crystal Tower

One thrusts into the other. It's impersonal. Robert's pushing Flint's face into the carpet as Robert jackhammers into him from behind. They both grunt and moan in sync of one another. It's fucking hot. And wrong. So wrong for me to voyeur... but I can't seem to look away.

A whimper escapes my throat, but only one guy's eyes leave the scene in front of him. Those eyes look so black, chemically so, like he dyed them to be without color. It's hard to decipher his facial features. All I can see is the emerald green blazer he wears without a shirt underneath. His abs, barely lit by the candlelight, have me gasping. I've never been this close to sex or guys, but it's so beyond thrilling to watch it unfold.

He starts to get up, and I bolt the way I came, not seeing the two guys finish.

"Fuck," I mutter, my skin flaming at the memory. I'd forgotten all about those guys and Jordan.

I look at him. His navy eyes appearing black now, colorless, dark, soul-sucking.

Rubbing my thighs together at the memory, I play with my lip piercings, needing a distraction from the lust permeating the air.

"Fuck is right, Colton. I remember you. Do you remember me?"

I don't answer, knowing it'll come out a squeak with my luck. My face is as hot as the candle's flame from that night. Men fucking with abandon. The sensuality of pure masculinity is the hottest shit ever. My core aches with the need to release. It's swollen. I can feel my clit with each step we take.

"Yeah." He chuckles. "You remember. That night, after

you snuck away, I rubbed one out three fucking times to tha little noise you made alone."

I blush more, biting the inside of my cheek to quench th groan.

"Little Miss Delinquent isn't so innocent-lookin anymore, is she?"

"What are you on about?" Ross interrupts our littl standoff.

My eyes can't help themselves. They trail down Jordan body, seeing his hard-as-shit dick pressing his pants. Fuck thi

"Colton here watched two Emeralds fuck for initiatio while I watched," Jordan explains.

"Initiation?" I stumble over the word.

"I'm an Emerald," he replies. "President of the Emeral Vestige."

I choke on a cough. *What? It's real?*

Despite my confusion, my body aches with need an desire. How is it we've met but I don't remember him othe than our interactions this year?

"You're probably wondering why we've only just met, he answers my unspoken question. "I'm a legacy. Like Lu here, I'm a generation brat. The difference between him and class wasn't a necessity until I wanted to meet you."

Raising an eyebrow, I ponder over this tidbit. It doesn make sense.

"Why me?" I ask.

Jordan sidles up to me, cupping my jaw, not soft, but no painfully either. "Colton," he tsks, with a shake of his gorgeou head. "This year, you're mine."

A scoff from behind him lets me know there isn't full approval.

What does this even mean? Do I have a say? What is with these guys and their claiming of me?

Shaking free of him, I try to escape before being barricaded in by Lux and Ross. Ten stands nearby, unhappiness on every sculpt of his jaw. The tick that clicks constantly only furthers that realization.

"Tonight is initiation, Colty," Ross sounds out.

"You're the newest pledge," Lux adds with a devilish grin.

"I don't want—"

"No one said you had a choice," Jordan butts in, his face one of excitement. "We need a replacement Hudson. Unluckily for you, you're the only one left."

Fear should overwhelm me. It should, but I'm not really sure what's going to happen, and I told Mel I would investigate what I could.

Mel.

"Where's Ridge?" I request, hoping they don't hear my desperation.

"Busy. Probably fucking that redheaded bitch." Lux hums approvingly.

I can't help the frown that takes over my face. I hoped there wouldn't be any of that. Not that I have a claim over any of these guys, but Bridger and I have a weird connection we've only ever tested in the dark.

"Little Goth Princess is sad," Ross snubs at me. He always

hits the hardest, doesn't he?

"That's because our Corpse Bride has an ache betwee her thighs for five dicks," Lux mocks.

"I had her first," Ten growls, his temperament makin me roll my eyes.

"Did you, though?" Lux goads.

"Shall we?" Jordan cuts their banter off, tipping my chi peering into my eyes. "Really fucking glad you're not wearin contacts. It'll make tonight more special."

"What's going to happen?" I try to hide the whimper c hesitancy.

Jordan nips at my lips. "You pledge your undying loyalt to Emeralds, and then you fuck every member of the club."

I gag at the imagery. "I-I won't," I stutter. Thinking c anyone other than these guys touching me has me shakin with trepidation and disgust. "I won't."

The second admission comes out stronger, less fearful.

"Who are the Emeralds, Colt?" Jordan asks as if I'r supposed to know.

"I don't know, but I'm not fucking a bunch of people t satisfy some sick game of yours. I'd rather die."

As soon as the words leave my mouth, I wonder if that what happened to Cass. Did he refuse to fuck them all? To b a part of some sick group that uses pleasure as a loyalty tool

"Guess you'll die then," Lux says darkly, towering over m

With the largest and driest swallow ever known to mar I scream.

CHAPTER TWENTY-TWO

PAST

"Col!" Cassidy yells from the other room.

He's the only one who calls me that. I've always felt it's somehow more masculine than my already boyish name.

What does he want now? I roll my eyes, putting my nail polish down while blowing on my toes in hopes of them drying faster. There's nothing I hate more than smeared nail polish. It's beyond frustrating. Moms always teases me for not getting pedicures, but the idea of other people touching my feet is beyond disgusting. Like, no thanks.

"Jesus, stop ignoring me!" he complains.

I stifle a giggle. Cass going into puberty has been a treat. He's impatient, hot-headed, and moody. PMSing without the period excuse, if you ask me.

Before I can get up, he storms in with an annoyed expression.

"Really, Col?" He narrows his gaze, zeroing in o my toes. "Can't you be like our moms and go get tha professionally done?"

"How about suck a dick, Cass?" His grimace has n smiling. "You go and have your feet touched by randon people and tell me how great that is."

Almost as if imagining doing exactly that, he cringe "Fair point."

"What's so urgent you have to yell?" I inquire, pulling m nail polish back out for a second coat. He sits at the edge of m bed, making himself home. Since starting at Arcadia, he's bee gone a lot. It's as if I've lost my best friend. Yang would sa she's my best friend, but my brother will always rank abov We used to be inseparable, until school came between us.

"I'm sorry, sis. It's just…" He pauses, his mind mullin over something. "The guys."

He stops entirely on those two words. As much as I wan to prod, he doesn't look like he exactly wants to talk to m even with his earlier urgency.

"You know I love you, right?" he asks.

The question comes out of nowhere, sending a shive down my spine. It's not the words, only how he stated then Something is wrong, whether he wants to tell me or no Something's up.

"Of course, Cass. What's up?" Going against my bette judgment of letting it fly, I'm poking. Cass doesn't keep secret from me, or at least, he never used to. Hell, I don't even knov who he's dating anymore.

"Fuck," he whispers under his breath, making me more worried. "Student Gov wants you."

If he didn't say it so somberly, I would be jumping up and down. Since Cass has been involved, he gets all the perks. He can drive to school, have his own dorm in the Crystal Tower, and they get to go off campus for whatever they want. Only seniors get the car privilege. We have to be escorted by a parent, guardian, or Third Year. It's beyond obnoxious.

"Really?" It comes out more timid than it should, but holding in my excitement is a must while he's freaking out.

He nods. It's not like Cass to be so... off-putting. He's the opposite of me—chipper, exuberant, happy. Yeah, I have my moments of elation, but it's my brother's default setting while mine borders more on the bored, lazy, and blah spectrum.

"When did they decide this?" I ask.

"Just barely. I called you to talk."

I'm trying to paint my pinkie toe when the bed dips, making me get polish over the edges of my nail. Complaining with a grunt, I grimace, but he doesn't laugh or apologize. I peer at him, seeing the true fear there.

"Talk to me," I practically beg. Seeing him this disturbed about something has me on edge. "You can always talk to me."

He sits next to me, taking the nail polish bottle from my hands and setting it on my nightstand. "Don't join, Col."

His words throw me off. Everything about this conversation is throwing me off.

"Why not?" I ask.

"Just... don't. Okay? I've thought about it, and I think it's a bad idea."

"You've thought about it in the last five seconds?" accuse.

Is he doing this because he doesn't want me to hav friends and opportunities? Wants it all to himself? It makes n sense. I've only ever heard great things, especially from Yan She's always bragging about how amazing it is.

"It doesn't seem like you're going to listen to m regardless," he huffs, standing. His form hovers over m My brother has definitely grown a lot in the last two year We used to be pretty matched out when we would fight ove stupid things, but he's easily twice my size now.

"Can't take advice if you don't offer anything," I complai and roll my eyes. "You come in here and tell me somethir I've wanted all semester and then demand me to not do i Sounds like you're jealous, Cass."

He grips his head, running his hands through the silver strands. "God, you're so fucking dense, Col. Jealous? Fuck off The entire string of words come off like a curse word. "Yo know what? Do it. It's your fucking funeral."

The bitter end of his sentence strikes me across the ski We don't fight. Cass and I aren't like normal siblings. Ther aren't really arguments, not about anything like this, but he stupid if he thinks I'll bend over backward to allow him to b the only one with privileges.

"Fine. I will."

"Great," he bites out.

"Great," I respond, flipping him off.

He huffs and leaves my room, slamming the door as hard as he can.

"You're Colt," a gravelly voice sounds from behind me, forcing me to turn.

When my eyes connect with hair as silvery as my pale blue eyes, my heart leaps. Boys. If there could be a slogan for me, it'd be *boys, boys, boys, I love all the boys.* It takes everything to not giggle at my thoughts, but a smile breaks free anyway.

Tennison Dellamore eyes me appreciatively. He acts like we haven't met or seen each other off and on for the last ten or so years. He and my brother have always been thick as thieves. Ross too.

"That'd be me," I muse, seeing a flicker of interest in his gaze. "But you should know that already."

He raises an eyebrow like he's confused. Instead of getting pissy, I decide to follow his lead.

"I'm Tennison," he offers, sidling closer to me, invading my personal space.

My breath hitches. The intensity in his expression isn't one you get from boys at Arcadia. Generally, they're a bunch of shy guys mixed with annoying fuckboys. But this one... he's intense in a soft way. Not too strong or pushy. Just right for me.

"Tennison," I repeat, watching a smirk tilt at his lips. "You act as if we haven't known each other our entire lives."

He chuckles, but I wink at him. It's always like me to flir
but for some reason, I want to be cautious with him, to mak
him want to stay.

"Colton. Cassidy's sister," he mentions as if mullir
over the new but not-so-new information. "I'm one of th
Enforcers."

Immediately, I'm sent back to the argument Cass an
I had last night. My face falls abruptly, the sadness from n
brother being harsh still fresh. He didn't eat dinner with u
last night and didn't come home.

"What's with the long face?" Tennison asks.

I grimace. "I'm sorry. What's up?" I try to change th
expression on my face, but the reminder of last night leaves
bubbling anxiety in my gut. As much as I hated him bossing n
around last night, I love my brother. He's never led me astray.

"A meeting. We want you there."

My face heats. The way he simply states that they war
me there makes me ache in places I've learned only burn fc
guys. "Yeah?"

His lips tilt again, and I'm melting. What is it with this guy
"Ten tonight, Crystal Tower."

No explanation, no directions, just a command.

I peer at my feet, hiding the burn beneath my skin b
looking away from his penetrating stare.

"And, Colton," he purrs, tilting my chin up at him. "Don
tell anyone. House rules. Come alone."

The hammering in my chest should scare me, but it onl
makes my body warm everywhere.

"Got it," I whisper.

He rubs a knuckle across my cheek, and I'm melting.

He walks away right after, leaving me a breathless and excited mess. Cass must just want to protect me from hot guys. That's it. Must be. He's always been so protective over me.

My nerves are shot as I trail to Crystal Tower later that night. It's pitch-black out, and I didn't know what to wear, so I put on sleep shorts, a tank, and a hoodie. It's not unusual for chicks to venture out in shorts, and mine aren't extremely short.

I don't know how to get into the tower. It's only for Student Gov. They have exclusive access. Out of the three buildings that house people, this one is more like a house than the hotel feel of the other two.

Before I reach the entrance, a hand clamps onto my arm. A squeak escapes me as I come face-to-face with a blond boy. It's too dark out to see his eyes or feel for his intentions, but he looks really familiar. Letting my arm go, he smiles. It's not seedy, but it doesn't help he scared me either.

"Must be Colton."

He doesn't ask, more like comments, as if random girls don't sneak around at night. He's wrong. We all sneak around. Some are just better than others. I'm sure he's well aware.

"You scared me!" I hiss.

A low chuckle leaves him, and I'm immediately draw
to the sound.

"I'm sorry," he placates, putting his hands up. "Didn
want you to get caught." He gestures to the door, and
security guard is there. "He decided to do a late run. Didn
want you to have a mark on your record."

The words read kind and in good faith, so I nod.

"Thanks," I whisper. It's against the rules to be out pa
ten. Curfew. Even without parents to breathe down our neck
our school does it for them.

"I'm Lennox DeLeon," he practically purrs.

My hands feel all sweaty at the way he announces h
name. It's proclaimed like he's a god rather than a school bo
They seem to forget we all grew up in the same small town, bu
I let them introduce themselves anyway, like I'm not awa
who they are.

"Colt," I respond, knowing he already knows. These guy
seem to be privy to it all.

"Happy to make your acquaintance, *Colt*."

I like how he says my name. Part secret, part reverenc
but all pleased.

"Let's head up the back way. It's how we get to and from
he explains.

Makes sense. It's how we sneak out at Ivory as well.

He leads me behind Crystal, and I see a back door. Ivor
has a fire ladder, not a door like this. It's almost like a real hous
how some have back entrances. We head through, trailing u
the stairs, and I see three other guys sitting in a half-circle o

206

couches. It's dimly lit, and I can't really make out the room much, other than it feels more homely than my tower.

It's definitely not a dormitory, more like a fancy mansion that caters to the rich, but since we're all wealthy, it only serves the Gov. Tennison included.

A smile breaks free when I see him. He returns it easily, leaning back, relaxing his entire stance. It has that same heat sizzling my skin. *Yeah, I like him.*

Lennox leads me to the loveseat in the center of the room. It's plush and leather, swallowing me whole as I sit. Remembering my lack of clothing, I adjust immediately, catching stares from each guy. They glance at one another, an unspoken conversation that has me both interested and nervous.

"You've already met me and Ten," Lennox explains. *Ten. Not Tennison.* "This is Bridger."

He points at this astute boy. He's got brown hair, or at least, it seems brown, and it's a little shaggy, curling at the ends. It gives him a charming appearance, like he's a sweet guy underneath the lack of facial expressions. "And this is—"

"Ross," the guy seated next to Ten announces. Unlike Bridger, he seems appeased at me being here. He stands up, sauntering over to me with purpose. His green eyes, even while the room is darker, show just fine. They're stunning and make his frosty blue hair seem even frostier. When he erases the space between us, he crouches to my eye level. "Nice to meet you, Colty."

The way he says Colty as if it's something to be cherished has me squeezing my legs together. "Hey," I squeak, my voice small and scared. Why are these guys looking at me as if I' a five-course meal?

"You're scaring her, Dare," Ten scolds. *Dare?*

"Why do they call you Dare?" I interrupt their staredow

"Oh, sweetness. Can't exactly tell you that on our fir meet, now can I?" Heat rises up my throat, making n swallow hard. Why do his eyes seem like they could eviscera my every secret with one look?

"We wanted you here to ask you to join," Lennc announces, sitting in the couch next to mine. "We need treasurer, and who'd be better than you?" *Someone actual good at math,* I joke in my head. Math isn't my best subject, bι numbers aren't hard. Not in this kind of way.

"Why me?" I sigh, not sure if it's out of nervousness c anticipation, but it comes out soft. Ross smirks at me, standir just to sit next to me. What's with these guys and smirking? makes them hotter to me. Most chicks would feel repelled b it, but these guys are making me feel something I've never fe for an Arcadia student. *Lust.*

"You're the perfect choice," Bridger sounds out froι my other side, making my heart race. His voice is like melte chocolate when I make homemade hot cocoa. It's sweet aη rough, almost like it's barely used. And I like that, knowing h doesn't talk often, but was willing to just now.

"He's right," Ten agrees. "Perfect."

My face feels too hot, and as Ross brushes his thig against my bare one, I'm feeling like I'll have a heat stroke if don't get some space or air. "Oh."

"What do you say, Diamond Girl?" Lennox requests, his eyebrow raised.

"Yes," I whisper.

"Good, then let's get started."

"S-Started?" I question with a stutter. I twine my fingers, the sweatiness making me internally cringe. It's really fucking hot in here.

"Yes, we play a game with all newcomers."

"How come Yang and Cass aren't here?" I ask, wondering why the other two members aren't here. Not that I told Yang, they said I couldn't.

"They're not part of new initiations," Lennox easily explains. "They'll know tomorrow."

I nod, understanding.

"Truth or dare?" Ten asks suddenly. I stare at him, wanting to pick dare because only wimps do *truths*, but I don't know their angle and truths can be just as cruel.

"Truth."

Everyone chuckles. "She's smart. See, perfect choice," Ross muses from next to me, his hand brushing my knee. I gulp, feeling tingles lick all over my body like little spiders. Fuck. Fuck. Fuck.

"Is it true you're a virgin?" Lux prods.

I balk, my mouth opening at his easy question. Easy for him, at least. To me, it's like hanging a banner on my neck saying *in desperate need of cherry picking*. He sees my unease and saunters over, crouching in front of me.

"Come on, Colton. Tell me your secret," he hums, making

the blood thrum in my veins, present and quick.

"Y-Yes," I admit, hiding my face and closing my eyes. H tilts my chin, his hand sure and strong.

"Look at me, pretty girl." I swoon at that name, feeling s many emotions all at once. The couch next to me moves an then there are hands on my arms. My eyes open on their ow accord, unable to keep looking away while being in a lion den.

Both Ross and Ten are kneeling at my feet. "It's incredib. sexy," Ten nearly hisses as I lean forward. It's like my boc doesn't want to stay away from them, but my mind tries t struggle over Cassidy's warning.

"Very," Ross confirms, brushing my thigh.

Between their heads, I see Bridger gazing in a heate interest that makes a small whimper leave my mouth. Lennox lustful gaze drills through me like a hot poker, and sweat line my spine.

"Your turn, Colty," Ross says, then saunters to the cha next to Bridger.

Ten waits another few breaths before dropping m chin and heading over to Lennox. They've left me all hot, an bothered in a lonely chair and I don't know why.

"Bridger," I whisper, almost uncertain of why he's m first choice. Maybe it's his voice I want to hear, or the stiffnes in his posture that doesn't reflect the absolute tumultuou flames in his eyes.

"Truth," he grunts.

It takes me by surprise, but the others just smile, knowin

something I don't.

"Why me?" I ask.

His eyes widen a fraction before he adjusts himself in his chair. He wasn't expecting this, but unlike the others, I think he'll be the most truthful.

"Because I want you," he finally lets out. It's rough, like it took everything in him to admit. "We all do."

We all do. Want me why? Why can't they stop being cryptic?

"Ten," Bridger deflects, no longer looking at me.

"Dare."

In that word, I feel *promise*. Whether proprietary or not, it's there.

"I dare you to undress to your boxers."

Ten smirks, confidence oozing off him in heaps. My entire body heats as he grips his shirt and takes it off. His shoes are next, and finally, he undoes his pants in a slow deliberate fashion, his molten gaze not leaving mine for a second. As his pants make their way down his legs, his erection pops up like a whip, making itself known. I grip my chest, unable to stop the hammering. I'm a virgin, not a saint. I know what a big dick looks like.

He sits back, widening his legs, giving off what Yang calls *big dick energy*. Now, I know what she meant because he's bleeding that energy, and from the tent he's sporting, it's not an inaccurate vibe.

"Colton," Ten vibrates, hands gripped on his thigh.

"Me, again?" It makes me nervous, and I know they're

not about to let me pick truth again.

"And don't you dare chicken out," Ross teases, amusement gleaming in his expression.

Lennox's cool appearance has me squirming. It's like he waiting for my move.

"Dare." The single word comes out a prayer, a hushe one in the wind, not expecting response.

Ten's face heats as he leans forward, placing his elbow on his thighs, a calculating expression present. "I dare you kiss every one of us."

Bridger adjusts in his chair, his face showing a little desir that he masks just as quickly. Why does he hide? Why does intrigue me so much that he does? It's like unwrapping a gi you never asked for, slowly un-taping each edge in patienc and care, knowing the result will be worth the time taken.

A jolt of lust spikes in me. I grab my hair, putting it a one way so my neck can breathe a little from the hotnes overwhelming me. Standing with confidence that's half-fals I go directly to Bridger.

Something about him makes me want to give hir my first taste. I think he needs this as much as I do, but fc completely different reasons.

He notices me picking him, and it's like he licked nine-volt battery, shocked and uncertain. Instead of leanin forward and kissing him with a peck, the stares of the othe guys has me sitting in his lap.

He's dressed to the nines, almost too much for this lat hour, like he wears a suit to bed. These guys don't wear th normal school attire. They're always wearing Gucci and Armani. Ten wore Dior today, so I know they're not ones to hide their wealth or privilege. It should bother me, but it doesn't. I almost wonder if it's because they're Gov. Maybe they get a free pass for more than I've heard.

When I'm fully settled on top of his slacks, I feel rock hardness beneath me. He's not as unaffected as he pretends. He groans while I'm scooting up, making sure there's not much space between us. Next to him, Ross is breathing heavily. It's the only noise I can hear besides Bridger's shallow breaths and my heart rate.

Once his eyes connect with my own, it dawns on me that they're black. Colorless. Depthless. A void. They're beautiful. Even if others see emptiness, I see an entire universe.

"You going to kiss me?" he grits, his jaw ticking from the action. Is that anger? Desperation? While I lean forward, my pussy drags across his length, and his jaw locks even tighter, like he's biting on diamonds.

Our breaths intermingle as the distance between us disappears and then he's pushing toward me, taking my mouth with his. It's so overwhelming and spicy, like he ate cinnamon gum or a toothpick. My belly burns with unbridled warmth, making my core ache with need.

His palms trail up my body and grip the back of my throat with care, but with enough strength to tell me who's in control. My hips rock into him, craving friction. A hiss escapes him, and groans ease out nearby, reminding me that I'm not alone. That thought only turns me on more.

Bridger's tongue slides into my mouth, tasting, dancin
giving me so much pleasure with simple flicks. Not even a fe
strokes more and he's pulling back, his chest heaving. He fe
it, too, the passion and need.

"That was so fucking hot," Ross lets out.

Bridger's forehead has a little sweat lining it, remindir
me how hot it's been in here since I walked in.

"My turn."

I don't get to stand up before Ross is hauling me onto h
lap. Unlike Bridger, he's not as controlled. His eyes are nea
desperate. This time, I don't even get to lean in. He grips m
face and slams it on him. It's sloppy and full of promise, an
we're both undulating our hips. A moan slips from my mout
before he's letting me go. In his eyes, there's a promise, and I lik
knowing he's not disgusted that I've already kissed someone els

Rising off from him, I stand, staring at Ten. He look
high. His eyes are half-mast and glassy, like he's spent ju
from watching me touch and taste two other guys. He drag
his lower lip through his teeth, and I clench my thighs befoi
making my way to him.

He gets up from his seat and meets me halfway. Grippin
my face like a lover would, he's soft, gentle, with absolut
endearing care. His tongue strokes me like a secret, whisperin
it on my lips. I allow it and breathe in a taste that shouldn
be on a seventeen-year-old's breath, something that has m
groaning. Beer, the stronger the better, is something I crav
and he tastes of it. Not the cheap Lite stuff, but somethin
more edgy and flavorful.

HERE LIVES A CORPSE

He licks inside my mouth, tracing each groove, and as messy as it sounds, it's not. It's passionate and consuming.

He's pulled away from me in the next beat, and Lennox almost glowers at us. Lust—pure, satanical, deadly almost—licks every hard and sharp feature. And his eyes, the ones I couldn't see earlier, they gleam. They're a soft hazel. Now, they're a light green, but I know they'll change with the sun and his moods. It's bound to.

"Come to me."

The demand isn't harsh, but it makes it no less challenging, so I do. I seek out his lips, brushing so softly. He doesn't reciprocate, but I can feel his unabated yearning as he shakes a little. It takes no longer than a few seconds before he's lifting me, forcing my legs around his hips.

He leads us to the love seat I originally sat on and hovers over me. Lennox doesn't rush. He takes his time, memorizing my mouth, savoring it, taking each guy's taste and mine for the keeping.

How they're able to all kiss me and not give me disappointment or a flicker of shame is an amazing feat on its own. Beautiful. Something to remember.

As he rocks into me, my body heats more and more, and with a few last thrusts, his clothed dick brings me to the hottest orgasm I've ever had, the first I've ever had from someone other than myself.

"Fuck!" I cry out, and they're all watching me lose myself.

Barely getting off my high, I hear a booming, "What the fuck?"

I know that voice, one I've heard since we were babie
My earliest memory is that voice saying my name and n
loving the comfort it brings.

When Lennox lifts off me, my brother's ice gaze prickl
with deadly intent. Dread overwhelms me as four guys face o
with my best friend.

I'm totally fucked.

CHAPTER TWENTY-THREE
PRESENT

Guess you'll die then.

A hand clamps down over my mouth before much noise escapes me. Not that it would matter. The buildings are all too far apart, and there's no one around to hear me. It only occurs to me now that the many students who have disappeared over the years could easily have been dead and buried out here. It wouldn't be a reach. This is Arcadia we're talking about.

Cassidy warned me. Even if he never brought it up again, his intent had been there.

"Can't have you screaming, now, can we?" Jordan whispers near my throat as he squeezes my mouth deftly, cutting my complaints off before they truly start.

I can't respond, and he doesn't seem to need me too. He's just like them—callous, greedy, and self-absorbed.

He leads me toward the cabin, along with all the others,

and I struggle every step of the way. We're getting farther ar
farther away from the Crystallites party. Where is Mel? Is sl
okay? That triggers another thrashing fit, and I'm not goin
to stop until they let me go. Out of every one of them, Bridge
is the last I would suspect to be a total psychopath, but mayt
that's what he would want, for me not to notice how crazy l
is deep down.

Eventually, they all must get frustrated because the fou
of them are carrying me as I try to wiggle free. It's not helpin
There's no give in their grip. It makes me wonder if Bridge
would be a part of their kidnapping, or if he would stick u
for me like he used to.

He's not the same. Get over it.

Do they not understand I don't want this? That
would rather die than fuck random people? No one reall
knows who the Emeralds are, right? It's an unspoken rule c
something because Jordan is the first I've actually met, othe
than apparently those guys from that night. Not like that wa
information I had been aware of. Sneaking in isn't what I'
call *in the know.*

Were they initiating members? Why do they all watch
Is it a lust kind of thing or more of a show-no-mercy kind c
bullshit persona? Maybe it's both, and they're all a bunch c
entitled rich fucks.

Not that any of us are any better. Since Cass died, it's no
who I am anymore, but once upon a time, you could fit me i
that box easily.

"The more you struggle, the harder I get, Corpse," Lu

grunts, holding onto my waist. None of them are hurting me, but instead, holding me hostage so I don't hurt them or myself.

If he says that to force me to stop, he's failed. It's not my fault he's sick and twisted. My fight won't falter even if it entices his perverted mind.

Attempting to smack him, I pull my arms from Ten, hating that he's a part of this, that he would do this to me, that he's exactly who I always figured he would turn out to be. What we shared, like everything involving these guys, was *fraudulent*. Not real.

I created this perfect story in my head, one where we would all be happy and together. What a load of shit. If there was any doubt that I was a teenager, this definitely proved that sentiment.

When I realize they're still holding my mouth, I gnash at Jordan's palm, finally getting my hands free to hit whoever is nearest. My foot connects with someone, and my hands collide with Ross. There are several *what the fuck*s and *Jesus, Corpse* grunted.

"Fuck! Calm down!" Ross shouts.

My heart aches with his betrayal. I hate them all. Tears prick my eyes, not from fear or sadness, but from pure electric abhorrence. At one point, I thought I liked them all. Only took them five months to change my mind.

I lost my brother in the process of realization, and that's what hurts the most.

"Stop kicking," Ten hisses.

It's annoying that they aren't inflicting pain while still

holding me against my will. It's like they want my complianc
but won't hurt me in the process. I can't tell if that's a
advantage or downfall. Either way, when my right foot kicl
Lux, I use it to my advantage. They finally let go, and I fa
straight on my ass, causing my skirt to rise entirely. Four se
of eyes connect with my bare thighs as I hit the moist gra
beneath me.

Before they can catch me again, I do what I do best.

Scream.

I scream so loudly someone yells, "Is someone o
there?" Scrambling to get up, Jordan levels me with a gla
that promises pain and I settle back on the ground. With m
luck, his glare is more sinister. Death, perhaps?

Another voice, a girl, calls out, "Are you okay?"

If only I had a rape whistle. While they probably won
stoop to that level of antagonizing, it would be so fuckin
useful right now.

The guys are zeroing in on my disadvantage. I get read
to screech, but Ross hastily jumps on me, caging me in. H
lips, rough and persistent, land on my open mouth, makin
this the most awkward, unwanted kiss of my life.

These guys take the cake for stealing kisses from me.

His tongue teases the roof of my mouth, and then I'
biting him. The coppery tinge of blood slicks our mouth
and he's frantically pushing off of me. His mouth has red an
black all over.

Maybe he should think twice before forcing himself on m
and while I'm wearing *Vampire Kiss* black lipstick, no less. I smil

at his unpleasant grimace, glad I caused him some pain. It's only fair. He and his fuckboy friends have done tenfold to me.

Seeing the smudges of my lipstick all over him makes me wonder what my face must look like. A black and green mess? Should have added that setting spray when finishing. Luckily, I never cried. That would cause one hell of a gothic mess. It's never pretty when my emotions get the better of me, or when I shower without removing my makeup first.

"Going to scream again?" Jordan asks, crouching down on my level. His mouth tilts in an amused smirk, part barbarian and *all* insolence. That smirk transforms his face from Adonis to pure demonic.

His eyes lower to my exposed ass before roaming back haphazardly and connecting with my eyes. My skirt is still brushed up from the fall, giving them a view to enjoy. Heat flames my skin, too many needle pinpricks for my taste, but it's too late to play shy and hide my bare skin. They've all already seen enough, some even everything.

"Fuck you," I spit, venom leaking from my tongue. It gives me enough confidence to rise, but of course he wouldn't have that. He places an indurate hand on my knee. Though gentle in its force, it's enough to stop me from getting up.

"You look like you sucked a goblin's dick, Dare," Lux mocks, pointing at the black smears on Ross' mouth and making a ghost blowjob gesture.

It distracts me from Jordan's invasive personality, the one that bleeds erudition and refinement. It's as condescending as it is attractive, heady and repulsive wrapped in a barbed wire choker.

A smile tugs free at the obvious discomfort Ross feel Lux always has the best and worst comebacks. No one ca quite challenge him like me in the clap-back department.

"Eat a dick, Lux," Ross bites back, wiping his mout repeatedly.

"You already did it for me. Why make me outshine yo in *another* area?"

"Jesus fuck, shut up, both of you," Ten chastises.

Jordan still watches me, and it makes any amusement d in result of his nearly demonic-eyed inscrutability. He sees an or something because he takes it upon himself to lean in close his other hand digging into the flesh of my opposite knee.

It's more invasive than his stare, like he sees everythin yet I haven't said a single word. In this position, he holds all tl power while I'm in the most unfavorable position. Not tha being surrounded by four assholes would ever be considere an advantage.

My fingers trail the ground, barely, hesitant to giv them notice, searching for a rock or anything that could b beneficial. As they only connect with the wet softened san disappointment unleashes inside me.

"You can act like you hate us all you want, sweethear but we all know you're into it, into all of us," Jordan explain

He's so damn sure of himself. His posture says it all. S does the know-all way he delivered that statement.

Rolling my eyes, I attempt to stand again. My ass is col and it's not exactly dry. Why no one searched for the sourc of the screams is beyond me. They are above daft to just wal away and think it was nothing. It hasn't even been a year since my brother's body was found fifty feet south of where we are right now. What if history is repeating itself at this very moment? They wouldn't know based off their ignorance to my desperation.

"I'm not going in that cabin with you."

My words break their heated banter, and Jordan smirks churlishly. It's the kind of lilt that makes girls do stupid shit but scares me. It's one that holds knowledge and reprise. Both aren't welcome.

"Sucks we're not taking no for an answer. What's the worst that can happen, Greenie?" he taunts, lifting his chin.

That ego needs an entire continent to hold it. He could probably afford one, too.

"Death," Lux cracks, breaking the tension, laughing and making goosebumps rise on my arms.

"What the prick said," I spit, putting up a false bravado from my lack of options.

Lux looks at me at the insult, and his jaw ticks. I'm the only person I know who doesn't take his shit without serving him a new dish in return. He gets under my skin, but not as much as I wreak havoc under his in retaliation.

Not sure who hates who more, *but it's probably me.*

"You only die if you don't comply," Jordan deadpans.

There's not a trace of humor, but if he has any semblance of cynical humor as the rest of these asses, it's meant to be funny. Staring at him as if he's the dumbest person on the planet, I wait out his retaliation-filled words.

"Don't say you won't. There's already a dead Hudso
Don't need the second and only child left to die too."

I launch at him for that, slapping at nothing because Ro
and Ten are holding me back. How dare he? How fucking da
he say shit about my brother when he can't defend himsel
And something so callous? That's low.

Sticks and stones will break my bones, but words w
murder me ever after.

"Don't you dare utter his name! You sick sonofabitch,'
spit, anger consuming my flight capabilities.

Jordan lets out a derisive laugh. It's almost wet, covere
in blood and stained, making my skin crawl. "Can't hand
facts, Colty?"

Pushing forward again, he smiles, and it's so diabolic
that I wish he would die. That's not something I ever wish o
anyone, but this piece of shit deserves my hatred.

"Dude, back off," Ten chides. I turn to his face and see h
disgust. "I didn't agree to this."

Jordan stalks to Ten, gripping his chin tightly. It
domineering in a way I didn't realize existed between thes
guys. It's an odd sight, but it strangely makes so much sense.

"Don't be such a pussy, Tennison. You know what yo
got into when you joined."

Joined?

No.

He wouldn't.

"What is he talking about?" I barely whisper, feeling m
gut seize with every accusation.

"Didn't they tell you, *Colton*?" Jordan snides. "Gov is Emeralds. Emeralds is Gov."

The words repeat and repeat and repeat, but they don't stick. They can't. I wasn't an Emerald. I didn't do the shit I heard them do. Yang didn't... No. This is... No. Plus Lux and Jordan can't be the President. That's not how anything works.

What the hell does this even mean?

"I can see those wheels turning," he mocks, his teeth showing as he half-scowls, half-smirks. It's unnerving, the way he's two sides of a coin at the same time. "Yang and you weren't worthy of the title yet. Yang, because of her gender. Cassidy, though..."

My skin crawls. What had Cass gotten himself into? It makes sense, though, why he told me no. Why there were bags under his eyes. Why he never came home on the weekends.

"D-Did—" I don't know how to ask. How does one ask the guys you planned on being with in some aspect if they all fucked and my brother...?

Bile rises, and I'm shoving Ten and Ross away as I heave, wanting to puke everywhere.

My heart catapults. My mind races, and my skin feels itchy and unbearable. I would rather be anywhere but here right now.

No one rushes me as my body heaves continuously. There's nothing left to purge. I haven't been eating, but my stomach doesn't seem to get the memo.

"Did we fuck him? That's what you've got to be wondering underneath those toxic locks of yours," Jordan prods somewhere from behind me.

His voice is closer than anticipated. When I turn to him, he's right here, inches away. Gross. The way his eyes hone on me remind me of a snake's.

"Ask, Corpse. Ask us."

CHAPTER TWENTY-FOUR

"Well?" Jordan prods, raising an eyebrow at me. The scathing glare that I send him doesn't stop him from pushing closer until his palms hold my shoulders. "Ask."

How can such a simple question make me quiver and shake with both fear and intrigue? As much as I don't want to know if my brother fucked each of these guys I'm attracted to, knowing anything more about him drives me.

"Did you fuck my brother?" My question is quiet, but in the silent woods of Arcadia, it's as deafening as a bomb that detonates between us all as they stare at me.

"Would that make you jealous?" Ross questions, his black and bloodied mouth curling into a cynical smirk. He pushes his way between Ten and Lux, making sure he's in my line of sight.

"She's not answering because the answer is yes. Isn't that right, Corpse?" Lux prods, folding his arms across his chest.

"Why do you care?" I ask, wanting the answer but not at the cost of their questions.

"Maybe it makes my dick hard, thinking you want it inside only you," Lux taunts, pushing Jordan off me so he can invade my space.

It's always him, isn't it? The one who sets me off, pushes me off my axis in hopes my balance entirely fails me. That's him, the meanest one, the one who took so much and offered so little in return.

His hands replace the ones Jordan put on me. The difference between the two is obvious. Lux's palms are like big veiny mitts, large and apparent, gripping me tighter and with more familiarity and aggression. He wants me to falter to fall back, and show fear.

I'm not scared of him.

No matter how much fear swims through me from not knowing what they did to help this town cover up Cassidy's murder, I'm still not scared for those reasons.

What terrifies me is how my heart beats faster, in tandem with my heavy breathing, indicating how his close proximity turns me on more than it should.

Having them all circling me like I'm prey makes me innately aware of what power they have over me. They shouldn't. They're worse than the plastic polluting the ocean yet they'll kill me all the same.

"Pretty sure everything makes your dick hard, Lux." feel nothing behind the bitter words leaving my lips, but he glares anyway.

Instead of retorting, having our wordy battles like usual, he hauls me to him, taking my mouth with his.

When will they learn? Do they not realize they steal kisses like the fucking boogeyman steals sleep from every child?

His mouth crushes mine, and I hate how perfect his lips feel against mine. Out of every Arcadia boy who's taken my mouth, his is righteous, burning, almost scorching in its wake.

I've waited for this moment, the time where he would take and take and take, reminding me how little power I have over my emotions when he's involved. Fuck. His mouth, the way he captures me with every pull and brush. His tongue teases, seeking permission, and it's in this moment, where I realize how well he kisses. I shouldn't want more, but do.

As I let him in, we both let out a little groan at the contact of our tongues. It's greedy and irreverent. It's a hostage takeover that turns deadly, and as his hands rise to my jaw, gripping me possessively, I lose all sense of right and wrong. I lose me, the girl who has fought tooth and nail to escape their thrall.

His hands leave my face and trail to my ass, hoisting me up, forcing my legs to wrap around his waist. If I was unsure of how he felt for me at any point, his rumbling noises and hard dick leave me without a doubt. He's as into me as I am him.

Whistles echo from around us as he grinds into me, breaking me from this stupor. Fuck. What have I fallen into? Why did I like it?

My stomach clenches from the repercussions of our actions. He won't care. He'll probably even brush it off, but I can't deny the sensations thrumming through me. It's always a game with them, but it's never been one for me.

He leaves a final bruising kiss on my lips, making my thigh ache with how much I clench them. Then, he lets me down, b when we're fully untangled, I see it in his eyes. *Change*. It's li he realized that made a difference for him, too.

"Now that you've got your rocks off, can we move along Jordan drawls, annoyance lacing each word. If you didn't p attention, it would be less apparent, but his eyes are dark. H almost jealous. Maybe even a little frustrated.

Talking shop doesn't appeal to me. Knowing if th fucked my brother won't either. Even if it led to answer knowing he touched them, it would ruin me.

"Inside," Ross suggests.

My eyes meet his before landing on a clenched-fist Te His jaw is taut, his cheeks almost hollow with how his ang seeps in waves flowing straight into me.

"Where's Mel?" I deflect, needing to at least know she okay. It's not like they're saints. Maybe she's their plan physically hurt me for real this time. They seem the type destroy and never ask questions after.

Ten turns and brushes past Ross to head inside the cabi Jordan rolls his eyes, giving me a once-over before turning wait for us to follow. Are they just going to ignore me?

"Jealous, Corpse?" Lux breaks the silence before grabbir my head and leading me to the one place that haunts me i more ways than one.

I'll never admit it to any of them, but yes, I am jealou Bridger and I had something special. Call it a connection, lus or even kindness when little was offered. Either way, him being with Mel unsettles me.

I can lie and claim it has everything to do with her well-being, but my heart would beat against its cage, calling me out for the fraud I am.

"Why does it matter?" It comes out smaller than it should, meek and fragile, like my stupid beating appendage. They've made me raw tonight. Every fucking one of them has messed with me in some shape or form. It's demoralizing and painful. Their mix of aggression and kindness gives me more whiplash than the Adamson's drama network. What makes it worse is they realize their power, and they use it.

He halts me from following the others. "Just admit it, Colt. You hate the idea of sharing us with anyone other than yourself."

I go to interrupt his quick judgement, but he grips my chin, holding it with his thumb and index finger, digging, grasping at my need to submit.

"Don't try and lie here. The only people you'd share us with is each other."

With those damning words, I swallow. It's true. I don't know why, but it is.

"Am I wrong?" he pushes, knowing I'm not answering him for a good reason.

"No."

I don't add or explain. I can't. Something about them being together doesn't turn me off or make me jealous, which makes zero sense. Them sharing me and me sharing them with one another should freak me out, disgust me even, but makes my thighs clench and my body heat up.

He tilts my head ever so gently, his eyes boring into min like he sees me. Not the Colt I've become, but the carefree o who had two loving parents, an older brother who loved he and four guys vying for her attention. The Colt who did know true heartbreak or pain. The soft Colton who want love and would experience the loss before the true gain.

"Kiss me, Corpse" he whispers, and I swear my hea momentarily stops at the huskiness in his voice. He's askin not pushing or taking, simply requesting with the intent need and not to quiet me or scare me.

Just for me.

Wanting me.

"Kiss me first," I reply breathily, waiting, anticipatin grasping for *something*.

"When a corpse and a man without a heart kiss, do he die?" He grips my jaw, and intoxicating warmth invad my skin. We're separated simply by a battle of wills, hi unwilling to plunge and me unable to succumb to him on more. "Or does she beat the odds and come back to life?"

"*Lennox*," I barely whisper before his mouth is on me agai

It's different this time. Softer. Kinder. Intentional. It not harsh and cruel, and the offset of our connection mak me ache in ways I shouldn't. It builds and builds, and all I ca do is relish the sensations before he undoubtedly returns the Lux who's always callous.

When he pulls away this time, his face only furth

confuses me. His eyes are closed, and his face is scrunched. Not in displeasure, no, more of disconcerting. It's as if he's as shocked and wondrous as I am about our connection.

It has never made sense.

When his hazel eyes connect with mine, I watch as they glimmer with confusion and lust, twining together like a puzzle, winding and winding as they attempt to unveil all the answers.

"You two done giving moony eyes?" Ten barks from the cabin's doors.

I stare at his stiff posture and know he's pissed. He has no right to be. His choices tore us apart, our relationship demolished by his actions, not mine.

"Be a good little bottom, Ten, and shut the fuck up," Lux bites out.

With those scathing words, I'm barely able to keep my mouth and expression closed. There's a story there, with all of them, and if it's the last thing I do in my lifetime, I'll learn every secret these guys hide.

CHAPTER TWENTY-FIVE

"I'd wondered if you two fucked with how long you we[re] alone, but even Lux over here isn't a two-pump chump li[ke] Ten," Jordan jests as soon as we're piled in the living room[.] kissed them all in a year ago.

"Fuck off, Walker," Lux bites, sidestepping me to s[it] across the big table.

The room is still as it was. A massive coffee table res[ts] in the center, engraved with the crest of Arcadia. It's a dark[er] wood, almost a black-brown. It fits their entire room [of] tastelessness.

The three couches make a large U, and the two recline[rs] across the table close the odd circle. The interior of the pla[ce] hasn't changed. The legacies are lining the wall, awards, ar[e] bullshit plaques that make zero sense also cover the gaud[y] damask wallpaper.

We could be on the set of a Tim Burton film, and I wouldn't be able to tell the difference. Even when all lit up, his place isn't any less chilling than when dimly lit.

As we all sit, I'm once again left alone in the smallest love seat couch. This room, the feelings surrounding it, and the goddamn placement of people—sans Bridger—makes me uneasy. It's like my initiation. The kisses. The lies. The thievery.

"Why are we here?" I break the bubble of silence. Unable to sit still, I move my leg to cross over the other then back again. I'm nervous.

Ross must've showered. He's now fresh-faced. The only things showing it wasn't a dream is his busted and swollen lips. They taunt me with their coloring, showing I've marked him, given him a little hostility in return. His lips tilt at me. He knows I'm analyzing them.

"We're here because you want answers, and the Emeralds can't have you searching anymore. You're endangering us all." Jordan speaks as if he's a teacher explaining the most mundane of situations and not threatening me without using the words.

"You never answered my first questions. What makes me believe you'll answer any?" The words come out discordant, uncharacteristically rude, even for me.

"Guess you've got to put on your big girl panties and hope for the best," he deadpans.

"Fuck this," I declare, standing and attempting to escape.

Before I get too far, Ross has a hand on my arm, and Ten is next to him, watching me, glaring, and pouting. Because that's what it is. He's pissed I've kissed several people. It's obvious.

"Not so fast, Greenie," Ten hisses. "Sit. Listen. Don't fucking argue."

Hearing such reproach from him isn't something I'm used to. I hate it. It's not like him. As asshole-y as he acts around *them*, there's a soft guy with a heart twice the size of mine. It's what always drew me to him in the first place.

He and Ross lead me back to the couch, reminding me of that night, making me wish I could erase it from my memories. That's where this all got screwed up, where our paths intertwined, and I felt destined to crave all of them.

"What do you know about Emeralds?" Jordan asks.

Everyone stays silent. Lux doesn't even look at me. His head is tipped back, avoiding this entire conversation. Ross sits on my right as Ten sits on my left, and Jordan opposite of us.

I think back to my first year here. Nothing clings about Emeralds, other than they're a ghost story, a myth. No one really knows who they are. Hell, I didn't even know these guys were involved. How stupid must I look?

How were you supposed to know?

"Absolutely nothing."

Jordan nods, rubbing his chin and standing. He makes his way out of the room, and I hear him rifling around for something before he's back. In his hands is a leather-bound scrapbook. It's old but in pristine condition. It looks more like a photo book than a scrapbook.

"Here," he sounds out, offering it to me, but I stare at

like he's nuts. When I don't reach out, he comes closer and places it in my lap. "Look."

The book weighs a ton. It takes a few seconds to grasp that they *really* want me to read whatever this is. On the front it's inscribed with Latin. *Limpieza de Sangre.*

"Purifying the Blood," Lux states numbly, void of any emotion.

There are snapdragons entwined with snakes, serpents and their fruitful blooms, almost like a crest or emblem. It looks familiar, but I can't seem to place where I've seen it before.

"What does that entail?" I ask.

"We keep the bloodlines pure. The founding families of Arcadia are the only members," he mildly explains. "Males of the bloodlines, that is."

"This is stupid," I mutter aloud. What are they, barbarians? Old aristocratic douchebags who have to have a lineage line back to the seventeenth century?

"It may sound pretentious, but it's just how it is around here," Lux says.

"So, Emeralds are like a fucking frat house?"

"No," Jordan practically spits. "We're a sodality of the rich and powerful. We have a purpose."

"And what's that? To gang bang?" I mock, not understanding what the fuck they can possibly do here that merits an old book detailing all of the members, their bloodlines, and purposes throughout the group.

"Don't be so goddamn naïve, Colt. It's unattractive," Jordan says disdainfully, giving me a death glare.

Okay, Mr. Seriously-fucking-mad.

"Then tell me what the fuck you're talking about—" start to yell, hating that he called me naïve.

The door opens, interrupting me, and in pops Bridg and Mel. My heart hurts. On his face is red lipstick, and hers smeared. I'm not sure why, but betrayal from both ends rat through me. It's like a fucking Ping-Pong of disappointme as my eyes roam their disheveled appearances. She would fuck him. He wouldn't fuck her.

Right?

Maybe I am naïve like Jordan says.

Maybe they're really fucking with me, and all last ye was a game.

"Where were you two?" I nearly accuse Mel, hating t trepidation in my tone.

Immediately, I'm taken aback at Bridger. He's stari at me with a mask of indifference. He doesn't show a sing emotion on his face until she blushes, seemingly scandalize

The red on her cheeks nearly match the smears on h face, and my stomach clenches. A smirk, evil and debilitatin covers his face. He could have wiped that off, hid the fact th they did whatever the fuck they did, but his intentions to hu me are clear, and it only further worsens my anger. Why is doing this?

"We… uh… got lost," Mel murmurs.

"On his dick maybe," Lux jokes.

I'm not feeling the teasing. When she asked abo homecoming, I'm sure she never would have known Bridg was my last guy. The one who doesn't kiss. Doesn't offer his mouth for the taking. Yet, he did. Right now. With someone he doesn't care about.

Everyone stares at me glaring at the red on his face. Ten seems annoyed. Ross is amused. Lux is... fuck I don't know what he is, but Jordan—that fuckwad—is smiling with so much pride. It's like he conjured this shit up himself and is immensely satisfied.

I stand. "Well, I'm going to—"

"No, you're not," Jordan practically barks, and that makes Mel realize the situation she walked in on isn't a pleasant one.

"Colt, are you okay?" she questions, her voice hard like steel.

"Yeah, Corpse, everything good?" Lux mocks, using the most derisive tone I've ever heard. He's still smiling in a chilling way. It's evil, far passed the soft boy he pretends to be on the outside for everyone but the guys and me.

"I'm fine," I answer to them both, but when I see Mel stiffen, it's like she knows I'm lying.

"Good. Then let's sit." She practically hops over to me as if she's all but forgotten the weird stance of every guy surrounding us. She sits next to me and fixes her makeup in a way that says she's using this time for something good.

I try to smile at her carefree ease, but something is off. Not with her, no, but with what these guys want. Why bring Mel here unless she's a part of it? Or maybe she was getting antsy too.

After she adjusts her makeup, she squeezes my thigh.

"Why is there mud on you?" she questions.

"Because she's a whore that spreads her legs for everyone,"
Jordan quips, showing his cards. Wasn't he supposed to be on
the down-low?

She looks at me, then glares at him. "I don't recall you
ever being called a whore for fucking half the school, Jordan.
So maybe lay off." Ten's voice booms.

The room bursts out in a ruckus of laughter. All but me,
Bridger, and Jordan, that is.

Mel butts in. "Before you say it's different, it's not. Women
have needs, too. At least Colt here owns that part of herself."

The room silences, and I'm not sure if I should hug her,
marry her, or kidnap her and run far the fuck away from
Arcadia. No situation is looking good for either of us.

Jordan's thunderous gaze should scare me, but without
knowing his angle, it's hard to be afraid of a loveless soul.

He's just sad.

And broken.

That's what he is. There's no other excuse.

"We were just telling Colt we missed her in Student Gov
and want her back," he lies through a very fake smile. He's
charming. So much so, he even fooled me.

They're all full of shit, but I let them lead. Anything to
keep Mel safe and out of this weird-ass shit they brought me
into.

She nods. "Well, I'll let her answer herself, but we all
know she's going to tell you where to stick the stick you keep
close to your ass."

I laugh at her southern drawl. She knows me. It may be a new friendship, but she's shown nothing but love and care for me. It's something I absolutely admire.

"So why are we here?" Mel asks, her voice low and confused.

"They kidnapped me," I mutter, and they all glare at me, but her eyes lighten with acknowledgement.

"She's being dramatic. We went to go to the party, and she pre-gamed. We didn't want her to embarrass herself."

It's Jordan who talks, and until an hour ago, he was considered an ally.

"Well, good thing she's got me," Mel states. She reaches out her hand.

No one stops her, probably because she's not a part of this and they don't know if she will cause trouble. Or at least, that's the only reason I can see that they're letting her take my hand and walking me out the door.

"Thank you," I whisper quietly. She doesn't even know how bad it got.

That they admitted to being Emeralds.

That they have initiation.

That I witnessed it once.

That my brother was an Emerald.

I'm barely breathing with how much fear races through me. What did they want, and why are they fucking insane psychos? Why am I only partially scared?

All of this should make me run, but curiosity wants me to know more.

Did they kill Cass? Did he die because he didn't fu[c]
them? What is happening around me?

My heart hammers as she leads me out.

"To the party?" she offers.

Usually, I'd say no, but something says being in a roo[m]
full of people will be a helluva lot safer than at my dorm.

"Let's," I say, looping our arms.

When I turn to look at the door behind me, I see all fi[ve]
guys watching. Foreboding is like a snakeskin. No matt[er]
how many times it sheds, it'll still be a warning that dang[er]
is near.

We make it to the Crystal Tower and are allowed [in]
immediately.

"Going to tell me what the fuck was happening ba[ck]
there?" Mel asks.

I peer at her, wondering how much to say and n[ot]
knowing how much to trust her. We became friends real[ly]
fast, and who knows if she's a ploy or not. After Jordan end[ed]
up being a part of my daily nightmares, who's to say she's n[ot]
involved?

"They wanted to scare me. Jordan picked me up for th[e]
party, pretending to be a nice guy. Came to find out he's n[ot]
a good guy. He's been a part of their plan to ruin my life sin[ce]
Cass died."

Her eyes widen. "Does that mean that he's in on whatev[er]

they're plotting?

"Probably," I admit. "For some reason, they think I know something about Cass' death, and they're trying to scare me for that information."

"Shit. That's pretty fucked up."

"Entirely fucked up," I confirm. "They're involved somehow. How else would he be dead and they all tried distracting me that night?" I know I'm halfway talking out of my ass with assumptions and half-telling truths.

"When was this?" she asks, and it occurs to me I've been hiding a big part of this.

"Last year for spring break, the guys and I spent most of the vacation at the cabin. We were all… I don't know, dating almost?"

Her eyes open even wider. If she tries any harder, they'll pop out.

"Well, we were all at the house and then got invited to an Emerald party."

"Wait, wait, wait. What is an Emerald party?"

That's when I realize I'm not giving her the entire story. She doesn't even know the ghost stories, the ones that aren't a myth at all.

"In 1910, this school was founded by these families. Several of their names have been erased from history, so I don't even know the names of them all, except obviously my last name and the other guys' too."

"You're really starting to freak me out. What kind of place is this?"

243

"An elitist colony that houses only the rich."

She nods emphatically, and I wish I had all the time the world to explain this. Something tells me my time on th earth will be cut short just like my brother's.

Mel grabs my wrist and leads me toward an abandon room. "Okay, spill."

"My brother used to tell me these stories when we we younger, ones our grandpa told him about the rules ar expectations of the Hudson family. Cass started by telli me that this town was forged in 1920, a town built by peop with secrets and a lot of money and wealth. There were the founding families. When one was wiped out or they ma the mistake of divulging secrets, they were removed from th books of history. It was like they never existed."

Mel's body shivers, and if she wasn't wearing Bridge coat, I would think it was from the cold and not the fear.

"There are only five family names I know of—Hudso Dellamore, Clemonte, DeLeon, and McAllister."

Her eyes widen. "You and the boys."

I nod. "Except Jordan. I don't know where he fits into of this."

"Maybe his name isn't Winthrop," she says.

It could be. He could have lied.

"Being a founding family has a lot of weight, so mu so, that in the later 1950s, they created a group called th Emerald Vestige."

Her eyes light up in understanding.

"I thought Cass was making shit up, but after tonight

think he was learning all along. He told me only men could be involved, that they're meant to set order to the town and keep it functioning, but what kind of organization has teenagers doing all the dirty work?"

"Just look at my dad. He has the twins doing all his dirty work since he legally can't," Mel adds.

That has my stomach all achy. "Back there, where they dragged me into, apparently that's the Emeralds' cabin."

"Oh my god," she whisper-hisses.

"That's where I stayed almost all of spring break... What if somehow that's why I didn't see Cass until right before he died?"

"Did they say anything that made you believe they did it?"

"They said that Emeralds are Student Gov and that the Student Gov is a front for Emerald business."

"Does that mean that all along, you were a part of something bigger—something more sinister?"

"That, or what my brother said still holds true. Emeralds are only meant to be boys. Women aren't allowed."

"Well, let's just reverse decades of feminism," she mocks, and I laugh because she's right.

"Whatever they're up to, I need to know. Want to do something extra diabolical?" I ask, hoping she walks away. Something about putting Melissa in danger doesn't sit well with me, no matter how I look at it.

"Only if we can have some cool codenames."

"What are you?" I balk. "Five?"

"Come on, Colt! Imagine the fun we'd have being a spy-like."

"Or dead. We could be dead."

She nods and then makes that *oh shit, you're right* face.

"How close are you and Bridger?" Though I'm asking for one reason, the deeper meaning has everything to do with how they came to the cabin disheveled.

She blushes, her face pink and embarrassed. I want to be happy for her. For him, even... maybe. I don't know. Hormones and emotions are confusing, and while I want be happy for them, it hurts so damn much.

"Seems like a bit," I mutter. "Can you pry some secret out of him?"

She smiles, thinking about it. Probably how she could and I cringe. "I can try."

Bridger is a tough nut to crack, but seeing him soft with her has me believing maybe I'm wrong.

"I'll try on the others," I say. "Ten and Ross may be the easiest for me."

"What if we can't figure it out?" she asks, a good and terrifying question.

"Then we're better off buried six-feet deep next to my brother."

Her face pales, and I want to take the words back, but I can't.

"Let's go act like we didn't just have a freaky conversation. Maybe we'll even spot the guys."

"And make sure to loosen up," Mel suggests. "You look

like you're on a warpath."

"I am," I muse.

"But they can't know that. Just look normal."

"Have you seen me?"

She makes a show out of looking me over from head to toe. "Yeah, I have. So, go be you."

"Thanks for the advice, ma'am. I'll take it under advisement."

"Fuck off," she sasses, giggling as we strut arm in arm into the madness.

Music blares around us, and the walls flash with strobe lights and color projectors. The Crystallites don't ever settle for second best. They definitely make sure to use every penny they can to make this place a grand scheme, but *Last Friday Night* by Katy Perry rings out. I cringe. Why can't they have some I Prevail or Falling in Reverse? These teens are definitely a lost cause if this is their go-to.

Mel nods over to the bar, and I let her drag me there. Being rich has its perks, such as hiring a real DJ, a bartender, and probably a drug dispensary.

She tells him she wants three shots of Jack, and I flinch. The last time I had that, my brother died. Thinking of it makes me super uncomfortable now.

I ask for whatever is on tap. Cheap beer is disgusting, but at least the glasses are huge and make me appear to be drinking.

"Can you only fill it a little over halfway?"

The barista looks at me as if I'm insane but nods and

does it anyway. Mel shoots three shots of whiskey down an
then hauls me with my already halfway gone beer to the table

Setting down my drink, she pulls me closer.

"Let's dance?" she suggests while I scrunch my face
dismay. "Come on, it's not that hard!"

"When you have two left feet, it is!"

"Live a little."

Doesn't she mean die a little? Because that's what
happen. Dying.

I give in, and she pulls me to the dance floor. The son
changes to some Bruno Mars song I don't recall. Mel breal
out, dancing, acting as if I'm used to this kind of behavic
She's not the best, but she has fun and puts her all into it.

It's loosening me up, and I shake my hips, and we're ju
two teens having fun. After three songs, I'm dying. I'm still n
used to this much exercise. When I go to tell her I'll be bac
she's already waving me off.

When rotating, I come face-to-face with Ten.

"You ran away, Greenie."

"And you're a dick," I grunt.

He grabs my shoulders, making sure to seem gentle, b
the look in his eyes is anything but.

"Dance with me."

It's not a suggestion. He doesn't give me an out. He
expecting it, and I'm going to give in like I always do, especial
now that I have a goal in mind.

I let him turn me around, bringing our bodies flush. F
lifts my arms, wrapping them around his neck as he star

dancing with me, reminding me what it feels like when our clothes are gone. I ache, my pussy throbbing with the acknowledgment. Hell, my whole body throbs, but that's more to do with the exertion than the need cloying for attention.

"Remember the last time you had your arms around me like this?" he breathes into my throat.

My skin breaks out in goosebumps, chills making my nipples peak.

"Can't say I do," I lie.

How could I forget? It's the night my brother was taken from me.

"You grinded against me while Ross sandwiched you in. Then we nearly all fucked."

I hiss when he bites the shell of my ear. That night was both the best and worst of my life. They played me like a fiddle, and I fell for it. Then they band together, and my brother died while Ten fucked the innocence out of me.

"Can you remember how good it was when my cock sank inside your little virgin cunt?"

I turn to him, seeing heat in his eyes, but there's more. There's regret. Something I feel every day.

"I remember you walking away," I say, my voice a lot stronger than I feel.

"You're remembering it wrong then," he bites back. "You're the one who walked away."

"I did not!" I yell.

The music decides then is a good time to go quiet. Everyone is now looking at me and Ten. When I peer around,

249

the rest of the boys are watching in amusement. All but Bridger who's nowhere in sight.

Great.

Ten grabs me by the waist and maneuvers me toward the stairs, away from everyone. Once he pushes me against the wall, my body shakes with both fear and awareness of the stiffness pressed against me.

"When Cass died, you forgot our friendship, our pact. You left me," he parrots.

"Yet, who didn't try to find me? Who didn't come to his funeral?"

"That's not fair," he complains and shakes his head. "You left."

"And you could have chased me. Showed up when they buried him! You didn't. You picked *them*." The words are practically spit from my mouth like a used piece of gum.

"What would you have me do?" he challenges, cupping my jaw. "Pick you when you couldn't even decide that you only wanted me?"

That was low. Even for him.

I push him away from me. "Don't act like you didn't get the best of it all. You fucked other chicks and still tried getting in my pants. Guess when the going got tough and you finally fucked me, it wasn't enough for you."

His eyes darken, and he pushes me against the wall again. "I'll never get enough, Colt. Fucking others isn't fucking *you*. My cock aches for what we shared. I haven't felt pleasure like I did when I sunk inside you. You're in my fucking soul, bab girl, and, fuck, if that doesn't drive me nuts."

"I'm not changing what I said. You got to fuck me and have your pick of the desperate Arcadia mill. Don't come at me acting like I chose anyone because it was all of you."

He shakes his head. Ever since Ten was younger, he never liked sharing. When we started messing around and I wanted his Pop Rocks or a lick of his spumoni ice cream, it nearly hurt him to share. That didn't stop me from trying to be his friend and get what I could out of him.

"I want you to want only me," he demands.

"Isn't that a little unfair since you didn't only want me?"

"That's where you're wrong. I wanted you so badly I had to escape inside others to stop the urge from pushing myself. You're all I thought about, and they took the edge off. They meant nothing."

"Well, to me, they ruined everything."

He grips my throat, rubbing circles over my pulse point. "Jealousy is hot on you, Greenie. My dick thinks so, too."

"Fuck you and your stupid dick," I curse, wanting to slap him.

He brings his lips to mine. "Isn't that what you did? Fuck this stupid dick and enjoyed it? But it wasn't enough, was it? You wanted all of theirs, too. You wanted us all to fuck and love it."

I whimper. My body aches with the truth of it, and my legs clench with desire. My heart hammers with a mixture of hatred and absolute lust.

"That's why you didn't choose. Is it the thought of me

251

sinking in you while others do too, or are you a glutton ar want us to fuck each other as well?"

A moan escapes my mouth before I can stop it. A smi tilts at his lips, and then he's kissing me. It's an undertakir stealing everything, all while I'm suffocating with desire.

He slips his tongue inside, and then he's devouring ea moan that tries to escape. He's thrusting against me like l wants to be inside me, and that's all that I can think about, hi pushing inside me while I scream about how much I hate hin

He breaks us apart and lowers to his knees. "Spread yo fucking legs, Colt."

I peer down at him and widen my stance.

"Wider."

It's the cruelest command, and for some reason, that h me wetter. He's such a prick, but he's still that sweet boy wl gave me his snacks even when he didn't want to.

He lifts my skirt, and then his head disappears underneat His tongue swipes across my barely covered clit. "Still tastir like the devil's fruit, Kid."

"Shut up," I bark as he's grabbing my thighs and pressir into me.

My back bows against the wall, and he laps me up wit every breath, his tongue laving, his teeth nipping, his grip c my thighs tightening. I'm moaning and arching into him . he feasts on me.

"Fuck, Ten," I moan, and he's going faster, mor aggressive, and then he's biting my clit and its ring, and I' done for.

I thrust against his mouth two times before my mewls echo around us. He lets my thighs go and brings our mouths together. I can taste myself on him, and it's such a magical experience. He's not scared to eat me out and then kiss me.

As soon as he starts undoing his pants, someone rounds the corner. When Ross is standing there, a wave of lust fills me, but his face is full of contempt.

"Your etiquette is poor," he mocks Ten. "She likes to be fingered when eaten. Maybe in the future, hit her g-spot, and she'll actually scream. Don't worry. Next time, I'll show you how it's done."

Ten scowls at him.

Feeling like the moment is over, I lower my skirt, adjusting, then give Ten a brief kiss before walking past Ross and back to the party.

They're going to be the death of each other.

And maybe then, they'll tell me everything I need to know.

CHAPTER TWENTY-SIX

"Sounds like you were busy over there," Lux muses, interrupti
my escape to the main room where all the party-goers see
to be. He's leaning against the wall in the hallway—not qu
blocking everyone, yet making sure they know if they pa
him, it's purely because he allows it.

"Surprised you could hear me. You seem to igno
everything I say."

"Regardless," he snubs, waving a hand. "I'm sure you'
got loads of questions, Corpse. Become an Emerald, and we
tell you everything."

"Even about Cass?"

He narrows his eyes on me, his face going through
barrage of emotions: The pinch between his eyebrows seer
painful. When they soften and he settles on indifference,
already know my answer.

"Get bent, Lux."

"You keep saying that, and I'm going to take it as an invitation."

Letting out a large sigh, I attempt to sidestep him. His hand clamps onto my wrist, his face still impassive as fuck, making me worry about his intentions. For one second, I feel at ease because he's Lux and he's never hurt me. Then it passes, remembering how he and the rest decided to use sex and orgasms to distract me from the truth.

"Let me go," I growl, my voice harsher than I've ever heard. Lux isn't the end game. Ross and Ten are. They're the weakest links, the softer ones, the two who actually care about me. Lux is too much of a loose cannon. He'll ruin me. As dumb as I've been, I would let him, not realizing until far too late to find out what his intentions are.

Instead of him listening to me and letting me go, his hold tightens. Lux's eyes glimmer with something akin to deviousness, and he pulls me closer to him, until we're nearly flush.

"Why would I ever let you go, Corpse? Have you forgotten? You're mine."

"You keep saying that," Jordan butts in, coming from somewhere in the mix of people, boxing me against Lux, his front to my back, "but she's *ours*."

Lux scoffs. "You're new here, Walker. This one has been mine far before anyone else's. Isn't that right, Col?"

Col. That fucking nickname. Swallowing the dryness, I shiver. Lux may not have taken my virginity, but he took a lot more.

"N-No," I mumble, trying to argue my point but faili
miserably. Lux makes me flustered, ever since we met, and
continues to unravel me like a broken thread, fraying awa
strand by strand.

"You see, Walker, I took her first orgasm. Wrenched
from her pale little body while she screamed for more."

Jordan pushes into me further, his hard erection at r
back. What is it with these guys? Do they all share? Most gu
would have a pissing match to distinguish who can have wh
but these five... they seem to poke the beast inside each oth
but want to defile me as a whole.

"Is that so?" Jordan asks, his voice carrying a tone
intrigue.

My body rubs against Lux from Jordan's movement, ar
he lets out a low hiss.

"Yup, she bit me so hard I bled."

My face ignites at that, warming to the point of feveris
My body shakes a little with shame, and I look away. Lu
grips my chin, raising it so we're eye-to-eye. His eyes are ho
dissecting while undressing me at the same time.

"Hottest moment of my life. Left a scar, and seeing th
red on her lips when she was done? Pretty sure that was m
number one spank bank image for weeks."

He tells Jordan all of this while looking directly into m
eyes. There's so much intention in his gaze, and it withers
shiver out of me.

"She's wiggling like she wants a rematch, DeLeon."

"Bet she'd cream all over if you watched us too."

I close my eyes, and Lux bites my cheek, forcing me to yelp and push away.

"Whatcha say, Corpse? Ready for me to fuck some life into you?"

"Never," I grumble.

He smirks, his dimple coming through with the gesture, making him all the more undeniable. "Never is far too long, Colt. My cock thinks we should renegotiate."

"You should stop talking to your dick, Lux. Pretty sure it's unhealthy."

He full-on laughs, amusement lighting his features. "Fine. If I kiss you and you moan, you have to let me make you come." "If you kiss me and I don't, you have to walk away and end this bullshit."

"I feel like I'm losing this game," Jordan pipes in. "How about both of you moan, I not only watch, I touch?"

"Fuck off, Walker," Lux hisses, his voice wary. Is he worried? Does he not want Jordan involved?

"Shut up and kiss me," I growl, wanting to end the standoff they're having and get this over with.

Lux takes no time to grip my face, closing the distance between our mouths. Swallowing back a moan that already wants to seep from my lips, I struggle to keep my heart beating at a safe rate. While one of his hands continues to hold my jaw, his other falls off.

It isn't until I feel it under my skirt that I squirm. He cups my sex possessively, rocking into me. Can he feel how wet I am? It's not only from Ten being between my legs five

257

minutes ago. Being around all of these guys has me desperate for a taste.

When his fingers part my pussy, I lose my battle and moan. His teasing doesn't stop there, though. He rubs his finger up and down my slit, avoiding the one place that's begging for attention.

Right before we break apart, I feel Jordan reaching around me, and until I hear the groan from Lux, I don't realize what has just happened.

"Looks like you both lost," Jordan muses when our lips part. He chuckles when I scoff.

"He cheated."

Lux bites my bottom lip, sucking it inside his mouth. "There are no rules when fucking you is on the line, Corpse."

"Don't worry, princess. He lost, too. You're both mine."

"Shit," I breathe, realizing I'm about to have a threesome with two guys I definitely hate more than I like, all while I'm supposed to be worming information out of Ten and Ross. *Not that they're forthcoming when I'm not fucking around with them.*

How have I not seen them pass?

Are they still in the stairway?

What the hell are they doing?

Lux twists me into Jordan's arms, and then Jordan tugging me to a room I've never been inside of before. When the door opens, shock hits me square in the chest.

"W-Why does this look like it's Cassidy's room?" I choke on my words.

Cass had two rooms? He shared his one with me at th

tower, just a few floors higher. Before, it struck that me he never hooked up with anyone. *Thank God.* But maybe this room was his to do just that? It looks almost identical to the one he has at home. The walls are a medium gray, a tint too light for dark and a shade too dark for light. Posters of his favorite bands line the walls, along with a couple posters of his favorite celebrities.

And the bed.

It's black.

Lux stops in front of the bed, turning to me. His piercing hazel eyes drip with malice. Not geared toward me, no, but it permeates the air as if he's giving off the aura.

"Why the fuck are we here, Walker?" Lux demands.

The way Lux's shoulders are bunched, preparing for a fight without a contender, has me trying to wiggle out of Jordan's grasp, but he tightens his fingers. Cool air wisps around me, chilling me. I'm no longer turned on.

"Just the first room I came to," he explains, indifferent.

I can't read Jordan. He's good at hiding his tells, and in this moment, where his voice doesn't waver, I'm unsure where his head's at.

"I'm not doing this. Not here," Lux argues.

This confuses me. None of these guys seemed to care about Cass. Why would he? If this is even his room…

"Too bad, I'm not looking for a new room. Get on the bed, Lennox," Jordan commands.

Lux freezes, his body stiff, but something must exchange between the two of them because Lux sits at the edge of the

bed. Jordan guides me toward him, his hands still cupping m
shoulders.

By the time I'm between Lux's knees, I'm consumed wi
heat once more. Fear swims through me, but the need to s
where this goes is more present.

Jordan's fingers trail to my hair, taking it all from o
side to the other. His lips connect with the sensitive flesh
my collar bone.

"Look at me," Lux demands. My eyes immediately lat
onto his. "I've missed those glaciers, Colt."

My heart clenches at the words. I've missed them to
just not from my own face.

"Undress her, Lennox."

Jordan's words have Lux scowling and me hummi
with energy. Lux doesn't seem to be submissive. It shows wi
his scowl and hatred, how it seeps from his every breath.

When I go to assist him because he's angry, Jordan sto
my pursuit. "No."

"Let me," I growl, knowing what Lux needs. Jordan m
think he knows, but he doesn't.

He lets me go, and I push Lux on the bed, straddling hi
His eyes darken. Leaning to his ear, I take a bite, my tee
grazing him harshly. He growls into the crook of my neck.

"Take."

It's one word, but it's enough for Lux to push through. H
grips my throat, forcing us both in a sitting position. He nee
control. Having it taken from him isn't a turn on. We've on
fucked around on a few occasions, but during those times, I

was the dominant one.

Submitting is natural for me, hot even. Wanting him to devour me wholly is something we're both used to. Jordan may not know this about Lux, but he'll understand soon.

"Stand," Lux hisses. When I pout, his grip on my neck tightens. "Always so fucking bratty." His bites my lip, his teeth tracking my piercings, forcing us both to stand. He lets me go, turning me around. "Take off your skirt, Colton."

When I go for the corseted strings, he grips my wrist. I angle my head toward him, wanting to know why he stopped me. "Safe word."

"Green," I answer automatically.

We never had these before. We never needed them, but with the deviousness in his expression and the aggression in his moves, it's necessary this time around.

"Good girl."

The praise has me warming from the inside out, my pussy damp with need.

"Now, undress."

I grip the pleather material, untying the bow, all while loosening the band of my skirt. Once I unbuckle the clips, it falls to my booted feet.

Jordan lets out a low whistle while Lux breathes heavily behind me. It's his way of showing control. No attention. Making me feel discomfort. For some reason, it makes me hotter, more desperate for this.

Going to the hem of my see-through blouse, I remove it, receiving a "fuck" from Jordan. All that's left of my clothing is

my boots, barely-there thong, and taped tits, so I turn to Lu
waiting for direction.

"Remove the lace, Colton. Then be a good little slut an
bend over." My face heats at his instructions, and a little ev
smirk tilts on his face. "Grip your ankles for me, and aft
Jordan and I have inspected that pink pussy of yours, you
wait for further direction."

Swallowing the nervousness down with my pride, I sli
off my panties and step out of them. With shame tickling m
bare skin, I bend in half, holding onto my boot-clad ankle
The cool air hits my core, a mixture of shame and chills cove
my skin.

Arousal coats my folds, I can feel it sliding against m
skin as they stand behind me. "Such a messy slut," Lux mus
aloud. "Dripping from your cunt like a leaking faucet."

I shake from the desire filling my system. There
something so erotic about being called a slut. It makes m
want to tease and get my ass spanked for it.

So, I do.

Wiggling my hips, I hope for punishment. It doesn't tak
long to come. *Thwack!* A palm connects with my skin, and I cr
out at the pain tingling my raised flesh.

"You're being bratty, Colton. We don't have time fc
bratty."

"He's right. We've been gone for too long already," Jorda
concurs.

I feel someone at my back, and somehow, I just know it
Lux. His palm rubs against my stinging cheek before he grab

t. "You're making a mess, Corpse. You're going to drip on the
floor."

Loud groans slip free from me as his fingers dance along
my spine. The sensation of them trailing down the crack of
my ass has me shifting, trying to gather friction.

Another *slap*. "You come when I allow it, not any time
sooner."

I let out a huff and earn another spank to my other
cheek. Unable to help myself, I yelp.

"Look at her mess, Walker."

Footsteps sound out, and then a finger glides down my
slit.

"Fucking filthy," Jordan agrees, and I whimper.

"Have a taste," Lux offers me up, like an animal on
display for the taking.

My heart beats rapidly at the noise of Jordan's knees
audibly hitting the ground. When a wet tongue laves at my
entrance, my body jumps on its own accord. Someone palms
my pussy and slaps it. My clit throbs with the ache of needing
to come mixed with the desire from the pain and punishment.

"If you get greedy again, Colt, I'm not going to let you
come."

"Fuck you," I hiss.

When this slap hits my pussy, I'm expecting it. Biting my
lips to prevent a scream, I can barely hold my tears at bay.

"Safe word, Colt."

"Green," I whimper, tears finally breaking free.

"That means go," Jordan muses, chuckling behind me.

"Use it," Lux orders.

"No," I hiss, not wanting to. I need this, the control bei taken, the pain, the shame of doing something that I nev imagined myself wanting to do.

"How did that taste, Walker?"

"Not sure. Might need another lick."

Lux must have offered because not even a breath lat Jordan's tongue flicks out against my heat. It takes eve ounce of control for me to not push back into him. When t pressure is gone, the sound of him smacking his lips has n skin heating more.

"Sweet as sin," he admits.

"Stand up, Corpse."

I shake from head to toe but seem to be able to stai okay. Jordan turns me to him and takes my mouth, kissir me. Whether this is planned or not, I allow him to lead. H grip on my face tightens, and he moves it to the side and tak my throat.

When he lowers, I see Lux leaning against the dress nearest us. He's calculative, his gaze unwavering. While Jorda thought he won some bet, it never would have worked. Lookir at a confident Lux, his darkened hazel eyes and the tick in h jaw, leaning with power while he watches is proof enough.

He may seem uncaring, but the stiff erection pressir against his suit lets me know he wants more. He just wants control the outcome.

Jordan's mouth connecting with my clit has me groanir loudly.

Lux smirks. "Since we don't have time to tamper your slutty nature, seems we'll need to fuck it out of you."

He saunters toward us while Jordan stays crouched between my thighs. His hands grip my lips, spreading them wide while his mouth tastes and teases.

Lux towers over me, his height almost comical against mine. He pushes me backward, the back of my knees hitting the bed in the same breath. Jordan loses his grip and waits for Lux.

"Condom," he barks at Jordan.

I watch as Jordan rifles through the drawers, finding a line of several. He tears two off and brings them over.

Lux now hovers over me, his face above my cunt, his hot breath teasing the wetness there. "Suit up, Walker."

I don't say what I want to say. *Why not you?* Since we messed around, all I've wanted is him. To taste him, touch him, feel what would never be mine.

Not watching Jordan, Lux sinks two fingers in me. "Eyes, Colt. Give me your eyes." Distracting me, I can't tell if Jordan put on the condom. It doesn't matter though. Lux, like the thief of all thoughts he is steals my attention.

Our gazes connect, and the heat in his is addictive.

"I'm going to let him fuck you now. Be a good slut and scream for me, okay?"

I nod, and he kisses my clit before pulling his fingers out. While Jordan kneels, Lux rises, comes to the side of the bed, and pushes the same two fingers in my mouth. "Clean up your mess, little slut."

And I do, sucking them until he pulls free.

Jordan harshly grips my knees, forcing my boot-clad fe
on the bed, and then he's thrusting into me.

My eyes roll back as his thick cock drills inside.

"So tight, princess."

I groan as he rotates his hips, bucking into me, and n
back arches.

Lux comes onto the bed, suit and all, his knees on eith
side of my head. His palm grips my throat as he leans dow
"I'm about to make a mess of you, Colton. Last chance. U
your safe word."

I can't really speak with him holding my oxygen bac
but I attempt at shaking my head. His rueful grin is enoug
to unnerve me. His hand unclenches around my throat, ar
he undoes his slacks, whipping out his cock. Fuck, it's bigg
than I remember. He spits into his palm then strokes himse
above me.

"I'm going to come," Jordan hisses as his speed quicken
He grips my hips, his fingers digging into my flesh as he ran
into me. My eyes close and he grunts out his release. Whe
I open them again, Lux's cock still stands proudly above n
while he strokes with ease.

"Need lube," Lux commands so I start to move, but I
stops me. "Not you."

"There was none," Jordan bites out, zipping up his jean

Lux growls then peers at Jordan. "Then get on your kne
and suck my cock, Walker. I know you're a fan."

Jordan says nothing, and when I look at him, the heat i
his gaze doesn't lie.

Jordan stalks over as Lux adjusts.

"Change of plans, Corpse. Looks like you're riding me."

"Thought you were going to fuck the life into me?" I taunt, disappointed that he took away my visual.

He stares at me with a heated gaze. "Is that why you're pouting? Sad you didn't get two cocks?"

I nod, hating the heat swarming me. Knowing they'd both be inside me makes me desperate.

"Ross was right, you're a greedy slut."

I narrow my eyes. He's teasing me.

He grips himself and strokes slowly. "Sit on my lap, slut. Show Jordan how much better my cock is."

I whimper but do as he says. Hovering above his bare length, I wonder how bad this would look. I just fucked Ross, messed around with Ten, allowed Jordan to fuck me, and I'm about to have a repeat with Lux.

He clamps my hips and forces me down his dick. We moan together as I'm seated fully on him. His eyes are closed, and it's the first time I've seen him appear soft. Saintly, even.

Rocking onto him, his gaze connects with mine.

"Greedy, greedy."

Then, he's bucking into me while I'm practically stuck. His hips roll and cant upward, impaling me over and over.

I tighten around him, feeling him stretch me with each upstroke.

"Everything I imagined," he grunts. "You even have red in your cheeks, Corpse."

His hand snakes down and begins flicking my clit, and

I writhe above him, my wetness making an audible sound
we rut together.

"Come for me. Cream all over my cock, Colton. I need
feel you fall apart."

And I do. My body detonates as he fucks into me, rubbi
me at the same time.

"Lux," I groan. "Harder."

His ass lifts us off the bed, the zipper of his slacks abradi
my skin as he thrusts harder into me. After several pumps,
grunts, and I feel the heat, the hotness of his orgasm pouri
into me, shaking me with another mini orgasm. *No condom?*

When I practically fall on top of him, he lets out a huff.

"Such a little slut. Fucking two guys in her brother's o
room. On his old bed…"

My high lasts all of two seconds as Jordan's words spit
me. No. *Nonononono.* I practically jump off of Lux, his relea
coating my thighs. I hurry to grab my top and skirt.

"Colt," Lux says, his voice exhausted.

I see him, though, his spent dick still out, flapping again
his messy slacks. Then I see Jordan, the smugness on his fa
makes me sick. He folds his arms against his chest, and I hur
to finish tying my skirt.

"Nice fuck, Colt. Didn't know vamps had such war
holes to sink into."

"What the fuck is wrong with you?" I hiss, adjusting m
last string.

He laughs, throwing his head back. "Just playing th
game. You know the rules, Colt. It's not my fault you decide

to slip on two dicks when your brother's body is still fresh in its grave."

"Fuck. You," I cry.

Tears leak from me, and I run from that room as fast as I can, not knowing why the fuck I allowed myself to think anything positive.

Rushing out of the tower, I hurry to Ivory.

They wanted me to play the game.

They wanted me to lose.

They wanted me to be docile.

Too bad I'm upping the ante, and if I've got to fuck my way to get the answers, that's what I'll do. They may have prodded at the beating organ protected by my ribcage, but they forgot I've already lost everything. Pretending to give them my heart will result in their pain, not mine.

I'm done playing by the rules.

I'm here to win.

My monsters are all I have left.

Unfortunately, dealing with monsters makes you become one.

CHAPTER TWENTY-SEVEN

LENNOX

Don't show weakness. Weakness isn't tolerated.

You can't be a king with a spine as solid as a wet nood[

Don't show love. Love isn't allowed.

You can't be a master with a heart as soft as a pin cushio[

Don't give niceties. Niceness isn't forgiven.

You can't be a ruler when your soul is as visible as th[
emblem on your sleeve.

I remind myself of this daily, of everything my fath[
taught me as he hit the words into me. His fists left permane[
brands on each bone he's broken. When he's in a really hars[
mood, I'm pieces rather than whole.

It's at those times when I show Colt my true face. I ha[
it, the fact that she completes me in ways no thing or perso[
ever has before. She just has to stare at me with those glass[

doll eyes and I'm a fucking goner. She softens me when I've avoided conceding to kindness my entire life.

My cruelty is only purposeful because getting close to a Hudson is forbidden. Dad made sure that me, Sebastian, and Drew were aware of it at a young age. He never said why, never explained what made them against the rules, but I'm sure there is a story as old as Arcadia.

DeLeons are meant to marry into the Clearwaters or Silverstones. They're where I'm destined to be. To build Dad's company and carry on a legacy I have no desire to be a part of, sacrifice is the only answer. Being the oldest has its downfalls. Pedestals are too high to climb, and there's no way I'll ever reach his standards of great. Perfection—that's what he wants, what I fear, and what will happen. Sacrifice, blood, tears, and every sweat gland of mine will perspire until he deems it enough.

I sit in the chair in Psych, watching Colt jot down every word shared from Bautista's mouth. It's cruel to watch her with this much intent. It's a curse, seeing her beauty and wanting to capture it entirely, enslave it to me, store it in chains, and never let it loose.

She's a distraction, a disease, and yet, I never want the cure.

Since the party, when me and Jordan shared her, she's avoided us all. Her hanging out with that bitch Melissa is becoming an issue. They're not playing the game, following the rules, or sticking to the traps we've set in motion.

One thing that differentiates Colton Hudson from every

rich bitch at Arcadia is the fact that she's cunning. Seei
everything from a different perspective gives her an an
none of us planned for.

She's a wild card. She's unstable. And she'll ru
everything.

She's basically hiding from everyone in plain sight. Bei
a pariah gives her the type of camouflage no one expected h
to have.

Colt bites her pen, her teeth digging into the black end
it. Colt is habitual. The same dress, makeup, and little nuanc
people don't register. The way she nibbles her pen from t
left only. Not the right, only ever the left. The way she cross
her legs under the desk, always wearing long socks that ma
me want to bite them all the way up to her thighs.

She's skinnier this year. Her body is lithe and almc
sick. Most people wouldn't notice, but I'm particular abo
information. I analyze it, dissect it, and then rip it apart f
my benefit. She's one of those things of mine, even if sh
forgotten that fact.

"Mr. DeLeon, are we boring you?" our teacher ask
interrupting my case study of Colton, the bloody corpse.

"Actually," I mock, "boring would be far mo
entertaining than your dribble."

"Out."

It's a single word, but it has me smirking. These teache
have forgotten who owns this school, all the power and mon
that lines their pockets. But it's okay. It gives me time to c
what's necessary for the next step. Disappointing *him* befo

I've had the chance to prove myself isn't something I can do. We only have six months before everything happens. Once it does, Cassidy Hudson won't be the only one buried six-feet under.

No one's safe.

Not even me.

"I'm sorry. Are you threatening to take me out of class?" I act the part, playing the saintly Lennox DeLeon, the class president, heir to the DeLeon fortune. It's a game. Every step I take is planned. A smirk tilts my lips as I feel the man's eyes staring at me all while I watch my toxic green goblin. She won't look at me, but that doesn't stop me from devouring every inch of her body, committing every ounce to memory.

She tastes as dangerous as one would think.

Addictive.

Savage.

Captivating.

"Not threatening, Mr. DeLeon," our teacher states. "It's happening. Leave."

I let out a derisive snort. "Sure. I'll get right on that."

He waits for me, his arms crossed, a scowl painted on his hardened features. The poor sod can't even tell how idiotic he's being. Whether I'm president or not, my father doesn't take lightly to teachers dismissing me, and I'm sure one of these loser Arcadia kids will be informing him or Twitter how I've been kicked out of class.

When I stand, Colt finally glances at me. Her cheeks are tinted that rouge color that always makes me hard, and I can't

help but to wink. She hates me, but she forgets hate-fucking[ ]
much nicer than Ten's and Ross' pussy lovemaking attempt[ ]

She'll learn.

I'll teach her.

She turns away, and I strut past her and out the doo[ ]
These losers don't know half of what my life is like. Th[ ]
never will. A king can have all the power, but it's his subjec[ ]
knowing his life that damages everything.

I'll keep my secrets, and these kids will learn that I bo[ ]
for no one. Not even *him*. If I die, I'll die with my pride.

"So, what do you think?" I ask Jordan later that nigh[ ]
I'm sitting on my bed, typing my essay for Humanities, whi[ ]
he leans against the headboard, spinning a pen in his finger[ ]
Jordan was supposed to be our plot twist. He went under th[ ]
radar with Colt, but it wasn't as fruitful as we'd hoped.

"She's hiding shit. Melissa, too. Not sure what they're u[ ]
to, but Bridger says Melissa is laying it on thick, if you catc[ ]
my drift."

"Colt isn't going to like that her best friend is fuckir[ ]
him," I point out, thinking of how *I* feel about Ridge touchir[ ]
someone other than Colt. He's not mine, but it doesn't mak[ ]
me want him touching someone else.

My mind travels to Ross. To Ten. Then back to Jordan.

Sharing has never been a problem with us. Not befo[ ]
Colt, at least. Now, it seems she's pitted us against each othe[ ]

We all want a taste. We all want her as ours. We all want to win her favor.

"It's all a part of the plan, Lennox. Can't win if we're not on top."

Grunting, I get off my bed, needing something to ease the stress. After setting my laptop on my dresser, I close it and run a hand through my hair.

Being a DeLeon is hard enough. Add the presidency, Colt, steadying my grade point average, and everything I've got to do to protect the Emeralds, I'm fucking exhausted, and the school year is still fresh.

I don't have time, yet it's all I need. I need it to slow, crash onto the rocks of Moonstone Lake, to drift and become simpler, but I'll never get my wish, not as long as I've got duties.

"Do they know?" Jordan asks, breaking me from my stupor.

"Know what?"

"That we fucked her. Together."

I think back to that night. I needed so much more. I've got to break her down, make her cry, and then lick her tears away as she begs me to come.

"No," I bite, wanting to punch him for bringing it up. They don't know. I've never kept secrets. Each time one of us hooked up with Colt, even before, we knew. When Ten fucked her, it was a joint decision.

This is the first time I've held back, and I don't know why. Maybe it's from Ross fucking her without asking. Maybe it's Ten kissing her when we decided to wait. Or maybe it's

because they've all had their taste while I've stayed back a
made sure she wouldn't completely break.

No matter the *why*, it's something we're risking
keeping silent.

"Are your little pets going to be jealous?"

My eyes land on him, his dark hair in disarray and I
navy blue eyes digging into my soul with a single glance.

"What's it to you?" I ask. They're not my pets. No matt
what we share.

"Maybe riling them up is what I want to do. Right befo
I fuck you."

"Not happening, Walker," I challenge, pointing a fing
at him.

He grabs a joint off the nightstand and lights up. H
chest deflates as he inhales deeply. His eyes relax as he hol
in the rich smoke. "I'll break you down, DeLeon. Then that a
is mine."

A sardonic laugh leaves me. This fucker thinks he's goi
to get a taste when none of the others have? He's reachir
even for him.

Ross, Ten, Ridge, and I grew up together. Ten was clos
to Cassidy. Bridger was closer to Jay, and Ross was mine. W
did stupid shit together, shared our first fuck together, ar
got wasted for the first time together. Jordan is new. He m
be the President of the Emeralds, his last name bestowing th
title, but he'll never be Ross.

"In your dreams, Walker."

"Dreams come true all the time. Watch."

I flip him the bird as he takes another long drag, and I leave him in my room, hoping he doesn't fuck up everything we've spent the last year planning.

Too bad Cass isn't here to see it.

CHAPTER TWENTY-EIGHT

Two months. I've avoided them for two months, and it's nearly Thanksgiving. I'm doing better physically. I can finally eat food. Between the doctor and therapist visits, finally being taken off my medication, and struggling with eating anything, it's been exhausting. It took a couple extra weeks, but my doctor gave me the all-clear for regular food. My physician, doesn't even require to see me. Rich people get away with everything, and apparently, my illness is another thing I could lie about and get away with.

I've been devouring too much food, though, and I'm constantly sick. It's an adjustment, and to stop my binging, I've had to busy myself.

Pizza and chocolate. I'm eating pizza and chocolate. And Pop Rocks.

God, I missed them.

That's not even in reference to Ten, even if whenever they explode in my mouth, I think of him. The night of the party, when I kissed and shared two of the five guys, it's unspoken.

In class, Lux is silent—waiting, I'm sure. Mel doesn't know I ran home because of them getting to me. She was too busy with Bridger, anyway.

Jordan's words from our time together are on replay, the ones about being fucked on my brother's old bed.

He got to me.

They all did.

Mel doesn't even know about what we did, and we pretty much live together at this point. Plotting the demise of five boys and finding Cassidy's killer aren't easy tasks. We're constantly trying to find out what possibly could have brought him harm, but without information, we're at a plateau.

The plan is to sneak into the Crystal Tower and snoop in Cassidy's old room—if that's what that room was. Then if we can get back into the cabin all while the boys are gone for their winter break in three weeks, we'll win. Our sleepovers recently consist of her staying for days at a time.

Fall break just started, and she wants me to fly to Tennessee to ease the tension in her house between her and her dad. Moms is in Europe right now, and Mom is in Australia signing a new deal for some stone—I didn't really listen on the phone call. I'm free.

Honestly, if it wasn't for the prospect of seeing and meeting her brothers, I'd run. The thought of meeting Prudence and Justice scares me shitless.

A mafia boss, twins, and a corpse walk into a bar.

Not a joke. This is what will happen.

Laughing at my own mental image, I wait for Mel come over. I got her a duplicate key. She doesn't even kno anymore.

"Hey, Col!" she hollers at the entrance.

"In here!" I return and hear her practically running dov the hall to my bedroom. When she steps in, I'm touching u my toenails with black polish. This one is different from t last one. It has metallic glitter that gives it a chrome effect.

"You look like you're trying out for Beetlejuice in th outfit, girl."

I stare at my striped shorts, black NF hoodie and Oog Boogie slippers, and can't help the laugh that comes out.

"I'd be a helluva lot cuter, and I definitely wouldn't gra my crotch every chance I get."

"That's what makes him so hot.'

"Ew," I groan, putting my finger in my mouth. "Tha just wrong, Mel."

She laughs and sits next to me. The bed dips, making n nearly paint my toe. "Sorry," she mumbles.

"You think he's hot?" I don't let it go, not wanting h to pretend she didn't just admit to thinking that dead dude attractive.

"Have you seen the way he turns into a snake?"

"Yeah, and gross."

"You have no taste," she argues.

"And you're a freak."

She grabs her chest. "How dare you?"

We both become a fit of giggles.

"You either have daddy issues, or you really need a daddy, and I'm not talking about your dad."

She blushes. Does she want one?

"What's that face for?" I ask, pushing her for information.

Her cheeks grow redder. "There's this guy I met when I went to Arcadia's Village. He was older, a lot older, and he was so incredibly handsome that I nearly melted."

"Ooooh, do tell. Did you do the big bang?"

"God, no. He was my dad's age and could have been a total skeeze."

"You're probably right, but men that are older usually know how to make it feel really good. If you know what I mean." I hit her shoulder with mine, and she laughs.

"I haven't had sex before," she admits.

I place my nail polish down and turn to her. "No shit?"

"No shit," she repeats. "I always wanted it to mean something, but come to think of it, maybe I just want to be owned by someone that knows what to do."

I smirk, thinking of my first time. "I lost mine last year before my brother passed away." I wince. He didn't pass. He was murdered. "I thought it'd be shitty and painful, but the guy I lost it to knew what he was doing. He made me come several times before we had sex."

Her eyes take on a conspiratorial glaze. "Maybe I just need that."

"Maybe," I muse and change the subject. "Want to go

281

searching while we're at your home? Bars. Fake IDs. Le
make it happen."

She nods enthusiastically. "Oh, man! I am so excited f
us to spend the time together…" She pulls out her cell, and h
eyes widen.

My phone vibrates, and I reach for it, distracting r
from her phone.

Girl! I miss you! Let's catch up? Yang's text makes me gri

*Yes! Phone call, or would you want to squash your shitty moc
and visit me?*

*Are you saying I'm high-maintenance, Colton? Because
it's true.*

I laugh out loud at that.

"Who's that?" Mel questions as my face hurts fro
smiling.

"Yang," I mention. "She's being a brat."

She smiles and nods, but I see something uncomfortat
there. "My dad's town car is outside. We need to go pronto.

She helps me blow on my nail polish, and since I did
get my normal three coats, I pack it in my purse and he
out. The driver stands in front of the car. He's older, bla
hair with a tinge of gray at the temples. I give Mel waggli
eyebrows, but she reddens and shakes her head. We load o
bags and are headed off.

The divider slides down, and the driver starts talkin
"We'll be at Arcadia International in an hour. Please drir
refreshments and let me know if you need anything."

While Mel is a stuttering mess next to me, I tell hi

thank you. The divider goes back up, and I jab her side.

"You could totally convince him to pop that cherry."

"Colt!" she hisses. I giggle. "I'm serious. He's easy on the eyes, and I bet he knows exactly where your clit is."

"Oh my god, shut up," she hisses.

I grab a bottle of water, sitting at the center of the vehicle, twisting the top, and drinking it in the next go. The cold hurts my throat, reminding me how much warm water is more appealing.

After we head out, we chat travel plans and decide we'll plan more when we know how the weather is looking. After getting to the airport, the driver takes our luggage, and we get on the big private jet. They serve us refreshments, making sure there's nothing more we need, and before we know it, we're in Tennessee.

When we arrive, there's a new driver. He's bald, stalky, wearing sunglasses that make him seem more like a security guard than an escort, but it doesn't seem to bother Mel. She's used to this kind of weird experience.

The black town car glides toward our destination, and the man doesn't say a single word.

"That's Fonzy. He doesn't talk."

"Like, ever?" I question, raising a critical brow.

Mel laughs and nods.

My gaze flicks toward the front, wondering if he's some scary mobster. You know, the *hands* of the operation, since it's obvious Mel's dad is the *brains*. Fonzy's narrowed expression sends shivers down my spine, almost like a confirmation.

"He's the silent type and gestures instead of speakin When I was younger, it always made me upset because I f alone a lot, but he seems to grow on you."

Her words draw my attention back to her, but when I p back, the divider is now up and I wonder how communicati is possible. Then, I think about Bridger and realize that may it works by getting used to the silence rather than enjoying

"We'll be at my house in twenty if you want to pow nap," she offers, all while focused on her cell.

I've never been much for social media. It would be drag if I died and not Cass. They don't really have proof of r life. I have a whopping hundred and eighty-seven thousa followers on Instagram, but I don't care. I don't upload, b they still stalk me, wanting information.

Cassidy had nearly half a million followers and bless their timelines at least two times a day. When he died, account skyrocketed, and people would tell stories about h he changed their lives and how they were close. All bullsh It drove me nuts when they acted like my brother mea something more than a follow on a page. He was my best frier *We* were close. They were fakes, and it grated on my nerves.

I'll admit it. After he died, I stalked all his socials just feel closer to him. To reiterate, it would be sad if I died. Ther no proof of my existence.

"Oh my god!" Mel exclaims, throwing me out of n reverie. She holds her phone as if it's precious, and that's unnerving.

"What?" I ask, unsure why she would be all excited.

"Ridge Clemonte is in Raleway," she mentions. "That's near Tremington." It's almost a whisper, like she doesn't know how to act at this information. Or maybe it's this new weird dynamic of her crushing on a psychopath that has me uncomfortable. It's not because I think he'll hurt her. It has everything to do with the green monster inside of me who wants to keep him to myself.

"Cool," I mutter, but I'm not happy he's here. That means he's doing sketchy shit since he's from Arcadia, and there's nothing out here for him.

What's your end game, Ridge?

"What's wrong?" She turns to me, her face scrunching in displeasure.

I hate that I'm an open book sometimes. People like Mel and Bridger and anyone else who point out flaws are able to notice the little things. I stare at her, wondering what she could possibly see in him. He's not nice. He's not sweet, and he's definitely not a charmer.

Taking another long drink of water, I flinch at the coldness of the liquid as it slithers down my throat.

Then why do you like him? The niggling in my head probes that lack of truth. To me, he's something different. He doesn't treat me like everyone else.

Worse. He treats you worse.

"I just thought it'd be us and your family," I lie almost patronizingly, hating how it sounds petty.

She almost seems to not believe me but chooses not to comment on it, anyway. "Don't worry. It'll just be us trying

to avoid the twins because I promise once you meet the
you'll be begging for some quality time with Ridge Clemon
They're insufferable."

"Hardly. I'd rather put a fork in my eye and use it as
meatball than spend any unnecessary time with Bridger."

"Whoa. That was a little graphic."

"Oh, I'm sorry. I'd rather electrocute myself in a batht
and become a French fry."

She cringes.

"Better?"

"I'm not going to say you have problems, but, girl, yo
have problems."

I let out a disparaging laugh. "I'm very much aware."

While she goes back to her phone, I stare at the plains
open fields, wondering where the hell I am and why does
mob boss not seem the type to be in a field like this. Does
bury his kills here? I mean, it would be the perfect place.

Why are you the way you are?

I really need to stop talking to myself.

Looking at my cell, I see the time. Usually, it would
time to take my medicine. Now, I'm realizing food needs to
my next priority.

"Can we order pizza?" I ask.

"While driving?" Mel questions, amusement lining h
brows.

I roll my eyes, and we both smile.

"Yeah, we can when we get home. I want to avoid Da
anyway."

Nodding with understanding, I relax as calm overtakes me. Maybe this is the break from the boys I needed.

As soon as we enter two massive gates, my breathing catches. Holy shit. In the distance, my eyes practically salivate at the sight. The house—which is definitely a mansion like all us Arcadia kids have—is massive. It reminds me of old Victorian homes that are brick and mortar with huge vast walls that could be a dungeon for the wars. It's gray and white-slated brick. It has a medieval appeal and even a bit of a creepy old-people-died-here vibe.

Is that a promise of something, or am I being dramatic?

CHAPTER TWENTY-NINE

"This is not at all what I imagined," I explain as soon as we standing outside the car.

She nods emphatically. "If Daddy didn't get this from family's inheritance, it would have been taken upon his arre but it's the Krane family's home. Passed down to the first son

"This is insane. But, like, what if there isn't a first son?"

She laughs.

"If there isn't a first son, it's skipped until there's a son. nod at her and she continues. "Honestly, I can't believe I gre up here. It feels more like a castle for a princess than a hom My brothers would always hide from me and tease me. It w hell, even if I loved them. I was isolated out here. Not man friends. It's a surprise I turned out normal."

I stare at the happy girl I've gotten to know and realiz how she doesn't seem to be secluded as she thinks. She's bee super flamboyant and nice.

"Well, I wouldn't have you any other way," I offer.

With that, she smiles, leading me inside. The big door opening itself reminds me of some weird cultist camp. This entire place gives me weird vibes, but I go with it.

As soon as we enter, a butler is taking our bags, halting my pursuit entirely. The inside does not represent the outside, and vice versa.

The inside reminds me more of the opulence of a castle, like my home but more natural. It has warm tans and browns. The only thing that freaks me out is the litter of hanging animal heads.

He's one of *those* guys.

I stare at a huge boar and its husks at the left of the foyer. It's massive and daunting. Next to it is a black bear that's absolutely terrifying. The opposite is lined with deer and bucks.

"You all right there?" Mel asks.

"Definitely, just a little thrown off." This weekend is going to be interesting, to say the least.

"These are prized wins, sweetheart," a broad man with a heavy voice says. He's tall, so tall that he has at least a foot on me. His shoulders are wide, and he seems to be all muscle. It's intimidating and I can see why people are scared of him.

His face is square and Grecian, like a man carved from an image of Sylvester Stallone. Mel looks nothing like him. Not the hair, not the nose, and definitely not the shape of her head. I stare at him as if he's a specimen and not a man who could cut me up into pieces and make sure I'm never found

With that image in my mind, I offer a hand. "Colto Hudson."

He takes it and isn't aggressive like you always hear books and movies. If anything, his big meaty palm engul mine with care.

"Hudson, like the diamonds?" he asks.

Of course, a man who lives off of the money of othe would know that.

I nod simply, not wanting to act all prim and proper.

"Wouldn't think Tasha had a daughter with such outspoken personality."

Outspoken is dick terms for odd. It's what my extend family said last year. Like, thanks guys. I wanted to be told can't be myself.

"They don't much care about anything anymore, sin I say, tacking on the moniker because I don't want to mal friends with a man wanted under the circumstances of killi hundreds.

"Hi, Daddy," Mel sounds out, interrupting the pregna pause of discomfort.

He peers around me. "Pumpkin," he sounds out joyfull but with an edge of sadness I understand. Mel avoids comir home at all costs, but she's here because I convinced he "What changed your mind?"

"My friend with an outspoken personality," she sa pointedly.

He has the respect to look ashamed at that, but h

290

embarrassment is short-lived when a door bursts open, and two guys walk in.

And shit.

They're hot.

They must be Justice and Prudence.

"Little sis!" one says.

At the same time, the other says, "there's the little shit!"

I can't help the giggle that escapes me. You can tell they're entirely different characters, even while being identical twins.

Their hair is messy. It's shewn in each direction, like the wind blew it, and then they put some spray in and ran their hands through to make it seem casual. It's a dark—nearly black—color that looks more like their father's. That's where the similarities end from them and Mel and their father.

"And who is this?" one of them asks, observing me with a piqued interest. His wine-colored eyes, somehow red, but still brown, with flecks of gold are looking me from head to toe like he'd devour me in seconds if I'd only let him.

"Justice," she scolds.

I look at Justice, seeing the sharp angles of his face and jaw. He reminds me of how all my favorite paranormal authors describe vampires—elegant, ethereal, striking. He smirks as I peer at him, raking my gaze over his body like it's a museum.

He saunters to me, leaning near my ear. "Like what you see, darlin'?" he asks with his smooth and sensual tone, and I'm melting in my boots.

The other brother pushes him out of the way, touching my chin like he's acquiring a new purchase. "Prudence Krane,

291

and who may you be, beautiful?"

I shiver, unable to look away from his rouge eyes. Li
his brother, they're tinny in color, but his are softer and mo
boyish somehow. Prudence has a scar on his upper lip.
makes a white mark, and for some reason, I want to lick it.

What the hell? Why am I like this? Why do these bo
have this effect on me? Isn't five enough? I've already got
handful of dickbags who can't seem to stop tormenting me

"Could you stop making eyes at my best friend and g
lost?" Mel grumps, pulling me back from his enamoring ga

He and his twin eat me alive with their eyes while the
faces appear impassive.

"My bad, sis. Didn't know you had staked claim."

"We're not fucking animals, Justice. She's not somethi
to claim."

I try and fail to hold in a laugh. "Y'all are wild," I mentic

Their father studies me, and it's reminding me I'm n
exactly safe in this place she calls home.

"We have reservations at Dellmonte's" her fath
mentions. "I'm Roderick. I didn't get to say before my bo
decided to rile themselves up."

I smile at him in kind, not wanting to make this vi
unpleasant.

"What's your name, beautiful?" Prudence questions, h
attention not leaving me at all.

"Colton," I whisper. It's almost shy and so unlike me.

"Everyone calls her Colt," Mel supplies. "So don't be
dick and call her asshole names."

They raise an eyebrow like the thought is blasphemous.

I turn to her with a smile. "You don't have to protect me, Mel."

"I'm well aware. These two just like to be dicks."

I nod in understanding. I know five others just like them who are currently at our school or with their horrible parents. Not a single one of them have decent ones; they were all raised by monsters.

"We aren't going with you guys tonight," Mel tells her dad whilst grabbing my arm. "Have fun without us. We're exhausted from our flight and finals."

The twins have a disappointed expression, but her dad seems almost heartbroken. "Okay, sweet pea. Taryn has delivered Colton's bags to the guest suite."

"Which one?"

"The lavender room."

She seems to accept this information, but Mel's face pinches in displeasure. Before I can make a remark, she tugs me away.

"When Mom designed the inside of this place, she had rooms designated for all people. They're color-coded for whether they have animals or not, whether there are children or not, et cetera."

I nod. "Smart woman."

"The smartest." Her eyes have this faraway look, one that says so much about her connection to her mom and how much it differs to the one she has with her dad.

She escorts me to the lavender room and then shows me

where everything is. It's immaculate here, soft, serene—wh
I imagine a nursery would look like for a loving family. Wh
she finally leaves, I go to the mirror, and I'm surprised to s
my contacts are not in. Recognizing my mistake by the i
blues that stare at me, I dig in my bag and put them on.

They've seen me fresh-faced and with my eyes. They'
seen *me*, not the me I've been hiding behind, but the small g
inside who's just a little too far past damaged, the one th
broke.

I put on my makeup and change out of my night shor
and crop top.

Shit.

I must have not made a good impression. Here I a
dressed in little to nothing while meeting new people. N
wonder her brothers looked at me like I was their next mea

My phone lights up, and I'm picking it up before seein
the caller ID.

"Girl!"

Yang's loud holler has me moving my phone away fro
my ear. I put it on speaker and begin to put some sweats ar
a cami on.

"Jesus, could you not scream off my ear?"

She laughs obnoxiously, and I already know she's tips
if not entirely trashed. "I'm sorry!" she both drags out and yel
simultaneously. "I just miss you."

By the time I've found my night tank, I smile. It's hol
and ratty, but it's the last thing I have from *before*.

"I really want to see you, Colt. How are the boys treatin

you?"

The need to scoff is there, but I don't. She knows what they've done, or at least, she knows what I've told her.

"Assholes, as per usual."

"Figures. They aren't exactly good guys. I told you this much when you started dating all of them."

"Ugh," I groan loudly. "I miss you, and I really wish you were here to help me deal with them."

"Like you'd want me anywhere near them. You may be nice, but you're territorial as fuck. No one would stand a chance."

I think back to Mel and Bridger, and all the things they could have done and be doing while she tries to get information.

Maybe a blowjob.

A handy…

Sad whimpers die in my throat, and I deflect by asking, "How's Duponte?"

"You already asked."

"That was months ago. I'm sorry you're evasive," I mock. "Hiding a new boy toy?"

"Why? You want him too?" She laughs, but I don't. "Shit, sorry. That was wrong."

"Fuck off," I bark, but it's not a harsh one. Her joke wasn't nice, but she's drinking, and it's not untrue that I have several guys in my life. "You're just jealous you don't have several dicks to ride."

"So, you admit you've been riding several?" She's full on

cackling now. "God, when I grow up, I want to be you."

"Ha." Putting my hair up in a bun, I sit at the edge of t massive bed.

"I'm serious! You have all these dudes that want you, a you're hot shit."

"Who's that?" Mel asks, entering the room.

"Her best friend. Who are you?" Yang questions, h voice too loud.

Mel cringes, her face showing discomfort. *I'm sorry, s* mouths.

I shake my head.

Mel answers, "Her other best friend."

"Gross."

"Really, Yang?" I groan. "You're nineteen, not five."

"It's okay," Mel responds. "Taking care of our girl whe you're not here."

"Whatevs!" Yang slurs. "Going to go fuck this rando a get wasted."

"Love you," I say, my voice somber, filled wi disappointment. Mel might think nothing of it, but Yang w being a dick.

Yang doesn't respond, and I hear the beep of the ca disconnecting.

"I'm thinking we should have a LOTR marathon," M recommends, offering me a smile. She's unbothered, and appreciate it.

"True nerd question." The words come out of n conspiratorially. "Which Lord of the Rings is your favorit

And don't be like Ross and pick The Two Towers."

She rolls her eyes and then laughs. "Wait, Ross likes LOTR?"

"He's a total ho for Arwen."

"I mean, he's not wrong," she comments.

I push her slightly. "No, that he's not. I'd fuck her."

Melissa's eyes shoot up.

"What?"

She just laughs. "Didn't know you were a girl kinda girl, Colt."

With a smirk, I kiss her cheek. "I'm an anything flies type of girl, especially if the connection is there."

She nods with understanding and gets up for snacks. "My favorite is the Fellowship, by the way." When our eyes meet, she has this look in her eyes. "Legolas riding in on that horse…" She fans her face, biting her lip. "I never thought a dude with long hair could be so hot."

We both laugh at that. Orlando Bloom in any state is hot. He's like an entire religion.

CHAPTER THIRTY

"So, sweetheart," Justice says the next morning.

Mel is still asleep, and I thought it would be a good id
to wander downstairs, maybe find cereal, and smoke a joi
before she wakes up.

I'm still in my sweats and holey cami, but luckily, i
black and won't show my nipples. The piercings, perhaps, b
no transparency will be had.

"Are you ignoring me?" His question comes out amus
and cheeky.

When I turn to him, I see his sharp jaw and the way
transforms when he smirks. He's so goddamn charming.

"No, just wondering if you flirt with all of your sister
friends."

He bites the inside of his cheek and fully smiles, his enti
face morphing with joy. It's so fucking adorable, his face wi

a big-ass smile.

I raise an eyebrow as he doesn't respond to me.

Sauntering over to cut the short distance between us, he stands in front of me, his face chalk full of cockiness, not the affronting kind, more of the type that bleeds regardless.

"You're the first friend Mellie has brought over in years, and you're also the only one I've found myself insanely attracted to."

"Is that so?"

He bites his bottom lip. I can tell it's not intentional. He notices and straightens a bit. Then he brings his forefinger to my chin. "Very much so, sweetheart."

"What's for breakfast?" Prudence asks, rounding the entryway with a big smile. His hair is in disarray, but it makes him seem boyish somehow instead of that sharp-jawed mafioso son look he had going for him last night.

"I'd say Colton here," Justice taunts, "but she seems like she'd want to be reeled in first."

My face flames at his words, and when Prudence looks at me, there's a distinguishable hunger. It's the same mirrored in his twin's expression. It warms me from head to toe, and fuck, it really shouldn't, but I can't help the way my thighs rub to create friction.

"She'd be a much bigger meal than breakfast, Just," Prudence mocks, smacking his brother's chest. "She'd need to be a five-course meal because there's no fucking way I could only sample her sweetness and let her go."

Fuck.

299

"Exactly," they reply in unison, and it takes me a seco
to realize I've said it aloud, and they're eyeing me w
expectance.

"Dad wants Mellie to come to dinner tonight."
Prudence who speaks. His face still holds a fiery tightness th
reminds me of my own desire.

"Please convince her to come," Justice practically begs

Whether it's because of my own broken family or t
two charming guys flirting with me, I nod.

They double kiss me on the cheek before showing r
where the cereal and industrial fridge is.

Later that night, I put on a black dress, one that cove
my thigh tattoos and scars. It's transparent in the cent
netted with mesh, and one of my favorites. I brush my ha
straightening it right after, and pin back my bangs. I almo
seem like myself again.

When I open my door, there's a man standing the
Much like the bald one at the front door, he's stalky and b
He doesn't say word but nods at me in greeting.

Mel comes bounding down the hall a moment later. "Y
finally look like yourself!" she shouts happily.

"Why are you yelling?"

"I'm just excited I don't have to suffer alone the rest
this week. Last night, just you and me? It was perfect. It's be
hard for me being here and not have someone on my side."

"What do you mean? Your brothers seem nice enough."

She gives me a sardonic *really* look. "Am I wrong?"

She laughs, placing her hands on her hips. Then she starts pacing. "My brothers accept my dad for who he is and even help him in his empire."

My eyes widen. Those two sweet flirts condone the darkness? They don't seem to have a cruel bone in their body. *That's what you thought about Jordan.* I close my eyes at that recollection.

"They're taking over for him when they're twenty-one. Since they turned eighteen, he's been training them for the inevitable."

"Wow." I don't know what else to say. From what she's mentioned, her father doesn't do nice things, even if he seems kind, and if those two are following in his footsteps, they must not be good guys either.

"Yeah, but enough about that. Let's go eat. They have a mean alligator soup."

I balk at her. *Gross.*

"So, Colton," Roderick starts, "what are your plans after Arcadia?"

We're sitting at a circular table. Melissa and her dad are opposite me while the twins are on either side of me. Their thighs and hands have bumped my bare thighs on several occasions, and the collective breath I've gathered has sent shockwaves through my system.

I'm glad I have somewhat of an idea, or this would be rea[l] freaking awkward. It seems parents—whether mine or oth[er] people's—always ask this question. It's like their ice-break[er], the easy flatline kind of topic that makes meals go quicker.

"I plan to go to Providence Hall."

His eyes widen as if he's impressed. "Are your parer[ts] happy about that?"

Unlike normal people when they ask a question, his fa[ce] gives nothing away. No eyebrow raises, no movement of [his] face at all. It's daunting, like being at a poker table with [a] milestone gambler.

Justice grips my thigh with his hand. When his finge[rs] tighten, a shudder zips through me.

"Honestly, they don't care. As long as I go to one of th[e] top five, they don't mind which one I pick." My focus is on ho[w] breathy or not my response came out. I could easily play it [off] as my illness, but at the same time, I've been better for weeks[.]

It's true about my parents not caring. Moms wants [me] close, but she's accepting of any of the colleges I choose [as] long as it's what I want. Mom wants me to go to Dupon[te] where Yang is, but it's not my kind of school. Duponte focus[es] on business, while Providence Hall focuses on creative arts[.]

He nods placidly. "Providence is an astute one, thoug[h]. Surely they must be proud?"

It takes everything in me not to scoff. How could [he] know they don't give two shits about what I do and wher[e I] do it? They don't. Moms can try and pretend, but I'm dead them, just like my brother.

"Like I said." I grab my glass of water and take a long sip. "They don't care."

He purses his lips but drops it.

Justice decides it's a great time to chime in, his skin still hot against mine. "So, got any plans tonight after dinner?" He waggles his eyebrows.

I practically cough on my next sip.

"Yeah, she's hanging out with me," Mel complains, giving her brothers a scathing glare.

"But she'd have so much more fun with us," they both gripe, laying it on way too thick. Prudence decides that's the best moment for his hand to grip my other thigh. My mind fizzles out. My breathing feels labored, and I swear sweat lines every inch of me.

Almost as if an idea pops into Mel's head at their suggestion, she smiles conspiratorially. "Where do y'all want to take her?"

Squaring my shoulders for an uncomfortable situation, I sip my drink in silence.

"We were thinking Bear & Brawl."

"That place is a cesspool," Mel groans. "Why not Herrington's instead?"

"Because we want to have fun, sis, not gouge our eyes out with people who think they're above it all."

While they have a staring contest with me stuck in the middle, literally, our food arrives. I went with chicken fried steak, mashed potatoes, collard greens, and pea soup. It smells

divine. Luckily, my nose and stomach are in agreeme
No queasiness at all. This will save me from an awkwa
conversation about my recovery.

"You good?" Mel whispers so no one can hear.

I nod and unwrap my spoon. The boys haven't stopp
watching me, but as I put the soup in my mouth and moa
their expressions go from wonder to hungry in two secon
flat. Justice openly gawks at me as if I'm the true meal he
and Prudence adjusts his pants while trying to keep a neut
face. It's endearing. Their hands disappear, and I'm sure i
because they don't trust themselves.

"So, Bear & Brawl... you down?" they ask me.

I'm not sure what the hell that is. Turning to Mel, I wa
for her explanation.

"It's a smaller club. Not seedy, but definitely where t
darker parts of Tremington elites go to get drunk, high, a
dance. Sometimes, there's even some people fucking."

My eyes widen. The fact she said that in front of h
father makes me uncomfortable in my seat, but he seer
unbothered by the entire conversation.

"Not sure if that's me," I admit to the boys.

For some reason, that makes them happier. They smi
in a way that sends both shivers and tingles across my body

"That means you're perfect for it," Prudence finally say

Their dad eats his massive steak in silence, but when
peer into his brown eyes, they seem calculated, wading o
the storm, but he's definitely paying attention. What man li
him wouldn't?

We don't go home to change after dinner. Instead, we go with the twins in their very rugged Jeep Wrangler, and they drive us out into the city.

Bear & Brawl seems like an okay place regardless of the terrible name. When they first brought it up, it sounded like a fight club, but the name doesn't depict its appearance. It's a massive club. The outside seems like a trendy venue, and the inside screams wealth.

Seedy, my ass. This place is nicer than most places in Arcadia Township.

I stare at the massive bar. We got in here so easily, didn't show ID or anything, but these guys probably have the entire town under their nose, and that's entirely too scary to think about.

"This is not what I expected," I yell toward Mel.

She nods in a way that says she's not impressed. I am, though. This is glamorous in a not-loud-but-not-subtle way.

She points to the bar, and I nod. I need a drink, and it needs to be pronto. Vodka is my poison. Whiskey is my cure, and rum is my lover. There's no going wrong here.

The boys follow us to the bar, and when we can't get the attention of the female bartender, it takes them one flick of their wrist for her to drop everything.

"She'll have a vodka tonic," he mentions and then motions

to Mel. He stares at me for a moment and then smirks. "Tl
beautiful one will have an Irish Trashcan."

My face flames at that. How would he possibly know I
a goner for some heavy drinks?

"Figured a girl of your caliber would need somethi.
that gives a pounding." With the word pounding, he bites t
inside of his cheek like he doesn't want to be obvious abo
his ogling.

His sister notices anyway. "Stop being a flirt and ,
away."

He grabs his chest as if he cares about her pushing hi
away. "You wound me."

"No, I don't. Now go find another girl to bother ar
leave my best friend alone."

He eyes me, asking me silently if that's what I want.

No, it definitely is not, and that reaction bothers me. I
not like I'm all about finding new guys when I have five at hon
that I don't know what to do with, and hate in the same breat
But these two, they're fun, and I need some fun in my life.

I smile at him and tilt my head, telling him to go witho
making Mel angry, and he pouts. Mel turns to grab her drin
and before he leaves, I wink and blow him a kiss. The wa
his face lights up and then darkens almost sends me into
tailspin of hormones. Shit. What did I say about boy craz
I'm pent-up with needs.

The bartender gives me a scathing glare before handi
me my drink.

"Think she spit in it?" I ask Mel.

She laughs, but her eyes are a little hazy. "That's Ronnie. She and my brothers dated."

"Brothers? As in both?" I ask.

She nods.

My body absolutely melts at that. Not because I've met one of their playthings, but because the thought of being shared is something I fantasize about often.

"She was obsessed with them, but they were only in it short-term."

"Do they do that often?" I ask, even knowing I shouldn't.

"Share or date?"

"Both."

She scrunches her face. "They haven't dated since this chick Serena got in the way of their brothership."

"Brothership?"

"They used to share her, date her, but she asked Justice for more, saying he was the one she chose, and she broke Prudence's heart. Since then, they decided not to date. It causes too many strings to be attached, and they really love their relationship for some reason."

My heart aches for Prudence and Justice. Imagine being best friends, literally with the other half of yourself, and thinking you're less somehow.

When I sip my drink, I practically moan. It's been so long since I've had a proper drink. After my diagnosis and the upending battle of being stuck with the inability to eat, I haven't had any booze. My body absorbs it too quickly, and the high goes just as fast.

"Whoa, there," Mel says. "Your eyes are looking glossy

I smile softly, feeling warm all over. "It happens. My bo metabolizes slowly, making the alcohol sit and burn faster.

She seems nervous when those words tumble o "Should you not be drinking?"

"I'm fine, for now. You should go dance, though," I off since she hasn't stopped looking at the dance floor since v walked in.

"Really?" she asks almost excitedly.

"Really," I repeat and shoo her away.

Not even a minute passes before a slimeball sidles u to me.

"Well, hello, Walking Dead. Want to dance?"

"That's a new one," I mock. "Get something more origir than that, and maybe I'll not tell you to go fuck yourself."

He scowls, his face turning hideous in an instant. "Yo stupid bitch, do you know who I am?" he barks and raises h hand.

This fucker wouldn't dare.

"Plotts!" Prudence barks.

The man stiffens. How does he know this guy and wh does that make me sad?

"Do you know this bitch?" Plotts—as Prudence calle him—asks.

"She's not a bitch, you piece of shit."

"He was literally about to hit me," I say.

Prudence's face takes on a scary shade. His eyes blacke and so does his features. In the low lighting of the club, h could even pass as an avenging angel about to smite this dude all the way off the planet.

"Was he now?" His voice is deepened to the point it's a hiss. It's gritty and dark and the depravity in it reminds me of something. I can't recall what it is, but it's there at the back of my mind, making my spine tingle.

"No," Plotts barks. "I was waving the waitress over."

It's a goddamn lie, but Prudence doesn't relax. If anything, he seems angrier.

"Ronnie!" Prudence barks, and she comes to him like a lost puppy. It's pathetic, really, the way she looks at him as if he's god. That's not a good look, and I shouldn't care, but it annoys me.

"What's up, buttercup?"

I internally gag.

Prudence puts on a very fake flirty smile. His nostrils are still flared, and his back is stiff and unhappy.

"Did this man wave you over?"

She looks at me when he asks, and her eyes narrow. The little bitch isn't going to be honest. She nods and says, "Yeah, the man wants an old fashioned."

I glare at her but breathe in through my nose. As I'm about to leave, hands clamp on my shoulders. For some reason, I don't feel disgusted, and when I look up and see Justice, I realize why.

His warmth spreads through me, making my cheeks warm. "Hey there, darlin'."

"Hey," I breathe, hating that his drawl does something

inside me that shouldn't happen.

He leans in close, and I can feel the air escape his mou
and skate over my neck, making my heart pound loudly.
not for the loud music, I swear the twins could hear it.

Ronnie looks at Justice's hands on me and lets out a hu

"This loser bothering you?" Justice asks.

I melt, fucking evaporate like ice cubes in a southe
iced tea. I can't help it.

He shares a look with his brother, and then some rando
person in a black suit and tie comes and carts the dude awa

Prudence takes the man's place and leans in opposite
his brother. "I'm sorry, sweetheart. It won't happen again."

My body shakes and warmth pools in my belly. What
happening to me?

"Thank you," I say to both of them and then go back f
my drink.

As I sip it, they watch me; one in interest, the other in bare
abated hunger. I'm a mess of hormones and desires. I ke
clenching my thighs to stop the pounding between my legs.

When they sit in stools next to me, I wonder what I'
supposed to do or say. The guys at Arcadia are always pushin
and I'm always caving, but it's like these two want me to mak
the first move.

After I empty my drink, my body becomes looser, ar
I'm starting to feel that fake braveness that comes with
buzz. I reach for both of their hands, and with my eyes, I as
them to follow.

I'm not a dancer. If anything, I'm the awkward perso

they make GIFs of and laugh at. But for some reason, having these two sandwich me on the dance floor is more appealing than anything.

They trail me and I wrap my arms around Prudence, bringing our bodies flush. Justice comes to my back, and we sway together. We're dancing off beat to the fast dubstep number they have playing, but that doesn't stop the ardor from growing between my thighs.

Justice's hands palm my hips, low and near my panty line. I groan, and Prudence brings our lips together. I'm so warm and consumed by their touch that I don't notice a looming figure nearby. It isn't until Prudence is ripped from my front that I realize we were entranced in one another.

I open my eyes to the blackest starless ones that haunt me every day.

"Bridger," I whisper, knowing he probably can't hear it. Shit.

311

CHAPTER THIRTY-ONE

Bridger's face, usually dead and unresponsive, is haunti
right now. His eyebrows dip in, chiseled onto his face like
demon, and the grimace he's sporting would scare anyor
His jaw is locked tight, and his face seems devilish.

"Colton," he bites out.

It's chilling, making sure to slice me deep, past the bone
and somewhere in my essence. No *Freak*. Or *Corpse*. Ju
Colton. He's not happy, but that's an understatement. He
more than furious and clinging onto psychotic.

"Bridger," I repeat, louder this time.

"The fuck are you doing?" he demands.

My face falls. I'm not doing anything any regula
teen wouldn't do. Have fun. Meet cute guys. Dance wit
said cute guys.

"Dancing," I bark, placing my hands on my hips, hatir

how he looks like he's about to strike.

Bridger looks behind me, and with his guard down, I see a flicker of jealousy on his face. It disappears almost immediately before his scowl returns.

"Who the fuck are these two?"

The twins wear pissed off glares, and for some reason, it makes me want to keep Bridger safe, and that awareness has me hating my life. This shouldn't be a thing. I shouldn't be worried about what they do to each other when I walk away, but I do. I hate it, but I definitely care.

"Prudence." Justice waves over to the brother Bridger ripped off me. "Justice," he says, pointing to himself.

"If you ever touch me like that again, dick, I'll end you," Prudence threatens, coming next to me to place a protective arm around my waist.

If looks could maim, Bridger would be eviscerating the palm on my hip. The possessive look in his eyes throws me. This is the most emotion I've witnessed on his face since we made out that one time. He's not one for emotions, and I'm surprised he's letting them out in a random club.

Which hits me.

"Why are you here?" I accuse. He's not the outgoing type, let alone the guy who will show up at a club.

"Ridge, there you are!" Mel's chirpy voice sounds out.

My blood runs cold, and my body nearly shakes with unabated anger. That fucking bastard.

"Oh, hey, Colt!" Mel exclaims, her face red and flushed.

It feels like homecoming all over again—the green

monster inside me, the burning ache of never being enou
for Bridger, and the desperate need to stake my claim on hi
They all drown me, making my skin crawl.

He doesn't get this kind of power.

He doesn't get to hurt me anymore.

He doesn't get... me.

"Ridge decided to meet me here," Mel explains, when n
a single fucking soul asked. "He said he was nearby, anywa

My eyes narrow, my blood way past simmering and
the verge of boiling. I'm so close to exploding. The only thi
that calms me is Justice leaning in.

"He's not worth it, darlin'. Let me take you home."

I nod at him, and Bridger's face shows malice for tw
seconds before that stupid mask is in place.

"I'm not feeling too hot, babe," I say to Mel.

She probably thinks it's my stomach.

"Rain check? I really want to dance some more."

The jealousy reaches inside me and squeezes before I no
She came here to lose her virginity. That was the plan, a
now she just might with the one guy who hurts me witho
blinking.

"Yeah," I mutter.

"We'll get her home," the boys reassure her. They lay
on thick for the benefit of the asshole standing in front of m

"We'll keep her safe," Prudence adds, gripping me tighte

Bridger's eyes travel to the hand on my waist, and h
nostrils flare again; the only thing giving away his anger
this very moment.

"Bye!" Mel says happily, probably grateful she won't have her brothers watch her every move and me bother her tryst with Bridger.

Fuck them both.

"Let's go, hmm?" Justice sounds in my ear.

"We'll take care of you, sweetheart," Prudence reassures, "in every way necessary."

I shiver and relent, not looking at Bridger, who lets Mel grind on him, ignoring how he looks at me with that callous smirk, and certainly denying the way my body wants to erupt with a green rage that has zero claim to that man.

We drive back to the mansion in silence. My heart hurts. My soul dies a little, and I'm so beyond pissed that my body feels the tension tenfold.

"Who was that guy?" Justice asks as soon as we're inside.

My body feels the adrenaline wane, and the booze take its place. It's weird, heavier than normal. Maybe the heart-racing rage that consumed me is now making me both exhausted and drunk.

"Bridger," I sort of slur.

Prudence grabs my arm. "Well, hey there, darlin'. You're not looking so hot." He shakes his head with a chuckle. "I mean, you're mighty fine, beautiful. You just seem out of sorts." He exchanges a look. "I only got her one drink."

"Who made it?" Justice questions.

"Ronnie."

"Fucking Christ, Pru. Didn't you stop to think that maybe,

just maybe, she's a psychopath and would drug Colton?"

I can't see the look on Prudence's face, but I can feel t
hatred rolling off him in waves.

"Fuck."

"Yeah, fuck. She's probably been doped up."

"That's low, even for Ronnie," Prudence says.

"Yeah, but she saw us both have a girl, and we were
exactly hiding our attraction."

I smile at that, unable to hide how much his wor
please me.

"Who was that guy?" Prudence asks me as soon as we
inside, lifting me into his arms, and he smells so delicious. I
has this elegant scent about him—sweet, manly, and smoo
like a Penn & Co. cologne I haven't smelled before. I ca
seem to focus on his question enough to answer because I
scent is intoxicating.

"You smell good," I groan, sniffing his chest loudly. "C
my god."

Oh my god is right. My inhibitions are very low right no

"You smell good, too, princess. Now, rest those pret
eyes so we can make sure you're okay."

I nod into his chest and breathe him in the entire way u
the winding stairs.

"We shouldn't have brought her there tonight," I he
Prudence whisper. They think I'm asleep, more than likely.

"Shut the fuck up, Pru. Not here." Justice's bark
probably as vicious as his bite. With a body built like
wrestler, he could probably take and give a beating.

316

I wonder why they're talking about me as if they've known me much longer than this trip.

They get me to my room. Pru sets me down and kisses my forehead softly, and a sigh escapes me. It's content, but I don't open my eyes. Justice comes over a second later and kisses exactly where his brother just did.

"Sleep, princess."

They don't realize I'm not asleep. Maybe whatever drugs this girl gave me will make me forget, but I don't want to forget how they smell and how much they make me feel.

I didn't expect to care either, boys.

After a few minutes, the fuzziness becomes too much, and my eyes shut. I'll deal with this all tomorrow, when my body doesn't feel achy and needy.

CHAPTER THIRTY-TWO

My head throbs as soon as my eyes open the next mornin
Two days in this place and I've already fucked with my hea
body, and possibly my recovery.

Regardless of how much I drank, I shouldn't feel th
way. Lethargy settles inside me, my body out of sorts but al
exhausted beyond repair. Despair isn't a light emotion, b
somehow, it feels extra heady this morning.

Mel.

Bridger.

Blurriness.

The constant stabbing pain in my eyes makes it hard
think back to last night. This seems much worse than wh
I drink too much and get a dehydrated hangover. My bo
feels gross and, shit. My face. I forgot to remove my makeu

After rushing to the bathroom where I put my wipes, I go at my face, feeling the sting of the removal as I try taking it off.

I pop out my contacts, feeling the dryness and slight burn from leaving them in overnight. Fuck, I really shouldn't have done that.

After taking a long and hot shower, brushing my teeth, and doing my skin care routine, I dress in sweats, a huge NF shirt that used to be Cassidy's, and my bunny slippers.

No one waits outside my door today, which surprises me. I only make it down the vast hallway before I see Justice standing in a doorway, looking right at me. My mouth waters at his shirtless body. He's so ripped. His abs are like his jaw, chiseled and defined. There's a massive crest over his chest. It looks vaguely familiar, but the more I stare at it, the less I realize from where. He could be an Adonis statue, and I would believe it, even with that tattoo on his chest.

"Sleep okay, princess?" he husks, his voice deep from sleep.

I shake my head, my eyes burning from forgetting to remove my contacts. Ugh. I never go to bed like this.

"Say the word, and I'll ease your pain," he teases.

I step toward him, and right before I make it, Pru steps out from behind him.

"Mornin', darlin'." Like his brother, his voice is syrupy and thick.

I love how they sound first thing in the morning—hot, sweet, and damn near irresistible. Southern comfort has a different meaning to it now.

Justice grabs a wet lock of my hair. "Never thought I find green hair so irresistible," he muses. When Pru lea around him, it brings me to believe these two sleep togethe He, too, is shirtless, but he's only wearing black boxer brief

"Jealous?" Pru taunts, raising a challenging eyebrow.

"Only that you two slept, and I feel like something too an ice pick to my brain."

My words have their face morphing in both anger an disappointment.

"Don't worry, princess. She'll pay for her actions la night."

Then it all hits me.

My drink.

That chick.

The pervy dude.

Bridger.

Bridger with Mel.

My stomach revolts, and as if they recognize my need escape, they move out of the way.

"It's the door on the left."

Inside their room, it's so them, blue and cool tones, bu shit, it's like its own apartment. There are two rooms and bathroom and a walk-in closet.

I make it to the bathroom and am hurling my guts out the next second. One of them holds my hair as the other rub my back.

"I'm *so* sorry," I apologize.

"Don't sweat it, beautiful. It happens." Pru reassures.

After I'm sure I'm done, I get up, rinse out my mouth, and pray that today doesn't continue with this grueling feeling, but the more I think of Bridger with my best friend, the more nauseated I get.

"We should get something in you," Justice says.

A giggle escapes me. It takes him a mere second to realize my mind wasn't in a clean place.

"That's not what I mean, but I'm not opposed in any way."

I smile at him, and we leave after they put shirts on. I only momentarily pout at that.

After going back to my room to brush my teeth, I make my way to the dining room. Roberta, the maid, cooks us breakfast, and the boys sandwich me in on either side of the table. I can't help but feel comforted.

As we eat, my body starts feeling better. I'm not as achy and agitated.

But Mel never came home last night, and that can't mean anything good.

I don't share.

I'm horrible at it.

But Bridger was never mine to have.

And he obviously has no qualms in proving that to me.

"What are the plans for today?" Just asks, his eyes intent on me.

I shrug, taking a bite out of my toast. My eyes are dead set on not looking at these two while emotions are piled on thick. That's my biggest downfall, finding comfort where I have none.

But that only lasts little time. Pru lifts my chin as I chewing. "What's wrong, beautiful?"

My body melts whenever he calls me that. He should have an effect on me, not this soon. This connection has to residual sadness from the last time I was with the boys, a seeing Bridger's lips smeared with Mel's mouth and how avoided them for the following few months.

"Nothing," I lie, feeling my lip tremble.

As if noticing how sad I truly am, Pru grabs me by t hips and puts me in his lap, my thighs on either side of hi Tears well in my eyes, and I just want to forget and get l for a while.

"Talk to me," he says, his eyes showing the utmc concern.

If the hardness underneath me wasn't present, I wou almost wonder if he didn't find me attractive after last nigh Who knows what embarrassing shit I did?

"Can we just go somewhere? Anywhere. I need distraction."

Justice touches my shoulder with comfort. "Anywhe princess. You name it."

Tears finally drip from my eyes, and I'm trying not to ful go emotional teen on these two. That's the last thing they nee

Standing with me still firmly in his lap, Pru grips my a with his huge palms and carries me off. They lead me back u the stairs, and when we make it to their room, I feel an o sense of peace wash over me.

"Let's cuddle, nap, and then we'll take you on a prop

outing."

My eyes well with tears. Pru sets me on their bed, and then they sandwich me in as I feel peace for the first time in weeks.

Sometimes, I wonder if I'm never meant to be alone, whether in reference to being single, sleeping in a bed by myself, or in general. Being surrounded by their warmth and strength makes me feel needed.

Pru brushes his hands through my hair, and Just rubs small circles into my back. Before I've realized, I'm out.

By the time I wake up, I'm feeling less exhausted and ready to rock the day. Hard flesh hits my butt as I rotate, and I realize it's Just's erection. My stomach warms, making heat brush across my face. How did I get to this point? Not just in Tennessee, but wanting to be close to two more guys?

As I attempt to adjust onto my back, Pru's hand grips my hip. "Keep wiggling, and we'll be stuck in this bed all day," Pru flirts and I try maneuvering to accommodate them both.

"Please keep wiggling. My dick likes being happy," Just groans tiredly. "I never knew waking up next to a girl would be so goddamn appealing."

"Y-You've never done this?" Shame flickers inside me momentarily, realizing I didn't even think over the question.

"Nah, we're not used to spending the night with others," Pru answers.

"What about Serena?" I ask.

God. I'm being brave and stupid all at once.

Just grumbles.

Pru chuckles. "Mel has a big fucking mouth."

Pulling the covers up, I duck beneath, not wanting the to see how red my face must be. It only causes them to tu toward me, laughing at my unabashed questions.

Fingers tug at the blanket covering my face, but I ke my eyes shut, squeezing too hard.

"Look at the princess. She's blushing."

A pathetic groan leaves me, and they're enjoying every mome

"Are you jealous, sweetheart?" Just's teasing tone tak on a little edge, like he enjoys the idea.

"I can't be," I bemoan. "We've just met. This is insane."

The blanket is off, and they're touching me and forci my eyes open. The intrigue and interest on both of their fac make my heart beat erratically. How is wanting them th easy? They're kind, whereas my monsters aren't.

"I kind of like that you care if you're the first," Pru mus He's biting his tongue, his teeth pinching the pink flesh as l amusement lights up his features.

"Me too. Guess it's a good thing that not even Sere was allowed to stay the night with us then, huh?"

Digging my teeth into my lip, I grind down on the fle needing to be aware that I'm awake, let alone alive. Perfecti isn't realistic, but somehow, these two were sent to me.

"Yeah, she wasn't you," Pru adds.

"We should get ready for our date."

I stare at these two boys and smile. "What about Melissa

They give me a sardonic expression, and I nod with a scrunch of my nose.

"Do you see Meli anywhere?" Pru jests, waving his hands about.

I scoot off the bed and roll my eyes as they smile as if they've won already.

Maybe they have.

"Looks like she's still gone with that dude. I'd say you're ours for the day."

The mention—or lack thereof mention—of Bridger has me sad, but it doesn't last. These two shoo me to my room, but at the same time, they walk me the entire way.

"Put on something comfortable," Justice offers.

"So, nothing?" I taunt.

His eyes darken, and he grabs my chin, holding me against the door to my guest room. "If that's what you want, sweets, say the word. We can say *fuck you* to the rest."

A shiver racks my frame, but I don't back down. I bringing our faces close, and the air sparks from our radiating lust.

"They say you should take a girl out for dinner before she spreads herself for dessert." It's teasing, but the words are so breathy it's hard to tell who I'm trying to convince.

Pru comes to my side, his fingers skating over my skin as he stares at us both. "Guess we should have an early dinner."

"Are you that hungry?"

Their eyes flick to each other and then to me.

"Like I haven't eaten in days." It's Justice who releases those words with bite.

"Get dressed, princess. The longer we're out here, t[he] more likely we are to hunt you down and keep you as t[he] prize." Pru's eyes twinkle.

The scorching way my skin seems to heat has me rubbi[ng] my thighs together.

Before they can further tempt me, I turn and head i[n] the room.

Cold shower?

Cold shower.

After I've showered—sans washing my hair—and calmed [my] vagina down, I dress in a short black mini pleated-argyle sk[irt.] It's the schoolgirl kind of design and was almost too much [to] resist. My top is another cynical one, *dead is the new black*. It'[s a] crop top, but I wore a fishnet camisole that covers my stoma[ch] while leaving enough to the imagination that you want mo[re.] Monochromatic colors my entire wardrobe. Winging [my] eyeliner and dusting my lips with gloss, I feel like me.

My boots are my last addition to the ensemble, but befo[re] I leave the room, I check my cell.

Sorry I didn't make it back. Hanging back with Ridge. It'[s a] message from Mel.

Boiling blood, that expression of an intense anger which you can't control, that's where I'm at.

Without texting her back, I head out, and it solidif[ies] tonight with the guys.

Whatever they want to do, I want it.

Even if I fuck them, and Mel hates me.

If petty was a shade, it would be black, and right now, it adorns every fucking inch of me. If Bridger wants to play and fuck around, I'll do the same. But worse.

"Wow." Pru's mouth falls open, making me feel hot and overwhelmed. "Fuck, princess."

"Goddamn," Justice groans.

I rotate, seeing him gripping the back of his neck. His eyes are widened, drawn to my body, and the way they make me feel is unlike anything I've felt before.

Unlike my monsters at Arcadia, these two aren't afraid of showing their appreciation for me without belittling me.

"My dick is not going to behave. We should just stay in."

I can't help the giggle that escapes me.

Justice's face almost seems to redden. He's embarrassed? The fact he finds me this hot makes me feel uncomfortable. I've never felt like the pretty girl, not since I stopped looking like my brother.

Cass.

My mind travels to him, to my monsters and what they know, to wanting more info, to hoping Mel is getting information and not just fucking him.

Annoyance consumes me. He's not hers.

"Ready?" Pru comments, coming up and touching my chin.

"Yeah."

But I'm not.

Is it a betrayal if they're not yours to betray?

CHAPTER THIRTY-THREE

After they feed me what they call *real* pizza—which is pre
fucking magnificent—they take me to a local fair. It's brig
and energetic. The energy hits on a different level. Even t
teens loitering seem laid-back.

I really need a joint.

"Do you mind if I smoke?" I ask them, hoping they wo
get upset. Many people are affronted at the sight of weed, b
it's something that calms me. Just being at an event such
this, my nerves are already frazzled.

"Only if we can join you."

It's such a simple response, but it lights me up inside.

They grab my hands, intertwining our fingers and le
me to the far north side of the amusement park. There's
Ferris wheel over here, a UFO ride, and a fried food shac

The funnel cakes are calling my name, but I'll wait until after I've smoked enough.

We make it toward the ride. Justice pulls out a few hundred dollar bills. "My girl wants to make out with me at the top of the ride. Give us twenty up there."

The ride attendant—a lanky guy in his mid-twenties—smiles at us and nods. "I'll make it thirty."

He lets us pass the rope and opens the little circular seat. After we're seated, he closes the cage, and the ride starts going up. The sky is dark, night has taken over the sky and the stars are invisible with the cloud coverage and air pollution, but I imagine this full moon and the lake that always calls me back home.

My tiny purse nestling my phone and everything else rests against my hip. As I unzip it and grab my lighter, my heart feels at ease. Pulling out my little box with my joints, I smile, and relief fills my lungs. There's something intoxicating about weed in a way that's indescribable.

Flicking my Zippo, I light up right as the ride hits the top. The twins watch my lips wrap around the joint, and the hunger they can't seem to hide presents itself like a promise.

I take a puff and hold it, offering them the smoke.

Pru's hand clasps mine as he leans over, kissing my fingers before wrapping his mouth around it. He sucks in, and his eyes never leave mine. I can't even look toward Justice because Pru's eyes draw me in a hypnotic-like trance.

After he lets out his drag, smoke wafts in the night, and my gaze stays on his strong throat and how much I want to line it with my lips.

"God, you're making it really hard to behave, sweethear Justice's dark voice forces my attention to him. His d imprints his jeans, pressing against the material aggressive He grabs the weed from Pru and takes a hit, but his gaze new wavers from mine.

We're fully stopped at the top, and Just stands and com toward me, crouching onto his knees. The little compartme we're in shakes a bit, and my breathing catches. Heights ha never made me falter, but it's a little different when you're a metal box that could fall and kill us all.

His fingers twiddle the blunt, he passes it back to me his eyes glide up my body appreciatively.

"Spread your thighs, Colt."

"Up here?" I swallow loudly, holding the stick betwe my two fingers while collectively holding my breath anticipation.

"Are you scared of getting caught with my face betwe your thighs, sweetheart?"

I don't nod because the idea itself excites me, even if fe is present, too.

"Open." This time when the single word comes out, i lustful and commanding.

I widen my thighs, and his hands roam the apex of the to my hips, his face full of anticipation. My heartrate pic up. Pru is here. My eyes collide with molten coppery on Like his twin's, they're filled with excitement. He palms h dick through his pants, his face relaxed—high—but it's n just from the weed.

"Smoke, sweetheart. Relax for me while I tongue-fuck you."

As soon as my lips wrap around my joint, he's flipping my skirt up, reaching forward for me. His tongue darts out, teasing my thighs. He traces slowly, taking his sweet time while I lay my head back, inhaling the ecstasy and waiting for him to give me a double dose.

He nips at my panty-clad pussy before pulling them down my legs, and I groan, grinding toward his face, wanting him to take from me, to give me pleasure, and to enjoy every second while his twin watches.

When I take a long drag, he flattens his tongue and laps at the wetness between my thighs. I let out a primal noise. He growls, flicking against my clit, and I cry out and place a hand in his dark hair, loving the softness.

My moans get louder, and I can feel Pru stand before seeing him. He covers my mouth with his as his brother eats me alive, fifty feet above people. The weed all but forgotten, I feel my pleasure building.

He laps at me as Pru takes every filthy whimper from my mouth. Justice's finger enters me, causing me to bow up, silently screaming my pleasure as it builds.

"Come for us, princess. Fall apart for us."

Just sucks on my clit once more, plunging a second finger inside me, curling it just right, and then I'm unraveling, crying out my release and moaning their names as if it's a requirement.

When Just sits up, his face is soaked, and the ravenous

look in his eyes has me crossing my legs, needing frictic
their cocks, anything...

The wheel turns, and I press out my blunt, wanting
take them home.

"Can we skip out?" The inner hussy inside me comes c
to ask the question.

Pru chuckles, but Just's wet face tells me he's on t
same page.

"Home so we can fuck," Just demands.

Before the door shuts behind us, Just lifts me, his finge
digging into my ass as if he can rip me in two just to fill r
up. He sets me on his massive bed—their massive bed—a
I drool as they shrug off their shirts. They come on either si
of me, sandwiching me much like at the Ferris wheel.

Pru kisses my neck, and Just caresses my jaw.

"Want to watch a movie?" Justice asks.

Right now, with them shirtless and my emotions hig
watching TV is the last thing on my mind.

I shake my head and grind back into Pru. When he le
out a husky groan, Justice's eyes flame. Pru's hand finds n
hip and grips tightly. His fingers dig into my piercings, ar
I'm near combustion already.

Justice cradles my jaw with both hands now, bringir
our faces together. Earlier, I had the luxury of tasting Pru ar
letting him devour my mouth. Now as Justice does the sam

I fall into it. His kiss is different. It's more sensual, guided, almost like a lover who wants to peel back every layer as he brings you to completion.

Then there's Pru behind me, gyrating his thick erection across my ass, making my thighs clench with every rotation. Pru's hand roves lower, cupping my heat.

"Fuck," I hiss.

"Have you ever been shared, beautiful?"

Shivers skate over me. The thought sending ripples of pleasure and anticipation over my skin.

"No," I whisper against Justice's lips.

He's moving to my neck and sucking there.

Liar. Jordan and Lux didn't have me at the same time, though. They had me separately in the same room.

"Do you want two cocks in you?" he husks, and his voice takes on the same deep tone it had this morning when they were shirtless.

"Yes," I confirm.

It's been a fantasy for ages—to be fucked by two guys as they both work together to bring me release. I never told the guys that because society seems to believe that being open and exploring with your sexuality makes you a slut.

But women have wants and desires too.

And that's what I want.

Both of them.

At the same time.

Pru bites the tendon that rests where my pulse races, and I moan loudly. That's when Justice moves, and Pru flips me

on my back, removing my skirt in a single beat. His eyes r
over the black lace boy shorts I'm sporting, and his eyes
me up hungrily. He doesn't meet my eyes for a moment as
greedily stares at my tattoos, and hopefully not my scars.

"So fucking hot," he rasps.

Heat licks my face, and I can't help the little grin th
slips through.

"He's right," Justice confirms.

When my eyes meet his, I'm glad I'm sprawled out. I
were standing, he would have made me fall right to his feet
a puddle of heat.

Justice leans over me, helping me up, and then sta
removing my bra and long-sleeved crop top.

Thinking of my arms being exposed scares me, and
stop him.

"What's wrong?" he asks immediately.

"I, uh…" I stumble over the words and reasons in n
head. "Can we just push it up?" I offer.

My arms being exposed isn't on my *ever again* list. May
that's what scared off Ross. No. I shake my head. No, he kiss
them in reverence. He doted on them as if they were beauti
and not ugly. Lux and Jordan didn't pay them a single glan
during our shared night, so maybe they're unnoticeable
everyone else but me.

He raises a pointed brow and concedes, sliding it
to my neck. Then his mouth is on my hip piercings, and I
tongue is swirling around them like he's been training for th
his entire life.

My gaze latches onto Just, and I notice him dropping his jeans. He's bare underneath, and his cock springs forward jutting out proudly. I lick my lips, unable to not think of what he tastes like. As if he knows where my mind lingers, he comes closer.

"Do those pouty lips want my cock?" he asks, and heat flames me when I nod. His face darkens. "I'm not soft and sweet, sweetheart. I like when you choke and cry around me."

I squeeze my legs at the imagery.

Pru hisses. "Fuck, she's hot for it, Just." As Just lines his thick head against my lips, smearing that little bead of cum off his tip onto me like lipstick, Pru lifts my bra and lets out the most satisfied groan.

Just's eyes flick to his. What most people find alluring about my breasts isn't their hefty size or their roundness, but the pierced rosy peaks in the center—this time with loops that are little crowns.

"Jesus fuck," Pru hisses.

At the same time, Just says, "Open wide."

He enters my mouth, inch by inch, and he's so massive that I have to remind myself to relax or I'll gag. Pru takes a nipple into his mouth while Just slowly thrusts in. When I'm bowing into Pru's mouth and moaning around Just's length, he starts going hard. I choke and gasp, all while tears flow freely.

"That's right, beautiful. Cry for me. Let me have those pretty tears." Just rubs my jaw as he thrusts in.

Then, Pru is lowering to my panties. His breath skates over the lace material, making me squirm. He doesn't do

anything but breathe heavily against me. I moan when he la
a rough closed-mouth kiss to me.

"I have a feeling this pussy is going to taste like heav
Colt. Are you going to cry for me?"

I try nodding around Just's length and fail.

"She's divine, Pru," Justice confirms, his hips bucki
toward me.

Pru's mouth wraps around my clit, on the outside
the mesh material, and I scream around Just, trying not
gag. Pru tongues the little metal piercing, but I can't see l
reaction as Just thrusts harder.

He pulls out a moment later, and his mouth is on r
throat, sucking, kissing, and nipping. His brother grinds l
teeth over me and starts gliding his tongue over the materi
I'm a mess of cries as they both work my body like their ov
personal instrument. I feel a pinch on my hips and hear a r
realizing Pru destroyed my panties. For some reason, th
only makes me hotter for him. How the hell did he possit
do that?

Justice shoots up and goes to the night stand, grabbi
two condoms and lube. I've never had anal sex before.

"I-I've…" I stutter.

"Never shared?" Pru asks at the same time as Justice asl
"Anal?"

I'm laughing at how they can have two different questio
while being so in sync elsewhere.

"The second one," I mutter, not wanting to say it.

"Don't worry, princess. I'll be gentle your first time."

First time.

First time.

Does that mean there will be a second?

As if hearing my question, he smirks. "Usually, there isn't, but Pru and I spoke while you napped, and we want to make an exception for you."

I all but moan at the idea. They stopped dating two years ago but want to be with me in some capacity.

"We can't," I murmur, the sadness enveloping me. "School… Mel…"

They groan.

"No sister talk while we're about to fuck you," Pru hisses. "This time is only meant for our cocks and your pussy."

Nodding with a flaming face, I watch as they silently communicate.

"We'll visit. Make the long-distance thing work."

I bite my lip at the prospect, contemplating.

"If that's too much for you, let us know, and we'll just enjoy these few days we have left."

Instead of speaking, I reach for Pru, since he's nearest, and crush my lips against his. He's holding my throat in the next moment and biting my lips as if it'll convince me to agree.

It just might.

He flips me on top of him and slides me down his length. I'm whimpering at the way he stuffs me. He's so big and thick. "I'm going to take this hot cunt of yours while Justice takes your ass. He's much gentler."

I look at Justice while he licks his lips and wonder if this

337

is the best idea. Lust clouds my brain and Pru thrusts up in me, making me cant my hips.

"You're meant to ride a cock, princess," he growls befc he flattens his palm on my stomach, gliding it slowly upwar When he reaches my nipples, he tugs and massages one aft another as I writhe on top.

Adjusting, Justice pushes me forward, guiding me so r ass is at his disposal. "We need to loosen you up," he direc "Don't bust a nut too early, Pru."

Prudence rolls his eyes, and I laugh. He seems offend by the thought.

Justice kneads my cheeks and begins spreading the wider. I moan when I feel his finger rubbing the pad of my ho He's gentle and teasing, making me practically wiggle for mo Then, I feel wetness and realize it's not lube. It's his mouth.

"Oh, fuck," I moan.

"Ah, shit," Pru grunts. "Whatever you're doing, bro, do stop. She's gripping my cock like a fucking vise."

He thrusts up into me as his brother slides his tong against my untouched flesh. Just's tongue pushes through tl ring, and I'm practically screaming.

"Fuck," Pru hisses. "Fuck, you're tight and fuckir drenched."

Pru brings his fingers to my clit and starts working n and playing with my piercing at the same time. After I'm literal mess of wetness and moans, Justice starts pushing finger in. When I tighten around him, he kisses my throat ar bites my ear.

"Relax, princess. Can't fuck you gently if you're gripping my finger this tightly."

I try to breathe, loosening up.

He bites my shoulder. "That's a good girl."

His tongue works magic against my skin, and his teeth mark me. I'm writhing on top of Pru, unable to help the way my body melts beneath their touch.

After it gets smoother, he's thrusting in tandem with his brother and I'm grinding for more friction. "Just like that, princess."

Then he's adding another, and the pinch only lasts a second before I'm humping Pru, wanting more, to feel fuller.

"She's a slut for us," Pru growls, holding my hips tightly.

That word.

It brings my thoughts to Lux, his name for me, his commands, and dirty talk. Somehow, he's here in the room with me, watching while leaning against the wall. My clit throbs at the imagery.

Pru's fingers dig into my sensitive flesh. There will be marks there tomorrow, and the thought only makes me needier. My pussy pulsates with desperation, and my body feels like it's on fire, ready to explode at any moment.

When I'm adjusted enough, Justice replaces his fingers with his thick length, and I whimper at the pressure. Pru grabs at my clit, swirling the pad of his thumb against it. Tears rush down my cheeks at all the sensations, and Justice fully seats himself inside me.

"Fucking hell," he grunts. When he twists my head to

take my mouth, my pussy gets wetter, beating like it's ready
cry, too. "Told you that you'd cry for me, princess."

He starts moving behind me, and I can feel them both insi
me. I've never felt fuller or more at ease. They work in tande
and I'm literally a sobbing mess of moans and whimpers.

"Fuck," Pru grinds out, thumbing my nub. "You're perfe
Colt, so fucking perfect. Your tight little body was made
take two cocks at once."

I cry out as my orgasm comes with several delibera
strokes. My body hums with so much fervor, I feel like I
dreaming, but Pru doesn't stop his ministrations. He pulls
my ring and pinches my clit, making me vibrate.

"I want you to explode on my cock, beautiful. I want
feel your wet juices soak me, okay?"

I nod as he works me, fucks me. Justice picks up his pac
and I'm practically ready to detonate.

"I'm going to come," Justice warns.

Pru bucks upward, fucking me so hard I see stars
clench, and then I'm squirting all over him. Justice grunts o
and stills inside me. As soon as that happens, Pru bucks in
me like he'll never have me again. Justice pulls out, leaving n
feeling empty. Prudence grips my tits, flipping us so he's c
top. He rams into me, and all I can do is hold on.

"Squeeze me, baby."

And I do. I fucking clench while he ruts a few more tim
before he's cursing my name in release.

"So fucking hot," he rasps, pulling out.

Both guys pull off their condoms, tying them off, ar

then Justice is carrying me to the huge jet tub in their shared bathroom. He runs the water, and I smile.

"You're the best of both worlds," I admit. "Fucks hard, cares harder."

Justice winks and brings our lips together. "Don't go spreading rumors, Colt. Can't have the world knowing I have a weak spot for emo chicks who ride cocks like a champ."

I blush but can't help the smile. "Think so?"

"Oh, sweetheart. I'm pretty sure if I wanted to fuck again, I couldn't. You know how to satisfy a guy." He kisses me one more time before leaving. He comes back with a bottle of bubble bath and adds it in. "Now, relax. Your ass is bound to be hurting."

The throbbing makes itself aware at his words. I'm not sure what the hell just transpired, but I feel a twinge in my chest making itself known. Feelings shouldn't grow this fast, yet here they are.

CHAPTER THIRTY-FOUR

After they bathe me together, both of them stuffing themselv[es] in the tub with me, I feel content. It's sweet and kind a[nd] makes me wonder why the dicks at Arcadia still get to r[un] since these two aren't jerks like that. They massage me, cle[an] me, and after they carry me out of the tub, I take a nap [in] both their arms. It isn't until a yelling Mel wakes me up tha[t I] realize this vacation wasn't about me. It was for her.

I'm probably a shitty friend.

"You've got to be fucking joking!" she hisses. I[n] exacerbated anger.

The sun shines through, and I know it's the following da[y.] Which means she was gone for over a day. With *hi[m.]* Images of her with Bridger infiltrate my cloudy mind, and [I] can't give a single fuck. I'll conduct the train all the way

Pettyville free of charge.

That's when it dawns on me. Being fucked, cuddled, and doted on by these two didn't stop my jealousy. I still want Bridger.

The guys don't care. I can see their expression.

"Not sure why you're mad. You're the one who ditched her to fuck some loser," Just barks.

He's not a loser.

Just a sociopath.

She growls and marches to the bed. "She's my best friend, not your fuck toy experiment."

"Mel," I chide. "It's okay. It was a one-time thing. It won't happen again."

"You're right. It won't. We're leaving."

My eyes widen. Shit. She must be pissed. "I'm sorry. I didn't mean to—"

"Stop. I get it. They're hot, and you were lonely. It happens." She glares at them. "But you two know the rules. My friends are off-limits. Find someone else."

"No," they both argue in unison, and I flinch.

"Colt is ours," Justice barks.

"No, she fucking isn't," Mel bites back.

"Yes, she is, and we'll be damned if you fuck up our happiness," Prudence jabs.

She balks while I sit in silence, hiding my face in my knees. Justice puts a reassuring hand on my back, rubbing up and down while Pru holds my hand under the blanket. They're too sweet, too kind. It's throwing me off.

"This is fucking ridiculous. Come on, Colt. We're goi
home."

I want to protest, to fight, but she brought me he
and it isn't fair to not be her friend first. I start to get up a
remember my lack of clothes. Mel closes her eyes and turns
walk out the door. "Get dressed. Wheels up in an hour."

With those parting words, she slams the door.

"Well, that went well," I joke.

"You're ours, Colt. Please, let's try," Pru begs, grippi
my chin.

He pulls me in for a kiss, his mouth warming me fro
the inside out. Then Justice pulls me to him and takes r
mouth right after, biting my lip for good measure.

"Can I think about it?" I ask, already knowing wha
want but not wanting to decide yet.

"Anything for you, beautiful," Pru murmurs.

"As long as you give us your number," Justice adds.

I laugh.

Rising from the bed, I get a smack on each ass cheek fro
both twins. They smirk at each other and then me.

"Get dressed, and apparently, head out."

They both jump up and ravage me, kissing and bitir
and I'm so close to staying so they can pump several orgasr
out of me for the road. They walk me to my room after I'
dressed and plug their numbers into my phone. I can't help t
warm and fuzzy feeling that zips through me at the thoug
of being with them, even if only on occasion.

"Before you go," I say, "can you make me a promise?"

They give me a skeptical look before they nod.

"No fucking that Ronnie chick."

Neither laugh, which I appreciate, and then they both crowd me. "No fucking that Bridger dude," Pru demands.

I never said his name.

That tingles a memory from the other night, but it's too fuzzy to grasp on to.

"Deal."

They both hold me—one to my back, one to my front.

"And, princess?"

I look at Pru.

"No fucking anyone. You're ours. This pussy…" He reaches down to cup the inside of my sweats. "Is ours and *only* ours."

I moan as he moves his fingers against my already swollen nub.

"And these," Pru adds, grabbing my tits then touching my lips and then finally my ass. "All of this is ours too. We aren't fond of sharing."

I nod at them and feel so many things, but cared for is on the top of that list.

"Except with each other," Justice adds.

"Hope you like swallowing your own words. You better do the same." I mean it to sound like a joke, but it comes off a little possessive, and my face heats at it.

"We will," they both say at once.

Then they're kissing me one last time and heading out the door.

"Until next time," Justice says as I'm waving.

It doesn't take long to pack, and then I'm in search of Mel.

She doesn't talk to me when I reach her, and really can't blame her, but at the same time, I want to know ho far she and Bridger went, and hate that any part of me car

We drive to their private air strip and are wheels within an hour, like she said. While we're in the air, I bre the silence.

"Are you really going to not talk to me?"

She rubs the bridge of her nose and her forehead befo peering at me. "I'm just annoyed. This isn't the first time th coerced my friends into their bed."

"They didn't—"

"Either way, I just didn't think you of all people wou fall for their traps."

"Wow," I mutter, incredulous. "You think I'm just a t for them?"

"That's how they work. I'm not sure why you didn't liste

"Maybe I felt sad and alone. Ever think of that?" I bite o

She looks at me and nods. "Doesn't change the fact th they're my brothers. Not only do I want to protect them, I' looking out for you."

"I know you care, but you were too busy with Bridger notice that being alone is fucking depressing."

She lets out a noise. "I was."

My interest isn't in the details. It's only stuck on one thing: did they fuck?

"Did you lose it?" I ask, knowing she'll understand the innuendo.

She bites her lips, her face red and flamed like an unripe cherry.

"You fucked him?" I nearly cry but coat it enough to seem mildly upset.

I'm not upset with her, just the circumstance. If I'd told her that he was mine, this would be a non-issue. I would have, if I felt I had the right to. The problem with Bridger is, he was never and will never be mine.

"Does it matter? Why do you care?"

Bees flurry inside me, stabbing my insides as I roll over her non-answer. The need to punch her rises. I'm not always violent, but right now, I could push her off this jet and smile as her body splat on the concrete.

"I care because he's mine," I hiss, hating my mistake immediately.

Her mouth falls open. Clearly, I threw her off as her head tilts at the information. "Excuse me?" she asks hotly.

"Bridger is my fourth guy from that night where they all asked me to the dance."

"The one you said *didn't* matter?"

"I lied!"

She balks. "You... lied..." Anger overcomes her normally nice expression. "What the fuck is wrong with you, Colt? I told you I liked him. You let me be around him? When he's part of

347

whatever fucked up thing you have going on?"

"And I told you to stay away!' I yell, hating her in t
moment.

She touched him.

She fucked what's mine.

I hate him.

I hate her because of him.

I hate, hate, hate, hate, hate.

My stomach is in knots and uncomfortable. They
this to me.

This shouldn't matter.

"Fuck this!" she hisses and gets up, moving to a se
across the jet.

I try to hold in the jealousy and ridiculousness of it al
don't own them, and they don't own me. We're nothing.

A couple hours later, she finally looks at me and attemp
to conversate. "I'm sorry I freaked out. Dad pissed me off
badly, saying I was being irresponsible and shit, and he ma
me want to leave. Even though my brothers and you did t
dirty, he's why we're going home. He didn't even fight me
it. But fuck you for not telling me."

"I'm so sorry."

She looks at me with disappointment, but it's almost li
she's used to it.

"It's okay. We will figure this out. At least now I wo

have to feel like shit when I'm not returning for winter and spring break."

I nod, knowing I'll be locking myself up in my room then. That's the worst time for me. I shut down and have to keep the pain at bay, and when it isn't there, I hurt myself and leave new marks to scar for later. Scars are meant to bleed, but they'll always heal eventually, even if the residual pain stays.

"I'm just not stoked for the next semester. I'm not sure how I survived this one," I surmise.

"Technically, you haven't. Your grades aren't the best."

I scrunch at her words. "I know. My parents will either not give a shit, or they'll set me up with a tutor."

She cringes. "Let's hope not. You don't take the shit I take. It won't be easy to help you out."

I nod, hating that she's right.

We chat about our classes and how finals are in the next six weeks. Neither of us are excited, but we're going to just go with the flow and hope we don't drown. The worst part? We are both crushing on the same guy and it's like the plane argument didn't happen. We just drop the fact we had our first fight.

The jet lands, and we're being shipped off to Arcadia.

"Think your driver will let us stop in town?" I ask.

"Maybe?"

He does, and I get a hair touch-dup while Mel cuts her hair in a shoulder-length bob. She's so fucking beautiful it's daunting. I want to be happy for her and Bridger. She deserves happiness, but thinking of her with him makes me want to commit murder, and it's not his murder I'm envisioning.

If she dies, she dies.

My heart beats erratically at that. It's irrational, isn't

She and I stop at the market store and stack up on ju

food. We're set for the next couple weeks. Maybe then, l

brothers—my new boyfriends?—will have sent us more.

By the time we're back on campus, I'm ready to pass t

fuck out. It's not even five in the afternoon, but it feels li

two days have passed, and I'm slowly dying.

She walks me to my room, and then we hug before s

leaves.

When I open the door, I'm not prepared for who is

the other side.

"Fuck."

"Fuck is right."

CHAPTER THIRTY-FIVE

"What are you doing here?" I hiss, glaring at Ross. Why is he in my room? I haven't even been here in nearly five days!

"Wanted to warn you," he responds, his shoulders tight, his face stiff.

"And? Out with it."

He places his hands in his pockets, his body oozing nervousness, but he doesn't say anything.

"I'm serious. If you're not going to spill whatever you need to spill, I'm going to hurt you."

"Don't go to the Winter Assembly."

I think of it. The staff usually splits it between doing a talent show and an award show type thing for the highest-ranking students. They're smart and don't tell you when the talent portion and when the reward portion is, so people are

C.L. MATTHEWS

forced to sit it out or lose the chance. It's not for another three weeks. He shouldn't be worried.

"Why the hell not?" I ask.

Not that I care. Nothing there appeals to me except when someone decides to try out their stripper pole skills.

"Just don't, Colton. Please."

Not Greenie, Vamp, or Corpse. Simply, Colton. What the fuck is going on?

"If you're not going to tell me why, I'm not going to avoid going to an assembly for you." I wasn't planning on going anyway, but he's making me nervous as hell. I've just gotten back from my trip, and he's sitting here warning me, but not telling me what's wrong or giving me a valid reason.

"Fuck, Colt!" Ross grabs his hair that's grown since school started. It's darker now, his natural roots showing through. He runs his fingers through it. The stress apparent on his face worries me, but I'm not sure what to say about it. "I'm trying to save you."

"You can't," I whisper. "I'm already dead."

His eyes lock onto mine, those greens practically bleeding. He's trying to level with me, tell me something, but unless those lips move, I can't be sure what it is.

"Don't go."

"My parents will be here." I'm telling the truth. They come every year. It's an alumni thing. "If I don't show, they notice."

His eyes widen. "A better reason to not show up."

"Don't say you guys are going Carrie on me," I joke

352

mean, come on. That was a weak attempt at being a dick, even back then.

His face darkens. "Don't say I didn't warn you," he hisses.

I'm struck stupid. Why is he being secretive, and why does it scare the shit out of me? I've been gone half of fall break. He shouldn't be here, yet he is. Why?

"Why are you here?" I ask. "Fall break doesn't end for another few days."

"I never left," he mentions, scratching his nose.

Never left? Something about those words scare me more than him pushing me to stay away.

"Why is that, Ross? Out of the five of you, you have the best home life."

He scoffs, rolling his eyes. It's such a boyish look for him that it throws me off.

"Yeah, a mom who drinks so much she doesn't know how to live, and a father who fucks every whore in Arcadia. Just dandy."

"I didn't say perfect, Dare. I said best out of all of us."

The sardonic laugh that leaves him gives me chills.

"You're so fucking blind to everything, Colton. You show up to Arcadia this year and act like you're supposed to be tough because Cass can't protect you anymore. And guess what? You aren't seeing the bigger picture, the things happening on the outside."

"You're being cryptic, and it isn't cute," I bite out, feeling my body's turmoil. I spent an entire night with the twins. They didn't let me sleep because they wanted to feel every inch of

353

me. Now, I'm supposed to try to absorb all the bullshit R
is spewing.

"Do you think the Emeralds are a secret for nothing?"
asks.

His question takes me back to the night of fake initiatic
to the scare tactic, to Bridger being with Mel, to the wei
Latin book that made zero sense, and to the way I left feeli
like I tumbled down Alice's Wonderland hole and wonderi
what the fuck happened.

It wasn't pretty.

This entire fucked up mess is confusing.

"Why did you fuck me?" I ask. "Why did you disappe
and pretend it didn't happen?" My tone shows the hurt, and
almost hate it.

Don't fuck Bridger, I hear the twins' voices in my hea
telling me I'm theirs. *Don't fuck anyone.*

Ross looks at me with a keen awareness, sadness filli
each pore, and it's unsettling.

"I can't be here." He shoves past me.

He can't even have a heart to fucking heart? Are y
joking?

"You're dead to me, Dare. Don't come back here."

His eyes latch onto mine one more time before he gra
the door knob. "After the assembly, that'll actually be true."

He slams the door after he exits, and I'm shaking fro
head to toe. It's not adrenaline or fear. It's pure unbridled rag
Something in him sets me off.

I grab the thing closet to me, which so happens to be r

Jack Skellington diffuser, and heave it at the wall. It splinters, cracking against sheetrock. The hiss of it when it lands makes me angrier. Nothing in my path is safe as I start throwing everything. The stuff off my TV stand, gone. The magazines, newspapers, and coasters on my coffee table, destroyed. My table aside the door, which holds all my pictures on the floor.

That's when the tears come, and my body thrums with despair. On the ground, where it should never be, is the photo of Cass and me. He has his arm around my neck as he whoops. I'd just made an acrylic painting that made it to national galleries. It was my depiction of the world from an elite person's view versus the view from someone who had nothing. It was separated by a metal grate, showing how the worlds could easily collide with each other even while worlds apart. The girls mirroring each other placed their palms against the border, their torture visible, silent, treacherous.

Cassidy's smile is happy, his face alight with humor and excitement. He was my biggest supporter. He dreamed harder for me, pushed me, and didn't let anything get in the way of my goals.

The tears come in heaps. They're swallowing me, drowning me, pulling me under the weight of their sadness and despair, taking and taking, hoping I'll suffocate.

"Why didn't I listen to you, Cass?" I stare at the image and the light that is no longer in those eyes, and sob for what feels like hours.

I didn't plan this, coming home and fucking breaking.

The plan was simple. Make it to winter break and see

my boys again. The twins are already distracting me. Thinki
I could ever find a shred of happiness when this place is
own personal hell was a bit of a stretch.

It's not where I want to be anymore.

Being in a loving environment for a steady few d
changed me.

It's insane how one single memory that could easily
swept under the rug is the driving force to making me wa
to leave here.

What if I ran?

Could I make it to Tennessee and survive?

Would the twins even want me?

I pull my phone out of my bra and unlock it. My ey
are met with a photo of the twins blowing me a kissy fac
laugh while tears still wet my face. They must have chang
my screen saver when they put their numbers in.

Immediately, a wave of despair fills me. I miss the
Their warmth. Their love. The way they touched my he
without doing more than being nice.

It's sad that they made me feel things so quickly and
unraveled just as fast.

I miss you guys, I send, creating a group chat for us thr

Immediately, two messages pop through.

*God, I've been waiting for you to text. We didn't get yo
number, princess.*

I laugh at Pru's message.

How much do you miss me?

Just's makes me feel warm in every way that matters.

Enough that I haven't packed or showered because I'd rather be talking to y'all.

Dots form and disappear and form and disappear. Repeat. Repeat. Repeat.

Does this mean you're going to sext us?

Of course, that's where Pru's head goes.

Not sure. Maybe you can convince me. I taunt, wondering if they're together. They probably are. They're attached at the hip.

If you two sext while I'm working, I'm going to be pissed. Justice's anger is palpable even through words.

Warmth spreads through me.

You're just jealous you can't jerk while you're with dad. I have no qualms at home. Alone. Lonely. Needing my girl.

Our girl, Justice corrects.

My dick is hard, Prudence sends back to the chat.

Mine too, asshole, Justice responds.

I'm sitting in a mess next to my room door, and all I can think about is how light my chest feels with these two consuming me completely.

Are you ignoring me, beautiful?

I can't help but smile at Pru's question.

I'm just enjoying your banter. Pretty sure it's turning me on.

I'm not pretty sure. I'm absolutely positive. Being fought over by two guys is hot, especially after our night together.

Fuck, they both text at the same time.

Which we definitely would if you weren't halfway across the world, but semantics. Pru sends a meme of someone saying *whyyyyy* all dramatically.

I giggle, and then another escapes me when Justice ser a side-eye emoji.

Imagine if you were both here, I'd be naked and probably fill Twice, I continue to torture. Problem is, it's me who's sad shit with the knowledge that they're so far.

Where are you? Justice asks.

On my living room floor.

Well, get that pretty ass up and get on your bed, princess.

My body melts with his message. I stand and lie on t bed in the next moment.

Then what?

Pull down those fishnets and take your panties with you.

I'm molten with his commands, wanting to be in t same room. But where is Pru? He disappeared.

Where's Pru?

Probably getting lubed up for some play time. Are you witho panties, sweetheart?

I nod and then realize he can't see me. *Yes.*

I want you to take those fingers and slide them down your boc Make sure to stop at those perky nipples and squeeze them for n Flick those dangling crowns for me too.

My hands grip my breasts through the material of n hoodie, and I cry out, remembering how they felt being tugg on by both Justice and Pru. My left hand lowers to my pus while my other stays on my breasts.

I bet you're so drenched for us. Justice knows the art sexting. That's for sure.

Tell us how wet you are, Pru finally responds, and my heart races.

Soaked, I moan when I rub the wetness around my clit.

Are you touching that pretty pussy, Colton? Pulling on that little hood piercing of yours?

I am. He's right. I pull on the little ring as pleasure zips through me.

Yes. It's all I can respond because I'm a goddamn mess.

That's when my phone starts to ring. Picking it up, I let out a sigh. "Hello."

"Hello, darlin'," Justice's voice rings through while I put it on speaker. It's husky and warm. His southern drawl is something I already miss.

"Hi, beautiful," I hear Pru say a second later.

"We're like nineties kids, three-ways," I jest.

"Don't say three-ways when my dick is this close to fucking combusting."

"I meant the call." I laugh. "But I'm down for that too."

One of them groans, and I feel my body only getting hotter.

"Are you touching yourself?" Justice asks.

"Yes," I breathily admit, not that he doesn't already know.

"Well, since my dick is going to be aching from the blue balls I'm bound to have after this phone call, you better yell my name."

"She's going to yell mine, actually," Pru comments.

I'm stifling a laugh. Having them argue over me is an ego boost I didn't realize I needed.

"Don't listen to him, Colt. Touch that wet cunt a
imagine it's us finger-fucking you."

I start rubbing over my clit and moan into the phone.

"That's right, beautiful. Let me hear you," Pru says or
groan.

Knowing he's touching himself with me while halfw
across the country has me literally panting.

"If I were there, I'd be eating that messy pussy while y
begged me for more."

I hiss as Just's words make me throb. I'm so fucking clo
to my orgasm.

"And while he ate you out, I'd be biting those supple t
and grinding my dick all over you."

"Ah, fuck," I moan.

"That's right, princess. Now tug those nipples for us. I
us hear you."

"Fuck, fuck, fuck," I chant as I rub myself and pin
myself at the same time.

"Shit," Prudence hisses, his voice near guttural. You c
hear the wet sounds of both of us moving.

"Now stick two fingers in you, baby. Use that thumb
your clit," Justice says, his voice so low and pained. "Imagi
I'm working you up to sink inside you."

I whimper and do as he says, letting out a long moan.

He clears his throat as if he's having a hard tir
swallowing. "By now, I'd be done and your cum would be in r
mouth. I'd be kissing from your inner thighs, biting each sto
and then hovering above you before I rammed inside you."

I can feel my climax rising, making my forehead sweat.

"Then I'd fuck you, sliding in and out, pounding into those tight walls until you screamed.

"After you wet my cock from that second orgasm, I'd fuck into you until my balls ached."

I'm a mess of moans, slick as I slide against my clit harder and harder, loving the intense warmth building inside me.

"Then I'd explode inside you. Since we were so worked up, we forgot a condom, and my seed would fill you to the brim. You'd shake from the intensity, crying out because you want more."

That's all it takes before I'm moaning both their names and shuddering from head to toe. My body quivers through my orgasm as I hear Prudence grunt his release.

"Fuck," he hisses. "That was so fucking hot."

"Yeah," I say, my vocal cords strained.

"Now, go take a shower, princess. We'll see you in a couple weeks."

"I miss you," I tell them.

"We miss you too. Don't forget our promise," Pru adds.

"Don't forget yours," I tease.

Then I hang up on them and shower.

That was a much-needed stress reliever.

CHAPTER THIRTY-SIX

JORDAN

Determination of death, do you know what that consists
Did your mind travel to an autopsy table? Maybe a TV sho
you watched which showed you your first experience of t
table where they carved up a human. Or maybe it was tho
words "cause of death." It's weird, isn't it? How our min
travel to the familiar, even if it's gruesome.

Determination of death.

What it consists of for me is the night where everythi
changed. Dead. Deceased. Heart beats no longer.

It wasn't supposed to happen. Not the death, not the la
of life, not the aftermath or the fall, but you never realize wl
you're about to lose until the loss has already risen.

One night changed my life. Our lives. Everyone's.

"What are you doing here?" Cassidy hisses. His pale hair see

frailer, thinner, almost a whisper to the wind, but he's fierce, even with his sunken cheeks and sharp jaw.

But something has changed. He won't tell me. Usually, he tells me everything like the little gossipmonger he is.

"Well?"

The way he pushes the words at Ridge has me shaken. It's not like Cassidy to be the aggressor. He's brutal when necessary. It's his protective trait, but he's anything but reckless.

Ridge doesn't take threats well. He's not soft. Nor is he stony. He's nothing.

If you could carve a box to reveal its secrets, slowly shredding down each inch until it was a masterpiece of pretty divots and edges, it would become nonexistent by the time you realized there are no emotions or motives to uncover.

Ridge—as all of us call him—is something else.

He would be scary if not for the way he softens for a certain little sister of Cassidy's. I once thought he didn't have a heart. I mean, how could he when he's emotionless?

Somehow though, one beats. Even if only for one girl.

"Don't ignore me, asshole!" *Cassidy's voice rises, the loudness breaking the stale air with a newfound tension.*

It's just us three—Ridge, Cass, and me. We're in the main gathering hall in Crystal Tower. Colt doesn't know, but this is where the Emeralds live. We meet at the cabin's basement, but this place in the tower is where we coalesce. This entire floor is our dedicated living space. Not only is it off-limits to everyone, it's nearly a secret. Hell, she doesn't even know I exist. I'm a shadow. The darkness in the late of night. Danger lurking in wait for the right time.

I'm a plot.

A ploy.

Their *weapon.*

"I'm here because we have business to see to," Bridger answ
with indifference. He places his hands against the railing, lean
against it. His face, as impassive as ever, doesn't even twitch wh
Cassidy comes closer.

"Business? Tonight is a Crystallites party at the cabin. Nothin
going to happen."

I stare at them both. I've heard stirrings. Bloodlines talk, a
the Grims have been practically vocalizing theirs. There's a ba
between the two oldest families—the Grims and the Marchett
Neither have kids our age, which means I'm the closest in line j
leading the Emeralds. The Grims—the oldest founding family, w
also has ties across the world—held the most secrets, dark ones, all
which terrify me. My father wasn't a saint. He got his hands dir
Like many—if not every*—founding family, he's a killer, but ev*
my old man knows his power doesn't compare to the Grims' Empi
They're so secretive they've been erased from the books.

There's been whispers amongst the adults at their charit
and galas that they're thinking of taking over Emerald busine
corrupting it once more, turning it into what it was created for.

There's a problem with this, though. Generations ago, t
founding families swept out three generational bloodlines, severi
their ties to the cause. This means all Emeralds and kids born sin
aren't fully aware of the past, not unless they read Limpieza *
Sangre*. It's the contract, really; the story of stories, all of them—t*
beginnings, the middles, and the ends.

"What are you dickbags doing?" Ross yells, walking through the room like he's annoyed.

"Cass is being a little bitch," I muse aloud, holding my spot as the bitter bitch of the group. That's what my father asked of me. It's what Mother expects, but most of all, it's what I pretend to be. If not, I would fail, and in my family, failing is the equivalent of a death sentence.

It's why I only have a little sister left. No one knows of Maximilian. It's as if he never existed.

"You're just mad you don't get to be the spotlight unless we're here," Cass bites, his eyes narrowing on me. Then they go to Ross, and Cass' blue crystals almost darken, hatred seeping out of them like venom.

"Aw, is poor little Hudson mad Rossy-boy dicks his sister?"

Cassidy's gaze bounces to mine, disdain dripping from every tired line on his face. What changed? He used to be able to hand it back to me. Unlike what everyone thinks of the star athlete, he's ruthless when it comes to those he loves. He doesn't cower, and he's the least weak link.

Ross throws his hands up. "I haven't—"

"Shut the fuck up, McAllister," Cass seethes, spittle leaving his mouth. "Let's get this shit over with. Gregor wants us at Site L early tomorrow. No drinking. No drugs." He glares at Bridger and Ross, then lands his eyes on me. "And no fucking touching Colton. She's off-limits."

"Aye, sir," I mock with a two-finger salute.

He scoffs and pushes past me. His sweat permeates the air, like a fog of tension. It's weird. He's been distant. Not the

boy I'd met before, but a new kind of tired, restless, and dec
to-the-world replacement.

When he leaves, I peer at Bridger. "What is happen.
with him?"

His eyes take on a different darkness, one he hides w
in front of others. He's a charmer when he wants to be, but
all know he's a sociopath in a good boy's human suit.

"Stay in your lane, Jordan, and keep an eye on Col
He stares at Ross. "You fuckers can't keep her safe alone. Y
tend to get distracted by pussy too easily."

This time, it's Ross who scoffs.

There's a battle here, one I've stayed far away from, l
what they don't know is that even if you win the battle, the w
hasn't even begun, and the girl isn't the prize for any.

"Keep your eyes peeled," Ross mutters to n
"Something doesn't feel right about tonight.

I stare at him. For the first time, I see it, the fear. Li
Cassidy's sweat, it's almost surrounding me, teasing the c
warning us all.

Too bad none of us listened.

I shake my head at the memory of Cassidy's last nig
We never truly saw eye-to-eye. The only reason he tolerat
me was because I never touched or went after Colt. It was
for lack of wanting. It was merely for the inability.

They had their rules, and as the ruling bloodline, I h
mine.

"She's back," Lux mutters.

I peer up at him, pretending I've been working on r

finals like I should be, but my mind keeps traveling to what was said to Colt right after we fucked her. *"Such a little slut. Fucking two guys in her brother's old room. On his old bed…"*

We've kept our distance since. Not by choice, either.

She's up to something. It's in the way she watches us and thinks we don't notice. Her friend, Melissa, isn't any less invasive. The difference between them is, Colt has all the power and the keys to the Emeralds' kingdom. She only has to use them correctly.

"Where'd she go?" I ask.

She disappeared for Thanksgiving. No warning. I left because Father required it. Lux left, too, to stay with me. Midas DeLeon isn't one for holidays with his sons. They usually vacation with my family. Lux and I ditched early, told them we had emergency school shit.

They believed us, but what they didn't know is what we planned.

"How the fuck are we going to be able to sneak in now?" The question leaves my lips in a curse.

Lux stares at me. "Why did you bring us to Cassidy's room?" he counters. His face is hardened.

Lux and I are always at war. He's the grenade, and I'm the pin who forces him to detonate. If not for me, he would be leading the Emerald Vestige. He would be ruling the school, but without me, he would fail.

"You could have stopped me," I point out.

"I didn't know that's where you were leading us. Ten's room is the last one on the left. I figured you were getting back

at him and going there. Now, answer me. Why did you ta
us there?"

He walks toward me, no aggression, just insolence. H
not happy, but he's unwilling to play all his cards. We wou
never survive if we ever went at it full-on. He's tumultuo
I'm reckless. We're a waiting disaster, but fuck, if he does
confuse the fuck out of me sexually. Before him, I did
question my preferences once. He's not my type. For one,
has a dick, and it never appealed to me in the least. Yet, h
somehow changed that for me.

"Tell me why it matters?" I ask, even though I know wh
It's the desire to hear him say it which drives me because
all know I won't.

"Why? He's fucking dead, Walker. Dead as a fucki
doornail." His chest puffs with angry drags of oxygen,
while his face contorts in pain.

Like me, he wasn't expecting the death of Cassidy. No
of us planned for bloodshed. We were supposed to distra
Colton. That's it. No one should've died.

"You're right. He fucking died, but that didn't stop y
from torturing Colt. It didn't deter you from fucking her ra
and it sure as hell didn't push you to tell me no, so what h
you so up in arms, Lennox? Is it because you're mad we we
in a dead man's room, or that you had to share her with me

His nostrils flare as he sucks in a ragged breath.

"Isn't that why we all hate each other, even while bei
brothers?" I ask.

"You are not my brother," he hisses.

"Why? Since I wasn't raised alongside you and the others, or because you want to fuck me? It's not my fault Maxim was here while I'd been in the dark. He could be here, and you'd be fine, wouldn't you?" I pester, and Lux growls, fisting his palms. "What, Lennox? Is the Saint of Arcadia finally cracking under pressure?"

He rushes me then, forcing me on my back. After ripping the book from my lap, he tosses it against the wall. "Shut the fuck up, Walker."

He fists my shirt's collar, the bed sinking from our shared weight, his face inches from mine, venom in his eyes and redness tinting his heated cheeks. He's always so well put together—the saint, the savior, the student body president.

"Tell me, DeLeon. Is the only reason why you hate me because of how much my older brother fucked you, and now you see his face when looking at me?"

He lets me go, his face falling with my words. The indent of him lightens, as if along with his speech, his soul's weight leaves him too.

"Guess you weren't aware that he told me everything," I add.

"I didn't even know you fucking existed," he spits, his face full of disdain. "You were the black sheep, the outcast, *unwanted*."

I smile. He's ruffled. His poor soft boy feathers are being plucked one by one, and he's not prepared for the massacre I'm about to cause.

"Yeah, I've always been the weak one to Father, but that's

not true. I didn't want to be involved. Maxim craved pow
craved blood, and craved you."

Lennox stiffens, his face one without emotions. "He di
anyway."

"Yet you never speak of his name."

"Seeing you is bad enough," he hisses through clench
teeth. The tick in his jaw appeals to me more and more eve
day, the sharpness from him. When Maxim was taken fro
Lennox, he changed. He hardened.

"Is it only bad since you can't have what you've alwa
wanted?" I ask.

"Fuck off," he barks, his face morphing into a longin;
feel deep in my chest.

I sit back up, bringing myself right to Lennox. When
turns his face back to me, I strike. Grabbing his jaw, I force I
lips to mine. He pushes me back, his eyes filled with a barra
of emotions. My chest rises and falls, crashing against t
shores of my ribs.

Then, he's pushing into me. His lips connect with mine
a furious takeover. He bites hard, the split forming soon aft
Blood as rusty and bitter as ever fills my senses. That's how
will be for us, rouge battlegrounds to lay our swords upon ai
paint them effervescent before the true war begins.

His tongue swipes against me, tasting the shared flavor
our loathing. It's bitter and sweet, a delicious combination
hate and lust. His hand wraps around my throat as we both low
back onto the bed. His legs box my hips in, and when I thru
against him, he growls like a beast untamed. He can act unfaze

get pissed, and even yell profanities until he can't see straight, but as our mouths demolish one another, there's no denying we both have pent-up issues only we have the answers to.

When we break apart, he jumps off me as if I've stabbed him. He wipes the remnants of my blood from his mouth with his perfectly messed-up button up, smearing the color around like paint. Then, he smirks and grimaces all at once.

"Don't ever fucking kiss me again, Walker. You're not Maxim, and you never will be."

"Your dick doesn't seem to be able to tell the difference," I mock, pointing at his tented slacks, "but don't worry, Lennox. If I wanted your ass, I'd take it."

His eyes narrow before he turns away.

When he slams the door to my room, I touch my lips, feeling the swell of them. My fingers graze the cut and feel the blood coating them. I'll bed Lennox in due time, but he won't be my only victory. A green-haired she-devil is on my list, too.

Fuck the *Limpieza de Sangre.* Purifying the blood won't happen until we find out who killed Cassidy, and since none of the guys seem to know, we're stuck wondering who the Judas is and if we'll survive another betrayal.

Trust no one, my father always says. *Rise above. Slaughter those who contend. Never, ever disgrace the family name.*

What's another mark against me? Maxim didn't die for anything special. He died because he liked sticking his dick in Lennox DeLeon.

The difference between my brother and I? I'll never get caught.

CHAPTER THIRTY-SEVEN

"Tonight?" Mel asks, two weeks later, as she's scrolli
through her phone.

I stare at her from the space at my desk. I'm doing r
final for Psych, and I've got to explain why Jeffrey Dahm
decided to eat people, but how do I explain a person's moti
when it seemed to be a brain dysfunction rather than t
desire to consume human flesh?

"Winter break isn't for another week," I mention, r
knowing where her head space is.

"They just announced on the Arcadia Post that they
leaving for a Student Government meeting for funding."

"What do they need funding for?" I scoff. "They're li
the rest of us, wealthy, wanting for nothing."

She eyes me, directing her phone screen my way, showi

me their post. Her face is curious, but there's also a little thrill in her eyes. She wants something without saying what that is.

"I can ask Ridge. See where he's going?" she offers a moment later.

I hide the way I feel about that particular suggestion. It makes me angry and possessive of him when there's no reason for it. He's *hers* now. She took him, and I have no hold over him anymore. If I ever did.

"Do that," I say nonchalantly, but in reality, I want to tell her to fuck off.

Right as I'm about to check the message board for any other posts, I notice a text from the twins. *Are you coming to Tennessee, or do we have to come to you, sweetheart?*

A smile breaks free, and for a moment, I forget what I'm trying to find out and what I'm supposed to be doing.

"What has you grinning like that?" Mel's voice sounds out.

Fuck. When she finds out I'm keeping in touch with them, she's going to freak the fuck out.

"Yang wants me to video chat with her this weekend."

Her face falls a little. "The *old* best friend," she emphasizes.

I want to roll my eyes. They've never met each other, and they both seem to want to be nowhere in the same vicinity. Neither have said it, but how they avoid each other when I'm on the phone with either of them is more than telling.

"Yeah," I lie, smiling at the newest texts.

Better not be ignoring me, Colt, or I'll have to redden your ass. My phone vibrates with Justice's text.

Then I'll add more strikes just because I'm your favorite, c you can't ignore me too. Prudence adds.

It takes everything in me to not laugh, but I feel the h flame my face.

Responding quickly, I nervously look around for M *With Mel. Talk to you soon.*

Instead of letting it go, I get a barrage of images of th sitting together, shirtless, with smirks.

If you two don't stop... I warn.

I'm really missing you, Just responds.

An image of him comes through. He's gripping sweats-clad dick. Then another ping. Unlike Just's pictu Pru's dragging down his gym shorts, the veins leading to thick erection, making my skin heat.

Now, I'm definitely ignoring you. Sending me these with being in touching distance? It's pouty and bratty, but I me every word.

Come visit. Just you and us. A week away. Pru tempts with his text.

I internally groan, wanting only that, but there are thin I need to do, to find out, like information about the Emera Vestige, about the guys, and my brother's murder. I can't ke delaying it over guys.

"You should invite her over tonight. She could help u Mel suggests, surprising me.

I consider it, thinking of Yang, of how she seem upset over Cass, but she didn't believe he was murdered. S thought I was having a mental breakdown, especially wh

I started cutting and stopped eating. She said I was clinging onto whatever kept his memory alive. She didn't understand.

"I can," I say, "if you think another hand will help."

Mel scrunches her face. "It could. She could be our lookout?"

Instead of doubting it, I text Yang. *Whatcha doing?*

Her text is immediate. *Pretending I'm doing a class assignment for Biochemistry.*

Gag.

I know, right?

How busy are you tonight? It's a nudge. She can be here in thirty minutes from Duponte if she drives.

Are you plotting something, Colty?

Is black my favorite color? Is pizza a lifestyle?

I'll head out in an hour? I can be there before dinner.

I love how she doesn't need an explanation. She's just going to drop everything to come out here. When we would sneak out and get into shit—like we did that one night at the cabin—she never acted as if I was insane. Yang went along with every plan of mine, no matter how asinine it was.

I'm at Ivory now. *eye roll emoji* I'll buzz you in.

Be there soon. Make sure you have something for me to eat.

It's as if you don't know me. I send the last text and look up to find Mel staring at me.

"I'm taking it she's coming?"

"Yeah," I answer. "Now, you two can finally meet and be best friends."

She rolls her eyes at me, but a small smile breaks free.

"She can't be half bad if she likes you."

"Can't tell if that's a compliment." It comes out sardon

and I laugh at the way she makes a *well...* face.

Not long passes before Mel orders a large pan piz

with stuffed crust, garlic crust, and peppers from Gregor's,

Italian shop at Arcadia Township. Yang agreed to stop a

pick the pizza up since we can't drive out there, and while I

a rebel on my best days, we're trying to be covert tonight.

We can't have anything go wrong.

Pounding at the door interrupts mine and Me

watching of Trashtube drama. That's what we call the sho

where commentators and K-pop stans go at it. Hopping

I rush to the door. When I peer through the peephole, I

Yang standing there.

"Gravedigger!" Yang yells when I open the door.

She sets the pizza on the coffee table before practica

tackle-hugging me. We're both giggling as we break apa

Like last year, her hair is nearly black. The only thing th

makes her appear different is the single neon blue coon t

where her hair parts.

Yang Milton is half-Vietnamese and half-South Africa

She's fairer skinned, like me, and short as hell. Her nose is ti

and her lips are full, but unlike me, she's naturally rail-thin

"I've missed you," I let out, giving her a once-over.

She's rocking her skinny jeans, Penn & Co. cashme

sweater, and booties that give her a boost in height.

When Mel comes out from beside me, I smile. "This is Melissa. Mel, this is Yang."

They awkwardly smile and wave at each other.

After Yang drops her overnight bag in my spare room, she comes back.

"What's the plan?" Yang asks as we're all watching Trashtube and shoving pizza down our throats.

I take another bite of the cheesy gooeyness. Raising an eyebrow at Mel, I give her the signal to be a part of the conversation and force her to speak.

"We're sneaking into the cabin at Moonstone Lake."

Yang's eyes go comically wide. She turns her face to me, questions rising but not leaving her lips.

"That didn't go so well last time," she mentions. "What are you thinking?"

I scrunch my face, hating the next part of this conversation. She'll either take it the good way or the way I'm afraid she will. "Cass was murdered."

She makes a *not again* face, and then she lets out a breath.

"I'm trying to find out if the Emerald Vestige hid it," I add before she can say anything.

She gulps. "They're a myth."

"They are not. They came after me at Homecoming."

"No fucking way," Yang balks, her eyes big and filled with interest.

"They threatened me, and I know they're involved." I won't tell her who. The less she knows, the safer she'll be.

"So, what are we breaking into the cabin for?"

"When we snuck in that night last year, I caug
an initiation," I mutter, my voice small. My face bur
remembering the way the two guys went at it.

After I watched the Emeralds fuck, I ran back
Crystal and didn't say a thing to Yang. She got caught by t
groundskeeper. He wrote her up for being out after hou
and we never spoke about it again.

"I want to get into that basement and see what I can fi
on Cass," I continue. "They said he was an Emerald, that
was initiated."

"I am shook." Her eyebrows trail near her hairline, an
feel like she's finally listening.

"Then six months later, he was murdered. I know it w
murder."

She doesn't argue or make a face. Yang just nods.

"How about I go to the cabin since I'm no longer
student and can get around easier?"

I look at her, worried. "Alone?"

"Yes. I'm guessing you have a double down plan a
that's why you needed me."

"It is, but we were just going to hit each one together a
take more time."

"Now, we can get it all done tonight. I'll go there. If I ta
too long, come find me."

"Okay, Mel will be going to Cassidy's old room in Crys
Tower, and I'll sneak into the dean's office."

Yang and Mel both look at me.

"Alone?" Yang asks.

I laugh at that, because I just asked her that.

"If the coast is clear, Mel can meet me and then maybe you, too. We'll share the documents and what we find. We'll meet up at Moonstone Lake, where the big rock is."

Yang nods, knowing exactly where that is, but Mel stares at me.

"You won't miss it. It's *huge* and unmistakable."

She nods, and we all put our hands together, getting dressed right after.

When we split up, I feel nervous. This is so dangerous.

CHAPTER THIRTY-EIGHT

We wait for Ivory and the other towers to hit curfew. By t
time the lights are out, we go our separate ways. Traili
down the stairs of the tower, a sense of foreboding weighs
me. Chills rack my frame, but I feel my breathing quieting li
my body responds to the fear of being heard.

The wind is mellow tonight, but that doesn't stop r
skin from prickling. It hasn't snowed yet, which is weird f
December, but I couldn't appreciate it more than I do no
It's cold enough that I couldn't rock a skirt or dress, so I we
for leggings, leg warmers, and a thick jacket. It's not poofy b
warm enough for if the temperature drops too much.

The normal lit area that leads to school is dark now a
seems almost eerie. They have night cameras, ones that w
detect me even if it's pitch-black.

My feet crunch the sticks leading to the pathway to Arcadia. My body feels stiff, nerves expanding across every inch of me. I've brought a switchblade knife, Mace, a flashlight, and a lock-picking kit I don't know how to use. My badge should get me in, but in case it doesn't, I don't want to fuck this all up.

By the time I hit campus, I'm covered in chills, and the wind has picked up, bringing with it a cold breeze and more worrisome thoughts. Are the others okay? Did they make it? Have they found anything?

Buzzing zips inside my stomach. The pizza isn't sitting well, and while none of the guys are here, the thought of them lying in wait is present on my mind.

I make it to the front of the school, and I try my badge. The light goes from red to green, and a resounding click fills the air. My breaths plume in front of me noticeably now, making me more aware of the already present chill. Pulling the door open, I realize it's darker than earlier. I grab my flashlight from my big pocket on the breast of my jacket and close the door behind me.

How can they not have an after-hour lookout?

My mind thinks of all the pranks pulled on everyone over the years—the graffiti, TP-ing of classrooms, and even the students taped naked on the gymnasium floor. It makes sense how people got away with so much shit.

Shining the light down the main hall that leads to the crossroads of every portion of the school, I feel more heaviness on my chest. The fear of being caught isn't what terrifies me. It's being alone. If someone killed me in this moment, I would

easily disappear. I'm alone, with no witnesses but the came
and empty halls.

My boots make their normal echoing smack on
linoleum. They're huge, and I'm a lazy walker, someone w
tends to drag more than necessary. At the moment, they're
loudest part of this mission, and I realize it's something I ne
to work on.

Before I can cross the main commons area to go towa
the office, my ears pick up a click.

Immediately, my heart races, and I reach for my kn
that was tucked in my bra. The thought of whether it wou
be safer with or without my light hits me square in the che:

Should I witness my death or be ignorantly slayed?

Before deciding, the choice is made for me. A figu
jumps out at me, making me squeal.

A hand covers my mouth, and I'm blinded by darkness
my light clatters onto the floor. I drop my flashlight. No wor
are spoken as I'm dragged toward a door. With it pitch-black
here, I'm not sure where I'm being led. My heart hammers insi
my chest, bringing forth a ringing sensation to my ears, all wh
my breathing is so erratic I may pass out simply from fear.

I mumble against the hand and realize if I play tl
correctly, I can attack. My knife is still clamped in my l
hand, and I can easily use it to defend myself. A plot forms
stomp to the foot, elbow to the gut, and a quick turn into t
attacker with my knife.

Survival may not be my outcome, but no one can ev
say I went down without trying.

That's when the scent of musk, a warmness that reminds me of home and familiarity, hits my nose. I stop all bodily movements, going limp in the arms of my captor. He nearly drops me. Loud grunts fill my ear as he struggles to drag my malleable limbs.

"Fuck, Colt. Stop being a pain in the ass," Lux hisses.

I smile, knowing my realization was right about his scent.

He stands me straight up, and I use that to my advantage, pushing him, but he seems to hit a wall. Flicking open the blade of my knife, I put it out in front of me. The light flickers on, and he stands near the door where my hand is pointed.

He's disheveled. His eyes are sunken, dark, tired. If he's been sleeping, it wouldn't be apparent based simply on his eyes. Lux appears exhausted, and not the kind where sleep can cure and ebb away. It's the kind that drags on for years, hanging over our heads until we take a blade to our skin, a pill to our mouth, or even a noose to our necks. It's the scary kind that brings worry, the troublesome anxiety that Lux is close to a cliff.

Walking toward him, I bring the metal beneath his throat to his jaw, not pressing it in but simply showing him I have the power.

"Why are you here?" I question, my words coming out more like a strike than impassive.

"Why are you sneaking out into the school when anyone could hurt you?"

"Don't deflect, Lux. For once in your goddamn life, drop

your mask."

His eyes shine hauntingly, dropping the "put-together act they cart around like the pink contacts I wear. "Wh are you going to get it into your thick skull, Corpse? St searching for answers you'll never get."

"Then tell me. Stop fucking blowing smoke up my and answer me, Lux." I peer up at him, his mouth so close, distracting and tempting.

No. He hurt me.

"There's nothing to say," Lux hisses, backing away fro me, and I let him. "It's done with. Drop it."

"He's dead, Lux! Nothing is done. Not until I ha answers."

He glares at me and pushes forward again, resting throat against my blade once more. I've never seen him lo so unhinged and inhuman.

"You will drop this, or someone will get hurt." H pushing into the metal. Blood breaks through his perfec smooth skin, prickling like the little lies he always tells so w

"Don't you dare threaten me!" I hiss harshly, my voi strained with fear and stress.

"I'm not telling this you as a threat, Corpse. I'm promisi you that if you don't let this go, someone *will* die."

My mouth drops open. He wouldn't... Unless he's w killed Cass.

"Don't look at me like that," he growls, pressing hard "Walk away while you're unscathed. You won't survive t next time."

I stare at him as if I don't recognize him, and maybe I don't. Maybe the soft side he saves for me in PE and when no one is around is as fake as Jordan's was.

Lux is not safe. He's dangerous. The sooner I accept that, the safer I'll be.

"Why him?" The one question I've asked myself for months, the one that's festered and soiled my insides like a living corrosive, slips free. It shows my cards, that I'll never be whole without my brother, never know true peace without answers, and never know what it's like to see his smiling face once more.

"Like you, he dug into things he knew better not to. If that's not reason enough, then I don't know what to tell you."

His words aren't callous. His explanation is subtle and leaves more questions than offers answers, but it's more than he ever gives me.

"Did I ever matter?" Another question, one I've kept close.

Like all the others, Lux holds me by the throat. His inability to be himself is visible to me, but it taints him, making him bitter.

His face falls for a split second, his eyes hardening to cover it up. "Would fucking me be easier if I lied and said you did?"

My gut churns. It boils with this uncanny hatred for him.

"Pretend all you want, Lennox, hurt me all you want to. It's not like the five of you have done anything less than destroy every part of me. Even if, in this moment, you need those hurtful words to live with yourself."

By the time I'm done, he's grabbed my knife-wield
wrist and forced the blade to bite at his skin. He move
away, a malicious tilt of his lips pointed at me.

"Tell me, Bloodsucker," he coos, his voice dripping w
venom, "miss me?"

He grabs the back of my neck, forcing my mouth to
crimson line on his throat. He doesn't have to direct me,
tell me what to do when we've done it before. He guides, an
lick. He squeezes, and I bite. He groans, and I moan at the w
his blood makes me feel complete. Disgust fills me, and I pu
away from him, abhorred at my own recklessness.

His eyes are dark, heated, desperate with need, a
while I want nothing more than to allow attraction to ru
me, I promised the twins I wouldn't fuck anyone.

Even this is cheating, breaking the rules I've vowed r
to break, but when he brings our mouths together forcefu
I don't stop him. As he brings the blade to my throat, pressi
softly, I barely cry out. His face moves, and his tongue da
out, lapping at the cut he's created.

That's when my entire body hums with intention, losi
its control.

He's my dark saint.

Tainted.

Troubled.

A liar.

He moves away, his face pinched with disturbance. "St
out of the Emeralds' darkness, Corpse. Don't end the Huds
bloodline by caring too much."

He hands me my knife, closing it. From his pocket, he brings out another flashlight and hands it to me. It's one of those skinny lights plumbers and mechanics use to hold in their mouths. He places a pair of goggle-type things over his eyes. When he turns, opening the door we came through, I feel emptiness take over.

And as Lux walks away without another word, I let him.

CHAPTER THIRTY-NINE

After the situation with Lux, I don't want to risk meeting [...] the lake. I text my best friends to meet back at my room. Sin[...] I didn't get any valuable information, it feels dumb to me[...] empty-handed.

"Did you learn anything new?" I ask Yang and Melissa [...] we sit cross-legged on my bed twenty minutes later.

"I got a ton of files. I hid them just in case," Yang explai[...]

I get up, walk toward the dresser, and grab my baggy th[...] contains five pre-rolled joints I made last week. Yang smir[...] her face lighting up with excitement while Mel stares at the[...] with boredom. She's not like me and Yang. We're notorio[...] potheads. It helps our anxieties, especially when it comes [...] finals, boys, and living in this fucked-up town.

"Did you?" Mel asks me, staring pointedly at the cut on my ne[...]

I forgot to cover it and act as if it's not there. I shake my head, not mentioning Lux. "I couldn't get into the office."

She raises an eyebrow, waiting for me to go on. Yang peers at us both as I pick up my lighter and start smoking. My shoulders relax a bit, and Yang looks ready to snatch it from me.

"Since we're all safe, maybe we should go again, and I'll get the shit at the bunker, and we'll meet at Opal, it's safest there, and they don't lock it at night. If anything goes down, we'll be safest there," Yang suggests.

I nod and look at Mel. "You should go with her," I explain.

She nods in agreement.

Yang shakes her head. "Unlike you, she knows how to pick a lock, I'm sure."

Mel's face reddens like her hair. She bites her lip. "She's not wrong. Dad taught me very little in the normal father department and went straight for the illegal shit."

We all laugh at that. Then, I stare at Yang, realizing I should admit what happened, or at least why I came back empty-handed.

"Someone followed me," I mutter.

Mel grabs her chest, flattening her palm. A gasp escapes them as they stare at me.

"I don't know who it was, but it's why I ran back here."

Their slack jaws tell me there's both anger and fear in this room now. They thought they were fine and could walk freely, but they must know that's not the case. It's best to keep them safe.

"We're going to leave our phones on at all times. If

we decide to go back out there, risks and all, we need to properly prepared."

They both nod, but they seem more spooked. I do blame them. I know Lux wasn't there to hurt me but to wa me, knowing he isn't gone on this supposed *trip* is a risk.

"I'm still in," Melissa says first, her face determined.

I nod, taking a long drag while calming my nerves.

Yang reaches for the smoke, and when I hand it to h she lets out a loud breath before speaking. "We're doing th We have our weapons of choice."

Mel pulls the small CZ Shadow from her bra then p it back inside. Then Yang pulls out a butterfly knife from h pocket and flicks it open.

"We'll keep communications open and meet up at Op Yang will only get the files, and you and I," Mel explai gesturing to me and then herself, "we'll find the files we ne and compare."

"I'm fucking scared," I admit with a self-deprecati laugh.

They look it too, and for once, Mel grabs the joint frc Yang and takes an inhale. She coughs, and we laugh at her.

When we finish it, we redress and leave our separa ways. We sneak out of the fire escape again. After we tr across campus with our flashlights, I take out my school bad and the door to the school opens. It's still the oddest and mc nonsensical thing. It may be locked at night for the world, b our badges don't stop working.

We sneak down the hallways, all the way to the dea

office. Mel picks the lock, and we enter. The cabinets are massive, nearly as tall as I am. They're labeled by letters, but after searching for all the boys' names, we quickly realize it's labeled by their last names first.

She goes through A – Eq, and I take over Er – I. When I spot a name I haven't seen in a long time, my breath catches. *Cassidy Hudson*. Why is this still here? He's gone. My fingers touch the little white tag with his name, and then I'm pulling it out.

My eyes are stuck on the folder, not wanting to see the contents, not wanting to invade his privacy even if he's gone.

While I'm still staring, Mel is searching in other cabinets.

"Oh my god!" she whisper-yells. Peering over at her, I spy her face faltering. "I couldn't find Jordan Winthrop, but I found a Jordan Edgington."

"That doesn't sound familiar."

"It's definitely him. His picture and information are in here."

I stare at the guy in the picture and wonder why he doesn't go by his real last name. But at the same time, this changes a lot.

He could be one of us.

One of the founding bloodlines.

We're looking at his papers, shuffling through notes, demerits... His file seems to go on and on.

We jump when we hear something outside the door.

"Fuck," we both say in unison.

Hurrying to hide, we shove the cabinets closed, and I

grab the two files. I hide under the desk while Mel slides in the closet.

"If I can get you out or vice versa, we'll meet at Opal st," I mutter quietly.

Mel nods frantically as we wait to be caught.

The door opens, and I hear… *giggling?*

"You're so hot." It's a husky male voice. It doesn't make sense. This is the dean's office and she's *not* a man.

"We shouldn't be here," a tittering female voice whispers, and then I'm hit with nostalgia.

No.

It couldn't be.

"Where else would we go, Tasha? Your wife is home."

Tears well in my eyes.

Mom.

"Shh. Just touch me."

Bile rises in my throat. This isn't happening. Mom said she stopped seeing men, that the only time she was unfaithful was when me and Cass were conceived.

It's all a lie.

She's here, right now, while Moms is probably at home cleaning or doing all the shit she already does and wondering where the fuck her wife is.

"Did you bring a condom?" my mom asks, and I die inside.

"Yes, especially after—"

"I cannot fucking believe you!" I scream and slide from underneath the desk. Luckily, I had enough sense to leave the file underneath and out of sight. Mel can get it.

"Colton, what are you doing here?" Mom says before the light turns on. Standing next to her is none other than Mr. Richter. My History teacher.

No.

No.

No.

Don't ruin that subject for me.

Fuck.

"The better question, *Mother*, is why you're here about to fuck my teacher when your wife—*my mom*—is at home."

"Don't talk to me like that," she remarks, folding her arms across her unbuttoned blouse.

Mr. Richter has the gall to look offended and sorry all at once.

"Is he my sperm donor?" I hiss. "Is that why he's always nice to me?"

"That's none of your business," my mom scolds. "Why are you in here?"

"Stop asking me stupid questions and respect me enough to tell me why you're stepping out on Moms."

"Your mother and I—" Mom starts before I stop her.

"Don't bullshit me. It's bad enough I wish I could trade places with Cassidy. Don't go making me want to end it all because of your stupidity." Maybe I should have allowed her to speak, but Mom always lies and she's cheating on Moms, so anything her or Richter say must be an excuse.

"We're not in love," she finishes her previous sentence.

"You mean, *you're* not. Moms is deathly in love w
you. She's so in love with you it's sickening, and look at y
coming to my school in the dead of night to not only che
but with a man. You disgust me."

I push past her and Mr. Richter, making sure to mak
scene so she'll follow. They both do. I'm happy to keep th
away from the door and lead them anywhere but back to N

"Stop!" Mom demands, and I'm far enough away tha
do. She slaps those obnoxious heels, tapping her way to r
"You will not tell your mother about this."

"Fuck you," I spit. "She has every right—"

My mom's slap connects with my face faster than r
mind can grapple the action. My cheek burns.

Richter comes over and grabs her hand. "What is wro
with you, Tasha? That's your fucking daughter."

She looks momentarily sad before shaking it off. Turni
to me, she raises her hand—making me flinch—but she ju
points a finger. "Not a fucking word, Colton."

Then, she's going back to the office, and I'm praying N
made it out okay.

I rush for the front doors, and I don't stop. The courtya
is black and empty, and my flashlight is still under the de
Chills wrack my frame as I make my way to Opal Tower. I
the farthest one from the school. Still clutching my face
wonder how my mom could hit me. She's never hit me.

A loud scream sounds out, stopping me mid-run. It's
chilling that my blood turns entirely cold.

"Help me!" a girl screeches.

It's Yang.

"Please, help me!" her voice carries over my bones.

My blood pumps with adrenaline as I race to her.

"Someone, anyone!"

Her bloodcurdling screams has me shaking from head to toe, but I still race after the sound.

"Some—"

When the last one is cut off, I just know. I'm bawling and screaming at the top of my lungs from the fear alone. "Yang!"

Nothing.

"Yang, answer me!" I scream.

Pulling out my phone, I dial Mel, hoping she's okay. My body feels every bit of dread at the possibility they're both hurt. I keep on running, searching as the phone rings, and when I finally find Yang's body on the ground, a part of me dies too.

"Please, talk to me," I whimper, knowing it's futile. I drop to my knees, wetness pooling under my kneecaps. Blood.

My body starts to quake with tears and sobs, and I'm too stuck in the moment to call the cops or respond when I hear Mel yelling on the other side of my phone.

"No!" I scream. My body shakes in horror. "No!"

Tears fly down my face, and my heart deflates. Yang's body is beneath mine, her eyes wide and scared. What fright she must have experienced to be here in the mud like she didn't matter.

My hands shake. My entire body trembles from a mix of despair, fear, and anger. All of it resides inside me. There's a battle to be won, a new game that pushes me forward.

I should have stopped pushing.

I should never have brought Mel into this—Yang, too for that matter.

But I kept digging.

Going to the tower was our first mistake. Digging through the dean's files was the next. But what solidified thi put a target on her back, and took her from me? It was ou choice, our choice to split up and not stick together. What w found may change everything, but how will we know? Yan hid everything to keep it safe. We were supposed to mee tonight and get the files.

She wasn't supposed to die.

She wasn't supposed to be involved.

She wasn't supposed to lose.

I'm moving away from her body, scrambling an vomiting. My throat is hoarse from screaming and sobbin When I reach her face again, people start coming toward m

It's late.

We weren't supposed to get caught.

This was our moment of clarity.

"You weren't supposed to die," I whisper against her ea "I love you so much. I'm so sorry. I'm so fucking sorry."

"What the hell happened?" Mel practically scream holding onto me as we stare into Yang's vacant eyes.

Time passes, and alarms blare around us. We hold ea other and sob above our friend, not knowing where to from here. When I'm pulled off her, my tears don't abate, b as the EMTs check her vitals, they shake their heads.

"She's gone. Time of death 1:01 a.m."

She's dead because of me, because of what I dragged her into. That's why she's dead.

None of the boys show up, not until she's being dragged away. That's when I spot Lux, and on his face is the haunting truth.

He told me this would happen.

He practically promised and predicted.

He was right. I won't survive this.

When I fall to the ground and blackness takes me, the only word that suffocates me is *revenge.*

TO BE CONTINUED...

ACKNOWLEDGEMENTS

m always thanking so many people... I'm sorry in advance.

Hubs. You're my soul. I could write a million emo words or how you give me life, but I won't. You're my happiness and hate tying it to you, but I can't help it.

Nicole, as my miracle editor, I cannot thank you enough. You've always made time for me and sacrificed your sanity or my peace of mind. I appreciate you so much.

Melmo, my second husband, though *he'll* argue that. Ha. love you. You came into my life at the right time and I'm rateful you're still here.

Dimples, my bossy Brit. I love your face. You're one of the rightest parts of my life. You guide me to do my best and forever orrect my messy manuscripts, which I'm forever grateful.

Nicki, my dude. Thank you for being here, for push
me, for writing insane notes that have single handedly put
in order for this book and the entire series. I love you me
than words and am so glad we found each other. And tha
you for reading this more times than I can count. You're
real MVP.

Cass and Britt, y'all mean the world to me. You're mo
than PAs, you're lifesavers and gems. I cannot imagine a wo
where you aren't by my side. I've never met two people wh
swear were meant to be by my side than you two.

Twin Bitch, no hugs, just drugs, and all the love.

Rina, you'll never see this, and I think that's what mal
it so bittersweet. I could not have finished this book so quicl
without our shared love and work ethic. You're the best, b
The very best.

Reread. GUYS. I love you so much. I love your consta
love. Your support. Your amazing ways of making me sm
and laugh and feel like I can accomplish anything. Thank ye

My Betas, which are pretty much Reread with a sprinl
of sarcasm. Hahaha! I love you guys, you're my backbone, 1
support, and my lifeline.

Team Trash Panda, you *guys*! You're literally the brai
to the operation. I'm so absolutely lucky and blessed to ha
a team filled with absolute amazing ladies who root for 1
and share the shit out of my books. I appreciate y'all so muc

Tits, my dude. I bet as soon as you see this, I'll get a barra
of messages and GIFs and I'm happy about it. Without yc
I'm pretty sure I couldn't complete much. You're my favor

nd biggest cheerleader. I love you more than tits and that's aying a shit ton.

Becca, Michelle, Ramz, Liza, Hazel, Kelsey, Mary, Kim, Colleen, and all the authors who pushed me to not only finish his but who were cheerleaders and supports during this rocess, thank you. You're the bomb and I love you.

Book Bitches, my dudes, my readers, you're why I am till here! Thank you for having faith in me and trying new ooks whenever I have a new taste.

To every author, blogger, reader, and human who loves acos... just kidding. (Or am I) Thank you for being YOU, upporting, loving my words, and just being here.

And to everyone I missed, it wasn't intentional. I LOVE OU ALL!

EST 1920

ODERINT DUM
METUANT

OTHER WORKS BY C.L. MATTHEWS

INHALE, EXHALE.
BREATHE
FIRSTS (CAPE HILL #1)
LASTS (CAPE HILL #2)
ALWAYS (CAPE HILL #3)
THE DATING GAMES: AUTHOR EDITION
WELCOME TO CAPE HILL (CAPE HILL VIPERS #1)

COMING SOON

STAGGER (DRIVEN WORLD NOVEL)
TURBULENT (SALVATION SOCIETY NOVEL)
HERE LIES A SAINT (HERE LIES #2)
HERE LOVES A SOCIOPATH (HERE LIES #3)
HERE PRAYS A SINNER (HERE LIES #4)
HERE SAVES A KILLER (HERE LIES #5)
DERNIER SOUFFLE
FOREVERS (CAPE HILL #4)

EST 1920

ODERINT DUM
METUANT

AND AS ALWAYS, IF YOU WANT TO FOLLOW ME,
I WELCOME Y'ALL WITH OPEN ARMS!

WEBSITE: CLMATTHEWSBOOKS.COM
FACEBOOK: @ CLMATTHEWSAUTHOR
INSTAGRAM: @CLMATTHEWSAUTHOR
TWITTER: @CLMATTHEWS121
TIKTOK: @CL_MATTHEWS
JOIN CL'S BOOK BITCHES: BIT.LY/CLSBBS

EST 1920

ODERINT DUM
METUANT

C.L. Matthews lives in lala-landia with her husband and invisible friends. She wants to riot the lack thereof authentic Mexican food in her state, but she's an introvert at heart. She enjoys tacos, Red Bull, and warm water, because she's crazy. She's an oddball, and realizes it's been mentioned before, just go with it. Her joys in life consist of writing unconventional romances, making book covers, causing havoc to her reader's hearts, and genre hopping when she needs a change of scenery. She's a special kind of weird and enjoys every moment of it.

Made in the USA
Middletown, DE
24 August 2023

37256758R00232